THE SISTERHOOD

Christine Beall, a dedicated young nurse, h[as]
just become a member of the Sisterhood.
Unaware, she is about to enter a garden o[f]
evil.

David Shelton, a talented surgeon on his way
up at last, has just joined the staff at Boston
Doctors Hospital. He is about to strike the tip
of a nightmare ...

What they share is overwhelming passion ...
and unbearable fear.

One holds the key to a terrifying secret. The
other suspects the awful, desperate truth.

The truth about ...

THE
SISTERHOOD

'Terrific ... a compelling suspense tale.'

Clive Cussler

'Euthanasia will never again be an abstract
subject to anyone who reads this grim,
compelling tale.'

Publishers Weekly

The Sisterhood

Michael Palmer

CORONET BOOKS
Hodder and Stoughton

Copyright © 1982 by Michael Palmer

First published in Great Britain 1982 by
Hodder and Stoughton Ltd

Coronet edition 1983

British Library C.I.P.

Palmer, Michael,
The sisterhood.—(Coronet books)
  I. Title
  813'.54[F]   PS3566.A/

  ISBN 0-340-33187-9

*The characters and situations in this book are
entirely imaginary and bear no relation to any real
person or actual happening*

This book is sold subject to the condition that
it shall not, by way of trade or otherwise, be
lent, re-sold, hired out or otherwise circulated
without the publisher's prior consent in any
form of binding or cover other than that in
which this is published and without a similar
condition including this condition being
imposed on the subsequent purchaser.

Printed and bound in Great Britain for
Hodder and Stoughton Paperbacks, a
division of Hodder and Stoughton Ltd.,
Mill Road, Dunton Green, Sevenoaks,
Kent (Editorial Office: 47 Bedford
Square, London, WC1 3DP) by
Cox & Wyman Ltd., Cardiff Road, Reading

DEDICATION

Love to my sons, Matthew and Daniel,
and to my parents

Acknowledgements

THE SISTERHOOD is the godchild of the very special people listed below. My gratitude to them goes much deeper than the words on this page could express.

To Jane Rotrosen Berkey, my agent and friend, for knowing I could long before I knew.

To my editors, Linda Grey, Jeanne Bernkopf and Sally Bown, for the style, wit and wisdom they have injected into this work.

To Donna Prince and Dr. Richard Dugas, for critical reading after critical reading.

To Attorney Mitchell Benjoya of Boston, and Dr. Steven I. Cohen of Providence, Rhode Island, for technical assistance.

To Clara and Fred Jewett, and the others who have taught me to live – and to write – one day at a time.

Finally, a special thanks to Jim Landis without whom, quite truthfully, none of this would have happened.

MSP
Boston 1982

PROLOGUE

"It's all right, Mama . . . I'm here, Mama . . ."

Fine fingers reached across the starched hospital sheet. Slowly, they closed about the puffy, white hand, restrained by adhesive tape and a leather strap to the side of the bed.

The patient, her other arm and both legs similarly bound, stared unblinking at the chipped ceiling. The rhythmic rise and fall of the sheet over her chest and the sweep of her tongue across cracked lips were the only outward signs of life. Her coarse, grey-black hair framed a face that had once been thought quite beautiful.

Now, skin clung tightly to bone, and dark circles of pain obscured her eyes. Although one could easily have placed her age at sixty-five, the woman was, in fact, only five months past her forty-fifth birthday – the day on which her terminal illness had been first diagnosed.

The girl sitting on one side of the brass bed tightened her grip, but turned her head away as a tear broke free and trickled down her cheek. She wore a heavy, navy blue coat and winter boots that dripped melting snow into a small pool on the brown linoleum floor.

Five long minutes passed; the only sounds came from other patients in other rooms. Finally, the girl slipped off her coat, moved her chair close to the side of the bed, and spoke again. "Mama, can you hear me? Does it still hurt as much? Mama, please. Tell me what I can do to help."

Another minute passed before the woman answered. Her voice, still soft and hoarse, filled the room. "Kill me! For God's sake, please kill me."

"Mama, stop talking like that. You don't know what you're saying. I'll get the nurse. She'll give you something."

"No, baby. It won't help. Nothing has helped the pain for

7

days. You can help me. You must help me.''

The girl, more confused and frightened than at any time in her fifteen years, looked up at the bottle dripping clear fluid into her mother's arm. She rose and took several tentative steps towards the door before the older woman's renewed pleas stopped her short.

Haltingly, she returned to the bedside, stopping a few feet away. An agonised cry came from a room somewhere down the corridor. Then another. The girl closed her eyes and clenched her teeth against the revulsion and hatred she felt for the place.

"Please come over here and help me," her mother begged. "Help me end this pain. Only you can do it. The pillow, baby. Just set it over my face and lean on it as hard as you can. It won't take long.''

"Mama, I . . . ''

"Please! I love you. If you love me, too, you won't let it hurt so anymore. They all say it's hopeless . . . don't let it hurt your mama anymore . . . '' Her eyes were desperate, pleading.

"I . . . I love you, Mama. I love you.''

The girl continued to whisper the words as she gently lifted her mother's head and removed the thin, firm pillow.

"I love you, Mama . . . '' she said again and again as she placed the pillow over the gaunt face and leaned on it with all her strength. She forced her mind back to the warm and happy times – long spring walks, baking lessons, steaming mugs of hot chocolate on snowy afternoons.

Her body was thin and light. Struggling for leverage, she grasped the pillow case and drew her knees up onto the bed. With each remembered scene, she pressed herself more firmly against the pillow. Bumpy rides to the lake, picnics at the water's edge, races to the raft . . .

The jerky movement beneath the sheet lessened then stopped.

Her sobs mixing with the rattle of sleet against the window-pane, the girl lay there, unaware of the fragment of pillow case which had ripped free and was now clutched in her hand.

After nearly half an hour, she rose, replaced the pillow, and softly kissed her dead mother's lips. Then she turned and walked resolutely down the corridor, out of the hospital, into the raw winter evening.

The date was February 17th. The year, 1932.

1

Boston
October 1

Morning sun splashed into the room moments before the first notes from the clock radio. David Shelton, eyes still closed, listened for a few seconds before silently guessing Vivaldi, *The Four Seasons,* probably the *Summer* concerto. It was a game he had played nearly every morning for years. However, the occasions on which he identified a piece correctly were rare enough to warrant a small celebration.

A soothing male voice, chosen by the station to blend with the dawn, identified the music as a Haydn symphony. David smiled to himself. You're getting sharper. The right continent, even the right century!

He turned his head towards the window and opened his eyes a slit, preparing for the next guessing game in his morning ritual. Hazy rainbows of sunlight filtered through his lashes. "No contest," he said aloud, squinting to make the colours flicker.

"What did you say?" The woman next to him mumbled sleepily, drawing her body tightly against his.

"Sparkling autumn day. Fifty, no, fifty-five degrees. Ne'er a cloud in the sky." David opened his eyes fully, confirmed his prediction, then rolled over, slipping his arm beneath her smooth back. "Happy October," he said, kissing her forehead, and running his free hand down her neck and across her breasts.

David studied her face as she awoke, marvelling at her uncluttered beauty. Ebony hair. High cheek bones. Full, sensuous mouth. Lauren Nichols was by all standards a stunning woman. Even at six a.m. For a moment, another woman's face flashed across his thoughts. In her own special way, Ginny too had always looked beautiful in the early morning. The image faded as he drew his fingers over Lauren's flat stomach and gently massaged the mound beneath the soft hair.

"Roll over, David, and I'll give you a back rub," Lauren said, sitting up suddenly.

"Ladies' choice," he murmured, rolling over and bunching the pillow beneath his head. "Last night was really wonderful," he added, feeling the thick muscles at the base of his neck relax at her touch. "You are something else, Nichols, do you know that?"

Behind his back, Lauren wearily forced the smile of an adult trying to share a youthful enthusiasm she had long outgrown. "David," she said, increasing the vigour of her massage, "do you think you might be able to get a haircut before the Art Society dinner dance next week?"

He flipped on to his back, staring at her with a mixture of confusion and dismay. "What has my hair got to do with our lovemaking?"

"Honey, I'm sorry," she said earnestly. "I really am. I have a thousand things hopping around in my head today. It was beautiful for me, too. Honest."

"Beautiful? You really mean that?" David said, immediately regaining his high spirits.

"There's still a hell of a lot of tension in your body, doc, but less each time. Last night was definitely the best yet."

The best yet. Progress, not perfection. That was all he could ask for, he decided. And certainly, over the six months since they had met, they had made progress.

Their life together was often an emotional roller coaster, quite unlike the easy, free-flowing years with Ginny. Still, their differences had not been insurmountable – her critical friends, his cynicism, the differing demands of their careers – and as each crisis passed, David sensed their caring grow. Although there were things he wished were different, he was grateful just to feel the caring, and the willingness to try.

It was this willingness David thought had died in him eight years before in screams and glass and twisted metal.

Realising that Lauren had said all she was going to on the subject of their physical relationship, David turned over once again. The back rub continued.

"You know," he said after a while, "of all the bets and guesses I've ever made with myself, you've been the most striking loss."

10

"How's that?"

"Well, I think it's safe to tell you now. On our first date, I bet myself a jumbo Luigi's special-with-everything-except-anchovies pizza that we would run out of things to say in a week."

"David!"

"I just couldn't imagine what an unsophisticated, stripes-with-plaids surgeon was going to find to talk about with a chic, jet-set newspaper reporter, that's all."

"And now you know, right?"

"What I know is that my body turned you on so much, you couldn't resist trying to play 'enry 'iggins with the rest of me." He laughed, spinning around to give her a bear hug, a manoeuvre that usually led to an out and out wrestling match. When Lauren showed no inclination to join in, he released her and leaned back on his hands.

"Something the matter?" he asked.

"David, did you have another nightmare last night? You were screaming out loud."

"Yes . . . I think I did," he answered slowly.

"Can you remember what it was this time?"

"The same one, I think. Fuzzier than other nights, but the same one. It doesn't happen so often any more."

"Which one?"

David felt the concern in her voice, but her expression held something more. Impatience? Irritation? He looked away. "The highway," he said softly. "It was the highway." The tone and rhythm of his words took on an eerie, detached quality as he drifted back into the nightmare. "All I see for a while is the windshield . . . the wipers are thrashing back and forth . . . faster and faster, fighting to keep pace with the rain. The white centre line keeps trying to snake under the car. I keep forcing it back with the wheel. Ginny's face is there for a moment . . . and Becky's, too . . . both asleep . . . both so peaceful . . . " David's eyes had closed. His words stopped, but the memory of the dream was unrelenting. Out of the darkness and the rain, the headlights began coming. Two at a time. Heading straight for him then splitting apart and flashing past, one on either side. Wave after blurry wave. Then, above the lights, he saw the face. The crazy drunken face, twisted and red with fire, eyes glowing

11

golden in the flames. His hands locked as he prayed the on-coming lights would split apart like all the others. But he knew they wouldn't. They never did. Then he heard the brakes screeching. He saw Ginny's eyes open and widen in terror. Finally, he heard the scream. Hers? His? He could never tell.

"David?"

Lauren's voice cut the scream short. He shuddered, then turned to her. His hands were shaking. He took a deep breath, then slowly exhaled. "Sorry. I guess I got lost there for a moment." He smiled sheepishly.

"David have you seen your doctor lately? Maybe you should get in touch with him." Lauren said.

"Ol' Brinker the Shrinker? He tapped me dry — head *and* purse — about three months ago and told me I had graduated. Don't worry. It's only a nightmare. Brinker told me they're normal in situations like mine."

"Well, I *am* worried."

"Lauren Nichols, you're frightened that I might come apart in the middle of the Art Society banquet and get your life membership cancelled!"

Lauren's laugh lacked conviction. "David, is there anything you take seriously? You laugh everything off as if you didn't care at all."

David's eyes clouded. "Lauren, you *know* I care. I care very deeply about a lot of things. I care about people, about pain, about life. As a surgeon, I see so much suffering that laughter is an essential tonic. The day I lose my ability to laugh is the day I lose my ability to cope." He stopped, sensing that with this sudden intensity he had over-reacted.

"I'm going to take a shower," Lauren said after a few moments. She was already out of bed, pulling on a blue velour dressing gown. "Why don't you make some breakfast? I'll get myself squeaky clean and we'll give this day a fresh start over a cup of coffee."

David sat staring out at the glittering new day until he heard the sound of water against tile. The day, possibly the most important one for him in years, was not starting out the way he had planned. By now he was to have told Lauren about the exciting turn of events at the hospital. Events which might well mark the beginning of the end of so much of the frustration and

12

disappointment that had plagued him recently. He wanted to share the tingling excitement he felt at facing this new beginning.

He put on a navy bathrobe and walked to the window. Four storeys below, a few early risers were crossing the still-shaded islands of Commonwealth Avenue. He wondered how many of them were feeling the same sense of anticipation he was. He smiled wistfully. How many times had he felt this way? High school, college, medical school. Ginny, Becky. So many beginnings. Beginnings as promising as this one. But of all the bright beginnings in his life since the accident and the nightmare year that had followed the deaths of his wife and daughter, this was the first one he really believed in.

Humming an off-key rendition of the Haydn Symphony, David shuffled to the kitchen. He was a muscular man, with broad shoulders and powerful arms that made him appear heavier than his 175 pounds. There were streaks of grey running through his black, bushy hair. His wide, youthful eyes ran the spectrum from bright blue to pale green depending on the light. Fine creases, once transient and now indelible, marked his forehead and the bridge of his nose.

The apartment, though small, gave the illusion of roominess, born largely of tall windows and ten foot ceilings – trademarks of many houses in the Back Bay section of the city. A long, narrow corridor connected the bedroom to the living room jam-packed with near-antique furniture, a dining alcove, and a tiny kitchen that faced an alleyway at the rear of the building. The front and bathroom doors faced one another midway down the corridor.

In the kitchen, David was throwing together the makings of a grand breakfast – orange juice, coffee, muffins and scrambled eggs. "Well and truly scrambled!" he thought to himself as he scraped the bottom of the pan. His expertise in the kitchen was a standing joke among friends, and his ambition was to write a cookery book for the single man. *Cooking For None* he would call it.

Lauren breezed into the dining alcove as he was setting their meal on the table. "Nicely done," she said, surveying his work. "You'll make a wonderful wife for someone some day." A few strands of glistening hair fell from beneath the towel she had

13

wrapped around her head. Her smile announced that she was starting the morning over again.

"So," David said deliberately. "What are your plans for today?" He was pleased at having fought back the impulse to blurt out his good news. He would disclose it casually, in the same matter-of-fact way Lauren so often told him about the luncheon she had been to at the White House or the assignment she had won to cover this or that Senator's campaign.

"David, do you have something you want to tell me?" she said.

"Pardon?" He aimed for perfect nonchalance.

Lauren smiled. "My college roommate once had a surprise party for me. Just before everyone jumped out and yelled, she had the same expression on her face as you do now."

"Well, I guess I do have a little good news. Dr. Wallace Huttner — the Dr. Wallace Huttner — is leaving town tomorrow for a few days."

"And?"

"And . . . he's asked me to make rounds with him this evening and to take over his patients until he gets back."

"Oh, David, that's wonderful," Lauren said. "Wallace Huttner! I'm impressed. The most widely acclaimed pair of hands to come out of Boston since Arthur Fiedler."

"Well, now we know that he is smart enough to recognise true surgical talent when he sees it! I'm covering his practice until he gets back from a three-day conference on the Cape."

"And there you sit, trying to impress me with how blasé you can act about the whole thing. What a funny duck you are, David."

The scrambled eggs, none too appetising to begin with, remained on her plate as Lauren fired one question after another at him.

"Huttner was written up in *Time*, do you know that?"

"So, he's operated on a few sheiks and prime ministers. He still puts his scrub suit on one leg at a time, just like the rest of us."

"Be serious for once, will you? Could this mean more money for you?"

David's eyes narrowed. He studied her face for a few seconds looking for more than superficial interest behind her question.

14

Although his lack of a typical surgeon's salary came up infrequently, a disagreement of some sort was sure to follow whenever it did. Lauren seemed unable or unwilling to accept the fickle economic realities of a medical speciality that was dependent on referrals from other physicians, especially in a city like Boston with its surfeit of doctors.

Even after two years at Boston Doctors Hospital he realised that many of his colleagues still had reservations about him. Word had filtered back. "Shelton? Oh, yes, I suppose I could refer this woman to him. But she's not the easiest person to deal with and, frankly, I'm not sure he could handle her. I mean that trouble he got into going to pieces after his wife and kid died. I'd like to help him out, I really would. But what would I look like to my patient if I send her to a surgeon and he comes unglued?"

It wasn't easy. He had never expected it would be. Lauren's concern over his financial situation was understandable, if somewhat discouraging. It would take time, he tried to explain. That's all, just some time.

David tiptoed around the issue. "Well, Huttner is chief of the department. It should mean more acceptance from the doctors who refer patients to surgeons." Any acceptance from most of them would be an improvement, he reflected ruefully. He still appeared in the operating room so infrequently that the nurses sometimes stood around after he entered waiting for the surgeon to arrive.

"Is he grooming you to be his partner?"

"Lauren, the man hardly knows me! He just saw the chance to throw a few crumbs in the direction of a doc who's struggling some, that's all."

"Well, Mr. Cool," she said smiling, "you don't fool me. You're as excited as I am about this! When do you take over for him?"

"I'm meeting him at the hospital at six. We should be done by eight or nine and . . . God, that reminds me. Joey and Terry Rosetti invited us for dinner, either tonight or tomorrow. I told them we'd – "

"I can't make it," Lauren said, rather too quickly. "I have to work."

David's attempts to draw Lauren into his long-standing friendship with the tavern owner and his wife always failed

15

and seemed to annoy her.

"In fact, I'm flying to Washington this morning." Lauren continued. "The President's going to announce details of his latest economic programme. The service wants me to cover it from the personal, human viewpoint. I'll probably be there for a couple of days."

"Okay. Well, in that case, you'll need all the nourishment you can get." He nodded at her untouched breakfast. "Want seconds on the eggs?"

Lauren glanced at her watch, stood up, and stretched. "Just leave them there until I get back from Washington." She walked halfway towards the bedroom before adding with a chuckle, "They can only improve with age." She dashed for the bedroom before David could give pursuit.

"You'll live to regret this," David called out. "Some day I'm going to become a famous chef and marry the Countess of Lusitania. Then I'll be lost to you forever."

Twenty minutes later, Lauren emerged from the bedroom, breathtaking in a burgundy suit and beige blouse. A silk scarf was draped loosely about her neck. "No caveman stuff, David," she said anticipating his hug and blocking it with an outstretched hand. "This outfit has to last me at least a day. Listen, I almost forgot. You might be able to help me out."

"Only in exchange for caveman stuff."

"David, this is serious."

"Okay. Shoot."

"Senator Cormier's office announced that he's entering your hospital in the next day or two for an operation. Gall bladder, I think."

"You sure? Cormier seems more the White Memorial than the Boston Doctors type."

Lauren nodded. "Do you think you could get in to see him? Or even better, get me in to see him? His campaign for a stiff windfall profits tax against the oil companies has made him really big stuff. An exclusive interview would be an ostrich-sized feather in my cap."

"I'll try, but I can't guarantee any – "

"Thanks, you're a dear."

Lauren wished him luck, squeezed his hands, and kissed him lightly on the mouth. Then, with a final, "Be a good boy,

16

now," she walked out of the apartment and down the hall to the elevator.

For several minutes, David stood silently by the door, breathing in her perfume, feeling a strange emptiness. "She could at least have tasted them," he said as he began to clear the table. "In spite of what they looked like."

The night watchman was fat. Fat and agonisingly slow. From the darkness of a recessed doorway, the nurse, a fragile-looking woman with hair the colour of pale sun, watched and waited as he lumbered down the corridor. Now and then he stopped to poke at the door of a storage room, or to check one of the bank of staff lockers lining the wall. But for the two of them, B-2 West, the sub-basement of the west wing of Boston Doctors Hospital, was deserted.

The nurse looked down at the grimy floor, mercilessly illuminated by bare light bulbs, and her skin began to tingle. Impatiently she glanced at her watch, and the corner of her mouth twitched. The watchman was taking forever. Forty-five, maybe fifty minutes of safe time – more than enough, provided there were no more hitches, she thought. Just relax.

Finally, the watchman locked the security box and plodded off in time to the tune he was whistling – the Colonel Bogey March. The woman waited an extra few seconds, moved quickly down the row of lockers to number 178, then dialled the combination printed on the card Dahlia had sent her. The thin, half-filled syringe was right where she had been told it would be. She briefly held it to the light, then dropped it into the front pocket of her spotless uniform. Checking the time again, she headed for the tunnel leading to the south wing. She caught the lift to Two South, then hurried into the rear stairwell and up two more flights. Slipping into room 438, she closed the door and leant against it heavily, catching her breath. Through the filtered dawn light, she could see the man asleep, his face turned towards her. From beneath the sheet, a catheter drained clear urine into a plastic collecting system.

John Chapman's recovery following kidney surgery had been uneventful. The woman smiled at the thought. Uneventful . . . until now.

She checked the corridor. A nurse's aide – the first arrival of her day shift – had just stepped out of the lift. The fragile tranquillity of night would soon break to the chaos of day. She must act now. Her pulse quickened as she moved to the bedside. There, on the nightstand, were the flowers, a glorious spray of lilies, and taped to the vase was the card, "Best wishes, Lily," she whispered to herself. She knew the words on the card – they were hers.

On the table next to the vase lay Chapman's silver necklace and medic-alert tag. She illuminated the disc with her penlight. "Diabetic. Allergic to Penicillin. Allergic to Bee Stings," it said. Again she smiled, as she drew out the syringe from her pocket.

The small syringe held the bee venom concentrate used by allergists to desensitise their high-risk patients. Although the dose would be fatal, it was still minute enough to escape detection during a conventional autopsy.

John Chapman's dark face was relaxed; even asleep he seemed to be smiling. The nurse pulled over a straight-backed chair and sat down. With one hand, she slipped the needle through the rubber stopper of his I.V. tubing. With the other, she gently shook him by the shoulder.

"Mr. Chapman, John, wake up," she cooed. "It's morning."

Chapman's eyes eased open. "Little Angel? Zat you?" His voice was a rich bass. A boyhood in Jamaica twenty-five years before still tinged the edges of his words. He focused on her and smiled. "My, but you are somethin' to gaze upon," he said. "Is it really morning or are you just one of my dreams?"

"No dream," she answered. "But I am a little early. My shift doesn't start for another half hour or so." She depressed the plunger, and the venom ran silently into the intravenous line. "I came in early just to see you."

"What?"

She didn't answer. Instead, she watched intently as a quizzical expression crossed Chapman's face.

"I . . . I feel funny, Angel," he said. "Real funny." Panic crept into his face. "I'm starting to tingle all over . . . Angel, somethin's happening to me. Somethin' awful. I feel like I'm going to die."

The woman looked blandly at his imploring eyes. You are, she thought. You are. At that instant the full force of the anaphylactic reaction hit him. The lining of John Chapman's nose and throat swelled nearly shut. The muscles surrounding his bronchial tubes went into spasm. The nurse spun round to be certain the door was closed. The reaction was more rapid, more spectacular, than she had ever imagined it would be.

"An . . . gel . . . please . . . " Chapman's words were barely audible. His eyes had swollen shut.

Instinctively, she checked for a pulse, but she knew that vascular collapse had already occurred. A second later, the last sliver of airspace in Chapman's respiratory passage closed. His body jerked twice in spasm, then he rolled onto his back and was still.

The nurse with pale sun hair held her breath during the final moments, then exhaled. Her face glowed with a beatific smile; once again, she had done her job well.

It was seven-thirty when David finished stacking the dishes in the sink and changed into a navy blue sweatsuit. He selected Copeland's "Rodeo" from his small record collection, and began a series of slow-motion stretching exercises.

The Copeland was a perfect choice, he thought as he dragged a set of weights out from behind the couch. For ten minutes, he lifted in various positions, pushing himself harder than usual until the tension of Lauren's unemotional departure left him.

The weights had come to be as much mental as physical therapy – a morning ritual for almost five years, begun the day David had decided to return to surgery by repeating the last two gruelling years of residency. That same day he smoked his last cigarette and ran his first mile. Within a few months, he had more than regained the stamina lost during three years away from the operating room.

Glistening from the work-out, he grabbed his stopwatch and keys, stuffing them into the pocket of his sweatsuit trousers as he stepped through the door.

He bypassed the narrow, rickety lift in favour of the stairs at the end of the hall. Trotting down four flights and across the dimly lit foyer of the building, he pushed through the front doors and out onto Commonwealth Avenue.

The sunlight hit him like a flashbulb. It was one of those days New Englanders boast about when they tell others that there is nowhere else on earth to live. One of those days that makes February little more than a distant memory, and helps them forget the muddy drizzle of April and the oppressive, steamy heat of mid-August.

Jogging a few blocks towards the esplanade, stiffness quickly gave way to a steady fluid rhythm. Elms and oaks flashed by, resplendent now with reds and oranges and golds. The air, unwilling to succumb yet to the commuters' exhaust fumes, tasted like mountain water.

David crossed over Storrow Drive and picked up his pace as he turned onto the tarmac path running parallel to the river. For a time he ran with his eyes nearly closed, breathing in the day and savouring the response of his muscles to the exertion.

He watched a lone oarsman sculling the Charles like some giant water bug. Even at such an early hour, there were people scattered along the grassy bank reading, sketching or just soaking in the morning. Cyclists sailed silently past him in both directions. Dogs tugged their masters along. Intense-faced students, wearing their books on their backs like hair shirts, shuffled reluctantly towards classrooms where sterile fluorescence would replace the bright autumn sun.

David checked his stopwatch and glanced around him. Under six minutes to the bridge. He had won his first bet of the run: sooner or later he would own a Rolls-Royce and an architect-designed house in the Berkshires. Wiping sweat from his eyes, he picked up his tempo a bit.

At the three mile mark, he turned and headed back. "It's getting better all the time," he sang out loud, matching each syllable to the slap of his shoes on the pavement. "Better . . . better . . . better."

Christ, it felt good to be alive again.

2

Christine Beall eased her light blue Mustang past the guard at Parking Lot C, smiling weakly in response to his wave. She cruised past several empty spaces without noticing them, then spotted one in the corner farthest from the gate and pulled in. Stepping onto the gravel, she adjusted her carefully tailored nurse's uniform and squinted up at the afternoon sun. But, preoccupied with other thoughts, other issues, she was oblivious to the magic of the brilliant autumn day.

Lot C was one of the three satellite parking areas appropriated by Doctors Hospital to meet the needs of an ever-expanding staff. Christine started towards the minibus stop, then decided she needed the three block walk, and the time to think, before reaching the hospital. Up ahead, two other evening shift nurses waved her to join them but, after a few quick steps, she stopped and motioned them to go on. Pausing by the window of a second-hand furniture store, she studied her image in the glass.

You look tired, she thought. Tired, worried . . . and scared.

She was not a tall woman, barely five foot four, and her sandy hair was tied back in a pony tail that she would pin up beneath her nurse's cap before starting work. Scattered freckles, still darkened by the summer sun, dotted the tops of both cheeks and the bridge of her nose.

"What are you going to do, kid?" she asked her reflection softly. "Are you really ready to embark on this whole thing? Peg-whoever-she-is may be ready. Charlotte Thomas may be ready. But are you?" She pressed her lips together and stared at the sidewalk. Finally, still undecided, she turned and walked down the block.

Boston Doctors Hospital was a massive glass and brick hydra complex, with three tentacles stretching north and west into Roxbury, and another three south and east towards the downtown area. Over the one hundred and five years of its existence,

21

construction of new, bigger and better extensions had been as much a part of the hospital's life as the white uniforms scurrying in and out of its maw.

Never able to snare a benefactor generous enough to endow an entire building, the hospital's trustees had adopted the unimaginative policy of identifying the tentacle extensions by the direction of their thrust. The sliding doors through which Christine entered the main lobby were located between Southeast and South.

She glanced at the large gold clock set in a marble slab above the information desk. Two thirty. She had another twenty or twenty-five minutes before having to take over from the day shift nurses.

She leaned against a stone column and surveyed the scene before her. Patients and visitors filled every available seat, while dozens more crowded around the information desk, or wove their way across from one wing to another. The activity, the size, the potential of the hospital still filled her with fascination and awe. There were certain days when she could almost sense a physical merging of her body with the fibre of the hospital, when she felt its pulse as surely as if it were her own. Slowly, she crossed the lobby and joined the flow heading down the main artery of the South wing.

Christine's floor, Four South, like most of the other floors in the seven storey wing, housed a mixture of medical and surgical patients, each with a private doctor. A few residents, widely scattered throughout the hospital, served as emergency back-up. On Four South, as on all other private floors in all other hospitals, nurses were the sole medical presence for most of each day.

Stepping out of the lift, Christine scanned the corridor, checking for an emergency trolley or other equipment that might suggest trouble in any of the rooms. The floor seemed normally busy, but an instinct, developed over her five years there, sensed that something was wrong.

She was nearing the nurses' station when the cries began – pitiful, piercing wails from the far end of the corridor. Christine raced towards the sound. As she passed room 412, she glanced in at Charlotte Thomas, who was sleeping, restlessly, through the commotion.

The cries were coming from 438 – John Chapman's room. At the doorway, Christine stopped short. The room was a shambles. Sweets, books, flowers and shattered vases covered the floor. On a chair near the bed, her face buried in her hands, sat John Chapman's wife, a proud, stocky woman Christine had met at the time of his admission. The bed was stripped and empty.

"Oh my God," Christine murmured. She crossed the room and knelt by the woman, whose cries had given way to helpless whimpers. "Mrs. Chapman?"

"My Johnny's dead. Gone. They all said he would be fine, and now he's dead." She was staring through her hands at the floor, talking more to herself than Christine.

"Mrs. Chapman, I'm Christine Beall, one of the evening nurses. Can I do anything for you? Get you anything?" Christine ached at the thought of John Chapman's death. The famous campaigner for blacks and other minorities had been up and doing well when she had left the hospital just sixteen hours before.

"No, no, I'll be all right," the woman finally managed. "I . . . I just can't believe my Johnny's dead."

Christine looked about. A few vases of flowers were intact, but most had been thrown to the floor or shattered against a wall. "Mrs. Chapman, who did this?"

The woman looked up. Her eyes were red and glassy, her features distorted. "I did," she said. "I came up to clean out Johnny's room. All of a sudden, it hit me that he was gone for ever. The next thing I remember, the nurse was trying to keep me from smashing any more of Johnny's gifts. He even got a card and a book from the governor, you know. My God, I hope I haven't ruined it. I – "

"You didn't ruin it, Mrs. Chapman. I have it right here. And here's the orange juice you wanted." A firm voice spoke from the doorway.

Christine turned round. Angela Martin nodded a greeting, then brought over the book and the juice. "I called your pastor, Mrs. Chapman," she said. "He'll be right over."

At the sight of Angela, immaculate and unruffled despite a difficult eight hour shift, the woman calmed perceptibly. "Thank you, child. You've been so kind to me. And you were

23

to my Johnny, too.'' She gestured at the mess. ''I . . . I'm sorry about this.''

''Nonsense,'' Angela said, ''I've called the cleaners. They'll take care of it. Come, let's wait in the quiet room until your pastor comes.'' She put a slender arm around the grieving woman's shoulders, and led her out.

Christine stood alone amid the wreckage, remembering her initial surprise at John Chapman's humour and erudite gentleness. Was there anything else she could do now for the man's widow? Not really, she decided. While Angela Martin was with her, the woman was in compassionate and skilled hands.

She started towards the door, then stopped and returned for the two undamaged vases of flowers. Mrs. Chapman might want to take them home, she thought.

As she picked them up, Christine glanced at the note taped to the green glass vase. Lilies . . . from Lily? Good grief, namesake flowers. What next? She shook her head. From the moment she had woken up that morning, the day had seemed beyond her control.

Her roommates, Lisa and Carole had both left for work when the phone began ringing. Christine made a quick thrust at her alarm clock, then identified the source of the insistent jangle. Eventually, she stumbled to the kitchen, certain that the ringing would stop as soon as she reached for the receiver. It did not.

''My name is Peg,'' the caller had said in a voice that was at once both soft and strong. ''I am one of the directors of your Sisterhood. There is a patient on your floor in Doctors Hospital whom I would like you to evaluate and, if you see fit, present for consideration to your Regional Screening Committee. It is not possible for me to do so myself without an awkwardness which might well be noticed, since I no longer actively practice nursing.''

Christine turned on the kitchen tap and splashed cold water over her face. Although mention of The Sisterhood had awoken her like a slap, she wanted to be sure she wasn't dreaming. ''No one has ever called me and asked me to . . . I mean . . . ''

The woman interrupted Christine's agitated stuttering. ''Please, Christine, just hear me out,'' she said. ''As is always the rule in our movement, you are under no obligation to do anything other than that which you believe in your heart to be right. I have known the woman about whom I am calling for many years. I feel certain that she would not want to survive the situation in which she now exists. She is in great pain and her condition, from what I have been able to learn, is without hope.''

At that moment, Christine knew, without being told, whom she was being asked to evaluate. "It's Charlotte, isn't it," she said more calmly. "Charlotte Thomas."

"Yes, Christine, it is."

"I . . . I've thought about her a great deal lately, especially with the agony she's been going through these past few days.''

"Were you planning to report her case yourself?" the caller asked.

"Last night. I almost called the Committee last night. Something stopped me from doing it. I don't know what it was. She is such a remarkable woman, I . . . " Christine's voice trailed away.

"The path we have chosen to follow will never be an easy one," the woman said. "Should it ever become easy, you will know that somehow you have lost your way."

"I understand," Christine said grimly. "My shift begins at three this afternoon. If it feels right to me then, I'll phone in her case report and let the Screening Committee decide."

"That is as much as I could possibly ask or expect, Christine. Perhaps sometime in the future, circumstances will allow us to meet. Goodbye."

"Goodbye," she said, but the woman had already hung up.

Before falling asleep the previous night, Christine had drawn up an ambitious list of projects for the day. Suddenly, with a single phone call, none of them mattered. She carried a pot of tea to the living room and sank into an easy chair, totally absorbed in thoughts of The Sisterhood of Life. Over the ten months following her initiation into the movement, a new meaning and purpose had entered her life. Now, she was being asked to test that purpose. With Charlotte's life at stake, the test would not be easy.

Engrossed in thoughts of Charlotte Thomas and John

Chapman's unexpected death, Christine wandered into the lounge to hang up her coat. Two of the day nurses had put aside the shift notes they were writing and were, instead, arguing about which of John Chapman's medications had most likely caused the fatal reaction. Christine had no inclination to join in. She greeted them with a nod, then said, "I'm going to see Charlotte for a few minutes. Send someone to get me in four-twelve if I'm not back by the time report is ready to start. Okay?" The women waved her off and resumed their conversation.

It had been nearly two weeks since Charlotte Thomas's operation. Two weeks during which Christine had walked into Room 412 dozens of times. In spite of the frequent visits, as she approached the door, a strange hope filled her as it often did when she was about to enter Charlotte's room. It persisted even though the practical, professional part of her knew it was unrealistic. She hoped to see Charlotte sitting in the vinyl chair next to her bed writing a letter. Her light brown hair would be piled carelessly on the back of her head, held in place by a floppy bow of pink yarn. She would look as healthy and radiant at sixty as she had probably looked at sixteen. A woman totally at peace with herself.

This was how she had looked each day during her admission in August for diagnostic tests. Christine imagined her voice, clear and pure, greeting her. "Ah, sweet Christine. My one woman pep squad, come to bring some cheer to the invalid . . . "

As she opened the door, Christine stopped and closed her eyes, shaking her head as if trying to bring herself back to the reality of Charlotte's condition.

Charlotte lay on her right side, propped up by several pillows, and seemed to be asleep. White-lipped, Christine tiptoed to her bedside. Charlotte's coarse breathing, nearly a snore, was laboured and unnatural. The oxygen prongs designed to fit in her nostrils had slipped to one cheek, exposing an angry redness caused by their continuous pressure. Hanging from the poles on either side of the bed, plastic bags dripped their fluid into her through clear plastic tubes.

Christine was close to tears as she reached down and gently

smoothed Charlotte's hair away from her puffed and pasty-yellow face. The woman's eyes fluttered for a second, then opened.

"Another day," Christine said, with cheer in her voice but sadness in her smile.

"Another day," Charlotte echoed weakly. "How's my girl?"

How typical, Christine thought. Lying there like that and she asks how *I* am. "A little tired, but otherwise all right," she managed. "How's *my* girl?"

Charlotte's lips twisted in a half-smile. She lifted a bruised hand and tugged lightly at the red rubber tube taped to the bridge of her nose and looping down into one nostril. "I don't like this," she whispered.

Christine shook her head. The tube had not been there when she had left last night. Her words were forced. "You . . . must have had some trouble with your stomach . . . The tube is keeping it from swelling with fluid. It's attached to a suction machine. That's the hissing sound you keep hearing." She looked away. The tubes, the bruises, the pain — Christine felt them as if they were her own. She knew that with Charlotte, her emotions were swaying her professional objectivity. Many times she had wanted to run from the room and turn Charlotte Thomas's care over to another nurse. But always she had stayed.

"How's that boyfriend of yours?" Charlotte asked.

The change in subject was her way of saying she understood. There was nothing that could be done about the tube. Christine knelt down and with accentuated girlish embarrassment said, "Charlotte, if you're talking about Jerry, he's not my boyfriend. In fact, I don't think I even like the man very much." This time Charlotte did managed a thin smile – and a wink. "Charlotte, it's true. I'll have none of your sly winks. He's a . . . a conceited, self-centred . . . prig."

Charlotte reached out and silently stroked her cheek. All at once, through the dim light, Christine fixed on her eyes. They held a strange, wonderful glow that she had never seen in them before. There was a force, a power in Charlotte's voice that Christine could almost feel. "The answers are all within you, my dearest Christine. Just listen to your heart. Whenever you really must know, listen to your heart." Her hand dropped

27

away. Her eyes closed. In seconds, Charlotte was in exhausted sleep.

Christine stared down at her, straining for the meaning behind her words. She isn't talking about Jerry at all, she thought. I just know she isn't . . . In stunned silence, she walked down the corridor.

The lounge was filling up. Eight nurses, six from the outgoing group and two from Christine's shift, were sitting around a table covered with papers, charts, coffee cups, ashtrays, and several bottles of hand lotion. One of the women, Gloria Webster, was still writing notes. Gloria was Christine's age, had bleached platinum hair and wore thick, phosphorescent eye make-up. She looked up, took a sip of coffee, then returned to her writing. At the same time, she spoke. "Hi, Beall."

"Hi, Gloria, busy day?"

The blonde continued writing. "Not too bad. The same old shit. Just more of it than usual, if ya know what I mean." She put down her coffee.

"Report finished?" Christine asked.

"In a minute. As usual, I'm the last one to start these damn shift notes. I think what we should do is just mimeograph one set and paste 'em in each chart. They all say the same thing anyway, if ya know what I mean."

Christine's brief laugh was purely for the sake of the other woman. Christine disliked Gloria's slap-dash approach, not only to paperwork but to people. As one of the nurses had observed wryly about her, "She doesn't give a shit about the patients."

The last two nurses arrived and took their places at the table. Report began with a discussion of the new patients who had come onto the floor during the two shifts since the evening crew had last been on. They were discussed in more detail than the rest of the patients would be. Even so, most of the remarks from around the table were not about the patients, but about their doctors.

"Sam Engles, patient of Dr. Bertram . . . "

" . . . Uh oh, Jack the Ripper strikes again."

"Bert the flirt, ten thumbs in the operating room but a dozen hands around the nurses."

28

"Stella Vecchione, patient of Dr. Malchman . . . "

"Good luck, Stella."

"Donald McGregor, patient of Dr. Armstrong . . . "

"She's nice, don'cha think?"

"Nice, but a bit senile."

"Edwina Burroughs, patient of Dr. Shelton . . . "

"Who?"

"Shelton, the cute one with the frizzy hair."

"Oh, I know who you mean. Isn't he on drugs or something?"

"What?"

"Drugs. Penny Schmidt on three said she heard from one of the O.R. nurses that Shelton was on drugs."

"Good ol' Penny. Always a kind word for everybody. I'll bet she could find dirt in a steriliser."

They went through the rest of the patients on the floor room by room.

"Beall, I guess you're gonna take four-twelve again, like always," Gloria said finally as she doused a half smoked cigarette in the bottom of a styrofoam cup. "Well, there's not much to report, except that things are even worse than they were yesterday, and that includes the bed sore, if ya know what I mean. Her temp and B.P. keep bouncing up and down. Nasotracheal suction is ordered every two hours. I did the bedsore, so you won't have to do it again for four hours. Christ, does that thing smell. Nothin' much else, I guess. Any questions?"

Christine fought back her indignant retort of anger and disgust at the woman's insensitivity, knowing it would fall on deaf ears, and merely shook her head.

The remainder of the report took ten minutes. Then the six day-nurses put on their coats and left. The torch of care had been passed.

After the lounge had emptied, Christine sat with Charlotte's chart and began reviewing it a page at a time. The process was painful. Page after page of notes, reports and procedures. The chronology of a medical nightmare. As she jotted significant items on a small pad, Christine's sense of resolve grew. It *was* enough. Just as Peg had said on the phone. She *would* present Charlotte's case to The Sisterhood.

She spent several minutes rewriting her notes and double checking to ensure she had omitted no important information. Satisfied, she opened her address book and copied a phone number on a scrap of paper. Then she hesitated. Her mouth was dry, and her stomach churned nervously. Come on, lady, she urged herself. If you're going to do it, then do it. As she stood up, she remembered Charlotte's eyes. The glow of peace, of infinite peace, was even clearer than before. " . . . Whenever you must really know, listen to your heart."

There was a pay phone at one end of the floor, partially shielded by a glass partition. The corridor was deserted. With every muscle tensed, Christine set the scrap of paper in front of her and dialled hesitantly. After two rings, a click sounded, then a short beep. A flat female voice said, "Good day. This is a recording. Ten seconds after my voice goes off, you will hear a tone. There will then be thirty seconds for you to leave your message, the time of your call, and a number where you can be reached. Your call will be returned as soon as possible. Thank you."

Christine waited for the tone. "This is Christine Beall, Four South, Boston Doctors Hospital. I would like to submit a patient for evaluation. The number at this pay phone is 555-7181. It is now three-fifty p.m. I'll be available at this number until eleven o'clock tonight. After that I can . . . " Before she could leave her home number, there was a sharp click as the recording machine shut off. She stood for a moment wondering whether to dial again. Then, overcome by renewed uncertainty, she returned the receiver to its cradle. If it's supposed to happen, it will happen, she thought.

Harrison Weller stared vacantly at the ceiling, unaware of Christine's entrance. The tiny Sony television suspended over his bed by a metal arm flashed the logo and closing music of "The Guiding Light". He took no obvious notice of it. He was seventy-five, but his narrow, craggy face had a serene, ageless quality.

"Mr. Weller, how are you doing?" Christine said crossing over to him. "Why do you have the curtains closed? It's beautiful outside, the sunlight will do you good."

He looked at her and forced a smile. "Charlene, isn't it?" he asked.

"Mr. Weller, you know my name. I've been in here nearly every day since you arrived. It's Christine."

"Sunny out, you say?" Weller's creaking voice reminded Christine of a high school actor trying to imitate an old man. He had arrived on the floor following repair of a fractured hip, and immediately had become a pet of the nurses. Over his ten days on Four South, he had been teased affectionately by the staff almost continuously, and addressed by any of a dozen nicknames – "Harry," "Cutie," even "Sonny." Although he never seemed to mind their endearments, neither had he responded to them. He often appeared confused or withdrawn, behaviour that had led his orthopaedic surgeon to label him senile.

Christine opened the curtains, flooding the room with late afternoon sun. She raised Weller to a sitting position and set herself down next to him so that he could see her face. The old man squinted at her for a moment, then broke out in a grin.

"Well, aren't you a pretty one," he said reaching up and lightly pinching her cheek.

Christine smiled and took his hand in hers. "How's your hip feeling, Mr. Weller?" she asked.

"My what?"

"Your hip," she spoke more deliberately, in a voice that was nearly a shout. "You had an operation on your hip. I want to know if you are having any pain."

"Pain? In my hip?"

She was about to try again when Weller added, "Nope. Not a twinge, 'cept sometimes when I move my foot over to the left."

Christine gasped. It was by far the most complicated response he had made to any question since she had met him. Her brows tightened as she strained to look beyond the labels and the nicknames. All at once realisation sparkled across her face.

"Mr. Weller," she shouted, "do you have a hearing aid?"

"Hearing aid?" Weller creaked. "Of course I have a hearing aid. Had one for years."

"Why aren't you wearing it?"

"Can't very well wear something that's in a drawer at home, now, can I?" he said as if the conclusion should have been obvious to her.

"What about your wife? Can't she bring it in for you?"

"Who, Sarah? Her arthritis has acted up so bad, she hasn't even been able to get out of the house to come and see me."

"Mr. Weller, I can send someone out to your house to get your hearing aid. Would you like that?"

"Why sure I would, Charlene," he said, squeezing her hand. "And while they're at it, tell 'em to fetch my glasses too. Sarah knows where they are. Can't see past the tip a my nose without 'em."

Christine's glow had blossomed into an excited smile.

"Mr. Weller, who's helping Sarah at home while *she's* sick?" she asked.

"Don't know for certain. Annie Grissom next door helps out some when she can."

"I can send a nurse to your house, Mr. Weller. If she thinks your wife needs one, she'll arrange for her to have a househelp."

"A what?"

She started to repeat herself, but stopped in mid sentence and threw her arms around him. "Don't worry, I'll take care of everything," she said in a voice that was half shout and half laugh.

Suddenly, Christine shuddered, then slowly loosened her embrace. She felt the eerie sensation of eyes watching her from behind. She spun around. Standing there, filling the doorway, was Dorothy Dalrymple, Director of Nursing for the hospital. She was in her mid-fifties, with close-cropped hair and a cherubic face. Her uniform stretched like a snowy expanse, enclosing a bulk of nearly two hundred pounds. Puffy ankles hung over the tops of her white clinic shoes. The fleshy folds around her eyes deepened as she appraised the scene.

Christine hopped off the bed, tugging her uniform straight. Although she had come to know Dalrymple professionally over the years, she had never felt completely at ease around the woman. Perhaps it was her imposing size, perhaps her lofty position. She had certainly been kind and open enough.

The director moved towards her, stopping a few feet away, hands on hips. "Well, Nurse Beall," she said reprovingly but unable to conceal a wry smile, "is this some new nursing technique, or have I walked in on a budding May-December romance?"

Christine smiled sheepishly and turned back to Weller. "Harrison," she said softly, "I told you we'd be discovered. We simply cannot go on meeting like this."

Christine squeezed his hand reassuringly, then followed Dalrymple out of the room.

Over the decade and a half she had headed the service at Boston Doctors, Dotty Dalrymple had become something of a legend for her fierce protection of "her nurses". Never considered a brilliant thinker, she was nevertheless well known throughout the medical community not only because of her bear-like charisma, but also because her identical twin, Dora, was the Nursing Director at Suburban Hospital, located some fifteen miles west of the city.

The two were called Tweedledum and Tweedledee — though never to their faces. They were, to the best of anyone's knowledge, the only nursing directors in the area who still faithfully wore their uniforms to work. It was one of the gestures that contributed to their popularity.

Dalrymple put a motherly paw on Christine's shoulder.

"So, Christine, what was that all about?" she asked.

Briefly, Christine recounted her discovery of the likely causes of Harrison Weller's "senility". The nursing director shared her excitement.

"You know," she said, "I spend so much of my time buried in paper work, labour negotiations, and hospital politics that sometimes I actually forget what nursing is all about." Christine nodded modestly. "The flair you show for your work reminds me that no matter how little respect physicians show us, no matter how they demean our intelligence or our judgement, we are still the ones who care for the patients. The ones who really know them as people. I honestly believe that most patients who recover from their illnesses are nursing saves, not doctor saves."

They walked down the corridor in silence for a bit, then Dalrymple stopped and turned to her. "Christine, you are a very special nurse. This hospital needs you, and more like you. Always feel free to talk with me about anything that troubles you. Anything."

Her words should have been reassuring, but something about her expression did not seem to fit with them. Christine felt suddenly cold and uncomfortable. She was searching for a response when the pay phone at the end of the hallway began ringing. She whirled to the sound as if it had been a gunshot.

"Well, it doesn't look like that telephone is going to answer itself, Christine," Dalrymple said, starting towards it.

"I'll get it," Christine blurted out, racing past the director and down the corridor.

She slowed down as she got to the phone, half hoping it would stop ringing before she could answer it. She hesitated then grabbed the receiver, reaching in her pocket for the pages of notes on Charlotte Thomas. Somehow, she knew with total certainty that the call was for her.

The voice was a woman's, stern with perhaps the hint of an accent. "I am calling Christine Beall, a nurse on this floor."

Christine closed her eyes briefly, took a deep breath, and said, "This is Christine Beall."

"Nurse Beall, my name is Evelyn. I am calling in answer to your message earlier this afternoon. I represent The New England Regional Screening Committee."

With anxious, darting eyes, Christine scanned the corridor. Dalrymple had gone. Staff and visitors milled around, but none within earshot. "I . . . I have a case I wish to present for evaluation and recommendation," she stammered, not quite certain she remembered the prescribed order in which their conversation was to proceed.

"Very well," the woman said. "I shall be taking notes, so please speak slowly and clearly. I won't interrupt unless I feel it is absolutely essential to do so. Please begin."

Christine's hands were shaking as she set the notes in front of her. Thirty seconds passed during which her thoughts and emotions were racing so fast she was unable to speak. Charlotte wants so much to have it end, she reasoned finally, it *must* be right.

"The patient in question is Mrs. Charlotte Thomas," she said in a slow, factual monotone that she hoped would mask the quiver in her voice. "She is a sixty-year-old white woman, a registered nurse. On September eighteenth, she had a Miles ressection and colostomy for cancer of the colon. Since her surgery, she has not done well at all. I have known Mrs. Thomas since her diagnostic admission in August, and have spent many hours talking with her both before and after her operation. She has always been a vigorous, active woman and has told me on several occasions that she could never face life as an invalid or crippled by pain. Up until this past July, she was working full time for a home health agency.''

Christine sensed that she was rambling. Her hands were wet and cold. She had known it wouldn't be easy. Peg had told her this morning that it shouldn't be. Still, she had not expected this kind of tension. And this was only the initial case report. What if they approved it? What if she actually had to . . .

"Nurse Beall, you may continue," Evelyn said. At that instant Christine heard footsteps close by. Panic-stricken, she whirled round. "Nurse Beall? Are you there?" Evelyn asked.

Dotty Dalrymple was standing a few feet away. Oh, God, Christine thought. Has she heard? "Nurse Beall, *are you there*?" The voice was more insistent.

Her knuckles whitened around the receiver. "Oh, ah, yes, Aunt Evelyn," she stuttered. "Hold on for a minute, can you? My nursing director is here." She set her arm down on the counter of the booth, but could still feel it shaking.

"Christine, are you all right?" Dalrymple said in a tone that seemed too bland, too matter-of-fact. "You look a little pale."

"Oh, no, I'm fine, Sister Dalrymple. It's my aunt. My Aunt Evelyn."

Dalrymple looked concerned. "As long as you're all right. You nearly jumped out of your skin when the phone rang before. Then when you didn't come back I was worried that perhaps something had . . . ''

Christine cut her off with a laugh that felt far too bright. "No, everything is fine. It's . . . my uncle, he had an operation today, and I was waiting to hear. Everything's fine." Lies, one after another. She couldn't remember the last time she had lied.

"Tell your aunt I'm glad everything is okay."

"I'll just be another couple of minutes, Sister." She could barely speak.

"No hurry, take your time." Dalrymple gave her a perfunctory smile, and headed down the hall. Christine felt as though she was going to be sick. The notes on Charlotte Thomas were a crumpled ball in her fist.

"Evelyn, are you still there?" she said weakly.

"Yes, Nurse Beall. Can you continue now?"

Christine forced herself to carry on. "Yes . . . yes, I'm okay. I mean, just a second while I arrange my notes." Her fingers felt stiff, unwilling to respond. First Peg's phone call, then the agony of John Chapman's wife, then Charlotte, and now Sister Dalrymple showing up on this, of all days, and seeming to be watching her more than any of the other nurses. As rising panic constricted her chest and throat, she tried to convince herself that her imagination was playing up, that she was over-reacting. Awkwardly, she smoothed the notes on the counter.

"The . . . the home health agency. Did I mention the home health agency?"

"Yes, you did," Evelyn said patiently.

"Oh, okay. Let's see. Oh, yes, I was here." The words blurred in and out of focus. "Mrs. Thomas has been on hyper-alimentation through an internal subclavian line for nearly two weeks and is still on intravenous antibiotics, hourly pulmonary therapy and continuous oxygen." At that moment, she realised that she had skipped a whole page. In fact, she was not certain what she had already covered. "Evelyn, I . . . I seem to have passed over some things. Is it all right to go back?"

"It's all right to do anything, dear. We'll be able to figure things out. Now just relax and give me what other information you have."

The woman's first warm words had an immediate effect. Christine took a deep breath, and felt much of her tension vanish. "Thank you," she said softly. Evelyn's reassurance had reminded her she was not functioning in isolation. She was part of a team, a movement, committed to the highest good. If her role was difficult, at times frightening, so were those of the rest of her sisters. For the first time, a note of calm appeared in her voice. "What I left out was that shortly after her surgery, she had to be operated on again for drainage of an extensive pelvic abscess. One week ago, she developed pneumonia, and last night a naso-gastric tube was inserted because of the possibility of an intestinal obstruction." She was still shaking, but now the words came more easily. "Her original cancer appears to have spread. Last week the radiologist's report on a liver scan noted 'multiple filling defects consistent with tumour.' Recently, she developed a large, painful sacral pressure sore and is now requiring round-the-clock Demerol as well as the usual local therapies. The physician's notes in her chart as of yesterday state that her pneumonia is worsening. Despite all her problems, she has been designated a full resuscitation should she arrest." Almost done, she thought. Thank God. "Mrs. Thomas is married, has two children and several grandchildren. That is the end of my presentation." She sighed deeply.

"When was the last case you handled, Nurse Beall?"

"The *only* case. Nearly a year ago. Mrs. Thomas would be my second." It wasn't like this the last time, she thought. That was beautiful, not an ordeal.

"Thank you for your call," Evelyn said, "and for your excellent case presentation. The Sisterhood of Life Regional Screening Committee will evaluate this patient and contact you within twenty-four hours. In the meantime, as you know, you are to take no action on your own."

"I understand." It was almost over.

"Oh, one more thing, Nurse Beall," Evelyn added, "The name of this patient's physician?"

"Her physician?"

"Yes."

"It's Dr. Huttner. Wallace Huttner, the Chief of Surgery here."

"Thank you," Evelyn said. "We'll be in touch."

3

David Shelton drummed impatiently on the arm of his chair and leafed through a three-month-old issue of *The American Journal of Surgery*. His excitement and anticipation at doing evening rounds with Wallace Huttner had been dulled by a wait which had now grown to nearly three quarters of an hour. Huttner must have encountered unexpected difficulty in the operating room.

For a time, David paced through the deserted surgeon's lounge, closing locker doors – a gesture that seemed, inexplicably, to restore some order to the situation. Forty-five minutes in an empty locker room had hardly formed part of his plans for the evening.

With mounting concern that Huttner might have forgotten their appointment altogether, he took off the suit he had dug out from the recesses of his closet for the occasion and changed into a set of scrub greens. He decided against putting on his own green canvas O.R. shoes, fearing that the shoes, a clean, new pair, would underline the fact that he had not spent much time in the operating room of late. He slipped paper shoe covers over his scuffed loafers and tucked the black electrical grounding strip in at the back.

The ritual of dressing for the O.R. had an immediate, buoying effect on his flagging spirits. Donning a paper mask and hair guard, he began absently humming the opening bars of *La Virgen de Macarena,* a melody he had first heard years before, heralding the arrival of the matador at a Mexico City bullfight.

Suddenly, he realised the significance of what he was singing and laughed out loud. Stopping before a mirror, he tucked several protruding tufts of hair under his cap and strode out to the surgical floor.

The Dickenson Surgical Suite, named after the first Chief of Surgery at the hospital, consisted of twenty-six rooms, devoid of windows, and occupying the entire seventh and eighth floors of the East Building. Wall clocks provided the only hint of what life might be doing outside the hospital. In atmosphere, politics, social order, even language, the surgical suite was a world within a world within a world.

From his earliest days as a medical student, David had dreamed of being a part of that world. He loved the sounds of machines and hushed voices echoing down the gleaming hallways, the tension in hours of meticulous surgery, the seconds of frantic action in a life-or-death crisis. Now, for the second time in his life, the dream was becoming reality.

Scanning the lime-tiled corridor, he saw signs of activity in only two of the operating rooms. The others had been scrubbed down and set up for the first cases of the next morning, then darkened for the night.

He bet himself that Huttner would be working in the room on the right and lost a weekend in Acapulco with Meryl Streep.

"Can I help you?" The circulating nurse met David at the doorway. She wore a wraparound, green scrub dress that failed to conceal her brawny linebacker's build. Turquoise eyes appraised him from between a paper mask and a cloth, flower-print hair cover.

At that moment, Huttner looked over from the table. "Ah, David, welcome," he called out. "Edna, that's Dr. Shelton. Will you get him a standing block please. Put it, ah . . . over there behind Dr. Prince." He nodded towards the resident who was assisting from the other side of the table.

David stepped onto the block and looked down into the incision.

"Started as a simple oversew of a bleeding ulcer," Huttner explained, unaware or, at least, not acknowledging that he was late for their rounds. "We encountered a little trouble when we got in, though, and I decided to go ahead with a hemigastrectomy and Bilroth anastomosis." David took note of Huttner's choice of pronouns and filed them away in the back of his mind with a wry smile.

Within a few seconds the rhythm in the room, disrupted by David's arrival, was re-established. It became rapidly apparent to him that Huttner's concentration, deftness, and control were quite extraordinary. No wasted words or motion. No outward evidence of indecisiveness. Although others in the room were playing their parts, he was clearly both conductor and principal soloist at this performance.

Suddenly, a pair of scissors slipped from Huttner's hand as the scrub nurse passed them to him, and hit the floor with a loud clatter. The surgeon's grey-blue eyes flashed. "Goddammit, Jeannie," he snapped, "will you pay attention!"

The nurse stiffened, then muttered an apology and carefully handed over another pair. David's eyes narrowed a fraction. From his vantage point the pass had seemed quite adequate. He glanced at the wall clock. Seven-thirty. Huttner, he realised, had probably been operating for the best part of twelve hours non-stop.

A minute later, Huttner surveyed his results then circled his head to relieve the tightness in his neck. "Okay, Rick, she's all yours. Go ahead and close," he said to the resident. "Standard post-op orders. I don't think she'll need the unit, but use your judgment when she's ready to come out of the recovery room. If there are any problems, contact Dr. Shelton. He'll be covering for me while I'm down at the vascular conference on the Cape. Any questions?"

David thought he saw a flicker of heightened respect appear in the eyes of the scrub nurse, which immediately rekindled his excitement about what the next three days held in store for him.

Huttner stepped back from the table, stripping off his blood-stained gown and gloves in a single motion, and headed for the lounge, with David close behind. Rather than collapsing in the nearest easy chair as David expected, Huttner walked casually to his locker, and took out his pipe and tobacco pouch. He filled, packed and lit the elegant meerschaum before settling in a thick, leather couch. With a wave of his pipe, he motioned David to join him on the sofa.

"Turnbull should have referred that woman for surgery two days ago," he said, referring to the intern who had failed to stop the bleeding ulcer. "I'll bet I wouldn't have had to take her stomach if he had." Huttner closed his eyes and massaged the bridge of his nose with long, carefully manicured fingers.

In his early sixties, Huttner appeared every bit the patrician depicted by his press clippings. He was a tall, angular man, an inch or two over six foot, with dark hair greying at the temples.

"I've been hearing some nice things about your work from

the nurses in the O.R., David," Huttner said in his cultured New England accent.

Nice things. David paused. Over the last eight years he had become wary of compliments, suspicious of hidden motives. But Huttner's flattery was genuine, he felt sure.

"Thank you, sir," he said. "As you saw tonight, some of them don't even know me yet. I mean, one major op every week or two is hardly the best basis for judging." David knew that Huttner might perform fifteen or more major operations for each one of his own, but his words held no trace of bitterness.

"Patience, David, patience," Huttner said. "I recall telling you that when you first came to see me about applying for staff privileges. You must remember that just as physicians are constantly hoisted up on pedestals, so are they also under continuous, magnified scrutiny." He tapped his fingertips together, carefully selecting his words. "Problems such as . . . ah . . . have befallen you are not quickly forgotten by the medical community. They are a threat, revealing a vulnerability that most doctors don't want to admit they have. Just keep doing good, conscientious work and the cases will come." He sat back pontifically and cupped his hands around the meerschaum.

"I hope so," David said, his smile a bit forced. "I want you to know how grateful I am for your trust and acceptance. It means a lot to me."

Huttner waved the remark away with his pipe. "Nonsense, I'm the one who is grateful. It's a relief to know that my patients will have a bright young Turk like you looking after them while I'm gone. As I recall, you trained at White Memorial, didn't you?"

"Yes, sir, I was Chief Resident there once upon a time."

"I never could seem to get accepted into that programme," Huttner said, shaking his head in what might have been wistfulness. "And it's 'Wally.' I get enough 'sirs' every day to fill King Arthur's Court."

David nodded, smiled and stopped himself at the last possible instant from saying, "Yes, sir."

Huttner bounced to his feet. "A quick shower, then I'll sign out to you on the floors." He tossed his scrub suit into a canvas hamper, then took a journal from his locker and handed it to David. "Take a look at this article of mine on radical surgery for metastatic breast disease. I'll be interested in what you think.''

With that, he strode into the shower room, calling out just before he turned on the water, ''Do you play tennis, David? We'll have to get together and have a few games before the weather closes in on us.''

''If I can remember which end of the racket to hold,'' David said softly to himself. He thumbed through the article. Printed in a rather obscure journal, it advocated radical breast, ovarian, and adrenal surgery for patients with widespread breast cancer. The concept was nothing revolutionary. However, horrible as the disease was, seeing the radical surgical approach laid out in print and scanning the tables of survival, brought a bitter taste to David's mouth. Survival at all costs. Was that really the ultimate aim? He slapped the journal shut and shoved it back in Huttner's locker.

The page operator was announcing the eight o'clock end to visiting hours when they started making rounds on the floors in the West building. Earlier, David had seen the two patients he had in the hospital, a ten-year-old boy in for repair of a hernia, and Edwina Burroughs, a forty-year-old woman whose factory job and four pregnancies had given her severe varicose veins, gnarled and twisted as the roots of a banyan tree.

Wallace Huttner had more than twenty-five patients scattered over three different buildings. Almost all of them were recovering from major surgery. On every floor, Huttner's arrival had an immediate effect. Horseplay around the nurses' station stopped. Voices were lowered. The charge nurse materialised, charts in hand, to accompany them on their rounds. Replies to Huttner's occasional questions were either stammered monosyllables, or nervous outpourings of excess information. Throughout, Huttner maintained an urbane politeness, moving briskly from one bedside to the next without so much as a hint of the fatigue David knew he must be feeling. The man was absolutely one of a kind, he thought to himself. A phenomenon.

Their rounds took on a comfortable pattern as they continued. Huttner allowed the charge nurse to lead them to the doorway of a room. Then he took the patient's chart from her and proceeded to the bedside. David, the charge nurse, and often the staff nurse

42

on the case followed. Next, Huttner handed the unopened chart to David, introduced him to the patient, and gave a brief history of the initial problem, operative procedure, and subsequent course of treatment, couching details in medical jargon that no one except a physician or nurse could possibly have understood.

Finally he conducted a brief physical examination while David flipped through the record, using a spiral-bound pad to record pertinent lab data and Huttner's overall approach and plan for the case. For the most part, he tried to remain inconspicuous, speaking when spoken to and keeping his questions to what seemed like an intelligent minimum.

From time to time, he glanced at Huttner. As far as he could tell, the man seemed satisfied that his charges were being left in capable hands. Before long, though, David began to wonder uneasily about Huttner's competence. Despite the unquestion- able – perhaps unparalleled – surgical skills, Wallace Huttner was sloppy: progress notes were brief and often lacked certain information, and abnormal laboratory results went undetected for several days before they were noticed and acted on. Small things. Subtle things. But unmistakable. It was not the kind of carelessness that would affect every patient, but inevitably it would be a contributory factor in some cases – a prolonged hospital stay, a second operation, even a death.

He must know, David thought to himself. It wasn't lack of pride or caring or skill – Huttner clearly possessed all three. The man was simply spread too thin, David decided. Too many cases. Too many committees, panels, and teaching obligations. How much could a man do in one day? Sooner or later he must either draw lines or make compromises or . . . get help. Maybe Lauren was right, he thought excitedly. Maybe Huttner *was* looking for a partner. Or maybe, David laughed to himself, Huttner had chosen him to cover the practice believing that of all the surgeons in the hospital, he was the least likely to notice these inadequa- cies. No matter. The oversights and omissions were small ones. He would go through the charts the next day and sort them all out quietly, without a fuss.

Minutes later, David's decision to keep silent was challenged. The patient was a man in his late fifties, a commercial fisherman named Anton Merchado. He had been admitted to the hospital several weeks earlier for an abdominal mass. Huttner had drained

43

and excised a cyst on the pancreas and Merchado was recovering nicely when he developed symptoms of an upper respiratory infection. In a telephoned order, Huttner had put the man on tetracycline, a widely used antibiotic.

The condition must have improved, David thought, because there was no further mention of it in Huttner's brief notes. However, the tetracycline order had never been rescinded. It had been in effect for nearly two weeks.

Anxious to speed up rounds, Huttner was giving his brief review of the man's history while he examined his heart, lungs and abdomen. David stood to one side, his attention focused more on the chart than on what the older surgeon was saying.

On the day before Merchado was to be discharged from the hospital, he had developed severe diarrhoea. Huttner's initial diagnosis was viral enteritis, but over a few days, the condition worsened. Early signs of dehydration began to appear.

David flipped from the progress notes to the laboratory reports and back. Huttner's mounting concern was mirrored in an increasing number of orders for laboratory tests and diagnostic procedures, all inconclusive. Efforts intensified, but there could be no doubt that Merchado was on a downhill slide.

As David read, an idea took root. He scanned page after page of laboratory reports, looking for the results of the stool cultures which had been ordered on several successive days.

"Well, what do you think?" Huttner said, turning to David. "David?"

"Oh, sorry." David looked up. "I noticed the man was still on tetracycline and was just looking to see if he might have developed staph colitis secondary to the treatment. It doesn't happen often, but . . . ."

"Tetracycline?" Huttner interrupted. "I ordered that to be stopped several days ago. Are they still giving it to him?"

Behind Huttner the charge nurse nodded her head.

"Well, no matter," Huttner said, hesitating slightly. David could almost hear him asking himself whether he had actually ordered it to be stopped or had just meant to. "The culture reports have all been negative. Why don't you write an order to take him off tetra. Go ahead and get another culture, if you want to."

David was about to do so when he noticed a culture report

at the bottom of the lengthy computer print-out that listed all results obtained on the patient to date. It read "9/24, STOOL SPEC: MODERATE GROWTH, S. AUREUS, SENSITIVI-TIES TO FOLLOW."

Staph Aureus, the most virulent form of the bacteria. David closed his eyes for a moment, hoping that when he looked at the sheet again, the words would be gone. It was several seconds before he decided to keep quiet about this and to correct the problem later. The hesitation was too long.

"What is it, David?" Huttner asked. "Have you found something?"

"Dammit," David hissed to himself. There was going to be no comfortable way around this. Out of the corner of one eye, he saw the two nurses standing motionless at the end of the bed. Did they know that in the next few moments the success of the evening and possibly of his career might be on the line?

Gritting his teeth, he passed Merchado's chart to Huttner, and pointed at the offensively impersonal line of type.

David's only reward was the same fiery look from Huttner that he had last seen directed at the O.R. scrub nurse.

"Mrs. Baird," Huttner growled, thrusting the chart at the charge nurse, "I want you to find out who is responsible for failing to call my attention to this report. Whoever it is, nurse or secretary, I want to see her in my office first thing Monday morning. Is that clear?"

The nurse, a stout veteran who had engaged in her share of hospital wars looked at the page, then shrugged and nodded her head. David wondered if Huttner would actually follow through what seemed so obvious an attempt to produce a scapegoat.

"Come along, Dr. Shelton," Huttner said curtly. "It's getting late and we still have several more patients to see."

It was nearly ten o'clock when they arrived on Four South to see the last of Huttner's patients, Charlotte Thomas. For the first time all evening, Huttner deviated from the routine. Taking the chart from the charge nurse, he said, "Come and sit down in the nurses' lounge for a bit, David. This next patient is by far my most complicated. I want to take a few minutes to go over her with you in some detail before we see her. Perhaps someone could bring us each a cup of coffee.'' The last remark was addressed to the nurse who managed a faint smile of acquiescence. ''White, no sugar for me, and for Dr. Shelton . . . ?''

''Black,'' David answered, thinking wryly that it would reflect his feelings nicely.

''Here you go, doctor,'' Huttner said, sliding the chart across to David. ''Leaf through it while we're waiting for coffee.''

Before reading a word, David could tell that Charlotte Thomas was in trouble. Her hospital record was voluminous. He thought back to his residency and a tall, gangly New Yorker named Gerald Fox, who was one year ahead of him. Fox had achieved immortality, at least in White Memorial Hospital, by Xeroxing a three-page list of maxims and definitions entitled, ''Fox's Golden Laws of Medicine.'' Among his humorous axioms were the definition of Complicated Case (When the combined diameters of all the tubes going into a patient's body exceeds his hat size), Gynaecologist (A spreader of old wives' tales), and Fatal Illness (A hospital chart more than an inch thick).

Coffee arrived just as David was scanning the admission history and physical examination. He heard Huttner say, ''Ah, Nurse Beall, thank you. You're an angel of mercy.''

He looked up from the chart. It was not the nurse Huttner had spoken to earlier, but a far younger woman David had never seen, or at least had never noticed before. For several seconds his entire world consisted only of two large, oval, burnt umber eyes. He felt his body flush with warmth. The eyes met his and seemed to smile.

''So, you are with our lady Charlotte again?'' Huttner asked.

''Huh? Oh yes.'' Only then did Christine break their long, silent gaze and turned to Huttner. ''She's not looking too well. I asked to bring the coffee in because I wanted to talk to you about h - ''

''How rude of me,'' Huttner interrupted. ''Nurse Beall, this is Dr. David Shelton. Perhaps you two have met?''

''No,'' Christine said icily. She was well acquainted with Huttner's lack of regard for the suggestions of nurses. Over the years she had given up even attempting to share hers with him. But Charlotte's situation was distressing enough for her to try. If Huttner would only agree to let up on his aggressive

treatment, to cancel the resuscitation order, she might not intervene even if the Screening Committee approved her proposal.
Despite his deliberate interruption, she felt determined to speak
her mind to Huttner. After all, it was *his* tube that was sticking
into Charlotte's nose. *His* order to prolong her suffering no
matter what. He could play puppet-master with his other
patients, but not with Charlotte. He would listen or . . . or have
his strings to her cut.

Huttner took no note of the chill in her voice. "Dr. Shelton
will be covering all my patients, including Mrs. Thomas for a
few days," he said.

Christine nodded at David and wondered whether he might
have the authority to temper Huttner's overzealous approach to
Charlotte, then realised there was no chance the surgical chief
would permit that. "Dr. Huttner," she said flatly, "I would
like to talk to you about Charlotte for a few minutes."

Huttner glanced at his watch. "Certainly, Nurse Beall," he
said. "Why don't you let us finish reviewing Charlotte's case
and examining her. Then you can go over things with Dr.
Shelton here. He'll know exactly what I want for this woman."
Huttner turned away and didn't see Christine's dagger-filled
look before she spun round and left the room.

Huttner took a sip of coffee, then began speaking without so
much as a word or gesture about the nurse who had just left.
"Mrs. Thomas is a registered nurse. In her late fifties, I think."
David glanced at the birthdate on the chart. She was nearly sixty-
one. "Her husband, Peter, is a professor at Harvard. Economics.
She was referred to me by an intern because of a suspected cancer
of the rectum. Several weeks ago, I performed a Miles ressection
on her. The tumour was an adenocarcinoma extending just
through the bowel wall. "However, all the nodes I took were
negative. I feel there's a very good chance that my clean-out may
have got the whole thing."

David looked up from the coffee stain he was absent-mindedly
erasing with his thumb. The five-year survival rate after removal
of rectal cancer with such extension was under 20%. A chance?
Certainly. A very good chance? Unlikely . . . but he judged it
wiser not to comment.

Comfortable in the blanket of his own words, Huttner
continued. "As always seems to happen when we work on

nurses or doctors, everything that could have gone sour post-operatively seems to have done so. First a pelvic abscess which I had to go back and drain. Next, pneumonia, and then a nasty decubitus ulcer over her sacrum. Yesterday, she developed signs of a bowel obstruction, and I had to slip down a tube. That seems to be correcting the problem, and I have a feeling that she may have turned the corner.''

Huttner folded his hands on the table in front of him, indicating that his presentation was done. An almost imperceptible tic had developed at the corner of his right eye. He must be absolutely exhausted, David thought. He returned to the chart. ''And if she needs to be operated on for the obstruction?'' he asked, already praying it would not happen.

''Then you go ahead and do it if that's your judgement. I'm leaving you in complete charge,'' Huttner said, somewhat testily.

No more questions, David resolved. Whatever you want to know, figure out for yourself. Just get through this night.

But already, another vital question to which only Huttner could supply the answer was worrying him. He *had* to ask.

''If she should arrest?'' he said softly.

''Dammit, man, she's not going to arrest!'' Huttner snapped with startling vehemence. Then, sensing the inappropriateness of his outburst, he took a deep breath, exhaled slowly, and added, ''At least I hope she doesn't. If she should, I want a full Code Ninety-nine called on her, including tracheal intubation and a respirator if need be. Clear?''

''Clear,'' David said. He looked down at the chart again. Whatever criticisms might be levelled at Wallace Huttner, under-treating Charlotte Thomas certainly could not be one of them. Thousands of dollars in laboratory work, hospital care and radiologic studies had already been done. However, on paper at least, the woman appeared far from ''turning the corner.''

''Shall we go and see the patient?'' Huttner's tone was more an order than a question.

David was about to follow when he noticed the report of Charlotte's liver scan. The words jumped at him from the page: ''Multiple filling defects consistent with tumour.'' He felt numb. Rarely had he heard of a patient surviving long with the spread of rectal cancer to the liver. Certainly, with this kind of disseminated disease, there could be no way to justify the aggressive therapy given Charlotte Thomas. If, as in the Merchado case, this report had somehow been overlooked, whatever remained of his good relationship with Huttner was about to disappear in a puff of smoke.

"What is it, doctor?" Huttner asked acidly.

"Oh . . . probably nothing," David said, uncomfortably. "I . . . ah . . . I was just reading this liver scan report."

"Hah!" Huttner's exclamation cut him short. "Multiple defects consistent with tumour, right?" He suddenly beamed with satisfaction. "Look at the name of the radiologist who gave us that report. G. Rybicki, M.D., the living Polish joke of radiologic medicine. He read the same thing on a scan as we did preoperatively, so I checked her liver out carefully in the O.R. Even sent off a biopsy. They are cysts, David. Multiple, congenital, totally benign cysts."

"I even went to the trouble of sending Rybicki a copy of the pathology report," Huttner continued. "He probably never even looked at it, as shown by this repetition of his initial misreading. Maybe we'd better just tear the report out of the chart." He crumpled the sheet in a ball and tossed it into the wastebasket. "Now, if you have no further questions, shall we go in to see the woman?"

"No further questions, your honour." David shook his head in amazement and smiled. There was something about Huttner's confident broad grin that went a long way towards dispelling David's misgivings about him.

Shoulder to shoulder, they walked down the corridor of Four South and into room 412.

4

The only light in room 412 came from an angle-poise treatment lamp, directed at an area just above Charlotte Thomas's exposed buttocks. Huttner strode to that side of the bed with David close behind, and moved the lamp back a foot. He stiffened perceptibly, and David's eyes quickly followed his gaze. The bedsore Huttner had described as "nasty" was far worse than that. It was a gaping hole six inches wide. The walls of the cavity were raw muscle, stained white by a drying poultice. A quarter-sized eye of sacral bone gleamed sightlessly at the centre. David stared in horror. He'd seen countless sores and wounds over the years, but nothing quite like this. Huttner straightened up, and threw David a grimacing half-smile.

"It's Dr. Huttner, Charlotte," Huttner announced as he flicked off the lamp and turned on the dim fluorescent light set in a cornice over her bed. He drew the sheet up above her waist, and walked to the other side of the bed. David followed, glancing at the I.V. bags, and the restraints which held her on her side; at the urinary catheter snaking from beneath the sheet; at the oxygen and suction tubes. Though ugly and uncomfortable for the patient, these were all tools of the medical trade that David noted, but accepted implicitly.

The first thing he noticed as he looked at Mrs. Thomas was the emptiness in her face — a blank soulless aura centring about her eyes, which were watching him through the dim light with a moist flatness. Even the sound of her breathing – soft, rhythmic cries – was hollow.

Charlotte Thomas had The Look as David had come to label it. She had lost the will to live, that extra energy essential to survive a life-threatening illness. The spark that often made the difference between a medical miracle and a mortality statistic was gone.

David wondered if Huttner saw the same things he did, sensed the same emptiness. As if in answer to his question, the tall surgeon knelt by the bed, slipping his hand under Charlotte's head and cradling it to one side so that she could look directly at his face. For nearly a minute they remained that way, doctor and patient frozen in a silent tableau. To David, Huttner's tenderness was as genuine as it was surprising.

"Not exactly feeling on top of the world, huh?" Huttner said finally.

Charlotte forced her lips together — an unsuccessful attempt at a smile — and shook her head. Huttner smoothed the hair from her forehead and ran his hand over her cheek.

"Well, your temperature is down near normal today for the first time in a while. I think we might be getting on top of that infection in your chest." He went on, carefully mixing encouraging news with questions that he knew would be answered negatively. "Is the pain in your back any less?" She shook her head. "Well, if things settle down the way I expect them to, we should be able to get that tube out of your nose in a day or two. I know how uncomfortable it must be. While I have you rolled over like this, let me take a listen to your chest, then I'll put you on your back and see if there are any new noises in your belly."

He examined her briefly, then glanced at the fluid levels in the intravenous bags and catheter drainage cylinder before kneeling beside her again. "You're going to make it, Charlotte. You must believe me," he said with gentle intensity.

This time, Charlotte did manage a rueful smile as she slowly shook her head.

"Please, just be patient, have faith and hang on a little longer," Huttner implored. "I know the pain you're going through. In many ways it's as awful for me as it is for you. But I also know that bit by bit, you're turning the corner. Before you know it, you'll be putting on lipstick and getting ready to see those beautiful grandchildren you've told me so much about." He paused. In the silence, David studied the man's face. His brows were drawn inwards, his jaw taut as a bow string. He seemed to be trying, through sheer will, to transfuse the energy of his words and hope. The woman showed no reaction. "My goodness, I almost forgot," Huttner said at last. "Charlotte, you are in for a treat. I know how tired you must be getting of

51

seeing my ugly mug every day. Well, you're going to get a break from that. I'm going off to a conference on the Cape for a few days. This handsome young doctor will be covering for me. He was the Chief Resident a few years ago at White Memorial. I couldn't even get accepted for an internship there. His name's David Shelton.'' Huttner motioned David over to the head of the bed.

David took Huttner's place, setting his arms on the sheet and resting his chin on them, six inches away from Charlotte's face. It seemed to take several seconds for her to focus on him.

"I'm David, Mrs. Thomas. How do you do?" He paused. "Is there anything you need right now? Anything I can get for you?" He waited until he felt certain no response was forthcoming, then made a move to stand up. Suddenly, Charlotte Thomas reached out a spongy, bruised hand and grasped his with surprising force.

"Dr. Shelton, please listen to me," she said in a husky, halting voice that had an unexpected strength. "Dr. Huttner is a wonderful man and a wonderful doctor. He wants so much to help me. You must make him understand. I do not want to be helped any more. All I want is to have these tubes taken out and to be kept comfortable until I go to sleep. You must make him understand that. This is torture for me. A nightmare. Please make him understand."

Her eyes flashed for an instant, then closed. She took several deep breaths, and settled heavily back on the pillow. Her breathing slowed down. It seemed to David that it might stop altogether, but within a minute it stabilised into a coarse, rhythmic snore.

All David could manage was a whispered, "You're going to be all right, Mrs. Thomas," as Huttner took him by the arm and led him out of the room.

In the hallway, the two men faced one another. Huttner was first to break the silence.

"Quite some night we've had for ourselves, isn't it?" he said, smiling in understanding.

"Yeah," David answered. He pawed at the floor with one foot. He would have said more but he was afraid that he might come apart in front of the man.

Huttner scrutinised his face, then said, "David, never forget that often patients with serious illness express the wish to die when they're at a stage of weakness and pain. I've been around for a long time. I've seen many patients as sick or sicker than Charlotte Thomas recover. This woman is going to make it. She is to get total, aggressive treatment and, if necessary, a full scale Code Ninety-nine resuscitation. Understand?"

"Yes, sir . . . I mean yes, Wally," David said automatically, searching his memory for the last time he had seen a sixty-year-old patient recover from the sort of severe, multi-system disease that beset Charlotte Thomas.

"We're in agreement, then," Huttner said, beaming at David's co-operation. "Let's go write a few orders on this woman, then we can call it a day."

David heaved an inward sigh of relief, and in an attempt to lift his spirits, bet himself a guitar and six months of introductory lessons that the last critical moment of the hectic evening had passed.

An instant later, a portly man, dressed in a turtle-neck sweater and tweed sportsjacket emerged from the visitors' lounge at the far end of the corridor and headed towards them. He was still thirty feet away when David knew with certainty that another wager had been lost. The anger in the man's stride was mirrored in his face and taut, white lips. His fists were held several inches away from his body on rigid arms.

David glanced over at Huttner, who showed a flicker of recognition but no other emotion.

"Professor Thomas?" David whispered.

Huttner nodded his head a fraction, then moved forward. David slowed and watched as the two men closed on one another like combatants at a medieval joust. The grandstand for their confrontation was the nurses' station, where several nurses, an aide and the ward secretary fell silent.

"Dr. Huttner, what the hell is going on here?" Thomas lashed out. "You told me there would be no more tubes and I get here to find a red rubber hose coming out of my wife's nose attached to some goddamn machine."

"Now Professor Thomas, just calm down for a minute," Huttner said evenly. "I tried to call you last night to let you know what was going on, but there was no answer. Let's go down to the visitors' lounge, and I'll be happy to go over the whole thing with you."

Thomas would not be mollified. "No, we'll have this whole business out here and now with these people as witnesses." He gestured at the gallery. "I came to you with Charlotte because our family doctor told us you were the best. To me the best meant not only that you would be the best in the operating room, but that you would be the best at treating my wife – as a human being, not just as some unfeeling piece of . . . of *carrion*."

The intensity and pain in Peter Thomas's voice was startling. Behind the nurses' station, Christine Beall cautiously turned her head towards Janet Poulos, the evening nursing supervisor. Poulos met her gaze impassively, then responded with an almost imperceptible nod. She was a slender woman, ten years older than Christine. Her coal-black hair was coiled in a tight bun, accentuating her narrow features and dark, feline eyes. A thin scar running parallel to her nose gave even her warmest smile a slight sneer, and undoubtedly contributed to her reputation among the nursing staff as being uncompromising and humourless.

Christine saw her in a far different light, for it was Janet who had supervised her initiation into The Sisterhood of Life. The secrecy of the movement was such that Janet remained the only Sisterhood member whom she knew by name and face. The nod acknowledged that Poulos, too, was assessing the drama unfolding before them.

"All right, Professor," Huttner said, a thin edge appearing in his voice. "If it is what you wish, we shall discuss matters right here. Do you have more to say, or do you want to know exactly what is happening with Charlotte?"

"Go on," Thomas said, relaxing his fists and leaning one elbow on the high counter in front of a totally bewildered ward secretary.

With the condescending patience of one who has learned that sooner or later he will win the day, Huttner systematically reviewed the developments that had led to his decision to insert an intestinal drainage tube in Charlotte Thomas. Then, more gently, he said, "It may not be obvious to you right now, Peter, but I believe that our treatments are starting to take hold. Charlotte could turn the corner any time now."

Peter Thomas looked down and retreated half a step. At that moment, it seemed to David as if Huttner had, in fact, won the man over. Then, as though in slow motion, Thomas brought his head up, shaking it back and forth as he spoke. "Dr. Huttner, I believe my wife is dying. I believe it, and I even accept it. I also believe that because of what you call *treatment,* she is dying by inches, without so much as a flicker of dignity. I want those tubes pulled out."

Behind the counter, a nurse whispered something to the woman next to her. Huttner silenced her with a look that could have frozen a volcano.

With an instantaneous, almost theatrical change in expression, he turned back, smiling calmly, to Peter Thomas. "Professor, please know that I understand how you're feeling, I really do," he reasoned. "But you must understand my position and my responsibility in this thing. We talked about it when you first brought Charlotte into my office, and you agreed that I was to be in complete charge. I offered to arrange for a second opinion, but you felt that none was necessary. Now here you are questioning my judgment. I'll tell you what. We have a built-in second opinion right here." Huttner motioned David over. "This is Dr. Shelton. He's an excellent young surgeon who was Chief Resident in Surgery at White Memorial. We've just examined Charlotte in great detail because Dr. Shelton will be covering my patients for the next few days. David, this is Peter Thomas. Tell him what your feelings are about Charlotte."

David stretched out his hand and Thomas shook it uncertainly. During the seconds they stood appraising one another, Thomas seemed perceptibly to calm down.

"Well, Dr. Shelton," he said finally, "What do *you* think of my wife's chances?"

David looked down momentarily and closed his eyes. Somewhere in a remote corner of his mind, a voice kept telling him that if he could just stall for a few minutes, his clock radio would go off, waking him up. With enormous effort, he brought his eyes up until they met Thomas's.

"Professor Thomas, I have just reviewed your wife's hospital record and met her for the first time," he said deliberately. "It really is impossible at this time for me to assess her whole situation accurately."

55

Thomas opened his mouth to object to what he considered an inadequate answer, but David stopped him with a raised hand. "However," he continued, in measured tones, "I will tell you that I see her as a critically ill woman whose chance of surviving this illness rests not only with receiving the best possible medical and nursing care – which I'm sure you won't deny she *has* – but also in having the will to make it through. *This* is the part I cannot assess yet. That strength comes not only from inside her, but from you, from Dr. Huttner, and from the rest of those who love and care for her.

"I know you'd like to hear a more clinical evaluation of her prospects, but right now I'm not in a position to give you that."

Out of the corner of his eyes, he saw Huttner beaming his approval. *Holy shit, I got out of it,* was all David could think. Then, even before Thomas responded, he felt angry with himself. He had not given even a hint of his true, bleak feelings about Charlotte's chances. As Thomas replied, his anger grew.

"You really don't see it, do you," Thomas said, looking wildly around him. "None of you do. Charlotte and I have been married for over thirty years. Thirty full and happy years. Don't you feel we should have some say as to what kind of agony she is put through to prolong what has until now been a totally rich and fulfilling life?"

This time David did not look away. For several seconds, there was a painful silence. Finally, he spoke. There was anguish in his voice, but also the power of conviction in his words. "Yes, I *do*. I feel exactly as you do, Mr. Thomas. Please believe me."

Again there was an agonising silence. David felt Huttner's eyes on him and sensed the world sinking beneath him. His tone softened. "But you must understand," he said. "I am not your wife's primary physician. Dr. Huttner is. And he is more experienced than I am in every respect of medicine and surgery. It is his final say as to what kind of treatment your wife will or will not receive. I will carry out his orders to the absolute best of my abilities."

Thomas glared at Huttner, then snapped, "I understand, all right. I understand completely." Spinning so fast that he nearly lost his balance, he stalked down the corridor towards his wife's room.

This outburst was the last straw for Huttner. It had been a long and trying day. He stepped back so that David and everyone at the nurses' station was included in his gaze. "I am going to say this one time and one time only." His tone was chilling. "Charlotte Thomas is to be treated as aggressively as necessary to save her life. Have I made myself clear? Good. Now all of you get back to your jobs. Dr. Shelton, perhaps you had better go home and get some rest. Straightening out my practice could prove an exhausting experience for you."

With that, he marched down the hall and followed Peter Thomas into room 412.

David stood alone in the centre of the corridor. The nurses behind the nurses' station some fifteen feet away were frozen and silent. He could feel the spotlight of their gaze turn on him, and with the nervousness of a first-nighter caught unawares he almost bolted. Then, out of the corner of his eye, he saw Christine Beall push herself off the counter and head in his direction. It was hardly the triumphant moment he would have picked for a second encounter with the woman.

As she came nearer, he looked away, inspecting a heel-mark by his shoe. He sensed her eyes measuring him. When they first met, he had been captivated by their gentle power and determination. Now, before their umber stare, he felt vaguely discomforted.

Moments before she spoke, he breathed in her perfume – a muted suggestion of spring. "Dr. Shelton, we're all very proud of the way you stood up for what you believe in," she said softly. "Don't worry. Things have a way of working out."

Her words and the way she said them startled him. They were not at all what he had expected. He repeated them in his mind but could not seem to grasp the feelings behind them. "Thanks . . . thanks a lot," he stumbled, preparing himself to meet her gaze. By the time he looked up, Christine was gone. Activity behind the nurses' station had returned to normal, but she had gone.

David decided to go and write new orders on Anton Merchado before putting the whole ghastly evening to rest. In the morning he would be on his own. As he shuffled away, hopes for the day to come sweetened the distasteful events of the past five hours.

"Things have a way of working out." He said Christine's words out loud as he pushed through the door to the stairway.

5

Christine stood in the deserted corridor after David had left, listening to the clamorous silence of night in the hospital. The sighs and coughs. The moans and laboured, sonorous respirations. Oxygen, gurgling through half a dozen safety bottles. The obedient beep of a monitor in duet with the mindless hiss-click of a respirator. And in the darkened rooms, the patients, thirty-six of them on Four South, locked in their own struggle – a struggle not for riches or power or even happiness, but merely to return to the outside world. To return to their lives.

In less than an hour, two hundred and sixty-three nurses would leave the hospital and head for diners or bars or home to mates and lovers. They would be replaced by one hundred and fifty-four others on the "graveyard shift", each struggling to maintain biological equilibrium in an occupation that demanded life and death decisions during hours when most of the world was sleeping.

At night, more than any time, Christine felt the awesome responsibility of her profession. Like any job, nursing had its routine. But beyond the drudgery and the complaints, beyond the routine and the deprecating attitude of many physicians, lay the most important thing – the patients. At times, it seemed, a silent conspiracy existed among physicians, administrators and nursing organisations to expunge from nurses any notion that their primary purpose was the care of those patients. The conspiracy even included the nurses themselves, many totally drained of the sense of caring and kindness which first brought them into the profession.

Christine gazed down the corridor towards room 412. Silently, she renewed a vow that she would never give in to confusion and pessimism. She would never stop caring. If a commitment to The Sisterhood of Life was the only way to honour that vow, so be it. Somehow, she knew that as long as she was part of The

Sisterhood, she had an outlet for the frustrations and heartache that had driven so many out of hospital nursing.

She remembered the day her commitment had taken root. It was a Sunday. Outside Doctors Hospital a winter storm raged. Inside the nurses' lounge on Four South another kind of storm was brewing. Much of its fury emanated from Christine and all of it was directed against a physician named Corkins who had just ordered an emergency tracheotomy on an eighty-year-old woman, the victim of a massive stroke which had left her paralysed, partially blind, and unable to speak. Christine had spent countless hours caring for her. Although the old woman was unable to move or talk, she had communicated with her eyes. To Christine, the message was clear: "Please, let me go to sleep. Let this living hell end." Now, with the operation, that hell would continue indefinitely.

For nearly an hour, Christine had sat in the nurses' lounge sharing her anger and her tears with Janet Poulos. Carefully, gradually, Janet had introduced her to The Sisterhood of Life.

Over the two days following the old woman's tracheotomy, Christine had spent many hours discussing her cheerless condition with Janet, at the same time learning more and more about The Sisterhood. Throughout her nursing career, she had been able to find joy in even the most distasteful aspects of daily patient care. But with each minute spent helping to prolong the agony of the old woman, Christine's frustration and anger grew. Disconnecting the respirator to suction the tube each hour. Frequent turnings. Urinary catheter changes. Deep intramuscular injections. Frantically trying to keep abreast of one incipient bed sore after another. And always the eyes looking at her, looking through her, their message even more desperate than before.

Finally, the commitment was there. Christine followed the directions given to her by Janet Poulos and reported the old woman's case to the Regional Screening Committee. A day later, she received their approval and instructions.

Towards the end of her shift, she slipped quietly into the woman's room. The drone of the respirator blended eerily with the howling winter wind outside. In the darkness, she felt the woman watching her. She bent over the bed, pressing the tears on her cheek against the woman's temple. After a few moments, she felt her nod – once and then again. She knew! Somehow, she knew. Christine gently kissed her forehead.

She brought her lips close to one ear and whispered, "I love you."

Reaching up, she disconnected the respirator, then waited in the darkness for five minutes before reconnecting it.

Nearly four hours into the next shift a nurse reported that she was unable to feel a pulse or obtain a blood pressure on the woman. A resident was called and after finding a straight line on her electrocardiogram, pronounced the woman dead. Later that morning her two sons, much relieved at the end of their mother's suffering, had the body taken to a local funeral home. Like the waters of a pond, disturbed momentarily by a pebble, the hospital returned to its normal state, the last ripples of the old woman's existence disappearing from its surface. By eleven a.m. her bed was filled by a young divorcée in for elective breast augmentation.

"Christine?"

She spun towards the voice. It was Janet Poulos.

"You okay?"

Christine nodded.

"It looked like you were posing for the cover of Nurse Beautiful."

"More like Nurse Troubled."

"That scene with Huttner and the Professor?"

"Yes."

"Want to talk about it?"

"No. I mean maybe a little. I mean you're the only one who . . ."

Janet silenced her with a raised hand. "The visitors' lounge is empty." She nodded towards the nurses' lounge. "From the looks of things in there, you've got about ten minutes before report. It's been sort of crazy up here tonight, hasn't it. I heard there were some problems after Mr. Chapman was found dead."

As they walked to the small visitors' lounge, Christine described the reaction of John Chapman's grief-stricken widow. Janet shook her head in disbelief.

"So she wrecked everything?"

"Almost. We managed to salvage two vases of flowers." Christine dropped onto a sofa and Janet took the chair opposite.

"Oh?"

"Yes. One of them was rather quirky, too."

Janet suddenly sat up straight. "How do you mean?" The question was asked matter-of-factly, but her expression suggested more than passing interest.

Chrstine glanced at her watch impatiently. They had only five minutes before report. "Oh, it was nothing, really. Probably just someone with an odd sense of humour. The flowers in the vase were lilies, and the card attached to them said something like 'Best wishes from Lily,' that's all."

"Oh, I see." Janet's voice was flat but her eyes were jumping. She scratched absentmindedly at the scar beside her nose, then suddenly changed the subject. "Are you thinking about submitting this Professor Thomas's wife to the Screening Committee?"

"I've already done it." Christine felt off-balance.

"And?"

"Nothing. I haven't heard yet whether she's been approved. You see Charlotte and I have grown very very close to one another – "

"Well, I say 'bravo for you.' " Janet broke in.

"What?"

"I hope she's approved."

"Janet, you don't even know the woman . . . or the situation. How can you possibly say . . . "

"I may not know her, but I know Huttner. Of all the pompous, conceited, self-righteous bastards who ever hid behind a goddamn M.D., Huttner is the worst. Wallace Huttner, M. Deity."

Janet's outburst was totally unexpected. For a time, Christine was speechless. Certainly, it was the overzealous, at times egotistical aggressiveness of physicians that had spawned The Sisterhood, but to Christine, it had always been a conflict of philosophies, not personalities. "Wh . . . what has Huttner's conceit got to do with Charlotte?" She felt confused and strangely apprehensive.

Janet calmed her with a wide smile. "Whoa, slow down," she said patting her on the knee. "I'm on your side. Remember?" Christine nodded, but was still rather bewildered. "I believe in The Sisterhood and what we're doing the same as you do. Why else would I have recruited you? All I was trying to say is that in cases like this Mrs. Thomas we get a . . . double benefit. We get to honour the wishes to the woman and her husband by re-establishing some dignity in her life, and at the same time, we get to remind a person like Huttner that he's not God. Agree?"

Christine relaxed and returned the smile. "Yes, I . . . guess we do." She rose to leave.

"If support is what you need," Janet said, "You've got mine. I think you did the right thing in presenting this woman, and now it's up to the Screening Committee to do its part."

Christine nodded her ackowledgement.

Janet continued as she reached the door. "You know, Christine," she said, pausing to study the younger woman's face, "it's quite all right to benefit from doing something you believe in. The goodness of any work isn't diminished by the fact that you might, in some way, profit from it. Do you understand?"

"I . . . I think so," Christine lied. "Thanks for talking with me. I'll let you know what the Committee decides."

"Thank you. And Chris? I'm here if you need me."

Still feeling uneasy about their conversation, Christine hurried to the nurses' lounge. She paused outside the door, trying to compose herself. Janet's explosion on the subject of Wallace Huttner had been startling, but it wasn't as disturbing as it had at first seemed. Janet had been part of The Sisterhood for years; she must have handled a number of cases. Proposing and carrying out a death, even a merciful death, was an emotionally charged, gut-wrenching business. Over the years, the necessity of facing the same decisions again and again was bound to take its toll in some way. In Janet's case, Christine decided, it was a bitterness towards those who made such awesome choices necessary.

She glanced down the hall in time to see Janet step into the lift. The woman was an excellent supervisor, and even more important, a nurse dedicated to the truest ideals of the profession. In the moment before she entered the nurses' lounge, Christine felt a surge of pride at the secrets she shared with her "sister"

6

Carl Perry steeled himself against the pain he knew would knife through his throat, then as gingerly as possible, swallowed. Pain, almost any pain, was better than the goddamn drooling he had been doing since the polyps or growths or whatever they were had been snipped off his vocal chords. It would be two more days of bed rest, intravenous fluids and writing notes in order to communicate before the danger of his vocal chords swelling shut would be past. At least that's what Dr. Curtis had told him.

He reached over and tugged at the band of adhesive tape that held the intravenous line in place on his right forearm. Several hairs popped free from his skin and he hissed a curse at the nurse who had neglected to shave the area clean. He stuck the edge of the tape down again.

"I.V. tape — complain to Drs. Hosp. Admin." he scribbled on a pad, tearing the note off and stuffing it in a drawer that was rapidly filling with other, similar reminders.

He flipped up the small mirror in his formica hospital tray and took stock of himself. Even with the scratches Curtis's instruments had made on the corners of his mouth, he liked what he saw. Deep blue eyes, tanned skin just leathery enough, square jaw, perfect teeth. He looked the way most other men of forty-eight could only dream of looking. The women saw it too, even the young ones. They fought for the chance to spend a few hours with him in the suite he kept at the Ritz. They all went home satisfied too.

What a perfect idea it had been to start the rumour around the singles bars that each year the girl who gave him the best lay would get a free Porsche courtesy of Perry's Foreign Motors. He might actually do it too, if the day ever came when his looks gave out on him.

Bored and uncomfortable on the sweaty sheets, he flipped on the television, then just as quickly turned it off. Nothing but the eleven o'clock news starting on every channel. He massaged the front of his blue silk pyjama trousers and felt the stirrings of an erection. No, not yet, he decided. Wait until you're really ready to go to sleep, then have at it.

At that moment, a nurse stepped into his room, closing the door carefully behind her. She was the same one who had sat on his bed and talked to him the night before the operation. A little old, maybe forty, he thought, but with a body that just wouldn't quit. Perry felt an immediate surge in the limp organ beneath his hand and again began massaging himself under the sheets, picturing the shapely nurse lying nude on his hotel suite bed, waiting for him.

"How are you doing, Mr. Perry?" she asked softly. She was standing less than a foot from him. Inviting him, he just knew it.

For a moment, Perry was torn by the dilemma of having to release himself in order to write a note. Finally, he scribbled. "Fine, sweetheart, how're you?"

"Is there anything I can get for you before I call it quits for the night?" she said, moving an inch closer.

Perry checked her left hand for a wedding ring. There was none, but that made little difference to his already mushroomed fantasy. "That depends . . . " he wrote.

"On what?"

Teasing him, tantalising — that's what she was doing. He decided to chance it. "Whether we make it now, or after I get out!"

He debated writing about the free Porsche, but rejected the notion as unnecessary.

"Do we do it alone, or invite your wife along with us?"

His new, giddy abstraction had her legs stretched upwards, heels resting on the wall over his bed. "Wife doesn't understand me," he wrote, playing along and adding a little smile face to the bottom of the page.

"Well, we'll see about everything when you're a little better," she said. "I'll admit that the idea of spending some nice time with you had crossed my mind." She toyed with the top button of her uniform and for a moment Perry thought she actually might undo it for him.

"You say when," he scribbled, slipping his free hand around her thigh.

"Soon." She smiled and stepped out of his grasp. "First, I have two presents for you. One is from your doctor, and one is from me. Which do you want first?"

Perry deliberated, then wrote, "Yours."

The woman left the room and returned holding something behind her back. Perry inhaled sharply at the way her uniform pulled tightly across her breasts. A "C" for sure, he thought. Absolutely. 34-C. He looked up at her beaming face, and noticed, for the first time, a thin scar running almost parallel to one side of her nose. A minor flaw, he decided. Candlelight, a little make-up, and *poof*, no more scar.

After giving him what seemed like a deliberately prolonged look at her, the nurse theatrically drew her hands from behind her back. She held a bouquet of flowers. Bright, purple flowers.

"Beautiful," he wrote.

"They're hyacinths," she said.

After a brief search for a vase, she set the flowers in the empty urine bottle that rested on his bedside table. Perry winced at her somewhat crude break with the romantic mood of the moment. Maybe she's into kinky sex, he thought, not at all certain he was ready to play someone else's game.

"Second present?" he wrote.

"Just some new medicine." She moved tantalisingly near as she produced a syringe full of clear liquid from her pocket and injected it in the tubing of his intravenous line.

He reached out and again grabbed her by the back of the thigh. This time she made no attempt to move away. Suddenly, he felt a strange tightness in his chest. His grip weakened, then, in less than a minute, disappeared altogether. With difficulty and mounting panic, he turned his head upwards and looked at the nurse. She was standing motionless, smiling benevolently down at him. He tried to scream, but only a soft hiss emerged from his swollen, paralysed vocal chords.

The air became as thick and heavy as molasses. No matter how hard he tried, he could not force it down into his lungs. His left arm dangled uselessly over the side of the bed.

"It's called pancuronium," the nurse said pleasantly. "A rapid acting form of curare. Just like on poison darts. You see, your wife understands you much better than you realised, Mr. Perry. She understands you so well, that she is willing to share a large portion of your insurance with us in order to eliminate you from her life.''

Perry tried to respond, but could no longer manage even a blink. A dull film seemed to cover all the objects in the room, as gradually, his panic yielded to a detached sense of euphoria. Through now immovable eyes and the thickening haze, he watched the nurse carefully unbutton the top two buttons of her uniform, exposing the deep cleft between her breasts.

''Don't worry about the flowers, Mr. Perry. I'll see to it that they get some water,'' were the last words that he heard.

Janet Poulos set Perry's arm on the bed, checked the darkened corridor of Three West, and calmly left the floor. As the stairway door closed behind her, she smiled in satisfaction. It had been an incredibly profitable day for The Garden. Just as Dahlia had promised it would be. First a masterful performance by Lily, and now she, Hyacinth, had done a very good job.

She laughed, and listened to the echo reverberate round the empty stairwell.

When she reached her office on One North, Janet settled behind her desk, then closed her eyes and relived the scene in Carl Perry's room. The sense of power – of ultimate control – was at least as thrilling as it had been at the bedside. It was an excitement that she, like all the others in The Garden had first discovered through The Sisterhood of Life. That they could be paid, and paid well for their efforts only sweetened the game. Janet blessed Dahlia for bringing Hyacinth to life.

Then, as so often happened after she handled a Sisterhood or Garden case, Janet began thinking about the man – the first man who had ever taken her, the only man she had ever loved. Was he a Professor of Surgery now as he had planned? Why had he never called again after that night? Well, he would certainly see her in a different light now. She had power, too. As much as the most powerful surgeon in the world. If he could only see her he would . . . Janet shrugged. ''Who cares,'' she said out loud. ''Who the hell cares anyhow.''

She picked up the telephone. It was time to share the excitement of the day with Dahlia.

7

At 11.37 p.m., Christine Beall was sitting in the Pinkerton mini-bus on the way from the hospital to Parking Lot C. Exhausted after the eventful seven hour shift, she declined an invitation for a nightcap from the four nurses riding with her and headed home.

Twenty miles away, in the dormitory suburb of Wellesley, Dr. George Curtis downed two fingers of brandy and shuffled back to bed from his oak-panelled study. His wife, who had turned on the bedside lamp and propped herself up on several pillows, looked at him anxiously.

"Well, how did it go with Mrs. Perry?" she asked.

Curtis sank down on the edge of the bed and sighed. "She's pretty shaken up, but all things considered, she seems to be holding together all right. I offered to go over there and talk to her, but she said it wouldn't be necessary, that she had people. Thank God, she didn't say anything about wanting an autopsy."

His wife frowned. "What do you mean 'thank God?' George, is something the matter?"

"Well, from what the resident on duty told me, Perry must have either had a coronary, or bled into his vocal chords where I did the surgery. Either way, his wife could try and make a case for negligence by saying he should have been cared for in the I.C.U. Without an autopsy, she's got no definite findings, so she's got no grounds for a suit, and I say 'Amen' to that."

"Amen, darling," his wife echoed as she turned off the light and rolled over next to him.

Christine drove slowly automatically, with glazed, unseeing eyes.

On the gaslit streets, the night world of the inner city was in full cry. The hookers and the hustlers, the junkies and the winos and the clusters of young men milling outside tavern doorways. It was a world that usually fascinated her, but tonight the people and the action went unnoticed. Her mind had begun playing out a far different scene.

It was a tennis match. Two women on a grassy, emerald court. Or perhaps it was only one, for she never saw them both at the same time. Just a bouncing figure in a white dress, swinging out with energetic, perfect strokes.

Totally immersed in the vision, she cruised through a red light, then onto a wide boulevard leading out of the city.

All at once, Christine realised why it seemed like a match. With each swing, each stroke, the woman's face changed. First it was Charlotte Thomas, radiant, laughing excitedly at every hit; then it was the drawn, sallow face of her own mother, a stern Dutch woman whose devotion to her five children had eventually worn her to a premature death.

The strokes came faster and faster, and with each of them a flashing change in the competitor's face until it was little more than a blur.

Suddenly, Christine glanced at the speedometer. She was going nearly eighty. Seconds later, a route sign flashed past. She was travelling in totally the wrong direction.

Shaking almost uncontrollably, she screeched to a stop on the hard shoulder and sat for several minutes gasping and heart pounding, before she was able to turn around and resume the drive home.

It was after midnight when she reached the quiet, tree-lined street where she and her roommates had lived for two years. The decision to search for an apartment in Brookline had been unanimous. "An old town with a young heart," Carole D'Elia had called it. After a three-week search, they found — and immediately fell in love with — the first floor apartment of a brown and white town house. Their landlady, a blue-haired widow called Ida Fine, lived upstairs. The day after they moved in, a large pot of soup outside their door heralded Ida's intentions to adopt the three of them. Christine had resented her intrusion in their lives at first, but Ida was irrepressible — and usually wise enough to sense when she had overstayed her welcome.

Christine, Carole and Lisa Heller were quite different from one another, but tailor-made for living together. Carole, an up-and-coming criminal lawyer, handled the bills, while Christine took care of the shopping and other day-to-day essentials of co-operative living. Lisa, a buyer for Filene's, was the social chairman.

With a sigh of relief and fatigue, Christine eased her Mustang up the driveway and into its customary spot next to Lisa's battered V.W. The two-car garage was so full of the "treasures" Ida was constantly promising to throw out, that there had never been room inside for more than their bicycles. As she walked around to the front, Christine noticed for the first time that lights were blazing in every room. A party. The last thing in the world she wanted to deal with. "Lisa strikes again," she muttered, shaking her head.

An unmistakable waft of marijuana hit her as soon as she opened the door. From the living room, the music of an old Eagles album mixed with the clinking of glasses and a half a dozen simultaneous conversations. She was racking her brains for somewhere else to sneak off to for the night when Lisa Heller popped out from the living room.

Three years younger than Christine and six inches taller, Lisa was dressed in what had become the unofficial uniform of the house, well worn jeans and a baggy man's shirt, pirated from some past lover. Her face had a perpetually intellectual, almost pious look to it that seemed, invariably, to attract men who were "into" Mahler and organic food, both of which Lisa abhorred.

"Aha! The prodigal daughter returneth to the fold." She giggled.

There was something disarming about Lisa that had always made even Christine's blackest moments seem more manageable. "Lisa," she said smiling around clenched teeth, "how many people are in there?"

"Oh, eight or ten or twelve or so. It's hard to count because some of them aren't really people, you know." She giggled again.

"Do me a favour, please," Christine pleaded. "Go get some rope and your raccoon coat, and see if you can sneak me past the door as your pet Irish wolfhound or something. I just want to go to bed."

70

"Ah, bed," Lisa said wistfully, steadying herself against the wall. "Soon, all that Gallo Chablis and fine Columbian dope in there will have us all in bed. The only question remaining is who will be bedded down with whom. Speaking of which . . . "

"Lisa, is *he* in there?"

"Big as life. It's his dope, doncha know."

Christine grimaced. "Dope or no dope, Lisa, Jerry Crosswaite is hanging on like a bad cold." She shook her head. "It's my own fault," she added with theatrical woe. "My cardinal rule, and I broke it."

"What rule is that?" Lisa punctuated the question with a hiccup.

"Never date a man more than once who has vanity plates on his car with *his* name on them." The two friends laughed and embraced.

Although seeing Jerry still had its pleasant moments, they were becoming fewer and farther between. Ever since his unilateral decision that they were "made for each other", Jerry had mounted an all-out campaign to make Christine "The Wife of the Youngest Senior Loan Officer in Boston Bank and Trust History". For weeks he had barraged her with roses, gifts and phone calls. To Christine's mounting chagrin, Lisa and Carole had become so swept up in the romantic adventure that they had undermined her efforts to discourage his ardour.

"Chrissy, will you stop complaining," Lisa said. "I mean you're over thirty, and he's a nice man with an Alfa. What more could a girl want?"

Christine wasn't totally certain she was being teased. "Lisa, he has fewer sides than a sheet of paper . . . "

"Well, babe, I wouldn't kick 'im out of bed," Lisa said.

"Stick around, Heller, you may get the chance to find out if you mean that." Christine brushed past her and into the living room.

Jerry Crosswaite set down his wine and began a piecemeal effort to rise from the couch and greet her. Christine forced a grin and waved for him to stay where he was. There were twelve others in the room, many of them looking even more gelatinous than Jerry.

"Brutal," Christine muttered, at the same time smiling irrepressibly at Carole D'Elia who was engrossed in a game of her own creation called "Scrabble for Dopes". In this version, to be played only with the aid of marijuana, any word, real or invented, would be counted as long as it could be satisfactorily defined for the other players.

Carole called her over. "Hey, Chrissy, you're the only one with any sense around here. Come and arbitrate. Is or is not 'ZOTL' the noun for a decorative arrangement of dead salamanders?"

"Absolutely," Christine said, giving her a hug from behind. None of the women sharing the house smoked marijuana regularly, but from time to time parties simply materialised, and as often as not pot was part of them. Despite the relative inactivity in the room, there was a sense of vitality which Christine felt every time she was with her roommates. She decided that their company might be just the tonic for her trying day. Even if it meant dealing with Jerry Crosswaite

"By the way," Carole said. "You had a call a little while ago. Some woman. Said she'd call back. No other message."

"A woman? Youngish?" Christine asked anxiously.

"Yes." Carole nodded authoritatively, polished off the rest of her wine, and wrote down her thirteen points.

Crosswaite had negotiated his way across the room and came up behind Christine, putting his hands on her shoulders. She whirled around as if struck by lightning.

"Hey, easy does it, Christine, it's only me," he said. He had discarded the jacket of his Brooks Brothers suit and had unbuttoned his vest — a move that for him was tantamount to letting his hair down. Only the fine, red roadmaps in his eyes detracted from the Playboy image he liked to project.

"Hi, Jerry," she said. "Sorry I missed the party."

His gesture swept the room. "Missed it, hell. It's been waiting for you. Lisa said you liked the necklace. I'm glad."

Christine glanced around for Lisa so that she could glare at her. "Jerry, I really wish you would stop sending me things. I . . . I just don't feel right accepting them."

"But Lisa told me . . . "

She cut him off, trying at the same time to keep her voice calm. "Jerry, I know what Lisa told you, and Carole, too. But neither of them is me. Look, you're a really nice man. They think a lot of you, so do I, but I'm getting very uncomfortable

72

with some of the gifts you've been sending and with a lot of the assumptions you've been making."

"Such as what?" Crosswaite said, an edge of hostility appearing in his voice.

She bit her lower lip and decided that she was simply not up to a confrontation. "Look, just forget it," she said. "We can work the whole thing through another time when there's a little more privacy and a little less wine."

"No, Chris, I want to discuss it now." Crosswaite's control disappeared completely. "I don't know what your game is, but you've led me along to the point where this relationship is really important to me. Now all of a sudden, you've gone frigid." His tone was loud enough to cut through to even the most somnolent in the room. Embarrassed looks began to flash from one to another, as Carole and Lisa rose to intervene. The banker continued. "I mean you were never any tiger in bed to begin with, but at least you were there. Now all of a sudden, you're a fucking glacier around me. I want an explanation!" Everyone froze.

Suddenly the ring of the telephone shattered the silence.

Carole rushed to the kitchen. "Chrissy, it's for you," she called out after a few seconds. "It's the woman who called before."

Christine unclenched her fists and took a deep breath before breaking her gaze away from Crosswaite.

There were three people in the kitchen. With an icy look, Christine sent them scurrying to the living room. Then she picked up the receiver.

"This is Christine Beall," she said sharply.

"Christine, this is Evelyn, from the Regional Screening Committee. Are you in a position where you can talk uninterrupted?"

"Yes, I am." Christine settled onto a high rock-maple stool.

"The Sisterhood of Life praises your deep concern and your professionalism," the woman said solemnly. "Your proposal regarding Mrs. Charlotte Thomas has been approved."

In the quiet kitchen, Christine began, ever so slightly, to tremble, as each word fell like a drop of water on hard, dry ground.

The woman continued. "The method selected will be intravenous morphine sulphate, administered at an appropriate time during your shift tomorrow evening. Two twenty-millilitre ampoules of morphine and a syringe will be beneath the front seat of your car tomorrow morning. Please be certain the passenger door is left open tonight. We shall lock it after the package has been delivered.

"We request that you administer both ampoules as a single injection. There will be no need to wait in the room afterwards. Please dispose of the vials and the syringe in a safe, secure manner. As is our policy, after your shift at the hospital is completed, you will please call the telephone recording machine and tape your case report. We all share the hope and the belief that the day will arrive when our work can become public knowledge. At that time, reports such as yours, nearly forty years' worth from nurses throughout the country, can be properly honoured and receive their due praise. In transmitting your report, there will be no need to repeat the patient's clinical history. Have you any questions?"

"No," Christine said softly, her white-knuckled fingers gripping the receiver. "No questions."

"Very well, then," the woman said. "Miss Beall, you can feel most proud of the dedication you show to your principles and your profession. Good night."

"Thank you. Good night," Christine replied. She was speaking to the dialling tone.

With a glance at the closed door to the living room, Christine pulled on a green cardigan of Lisa's which was draped over a chair. Quietly, she slipped out of the back door of the apartment.

The night sky was endless. Christine shivered against the autumn chill and pulled the sweater tightly about her. In the next street, a car roared around a corner. As the engine noise faded, a silence as deep as the night settled in around her. She looked at the stars – and suddenly felt desperately alone. She felt like a tiny speck in the universe, and the enormity of the decision she had made weighed down upon her. Panic and uncertainty constricted her throat and chest but the words ringing over and over again in her head were Charlotte's: whenever you must really know . . . whenever you must really know . . . She walked slowly over to her car and unlocked the passenger door.

8

David began his first day as Wallace Huttner's replacement by identifying Berlioz as Mendelssohn, but bounced back moments later by correctly forecasting that outside his window a day of change was on the way.

There was a dry chill in the air that kept him from working up the heavy sweat he liked during his run by the river. To the east, an anaemic sun was gradually losing its battle for control to an advancing army of heavy, dark clouds, each with a glossy white border. The day mirrored his mood: the difficult evening rounds with Huttner had left him with a vague sense of discomfort and foreboding that neither a night of fitful sleep nor his morning work-out had totally dispelled.

He had planned to make morning rounds along the same route he and Huttner had taken the previous night, but, once in the hospital, he was impatient to see how Anton Merchado was doing on his new treatment regimen.

The fisherman's bronzed, weathered face broke into a wide grin as soon as David entered his room. With that single smile, David's morning suddenly looked brighter.

"I had a turd, Doc!" Merchado's gravelly voice held all the pride of a mother who had just given birth. "This morning. One, long, plop-in-the-water turd. Doc, I can't thank you enough. I never thought I'd ever have one again."

"Well, don't get too excited about it, Mr. Merchado," David said, unable to resist a smile. "You certainly look better than you did last night, but I don't think the diarrhoea is gone for good. At least not just yet."

"My fever is down, too, and the cramps are almost gone," Merchado added, as David probed his abdomen for areas of tenderness, and listened for a minute with his stethoscope.

"Sounds good," David said, placing the instrument back in

75

his jacket pocket. "But still no solid food. Just sips of liquids and several more days of the new antibiotic and intravenous fluids. You can tell your family that you'll be in the hospital for another week if things keep going well. Maybe even a little longer than that."

"Will you be my doctor when I get out?" he asked.

"No, only for a few days, then Dr. Huttner will be back. You're fortunate to have him, Mr. Merchado. He's one of the finest surgeons I've ever seen."

"Maybe . . . and then again, maybe not." Merchado's squint and wise smile said that he would push the matter no further. "But you leave your card with me just the same. I have a bunch of relatives that are gonna be beating down your door to get you to do some kind of operation on them. Even if they got nothing wrong."

With a grin that understated his delight, David left the room, then looked at the list of patients he had to see that morning. The names filled both sides of the file card on which he had printed them. His spirits soared. For so many years he had not allowed himself even to daydream of having such a case load. As he neared the end of the corridor, he gave a gleeful yodel and danced through the stairway door. Behind him, two plump dowager nurses watched his performance, then exchanged disapproving expressions and several "tsks" before heading pompously to their charges.

David's rounds were more exhilarating than anything he had done in medicine in years. Even Charlotte Thomas seemed to have brightened up a little, although simply seeing her with the benefit of daylight may have had something to do with that impression. Her bed was cranked to a forty-five degree angle and an aide was spoon-feeding her tiny chips of ice, one at a time. David tried to gauge how she was feeling, but her only response was a weak smile and a nod. He examined her abdomen, wincing inwardly at the total absence of bowel sounds. No cause for panic yet, but each day without sounds made the possibility of yet another operation more likely. For a moment, David toyed with the notion of stopping even the ice chip feedings, then, with one last look at Charlotte he decided to leave things as they were.

At the nurses' station, he wrote a lengthy progress note and some orders for measures he hoped might improve her condition. By the time he finished it was nearly one o'clock. He had twenty minutes for coffee and a sandwich before he was due in his own office. Five and a half hours had passed in what seemed almost no time at all. He tried to remember the last time it had been like this and realised it had probably been eight years. Not, he reflected ruefully, since the accident.

Even his afternoon office hours, at times embarrassingly slow, were made pleasantly hectic today by frequent phone calls from the hospital nurses to clarify orders or discuss problems.

At precisely five o'clock, as the door closed behind the last patient, David's office nurse, Mrs. Houlihan yelled, "Dr. Shelton, there's a call for you from Dr. Armstrong. Her secretary is putting her on. You can pick up on three."

"Very funny," David shouted back from his office. He had only one telephone: its number happened to end in three. It was good to see Houlihan enjoying the unaccustomed busy day as much as he was.

"I'm off to cook up some hash for my brood. Good night, doctor," she called out.

"Good night, Houlihan," David answered.

Moments later, Dr. Margaret Armstrong came on the line. As the first female Chief of Cardiology at a major hospital, Armstrong had earned nearly as much of a reputation in her field as had Wallace Huttner in his. Of all those on the medical staff of Doctors Hospital, she had been the most cordial and helpful to David, especially during his first year. Although she referred her patients to cardiac surgeons almost exclusively, or, where appropriate, to Huttner, she had on several occasions sent a case to David, taking pains each time to send him a thank-you note for the excellent care he delivered.

"David? How are things going?" she asked.

"Busy today, but enjoying every minute, Dr. Armstrong." Perhaps it was her regal bearing, her aristocratic air; perhaps it was the twenty or so years difference in their ages – whatever the reason, David had never once had the impulse to address Margaret Armstrong by her first name. Nor had he ever been encouraged to.

"Well, I'm calling to see if I can make it busier for you," Armstrong said. "To be perfectly honest, I called Wally

Huttner's office first, but I was pleased to hear that you're covering for him.''

"Thanks. Fire away.''

"It's an elderly gentleman named Butterworth. Aldous Butterworth, if you will. He's seventy-seven, but bright and spry as a puppy. He was doing fine for a week following a minor coronary until just a little while ago when he suddenly started complaining about tingling and pain in his right leg. His pulses have disappeared from the groin down.''

"Embolus?'' David asked, more out of courtesy than any uncertainty about the diagnosis.

"I would think so, David. The leg is already developing some pallor. Are you in the mood to fish us out a clot?''

"Happy to,'' David beamed. "Have you gone over the risks with him?''

"Yes, but it wouldn't hurt for you to do it again. David, I'm a bit worried about general anaesthesia in this man. Do you think it might be possible to . . . ''

David was so excited about capping his day with a major op that he actually cut her short. "Do him under local? Absolutely!''

"I knew I could count on you,'' Armstrong said. "I am most anxious to hear how things go. Aldous is a dear old friend. Listen, there's an Executive Committee meeting in an hour, and as Chief of Staff in this madhouse, I have to attend. Could I meet you somewhere later this evening?''

"Sure,'' David said. "I have several patients to see before I head home. How about Four South? I've got a woman to see there with total body failure. Maybe you can even come up with some ideas.''

"Glad to try,'' Armstrong said. "Eight o'clock?''

"Eight o'clock,'' David echoed.

Hands scrubbed and clasped protectively in front of him, David backed into Operating Room 10, then slipped into a surgical gown and began making preparations to orchestrate and conduct his own symphony. Aldous Butterworth seemed small and vulnerable stretched out on the narrow operating table.

David ordered Butterworth's right foot to be placed in a clear,

78

plastic bag to keep it visible without contaminating his operative field. The foot was the colour of white marble.

Using small injections, he deadened an area of the man's right groin. With no pulse to guide him, David knew that the femoral artery could be an inch or more away from his incision. A miscalculation, and he faced an operation so difficult that a second incision might be the only solution. Focus in, he thought. Visualise it.

"Scalpel, please," he said, taking the instrument from the scrub nurse. He paused, closed his eyes, and breathed in the electricity of the moment. The cold steel tingled in his grasp, and he felt his senses sharpened to the finest point. Under the crispness of his mask, he smiled. He was ready. Looking up, he surveyed the expectant faces watching him, waiting for him. With a slight nod to the anaesthetist and a final glance at Butterworth's bloodless foot, he made his decisive incision. The taut skin sprang apart, immediately exposing the femoral artery. "Bullseye," he whispered.

The artery lay stiff and heavy with clotted blood. In minutes, David had isolated and loosely clamped it with two thin strips of cloth tape placed two inches apart. So far so good. Pressing the point of the scalpel into the vessel wall, he made a small incision between the tapes. Thick, dark blood oozed through the cut. Gently, he eased a long, thin tube with a deflated balloon at the tip down the inside of the artery towards the foot. When he thought the tip was in position near the foot, he blew up the balloon and slowly pulled the tube back through the incision. Two feet of stringy, dark clot were pushed out before David lifted the balloon free. Repeating the procedure in the opposite direction, he removed the thicker clot that had caused the obstruction. After irrigating with blood thinner, he was ready to close. He tightened the cloth tapes to prevent blood flow through the artery, then closed his incision in the vessel with a series of tiny sutures.

Outwardly very calm, inwardly very tense, David looked up for the second time in twenty minutes at the circle of eyes which watched him from the strips between caps and masks. He took a silent, deep breath, held it, and released the tapes. Instantly, Butterworth's foot flushed with life-giving colour. A cheer burst out from the team. Textbook perfect. The whole thing, textbook perfect. In exhilaration, he called out the good news to Butterworth, who had slept through the entire operation.

"That was *really* fine work, Dr. Shelton . . . really *fine* work . . . *really fine* work." David repeated the words of the veteran scrub nurse over and over, trying to reproduce her inflection exactly. He had dictated an operative note, showered and dressed, and was now striding jauntily down the corridor of Four South to share the news of Butterworth's successful operation with Dr. Armstrong.

Margaret Armstrong had already arrived on the floor and was sitting at the nurses' station drinking coffee and chatting with Christine Beall and the Charge Nurse, Winnie Edgerly. As David approached them, his eyes were drawn to Christine as she looked up at him. Her eyes and her smile seemed to be saying a thousand different things to him at the same time. Or maybe they were his words, his thoughts, not hers. Lauren's jewel-perfect face flashed in his mind, but faded as the tawny eyes engulfed him.

Dr. Armstrong's voice broke the spell. " 'Lo, David," she called out merrily. "Word is sweeping the hospital about my little man's new foot. Bravo. Come, we shall toast your successful operation with a cup of this coffee." She glanced in her cup, grimaced, then added, "If, in fact, that is what this is."

She wore a black skirt and light blue cashmere sweater, adorned simply with an elegant gold butterfly pin. Her white clinic coat, unbuttoned, was knee-length – the type reserved unofficially only for professors, or those with sufficient seniority in the teaching community. Her dark, wavy hair was cut short in a style perfect for her bright, blue eyes and finely carved features. There was an air about her, an energy, that commanded immediate attention and respect. An article written six years before about her contributions to her field had dubbed her the Grande Dame of American Cardiology; she had been only fifty-eight years old at the time.

Pouring David a cup of coffee, Dr. Armstrong introduced him to the nurses as the "hero of the day", and, with a mischievous wink at Christine, added that David was to the best of her knowledge still single. He laughed, but blushed and looked down in genuine embarrassment, realising at the same time that he was carefully avoiding any further eye contact with Christine. Seconds later, Armstrong had him describing Butterworth's operation blow by blow. For the moment, the danger of having to analyse his feelings for Christine had passed.

"Well," Dr. Armstrong said finally, after David had described the rosy hue of the old man's foot when he had released the tapes. "I stopped by the recovery room to see Aldous and he doesn't remember a thing. Snoozed his way through the whole ordeal. Here he is in danger of losing a leg or worse, and he sleeps through the procedure. That is my idea of good local anaesthesia, what?"

"I think I put him to sleep while I was trying to explain what I was going to do to him," David said.

Armstrong and the two nurses laughed appreciatively, then Armstrong said, "David, you mentioned something about having a complicated patient here on Four South. Is it Charlotte Thomas?"

"Well, as a matter of fact, it is," David said. "How did you know? Are you a psychic as well as a cardiologist?"

"Nothing that exotic, I'm afraid. The nurses and I deduced that she was the only one on the floor who fitted the bill, so I took the chance and went over her chart."

"And?"

"And, you're right. She is rapidly developing total body failure. In fact, I have only one observation to add to the excellent note you wrote this morning outlining her many problems. Your Mrs. Thomas has, on top of everything else, definite signs of coronary artery disease on her electrocardiogram. At least in *my* interpretation of her electrocardiogram," she added modestly. "I really have nothing dramatic to contribute to what is already being done. Does it seem as though the bowel obstruction will require re-exploration?"

"God, I hope not," David said, with feeling. "It would mean her third major operation in less than three weeks."

"Dr. Shelton, I have a question," Christine said, suddenly.

He responded quickly. "It's 555-2016."

"What is?"

"My phone number!" David said, immediately realising that he should have learned more about Christine Beall before testing

81

out his sense of humour on her.

Nurse Edgerly laughed briefly, but Christine did not crack the slightest smile. "It's not funny," she said. "Charlotte Thomas is probably sicker and in more pain than any other patient in this hospital."

David muttered an apology, but Christine went on, "What concerns me, is why, if she has so many seemingly incurable problems, Dr. Huttner has made her a full Code Ninety-nine? Especially after what happened last night."

"Last night?" Armstrong asked. "What happened last night?"

David paused, uncertain which of them she was addressing. Christine sat back, looking expectantly at him for his version.

"Well," he said finally, "Mrs. Thomas's husband and Dr. Huttner got into a discussion about the aggressive approach Huttner has elected to take in her treatment. Professor Thomas was frustrated and more than a little angry. Understandable, I guess, and certainly something we're all used to handling."

"And how *did* Wally handle it?" Armstrong leaned forward with interest, absently rolling her coffee cup back and forth between her hands.

"As well as could be expected under the circumstances, I think," David said. "He may have over-reacted a bit. He stuck by his philosophical guns. Refused to alter his treatment plan regardless of what Thomas, who was under obvious strain and pressure, demanded him to do. Finally, Huttner drew *me* into the whole thing. I'm afraid my opinion and the way I expressed it were not quite what he wanted to hear in that situation." David managed a rueful grin at his own understatement.

"And how *do* you feel about the whole thing, David?"

Dr. Armstrong's voice was soft. There was an openness in her expression that made him certain there would be no recrimination.

"I think it's a bitch of a situation, if you'll pardon the expression," he said. "I mean it's always harder to decide *not* to use treatment on a patient than it is to just go ahead and employ every medicine, machine and operation you can think of. That's why we end up with so many patients who drag on as little more than vegetables.

"Having watched several of my own family members die

82

prolonged and painful deaths, I personally think there are times when a doctor must make the decision to hold off and let nature take its course. Don't you agree?''

Hold off . . . let nature take its course . . . . There was something about the words, the way they were said. Margaret Armstrong closed her eyes as they echoed in her mind, then yielded to other words. The voice of a young girl.

"It's all right, Mama . . . I'm here, Mama."

"Don't you agree, Dr. Armstrong?''

"Mama, tell me what I can do to help . . . Does it still hurt as much? Tell me what I can do to help . . . Please tell me what I can do . . . "

"Dr. Armstrong?''

"Oh, yes," she shook her head slightly. "Well, David, I'm afraid I agree much more with Dr. Huttner's approach than with yours." How long had she drifted off? Were they expecting an explanation?

"How do you mean?''

No, she decided. No explanations. "The way I see it, following your philosphy, a physician would constantly be confronted with the need to play God. To decide who is to live and who is to die. A medical Nero. Thumbs up, we put in an intravenous. Thumbs down, we don't.''

David responded with an emotion and forcefulness that startled even himself. "I believe that the major responsibility of a physician is not constantly to do battle against death, but to do what he can to lessen pain and improve the quality of patients' lives. I mean," he went on with less vehemence, "should every treatment, every operation possible be used on a patient, even though we know there's only a one in a million or even a one in ten thousand chance that it will help?'' In the silence that followed, he sensed that, once again, he'd used a verbal cannon where a sling-shot would have sufficed.

At this point, Winnie Edgerly, a straight-forward if somewhat plodding woman of about fifty, felt moved to enter the discussion. "I cast my vote with Dr. Armstrong," she said earnestly. "I wouldn't want any tubes pulled out of *me* if there was the even slightest chance. I mean, who knows what might happen, or what might come along at the last minute to help? Right?''

"Please don't get me wrong, Nurse Edgerly," David said,

carefully minimising the intensity in his voice. "I'm not advocating pulling out tubes from anyone. I'm arguing that we should all think twice – or more than twice – before putting the tubes down someone in the first place. Sure they *can* help, but they can also prolong hopeless agony. Do you understand what I mean?"

Edgerly nodded, but David could see that she did not agree.

Finally, Dr. Armstrong said, "So, David, how does all this apply to your Mrs. Thomas?"

"It doesn't," he said curtly. "The treatment for Mrs. Thomas has been clearly spelled out by Dr. Huttner. It's my responsibility to carry out those plans to the best of my ability. That's all there is to it."

Armstrong seemed about to say something further, when the overhead page sounded, summoning David to the emergency ward. "It never rains, but it pours." He smiled at Dr. Armstrong.

"But I'll bet you don't mind getting wet like this at all," she said. "I'm very happy for you, David."

"Thank you, Dr. Armstrong." He swallowed the last of his coffee. "Thank you for everything."

With a nod to Nurse Edgerly and a longer look at Christine, David headed off towards the emergency ward.

Christine sat silently behind the nurses' station as the others dispersed to go about their business. There was a puzzled, almost ironic expression on her face. She slipped her right hand into the pocket of her uniform and, for a moment or two, fingered the large syringe and two ampoules of morphine which she had wrapped in a handkerchief and stuffed inside. Then she rose and walked with forced nonchalance down the hall towards room 412.

9

"Do you do hands, Dr. Shelton," asked Harry Weiss, the hawk-nosed resident who had called David to the emergency ward.

"Show me what you have," David said.

The emergency ward was in its usual state of mid-evening chaos. Two dozen patients variously uncomfortable and angry sat in the crowded waiting room. Trolley stretchers glided past like freighters in a busy port, bearing their human cargo to X-ray, the short-term observation ward or an in-patient room. Telephones jangled. A dozen different conversations competed with one another. David caught snatches of several of them as the resident led him to Trauma Room 8. "What do you mean you can't have the results for an hour? This man is bleeding out. We need them now . . . " "Mrs. Ramirez, I understand how you feel, but I can't help you. There is simply no Juan Ramirez on the emergency ward at this time . . . " "Now, you're going to feel a little pin prick . . . "

The patient David had been called about was a forty-year-old labourer who had lost a brief but unmistakably furious encounter with his power saw. The top halves of two fingers were gone completely, and a third was held together at the first knuckle by a sliver of tendon. Another no-win situation, David thought to himself as he evaluated the damaged hand. He spoke briefly with the man, who had stopped his profuse sweating but was still the colour of sun-bleached bone. Then he guided the overwrought young resident into the hallway. David had to decide whether to do the repair himself or to spend the extra time to take the resident through it. He chose to take the time, remembering the many late nights when other surgeons had made the extra effort to teach him. It was nearly half an hour before he felt confident that Weiss could complete the repair on his own.

Four South was unusually quiet as David stepped out of the

lift and started down the corridor towards room 412. A burst of laughter from the nurses' lounge suggested it was coffee break time, at least for some of the staff. His thoughts turned to Christine Beall, and he half hoped that she might step out of one of the rooms as he was passing. She's interesting-looking and has strange eyes, David thought. But it's more than that. She seems so intense, so caring . . . Oh, but come off it. Lauren is beautiful and has incredible eyes. You're only reacting like this because she's away. Face it, with Lauren you have everything you've ever wanted in a woman — beauty, brains, independence. Right? Even so . . .

The lights in Charlotte Thomas's room were off. David stood at the doorway, staring through the darkness towards her bed. The gastro-intestinal drainage machine, set for intermittent suction, whirred, stopped, then whirred again. Bubbles of oxygen tinkled through the water of the safety bottle on the wall. He debated whether or not to disturb her in order to check findings he knew would be unchanged. Finally, he walked across the room and turned on the fluorescent light over her bed.

Charlotte was lying on her back, a tranquil half-smile on her face. It took David several seconds to realise that she was not breathing.

With a gasp, he instinctively reached across her neck and checked for a carotid pulse. For an instant he thought he felt one, but then knew that it was his own heart, pounding through his fingertips. With both fists he delivered a sharp blow to the centre of Charlotte's chest. Then he gave two deep mouth-to-mouth breaths and several quick compressions to her breastbone. Another carotid check still showed nothing.

He raced to the doorway. "Code Ninety-nine four-twelve," he screamed down the deserted corridor. "Code Ninety-nine four-twelve." He ran back inside, and resumed his one-man resuscitation.

Thirty seconds passed in what seemed like a year before Winnie Edgerly burst into the room pushing the emergency trolley. At the same instant, the page operator, alerted from the nurses' station, announced, "Code Ninety-nine, Four South. Code Ninety-nine, Four South . . . Code Ninety-nine, Four South."

Seconds later, room 412 began to fill with people and

machines. Edgerly inserted a short oral airway into Charlotte's mouth and began providing respirations as best she could with a breathing bag. David continued the external cardiac compression. An aide rushed in, then wandered meekly to one side of the room, waiting for someone to tell her what to do. Two more nurses raced in, followed by Christine, pushing an electrocardiograph machine. Leads from the machine were strapped tightly to Charlotte's wrists and ankles.

A resident appeared, then another, and finally the anaesthetist, a huge oriental who introduced himself hurriedly as Dr. Kim. He replaced Edgerly at the head of the bed and looked over at David, who had handed the job of cardiac massage over to one of the residents and had moved to man the cardiograph.

"Tube her?" Dr. Kim asked. David nodded.

As the room filled with still more people, including the inhalation and laboratory technicians, Kim set about his task. He picked up a steel laryngoscope and inserted its right-angle, lighted blade deeply into Charlotte's throat, lifting up against the base of her tongue to expose the delicate, silver half-moons of her vocal chords.

"Give me a seven-point-five tube," he said to the nurse assisting at his side. The clear plastic tube, with a diameter of three quarters of an inch, had a deflated plastic balloon wrapped just above the tip. Skilfully, the large man slipped the tube between Charlotte's vocal chords and down into her trachea. He used a syringe to blow up the balloon, sealing the area around the tube against air leaks. Then he attached the black Ambu breathing bag to the outside end of the tube, connected oxygen to the bag, and began supplying Charlotte with lungfuls of oxygen at a rate of thirty per minute.

Christine stood and watched as David tried to centre the needle on the cardiograph. All at once, her eyes riveted on the slashing strokes of the stylus. There was a rhythm, a persistent, regular rhythm. "Oh, my God, he's bringing her back!" Her thoughts screamed the words. The one possibility she had never considered, and now it was happening. With every beat, a new horrifying images occurred to her. Charlotte, hooked to a respirator. More tubes. Day upon endless day of wondering if the woman's oxygen-deprived brain would awaken. *What had she done?*

The finely lined paper flowed from the machine like lava, forming a jumbled pile at David's feet. The rhythmic bursts continued.

"Hold it for a second!" David called for the resident to halt his thrusting cardiac compressions in order to get a true reading from the machine.

Instantly, the pulsing jumps of the needle disappeared, replaced by only a fine quiver. The pattern had been artificial – a response to the efforts of the resident.

Christine had misinterpreted the cardiograph. She felt near collapse.

"Her rhythm looks like fine fibrillation. Please resume pumping." David's voice was firm, but calm. Christine sensed a measure of control return. "Christine, please get set to give her four hundred joules."

The order registered slowly. Too slowly.

"Nurse Beall!" David snapped the words.

"Oh, yes Doctor. Right away." Christine rushed to the defibrillator machine. Was everyone staring at her? She couldn't bring herself to look up. Turning the dial on the machine to 400, she squirted contact jelly on the two steel paddles and handed them to David.

David motioned the resident away. Then he quickly pressed one paddle along the inside of Charlotte's left breast and the other one six inches below her left armpit.

"Everyone away from the bed," he called out. "Ready? Now!"

He depressed the red button on the top of the right-hand paddle. A dull thunk sounded as four hundred joules of electricity shot through Charlotte's chest and on through the rest of her body. Like a marionette, her arms flipped towards the ceiling, then dropped limply to the bed. Her body arched rigidly for an instant, then was still. The cardiograph tracing showed no change.

The resident resumed his pumping, but soon motioned to the medical student standing nearby that he was tiring. The two made a smooth change.

Immediately, David began ordering medications to be given through Charlotte's intravenous lines. Bicarbonate to counteract the mounting lactic acid in her blood and tissues, adrenalin to stimulate cardiac activity, even glucose on the chance that her sugar may have dropped too low for some reason. No change. Another adrenalin injection followed closely by two more four hundred joule countershocks. Still nothing. Calcium, more bicarbonate, a fourth shock. The cardiogram now showed a straight line. Even the fine fibrillation was gone. The resident again took his place over from the student and the pumping continued. At the head of the bed, the massive anaesthetist stood implacably squeezing the Ambu bag, which seemed like little more than a pliant black softball in his thick hands.

"Hook an amp of adrenalin to a cardiac needle please," David ordered. Although an injection through the subclavian intravenous line should end up in the heart, perhaps the tip had somehow become dislodged. He put his hand along the left side of Charlotte's breastbone and used his fingers to count down four rib spaces. Holding the ampoule of adrenalin in his other hand, he plunged the four and a half inch needle attached to it straight down into Charlotte's chest. Almost immediately a plume of dark blood jetted into the ampoule. A direct hit. The needle was lodged in some part of the heart. Behind him, Christine held her breath and looked away.

David shot in the adrenalin. For a moment, the cardiograph needle began jumping, and with it, his own pulse. Then he noticed that the medical student was rocking back and forth, inadvertently bumping into Charlotte's left arm dangling off the bed each time. He motioned the student away from the bed. Instantly, the tracing was again a flat line.

Christine felt the tension in the room slowly dissolving. It was almost over. She stared at the floor.

David looked at the anaesthetic with a shrug that asked, "Any ideas?"

Dr. Kim stared back placidly and said, "Will you open her chest?"

For a few seconds, David actually considered the idea. "How are her pupils?" He was stalling, he knew it.

"Fixed and dilated," Kim replied.

David gazed off into one corner of the room. Could be, *should* he do more? His eyes closed tightly, then opened. Finally, he reached over and flicked off the cardiograph. "That's it. Thank you, everybody." It was all he could manage to say.

The room began to empty. David stood there for a time, looking down at Charlotte's lifeless form. Despite the tubes and the bruises, and the circular electrical burns on her chest, there was something beautifully peaceful about the woman.

Peaceful, at last.

All at once, the impact of what had happened began to register. His hands and armpits became cold and damp with sweat.

As he walked out of room 412 to call Wallace Huttner, David was shaking. Deep inside him was the chilly feeling that somehow, he was just stepping into, rather than out of, a nightmare. He glanced at the wall clock. How long had they worked on her? Forty-five minutes? An hour? "What the hell difference does it make," he muttered as he sat down at the nurses' station to write a death note in Charlotte Thomas's chart.

"You all right?" Christine asked softly as she set a cup of muddy coffee in front of him.

"Huh? Oh, yeah, I'm okay. Thanks," David said, resting his chin on the counter and studying the styrofoam cup at close range. "Thanks for the coffee."

"I'm sorry she didn't make it through for you," she added.

David continued staring at the cup, as if searching for the answer to some kind of cosmic mystery.

"Potassium!" he exclaimed suddenly.

Christine, who had moved to leave the uncomfortable silence, turned back to him. "What about potassium?"

He looked up. "Something wasn't right in there, Christine. I mean over and above the obvious. I may be wrong, but I can't remember handling a cardiac arrest where I couldn't get a flicker of cardiac activity back, even when quite a bit of time had elapsed between the arrest and the Code Ninety-nine. Shit! I wish there had been time to get a potassium level on her. Potassium, calcium — I don't know what, but something was wrong there."

"Can't you get a potassium level done now?" Christine asked.

"Sure, but it won't be much help. During resuscitation and after death, potassium is released into the bloodstream from the tissues, so the levels are usually high anyway." He clenched his fists in frustration.

Christine felt a knot in her stomach. "H-How could her

90

potassium level have got out of line in the first place?''

"Lots of ways." David was too distracted to notice her worried expression. "Sudden kidney failure, a blood clot, even a medication error. It makes no difference now. I'm probably way out anyway. Dead is dead." He realised how distressed she must be feeling. "I . . . I'm sorry," he said. "I didn't mean that. I'm afraid the pleasant task of calling Dr. Huttner on the Cape has me a little rattled. I don't think this is the sort of news he'd be too happy about me saving until he gets back. Look, maybe sometime we can sit and talk about Mrs. Thomas. Okay?"

Christine looked away. "Maybe sometime . . ." she whispered to herself.

David fished out the number Huttner had given him. After the usual hassles with the hospital switchboard operator, his call was put through. Huttner's hello left no doubt that he had been asleep.

"Great start," David muttered, looking upwards for some kind of celestial help. "Dr. Huttner, this is David Shelton," he said into the receiver.

"Yes, what is it David?" His first words held an edge of impatience.

David knew then that he should have waited until the next day to call. "It's about Charlotte, Dr. Huttner. Charlotte Thomas." His head began to thud dully.

"Well, what about her?"

"About an hour and a half ago she was found pulseless in her bed. We worked on her, a full Code Ninety-nine for nearly an hour, but no response at all. She's dead, Dr. Huttner."

"What do you mean you worked on her? What in the hell happened, man? I checked on her before I left this morning, and she seemed stable enough."

David had not anticipated an easy time of it with Huttner, but neither had he expected a war.

"I . . . I don't know what happened," he said. "Maybe hyperkalemia. She had a brief period of fine fibrillation on her cardiogram, then nothing. Flat line. No matter what. Absolutely nothing."

"Hyperkalemia?" Huttner's tone was now more one of

astonishment than anger. "She's never had problems with her potassium in the past."

"Do you want me to call Mr. Thomas?" David asked finally.

"No, leave that to me. It's what he wanted anyway." Huttner's voice drifted away then picked up with renewed intensity. "What you can do for me is to get in touch with Ahmed Hadawi, the Chief of Pathology. Tell him there'll be a post-mortem on this woman tomorrow. I want to know exactly what happened. If for some reason Thomas won't consent, I'll notify Hadawi myself that it's off. You tell him we'll be at the Autopsy Suite tomorrow morning at eight sharp with a signed permission from Peter Thomas. Good night."

"Good night," David said, a minute or so after Huttner had hung up. He set the receiver down, then sighed softly, "Good grief."

The nurses' station was quiet — David was alone but for a ward secretary painfully trying not to notice him. Eyes closed, he sat rubbing his temples, struggling to sort out the unpleasant emotions swirling within him. Confusion? Sure, that was understandable. Depression? A little, perhaps. He had lost a patient. Loneliness? Dammit, he wished Lauren were home.

But there was something else. It was hazy and diffuse. Difficult to focus on. But there *was* something, some other feeling. Several minutes passed before David began to understand. Underlying all his reactions, all his emotions, was a vague nebula of fear. Trembling for reasons which were not at all clear to him, he dialled Lauren's number, hanging up only after the tenth ring. Even though he had unfinished business in the hospital, he felt the urgent need to get out. He would call Hadawi from home, he decided.

"This is Christine Beall of Boston Doctors Hospital," Christine said in a measured monotone onto the recording machine. "In the name of compassionate medical care, and on instructions of The Sisterhood of Life, I have, on October 2nd, helped to end the hopeless pain and suffering of Mrs. Charlotte Thomas with an intravenous injection of morphine sulphate. The prolongation of unnecessary human suffering is to be despised, and the dignity of human life and human death to be preserved at all costs. End of report.''

She hung up. Though she had no qualms about the rightness of what she had done, David's despondency had pained her. On an impulse, she picked up the receiver and dialled Jerry Crosswaite's number. With the sound of his voice, the impulse vanished.

"Hello," he said, "Hello . . . Hello?''

Christine gently set the receiver back.

In the shadows at the far end of the hall, Janet Poulos observed Christine as she left report and made the call she felt certain was her case report on Charlotte Thomas.

"Sound her out about The Garden," Dahlia had urged. "Be careful what you say, but sound her out.''

Janet countered with her belief that Beall was far too new in The Sisterhood to be ready for The Garden, but Dahlia had insisted.

"Just remember," she said, "what would have happened to you three years ago had I decided *you* weren't ready. As I recall, you were thinking about taking your own life before I phoned.''

In fact, Janet had passed beyond the thinking stage by then. At the moment of Dahlia's call, she had over a hundred sleeping pills laid out on her bedspread. Self-loathing and a profound sense of impotence had pushed her to the brink of suicide.

For years she had lived on hatred – hatred towards physicians in general, and one in particular. She had joined The Sisterhood to get the organisation's help in putting certain M.D.s in their place. Where necessary, she had even manufactured data on patients to get the Regional Screening Committee's approval and recommendations.

However, after six years and nearly two dozen cases, what little satisfaction she had gained from such activities had disappeared.

Then, with a single phone call, everything had changed. Dahlia knew about Janet's falsified laboratory and X-ray reports, about her hatred for physicians and their power, about many intimate details of her life. She knew, but she took no action to stop her.

Over the year after she joined The Garden, Janet was brought along slowly. Every few weeks, Dahlia would transmit the name of a patient in the north-east who had been approved by The Sisterhood for euthanasia. Janet would arrange a meeting with the distraught family of the patient, and offer a merciful death for their loved one in exchange for a substantial payment. The contract, once made, was then unwittingly honoured by the Sisterhood nurse who had initially proposed the case.

It was a wonderful, lucrative diversion, but The Garden had much, much more in store for Hyacinth. Other flowers blossomed within Doctors Hospital. One of them, Lily, was transplanted from the ranks of The Sisterhood by Janet herself. Soon, both women were given other responsibilities, primarily in the area of direct patient contact Dahlia had called them. They were no longer bound to Sisterhood cases. Euthanasia was not a concern – the new cases had proven more rewarding in every sense. John Chapman and Carl Perry were just two of them.

As Christine rang off, Janet moved towards her. Dahlia had reasoned that after handling a case as traumatic as Charlotte Thomas's, Beall might be ready. Hyacinth still had strong doubts. She would talk with the woman, but only until her own suspicions were confirmed. Beall would need a few more years of tongue lashings from physicians who, as often as not, were deadly weapons in their own right. She would need a few more thankless Sisterhood cases.

Then she might be ready.

Christine saw Janet coming, and waited.

"It's done?" Janet asked solemnly. Christine nodded. "Talk for a few minutes?" Again she nodded. In silence, they walked to the visitors' lounge. Christine dropped onto the sofa and, this time, Janet sat next to her.

"It's never easy, is it?" Janet folded one leg beneath her and watched as Christine picked nervously at the edge of the coffee table.

"I'm okay, Janet. Really. I know what I did — what we're doing — is right. I know how badly Charlotte wanted it to end. Her liver riddled with cancer, and Dr. Huttner wanted to keep sticking tubes in her. It was right." Her voice was strained, but under control.

"You'll get no arguments from me, kid," Janet said, reaching

94

over and squeezing her hand reassuringly. Christine squeezed back. "It's just too bad that we're the ones who have to shoulder all the darn responsibility, that's all." Christine responded with a nod and a rueful shrug. Perhaps Dahlia was right. Janet decided to push a bit further. "All that responsibility, and what do we have to show for it? Nothing."

Christine spun towards her, eyes flashing. "Janet! What on earth do you mean, nothing?"

Time to retreat, Janet decided. For once in her life, at least, Dahlia had misjudged. Beall's naive, idealistic flame had not yet been doused. She took pains to meet Christine's gaze levelly. "I mean that after all these years, after all the hundreds, the thousands of Sisterhood recruits, nothing has changed in the attitude of the medical profession."

"Oh." Christine relaxed.

"So, until things change, we do what we have to do. Right?"

"Right."

"Listen, Christine. Let's have dinner sometime soon. We have a lot in common, you and I, but this is hardly the place to discuss our mutual interests. Check your schedule and I'll check mine. We'll set something up in the next few days. Okay?"

"Okay. And, Janet, thanks for your concern. I'm sorry I snapped at you. This day's been a bitch, that's all."

Janet smiled warmly. "If you can't snap at your sister, who can you snap at. Right?"

"Right."

Janet rose. "I've got to get Charlotte taken care of. Her husband left word he won't be coming in to see her. Call me at home anytime you need to talk." With a wave, she left. At least Dahlia would know she had tried. Beall simply wasn't ready. Too bad.

Christine returned in time for the end of report. Restless, and sated with nursing and with Boston Doctors Hospital, she stood against a wall until the final patient had been discussed, then left before any of the others. Ahead of her, waiting for the lift were Janet and an orderly. On a trolley stretcher between them lay the sheet-covered body of Charlotte Thomas.

Held fast by the scene and her thoughts, Christine watched as the stretcher was manoeuvred into the lift. Not until the doors had closed was she able to move again.

10

Fox's Golden Laws of Medicine defined Pathologist as "The specialist who learns all by cutting corners to get straight to the heart of the matter, leaving no gall or kidney stone unturned."

As usual, the recollection of one of Gerald Fox's immortal definitions forced a smile out of David, despite his discomfort at the prospect of having to observe the autopsy on Charlotte Thomas.

He was already ten minutes late, but he knew that he had missed nothing except perhaps the preparation of Charlotte's body and the first incision. Although Fox's observations were usually right on the mark, David had never felt that his cynical maxim about pathologists was totally accurate. He thought back to his first exposure to forensic pathology, a lecture given by the county coroner just before David's group of second year medical students was ushered in to view their first autopsy.

"Cause of death, ladies and gentlemen," the old pathologist had said. "That is what we in forensic medicine are asked to determine for our medical and legal colleagues. In fact, nobody other than God Himself knows what causes a person to die. Nobody. Rather, what we can determine is the condition of each organ in a patient's body at the time of his or her death. From this knowledge, we can deduce with some accuracy the reason for cessation of cardiac, cerebral or pulmonary function — the only true causes of death.

"For example, if a patient is killed by a gunshot wound through the heart, we may say quite safely that death was due to cardiac standstill from a penetrating wound to the heart muscle itself. But what of the patient with a disease like cancer? We might be able to locate cancerous tissue in the liver, brain, lungs or other organs, and certainly, in one respect, may say that cancer is the cause of death. Determining the immediate cause, however, is nigh impossible. Did the heart stop because it was poisoned by some as yet unknown substance secreted by the cancerous cells? Or did lack of sufficient fluid volume, for reasons perhaps unrelated to the cancer itself, cause such an impairment in circulation that the heart could no longer function, and simply stopped?

"You must keep this in mind whenever you read such diagnoses as 'cancer' or 'emphysema,' or 'arteriosclerosis' as the cause of a patient's death. They may have been a cause leading to death, but as to the direct cause of death — that, my friends, remains a mystery in the vast majority of cases."

A mystery. David hesitated outside the two opaque glass doors labelled "AUTOPSY SUITE," in gold leaf letters. A sleepless night and chaotic morning had left him tense and uneasy. The prospect of Charlotte's autopsy only aggravated those feelings.

Then there was Huttner. Cape Cod was only seventy miles away, close enough for him to make the drive up that morning without much difficulty. Whether or not he would choose to return there after witnessing the autopsy was a different story. David bet himself a long-overdue and much-feared trip to the dentist that Huttner would elect to stay in Boston and resume control of his practice. He thought of turning the bet around so that at least he wouldn't have to face both the drill *and* the loss of his new found responsibilities if Huttner stayed. In the end, however, he decided that if he lost, he would be able to submerge the misery of a visit to the tooth merchant in other, more substantial miseries.

Needles of formalin vapour stung his nostrils as he entered the suite. It was a long room, nearly twenty-five yards from end to end. High ceilings and an excess of fluorescent light obscured, in part, the fact that there were no windows. Seven steel autopsy tables, each fitted with a water hose and drainage system, were evenly spaced across the ivory-coloured linoleum floor. In addition to the hose, used for cleaning organs during an autopsy and the table afterwards, every station had its own sink, blackboard and suspended scale. A large red number, from "1" to "7" inlaid in the floor, was the only feature distinguishing them apart. Except, that is, for Station 4.

On either side of that table six tiers of wooden seats had been built, identical to those in school gymnasiums. At certain times, the seats were filled with students in various stages of boredom, revulsion or fascination. At other times, the stands held groups of residents in pathology or surgery, craning to study the dissecting skills of a senior pathologist. Station 4 was the centre court of the Doctors Hospital Autopsy Suite.

At 8.15 on the morning of October 3rd, Stations 1, 4, and 6 were in operation, and a sheet-wrapped body lay on the table at Station 2. Wallace Huttner was standing, arms folded, at Station 4. The seats were empty but for a resident scheduled to post the body on table 2, and three medical students. As David approached, he caught sight of Charlotte's open-mouthed, chalk-coloured face. He bit his lower lip, swallowed the bile rising from his stomach and decided that it would be best to concentrate on the rest of her anatomy. He could deal reasonably well with autopsies as long as he viewed them purely as examinations of parts of a body. The nearer he allowed himself to get to the human aspect, the more unpleasant the procedure became.

Ahmed Hadawi, a quick, dark little man with disproportionately large hands, had made his initial incision, and was elbow-deep in the chest cavity, busily separating the chest and abdominal organs from their attachments to the neck and body wall. He made a soft clucking noise with his tongue as he worked, but otherwise seemed without emotion or expression. Occasionally, he bent over and murmured a few words into a pedal-operated dictaphone.

Huttner nodded coolly in response to David's greeting. His stance and manner bore no hint of the relaxed, interested, almost fatherly physician who had sat with David in the surgeons' lounge just thirty-six hours before. After the nod, he returned his attention to the dissection, carefully avoiding further eye contact. David looked at the man helplessly.

"Now, then, we are ready to take a look inside," Hadawi said, looking up. The resident stepped down from the wooden seats to get a better view and Huttner stiffened slightly as the pathologist began pointing out the anatomical status of each of Charlotte's organs as they existed at the instant of her death.

"The heart," he began, "is moderately enlarged, with thickening of the muscle and dilatation of all chambers. There is a small, fresh puncture wound through the anterior left ventricle which I assume is the result of Dr. Shelton's commendably accurate intracardiac injection.''

David thought that the moment might be right for a modest smile and nod, but then realised that no one was looking at him. He smiled and nodded anyway.

The little pathologist continued speaking as he dissected. ''There is fairly advanced narrowing of all coronary arteries, although there is no gross evidence of real damage such as might be caused by a myocardial infarction.'' Margaret Armstrong's interpretation of Charlotte's electrocardiogram had been right on the button, David thought. ''Keep in mind,'' Hadawi added, ''that evidence of an acute infarction, say less than twenty-four hours old, is often seen only in microscopic examination of the heart muscle itself, and then only if we happen to catch just the right section.''

''I want to be notified as soon as those slides have been examined,'' Huttner ordered, more, it seemed to David, out of a need to make some kind of statement than anything else. Hadawi glanced up at him and, with no more acknowledgement than that, turned his attention to the lungs. Both lungs were more than half consolidated by the heavy fluid of infection. Even if there had been no other problems, it seemed entirely possible that Charlotte would have been unable to survive her extensive pneumonia. David wondered if he should feel some sort of relief at this.

The remainder of the examination was impressive mainly for what it did not show. Pending, of course, microscopic examination of the abdominal lymph nodes, Hadawi announced that he was unable to find any evidence of residual cancer in the woman's body. The liver cysts, which had been misdiagnosed by the radiologist, Rybicki, were scattered throughout the organ, and similar fluid-filled sacs were found in both kidneys. ''Polycystic involvement of hepatic and renal parenchyma,'' Hadawi said into his dictaphone.

Finally, the pathologist stepped away from the table. ''I have a few remaining things to do on this body,'' he said. ''but they will have no bearing on my findings. To all intents and purposes, Wally, we are done. Most significant of what I have to tell you is that this woman's pressure sore was extending beneath her skin to the point where I doubt that even with multiple grafts it would ever have healed. Infection of the sacral bones had already begun and would have been almost impossible to treat.

"She has enough coronary arteriosclerosis for me to feel the final straw was probably cardiac. I intend to sign her out as cardiovascular collapse secondary to her pulmonary and bed sore infections. An additional stress undoubtedly came from her partial small bowel obstruction which, as you saw, was due to adhesions from recent surgery."

David decided it was time to speak up. "Dr. Hadawi, Dr. Huttner, if we could sit down over here, there are a few questions that I have." He could not bear the thought of having to discuss Charlotte's case over her gaping, dissected body. Hadawi responded with a brief, understanding grin and took a seat. Huttner, who still held his arms around himself, followed reluctantly. Nowhere in his eyes or manner was there a hint of disappointment or guilt. David judged the expression on his face to reflect something between disgust and seething fury. Regardless of her underlying disease, Charlotte Thomas had walked into the hospital as Huttner's patient, had been operated on, and had died. That made her a post-operative mortality. Her operation, and the many complications which ensued, would be discussed in depth at Surgical Death Rounds. Hardly a prospect that would sit well with this man, David realised. He was far more accustomed to asking the questions than to answering them.

"Now, David," Hadawi said, "just what is it that troubles you about what you have seen?"

"Well most of my concern centres on her heart, which seemed so unresponsive to everything I tried during the Code Ninety-nine. It may have been simply that too much time elapsed between the moment of her cardiac arrest and the time I started working on her, but it just didn't feel like that. I wonder if perhaps her potassium could somehow have risen too high and caused a fatal cardiac arrhythmia."

"That is always a possibility," Hadawi said patiently. "I've saved several vials of blood. I'll be happy to have her potassium level checked. However, you must keep in mind the limits of accuracy of such a measurement done in a post-mortem patient, especially one who has received prolonged external cardiac compression."

Finally, Huttner spoke. It was no surprise to David that he

was unwilling to surrender his unblemished reputation without a fight. "Look, Ahmed," he said. "I'm not totally satisfied with all this. Dr. Shelton here has a point. Since there's nothing obvious on gross exam to explain this woman's sudden death, then we should look further before signing her out as something as non-specific as cardiovascular collapse. Maybe some nurse made a medication error on her and caused an allergic, anaphylactic reaction of some kind. She was known to be allergic to penicillin."

Hadawi was obviously used to dealing with Huttner's ego. He merely shrugged and said, "If you wish, I shall be happy to order a penicillin level on her blood. Is there anything else you would like?"

Huttner seized the chance to avoid a Surgical Death Rounds presentation as a drowning sailor might grasp a passing chunk of driftwood. A medication error would provide him with instant absolution.

"Yes, there are some other things I think should be done," Huttner said in a professorial tone full of significant pauses. He seemed actually to be savouring his own words. "I think she should have a complete chemical screen. Antibiotic levels, electrolytes, toxins, the works."

"With no specific idea of what we're searching for, that will be expensive," Hadawi said softly, as if anticipating the outburst that would follow even this mild objection.

"Damn the money, man," Huttner fired back. "This is a human life we're talking about here. You just do the damn tests and get me the results."

"As you wish, Wally."

Huttner nodded his satisfaction abruptly, then started to leave. As he passed David, he snapped his fingers. "I almost forgot, David," he said over his shoulder. "The Cape Vascular Conference really wasn't all that it was cut out to be. I've decided not to go back. Thank you for your help yesterday. I think there's a meeting in January I might want to attend. Perhaps we can work out another coverage arrangement then."

His voice, David thought, held every bit as much sincerity as Don Juan saying, "Of course I'll respect you in the morning."

11

In his selection of a hospital, as in all the other affairs in his life, Senator Richard Cormier was his own man. While many Washington politicians considered it a status symbol to be cared for at Bethesda Naval or Walter Reed, Cormier over-ruled the objections of his aides and insisted that he be operated on by Dr. Louis Ketchem at Boston Doctors. "Always trust your own kind," he said. "Louie's an old war horse just like me. Either he does the cutting, or I don't get cut."

The walls of Cormier's room were covered top to bottom with cards, and cartons containing several hundred more were stacked neatly in one corner. In addition to a nurse and the Senator, the presence of a secretary and two aides helped to create an atmosphere almost as chaotic as that perpetually found in his Washington office.

"Senator Cormier, I must give you your pre-op meds, and these people will have to leave your room." The nurse, an ample matron named Fuller projected just the right amount of authority to get the Senator to comply with a request.

Cormier ran his fingers through his thick, silver hair and squinted up at the nurse. "Ten more minutes."

"Two," she said firmly.

"Five." The bargaining brought a sparkle to his eyes.

"All right, five," she said. "But one minute longer, and I use the square needle to give you this medication." She bustled out of the room, turning at the doorway to give Cormier a glare that said she was serious. The Senator winked at her.

"Okay, Beth, time to get packed up," he said to his secretary. "Remember, I want a thank-you sent to everyone who put a return address on his card. I signed what seemed like a thousand of them yesterday, but if you run out, have some more printed up and I'll sign them after the operation. Gary, call Lionel

103

Herbert and tell him to fly up here for a meeting the day after tomorrow. Tell him to be prepared to make some concessions on that energy package, or by God it's back to the drawing board again for his boss and those oil people he's so damn friendly with. Bobby, call my niece and tell her I'm fine, not to worry, and most of all, not to be upset that she couldn't leave the kids to fly here. I'll call her myself as soon as they let me back near my phone. Oh, and Bobby, have you got all the names of people who sent flowers? I want to send each of them a personal note. Do you think it would hurt anyone's feelings if I told them to send candy next time? This place looks like a funeral parlour and smells like a bordello."

Bobby Crisp, a young lawyer sharp and eager as his name, smiled over at his boss. "Your confidence in me must be growing, Senator," he said. "This is only the fourth time you've told me to do the same thing. When I first started working for you, it was seven! Everything's taken care off, I'll bring the list up for you as soon as you're ready to write, which will probably be half an hour after you come out of the anaesthesia, if I know you. By the way, do you know someone named Camellia?"

"Who?" Cormier asked.

"Camellia. See those pink and white flowers over there on the table? They came this morning with a note that just said 'Thank you for everything. Camellia.' "

"Men," Beth said scornfully. "Those pink and white flowers, as you call them, *are* camellias. Let me see that note." She read it and shrugged. "That's what it says all right."

"Thanks for checking," Crisp said. "I got low marks in reading throughout law school."

"Now, now, settle down, you two," Cormier said. He rubbed his chin. "Camellia's a strange enough name for me to remember it. Camellias from Camellia, eh? . . . " His voice drifted off as he tried to connect the name with a person. Finally, he shook his head. "Well, I guess a little memory lapse here and there is a small price to pay for the frustration I'm able to cause on The Hill with the rest of my senility. Whoever she is, she'll just have to live without a thank-you note."

At that moment, Nurse Fuller reappeared at the door. "I said five minutes, and it's already more than that," she said. "I swear, Senator, you are the most obstinate, pig-headed patient I've ever had."

"Okay, okay, we're done," Cormier said, waving the other three out of his room. "You know, Nurse Fuller, if you don't sweeten up soon, you're going to move from the sleek-cruiser class into the battle-axe category!" He grinned and added, "but even then you'll still be my favourite nurse. Go easy with that needle, now."

The nurse swabbed at a place on Cormier's left buttock, and gave him the injection of pre-operative medication. Fifteen minutes later, his mouth began feeling dry, and a warm glow of detachment spread through him. Like the beacon from a lighthouse, the corridor ceiling lights flashed past as he was wheeled to the operating room.

Louis Ketchem was a towering, slope-shouldered veteran of more than twenty-five years as a surgeon. Over that span, he had performed hundreds of gall bladder operations. None had ever gone smoother than Senator Richard Cormier's. The removal of the inflamed, stone-filled sac was uneventful, except for the usual amount of bleeding from the adjacent liver. As he had done hundreds of times, Ketchem ordered a unit of blood to be trans-fused over the last half hour of the operation.

The anaesthetist, John Singleberry, took the plastic bag of blood from the circulating nurse, a young woman named Jacqueline Miller. He double-checked the number on the bag before attaching it to the intravenous line. To speed the infusion, he slipped an air sleeve around the bag and pumped it up. Cormier, anaesthetised and receiving oxygen from a respirator, slept a deep, dreamless sleep as the blood wound down the tubing towards his arm like a crimson serpent.

At the instant the blood slid beneath the green paper drape, Jacqueline Miller turned away. The drug she had been instructed to use, the drug she had injected into the plastic bag, was ouabain, the fastest acting and most powerful form of digitalis. A drug so rapidly cleared from the bloodstream, so difficult to find on chemical analysis, that even the massive dose she had used was virtually undetectable. Three minutes were all the ouabain took.

Without warning, the cardiac monitor leapt from slow and regular beats to a totally chaotic pattern. John Singleberry glanced at the golden light slashing up and down on the screen overhead and stood for several seconds staring at it in disbelief.

"Holy shit, Louis," Singleberry screamed. "He's fibrillating!"

Ketchem, who had not encountered a cardiac arrest in the operating room in years stood paralysed, both hands still inside Cormier's abdomen. His orders, when he was finally able to give them, were inadequate. But for the work of the nurses, including Jacqueline Miller, several minutes might have passed with no positive action. Sterile drapes were quickly stuffed into the incision, and two unsuccessful countershocks were given. Seconds later the monitor pattern showed a straight line.

Without warning, Ketchem grabbed a scalpel, extended his incision, and slashed an opening through the bottom of Cormier's diaphragm. Reaching through the opening, he grasped the man's heart and began rhythmically squeezing. A nurse ran for help, but everyone in the operating room already knew it was over. Ketchem pumped, then stopped and checked the monitor. Straight line. He pumped some more.

For twenty minutes he pumped, with absolutely no effect on the golden light. Finally, he stopped. For more than a minute, no one in the room moved. Ketchem bit his lower lip and peered over his mask at the body of his friend. Then, two nurses took him by the arms and helped him move away from the operating table, back to the surgeons' lounge.

Standing to one side, Jacqueline Miller closed her eyes, fearing they might reflect the excited smile beneath her mask. The greatest adventure in her life was ending in triumph. Oh, Dahlia had told her where to go and what to say, but she had been the one to actually pull it off. Little Jackie Miller, ordering around one of the richest, most powerful oilmen in the world.

She tingled at the irony of it all: from girlhood in a squalid tenement to a secret meeting in Oklahoma with the President of Beecher Oil. What would Mister Jed Beecher have said if he knew that the woman who was giving him instructions, the woman who was taking his quarter of a million dollars, the woman who was dictating his every move had just taken her first aeroplane flight.

Jacqueline silently cheered the good fortune that had brought Dahlia and The Garden into her life. She still knew little about either of them, but for the present she really didn't care. When Dahlia was ready to disclose her identity, she would, and that was all there was to that. As long as the excitement and the monthly payments were there, Camellia would do what she was asked, and keep her eyes and ears open for cases which might be of interest to The Garden. As for The Sisterhood of Life, they would simply have to survive without further participation from Jackie Miller. No more free rides for them.

Mexico. Jamaica. Greece. Paris. Jacqueline ticked the places off in her mind. One more case like this, and she would be able to see all of them. The prospects were dizzying.

Behind her, on the narrow operating table, covered to the neck by a sheet, Senator Richard Cormier looked as he had throughout his operation. But his dreamless sleep would last forever.

"Ladies and gentlemen, if you would all find seats, we can get started, and hopefully make it through this business in a reasonable amount of time."

It was eight o'clock on the evening of Sunday, October 5, two days after the post-mortem examination on Charlotte Thomas. The cosy West Wing conference room of Boston Doctors Hospital was more than half full with the milling group of twenty-five summoned by Detective Lieutenant John Dockerty. Margaret Armstrong, in her capacity as Chief of Staff, had issued the invitations, and now sat beside Dockerty at a heavy oak table facing four rows of folding chairs. Flanking the rows were a variety of well-worn vinyl couches and hand-me-down easy chairs.

Dockerty was a thin rumpled man in his late forties, and wore a gabardine suit that appeared too large for him by at least two sizes. His lack-lustre, green eyes scanned the group, then turned to a sheaf of papers on the table in front of him. As he looked down, an errant wisp of thinning, reddish-brown hair dropped over one eye. He absently swept the strands back in place, only to repeat the ritual moments later.

His languid, almost distracted air suggested he had encountered most of what life can offer. In fact, he had spent more than fifteen years on the Boston police force carefully cultivating that demeanour, and learning how best to utilise it.

He looked over the room again, then spoke to Margaret Armstrong out of the corner of his mouth. "This group is obviously more adept at giving orders than they are at taking them."

Armstrong laughed her agreement, then banged a notebook on the table. "Would you all please find seats," she called out. "If we can't show Lt. Dockerty co-operation, at least we can show him manners." In less than a minute, everyone had found a place.

The hospital administrator and two of his assistants sat to one side of the second row of folding chairs. He was a paunchy, foppish man who had run away from his Brooklyn home at seventeen and changed his name from Isaac Lifshitz to Edward Lipton III. For years he had kept his job by pitting his enemies against one another so skilfully that none of them could ever rally enough support to oust him.

In the second and third rows opposite the administrators, Wallace Huttner sat with Ahmed Hadawi, and the other members of the Medical Staff Executive Committee. Occupying the chair just to Huttner's right was Peter Thomas.

The couches and easy chairs along one wall were the domain of the nurses. Eight of them, all in street clothes, were grouped around Dotty Dalrymple, who appeared volcanic in a plain black dress. Janet Poulos was there, along with Christine, Winnie Edgerly, and several other nurses from Four South, including Angela Martin.

Across the room from the nurses, David sat in a green lounger whose springs had long since given out. He sat alone until the very last minute when Howard Kim, the anaesthetist who had helped with Charlotte's unsuccessful resuscitation, lumbered in and lowered himself into the wing chair to David's right.

"I want to thank you for coming at such short notice," Dockerty began. "The first thing you can all do for me is to relax. This isn't going to be the sort of dramatic encounter you might have expected from watching Colombo or reading Agatha Christie novels. Theatrics have never been my bag, so to speak." His friendly manner seemed instantly to ease the tension in the room. "What we're here for tonight is simply to exchange information in the matter of Mrs. Charlotte Thomas; a matter involving all of you in one way or another. Hopefully, we can piece together exactly what happened on the day of her death."

Dockerty looked down at Margaret Armstrong, who nodded her approval of his opening remarks. Then, sweeping his hair back in place, he said, "Dr. Hadawi, suppose we start with your report?" The little pathologist rose, then paused, uncertain whether or not to remain in his seat. With a slight gesture, Dockerty motioned him to the chair next to his own.

Hadawi spread a few sheets of notes on the table in front of him, then said, "On October 3, I performed a post-mortem examination on the woman in question. The gross examination showed that she had a deep pressure sore over her sacrum, moderately advanced coronary artery narrowing, and an extensive pneumonia. It was my initial impression that she had died from sudden cardiac arrest caused by her infections and the generally debilitated condition resulting from her two operations."

"Dr. Hadawi, is that your impression now?" Dockerty asked.

"No, it is not. The patient's physicians, Dr. Wallace Huttner and Dr. David Shelton, were present at the autopsy. They requested a detailed chemical analysis of her blood."

"Help me out here, Dr. Hadawi," Dockerty cut in. "Don't you do these chemical analyses routinely on each — er — patient?"

Hadawi smiled wryly and folded his hands on the table. "I wish that were possible," he said. "Unfortunately, the cost of post-mortem examinations must be borne by the institution involved, and it is hardly an inexpensive proposition with all the sophisticated equipment and extra clerical help involved. While we would never knowingly omit a critical stain or test, the pathology department must nevertheless temper its zeal with judgment to enable us to stay within our budget." He paused for a moment and gave a prolonged, rather hostile look at Edward Lipton III.

"Please proceed," Dockerty said, scribbling a few words on the pad in front of him.

Hadawi referred to his notes. "Of the many chemical analyses which were done, two came back with abnormally high levels. The first of these, potassium, was seven-point-four where the normal upper limit is five-point-zero. The second was the blood morphine level, which was elevated far above that found in a patient receiving the usual doses of morphine sulphate for pain."

"Dr. Hadawi, would you please share your impression of these findings?" Dockerty's voice was calm and smooth.

"Well, my impression of the potassium elevation — and please keep in mind that it is only an opinion — is that it is artificially high, a reflection of events occurring in the tissues during and just after the cardiac arrest. The morphine elevation is an entirely different story. Without question, the level measured in

110

this woman was critically high. Easily, although not necessarily, high enough to have caused cessation of respiration and, ultimately, death.''

Dockerty spent a few seconds distractedly combing his hair with his fingers. "Doctor, you imply that death was caused by an overdose of morphine.'' Hadawi nodded. "Tell me, do you think an overdose of this size could have been accidental?''

Hadawi drew in a short breath, looked at the detective, then shook his head. "No,'' he said slowly. "No, I do not believe that is possible.''

There was not a whisper or movement in the room. For several seconds Dockerty allowed the eerie silence to reign. Then he said softly, "That, ladies and gentlemen, makes Charlotte Thomas's death murder. And her murder is why we are assembled here.'' Again there was silence. Hadawi shifted uncomfortably in his seat, anxious to finish his testimony.

"Thank you for your help, Doctor,'' Dockerty said to him. As Hadawi stood to go, the detective added, "Oh, one more small thing. You mentioned that the chemical tests were ordered by Mrs. Thomas's doctors, ah . . . '' he glanced at his notes, "Dr. Huttner and Dr. Shelton. Do you remember which one of them specifically asked for the tests?''

Hadawi's dark eyes narrowed as he searched Dockerty's face for some hint of the significance of his question. Finally, with a bewildered shrug he said, "Well, as I recall, Dr. Shelton requested the potassium level. The rest of the tests were ordered by Dr. Huttner.''

Dockerty nodded the pathologist back to his seat, whispering another "thank you" at the same time. He searched the room for a moment before saying, "Dr. Shelton?''

Howard Kim reached up a massive paw and patted David on the back as he inched sideways past the giant. David had known for a day about the abnormal blood tests, had even heard the wildfire rumour round the wards that some kind of police investigation was under way. Although Dr. Armstrong had not told him that he would be asked to make a statement, he was not at all surprised to be called by the detective.

Dockerty smiled, shook his hand firmly and motioned him to the seat vacated by Hadawi. Seeming at times disinterested, he led him minute by minute through the events that followed

111

Charlotte Thomas's cardiac arrest. Gradually, David's statements became free-flowing and animated; Dockerty's style made it easy for him to talk. Soon, he was sharing information with the dishevelled lieutenant in the relaxed manner of two friends in an alehouse. Without changing the pace or tone of their conversation, Dockerty then said, "Tell me, Dr. Shelton. I understand that shortly before Mrs. Thomas was found by you to be without pulse or respiration, you had a discussion about her, and about seriously ill patients in general, with Dr. Armstrong here and some of the nurses, namely, ah — " he consulted his notes " — nurses Edgerly, Gold, and Beall. Do you mind telling me what you had to say in that discussion?"

For five seconds, stretching to ten, then fifteen, David was unable to speak. The question didn't fit. It made no sense unless . . . His mind suddenly began spinning through the implications of Dockerty's question to Hadawi about who had actually ordered the test that had disclosed the high morphine level. The indefinable sense of fear, so vague among his feelings that night on Four South, now surged through him. His temples began to throb. His hands grew stiff and numb. *Holy shit, he's going after me! He's going after me!*

At that moment, he realised that Dockerty's eyes had changed from liquid to steel, and were locked on his, trying to pierce his very thoughts. David knew it had already taken him far too long to reply to the question. He inhaled deeply and fought the panic. *Loosen up and stop reading so much into this,* he told himself. *Just tell the man what he wants to know.*

"Dr. Shelton, do you recall the incident I'm asking about?" The deliberate patience in Dockerty's voice had a cutting edge.

Even before he answered, David sensed that his words would be stammered and clumsy. "I simply told them . . . that a patient who is . . . in great pain with little hope of surviving his or her illness might . . . might be treated with some temperance. Especially if the therapy planned is . . . particularly painful or . . . dehumanising . . . " He battled back the urge to say more, consciously avoiding the panicky loquacity that comes with trying to justify a questioned action.

Dockerty ran his tongue slowly over his teeth. He bounced the rubber end of his pencil on the table. He scratched his head. "Dr. Shelton," he said finally, "do you think that withholding

112

treatment from a sick person is a form of mercy killing? Of euthanasia?''

"No, I don't think it's a form of killing of any kind." Molten drops of anger began to smoulder beneath his fear. His voice grew strained. His words came too rapidly. "It is good, sensitive clinical judgment. It is what being a doctor is all about. For God's sake, I've never advocated shutting off a respirator or giving anything lethal to a patient."

"Never?" Dockerty's question was like a soft but deadly stab.

David exploded. "Dammit, Lieutenant, I've had more than enough of your insinuations!" He was totally oblivious now to all the others in the room. "If you have an accusation to make, then make it. And while you're at it, explain why *I* was the one who kept saying that something wasn't right during the resuscitation. Why *I* was the one who requested the potass . . . '' The word froze in his mouth. He realised even before Dockerty spoke, what the detective was driving at. "Damn," he hissed his frustration.

"I have had the chance, Dr. Shelton, to speak briefly with some of the other physicians and nurses who were with you in Charlotte Thomas's room. Like you, several of them were concerned that something was not quite right. Apparently the problem was obvious enough for others besides you to spot. Whether or not they would have gone so far as to ask for blood tests on this woman we'll never know because you did. At least, you asked for the potassium level."

"Are you trying to say I did that to cover myself, to ensure that nobody thought about anything like morphine?" Dockerty shrugged blandly. "This is ridiculous! This is really insane!" David cried.

"Dr. Shelton," Dockerty said calmly. "Please get hold of yourself. I am not accusing you or anyone else of anything."

"Are you finished with me now?" David spat it out.

"Yes, thank you." Once again Dockerty appeared as mechanical as he had throughout most of the inquiry. As David stalked back to his seat, he noticed that Wallace Huttner sat staring at him with cold, steely eyes. Involuntarily, David shuddered.

Dockerty whispered with Dr. Armstrong for several seconds, then called Dorothy Dalrymple. The Nursing Director extracted herself from her seat with the side to side movements of a cork coming free from its bottle. Once released from her chair, she glided to the front with paradoxical grace. She shook hands politely with Dockerty, then adjusted herself on the oak chair and smiled that she was ready.

Dockerty led her through a description of Charlotte Thomas's appearance during the day prior to her death, as summarised in the nurses' notes. "The nurses' notes are generally written at the end of each shift," Dalrymple explained. "Therefore, the notes from the October 2 evening shift were not done until the patient's death. However, the nurse who cared for Mrs. Thomas that night, Christine Beall, saw her at seven o'clock, approximately two hours before her death. Her notes state that the patient was, and I quote, 'alert, oriented, and somewhat less depressed than she has been recently'. Nurse Beall further writes that her vital signs – pulse, respiration, temperature, and blood pressure – were all stable." Dalrymple swung her massive shoulders and head towards the group of the nurses. "Nurse Beall, do you have anything to add to what I have told the lieutenant?"

Christine, who had been totally distracted since David's outburst, was not listening. She had heard about the discovery of morphine in Charlotte's body less than twenty-four hours before. The information had come through a telephone call from Peg, the nurse who had asked her to evaluate Charlotte Thomas in the first place. "Christine, I want to keep you abreast of what is going on here, without worrying you unduly," Peg had said. "There is going to be some kind of inquiry into the case tomorrow night, I've been told. A policeman will be there. However, your Sister Janet Poulos has reviewed your notes in the patient's chart. There is nothing there, she feels, that will implicate you in any way. It is our belief that the investigation will be short-lived and fruitless, and that Charlotte Thomas's death will be attributed to an individual whose name and motives will never be discovered. All Sisterhood operations at your hospital will be curtailed indefinitely and the entire matter should just blow over. You are in no danger whatsoever, Christine, please believe that."

Christine, lips pressed tightly together, was staring at the ceiling when Dalrymple addressed her.

114

Several seats away, Janet Poulos watched helplessly, every muscle tensed at the prospect of Christine leaping to her feet and shouting her confession to all, crying out the only other Sisterhood name she knew: Janet's. God, she wished there had been enough warning to call Dahlia. Dahlia would have known exactly how to handle things.

Janet's gaze moved past Christine to where Angela Martin sat, her cool blue eyes fixed on Dalrymple, her golden hair immaculately in place. The woman was absolutely nerveless. Even if it had been her name that Christine Beall knew, Janet doubted whether Angela would have been ruffled. Almost ten years as members of The Sisterhood and they had never even known one another. Now, they were best friends, sharing the excitement and rewards of The Garden, and speculating about the mysterious woman who had brought them together.

Did Dahlia have eyes and ears present in the room other than Lily's and Hyacinth's? Quite possibly, Janet acknowledged. The woman remained only a whispered voice on the telephone, but time and again Janet had been impressed with her cold logic and endless sources of information. Thanks to her, The Garden was growing steadily – in other hospitals as well as in Boston Doctors. Anywhere there was a Sisterhood of Life member, there was a potential flower. Dahlia had perhaps been hasty about Beall, but she remained a woman of near perfect judgment whom Janet wanted desperately to meet.

Powerless for the moment, Janet slid back in her seat and watched.

"Nurse Beall?" Dalrymple called again. Winnie Edgerly nudged Christine. "I asked if you had anything to add to what I have told the lieutenant."

Christine swallowed hard, but when she tried to speak, only a sandpaper rasp emerged. She cleared her throat, and tightened her grip on the arms of her seat.

"I'm sorry," she managed. "No, I have nothing to add."

Janet breathed a sigh of relief and closed her eyes. Beall had come through.

Christine looked across to where David sat, head resting on one hand, staring vacantly at Dalrymple and Dockerty. She could feel as much as see his isolation. In fact, she realised, she too was on her own. Despite the calls from Peg, the words from Janet and the knowledge that the vast Sisterhood of Life was behind her, Christine felt marooned. At that moment, she wanted to run to David and, somehow, reassure him. To tell him that she, more than anyone else, knew he had nothing to do with Charlotte's death. "Everything will be all right," she told herself over and over again. "Just leave things alone and they will be all right." She forced her concentration back to the scene before her.

"Miss Dalrymple," Dockerty continued, "you have a list of the medications given to Mrs. Thomas?"

Dalrymple nodded. "She was receiving chloramphenicol, which is an antibiotic, and Demerol, which is an analgesic."

"No morphine?"

"No morphine," she echoed, shaking her head for emphasis.

"No morphine . . ." Dockerty let the words drift away, but his voice was nonetheless loud enough for all those present to hear. "Tell me," he said, "is it possible for one of the nurses or other hospital personnel to obtain morphine sulphate in the quantities Dr. Hadawi has suggested were given to Mrs. Thomas?"

Dalrymple thought the question through before replying. "The answer is, of course, that anyone can get his hands on any drug if he has enough money and is willing to go outside the legal channels to do so. However, I can state that it would be virtually impossible for one of my nurses – or anyone else for that matter – to get away with more than a tiny quantity of narcotics from the hospital. You see, only a small amount of injectable narcotic is kept on each floor, and that is meticulously checked by two nurses at each shift change, one from the group that is leaving, and one from the group that is coming on. The night nursing supervisor has access to the hospital pharmacy, but even there the narcotics are locked up securely, and only the hospital pharmacists have keys. So," she concluded, shifting her bulk in the chair and folding her hands in a large, puffy ball, "assuming we're talking about a legal source, only a pharmacist or a physician could obtain a substantial amount of morphine at a single time."

Dockerty nodded and again conferred in whispers with Dr. Armstrong. "Miss Dalrymple," he said finally, "do the nurses' notes indicate whether there were any visitors to Charlotte

Thomas's room on the night of her death?''

"Visitors to a patient's room, other than physicians, are not usually recorded in nurses' notes. Certainly, none were mentioned in this case.''

"Not even the physician who found Mrs. Thomas without pulse or respiration?'' Dockerty asked.

Dalrymple's expression suggested that she did not approve of the detective's oblique reference. "No,'' she said deliberately, "there was no mention of Dr. Shelton entering the patient's room. However, I hasten to add that most of the nurses were on break at the time of the cardiac arrest so there was no one on the floor at the time to see him arrive.''

Dockerty seemed to ignore her last point. "That will be all, thank you very much,'' he said. As he nodded the woman back to her seat, David again exploded.

"Lieutenant, I've had just about enough of this!'' He stumbled to his feet and grasped the chair in front of him. Suddenly, the modest conference room seemed tiny, and unbearably warm. To his left, Howard Kim's moonface looked up at him impassively. "I don't understand why you think what you do, or even what you are driving at, but let me state here and now that I would never administer a drug or any treatment to a patient for the express purpose of harming him in any way.'' In the seconds that followed, David heard an inner voice telling him that, once again, he was sailing on his own words towards a maelstrom.

In a strangled voice, he said, "Lieutenant Dockerty, why are you accusing me? Surely there are plenty of others who could have been into her room before me.''

"Dr. Shelton,'' Dockerty said evenly, "I have not accused you of anything. If you will just – ''

"No!'' David shouted. "This whole inquiry is a sham. Some kind of perverse kangaroo court. A first year law student could conduct a more impartial hearing than this. If you want to frame me for something, then do it in court where at least you have to answer to a judge.'' He stopped, grasping for some morsel of self-control, and realising he had totally over-reacted.

"Very well,'' Dockerty said, "I think we've heard enough for now. I'll be contacting some of you individually in the near future. Thank you all for coming.'' He whispered some final

117

words to Dr. Armstrong, then packed his notes together, and left the room without as much as a glance at David's stationary figure.

By the time David had calmed down enough to release the wooden seat back and look around, the West conference room was nearly empty. Christine and the other nurses had gone. So had Howard Kim. As he scanned the back of the room, his gaze met Wallace Huttner's. The tall surgeon's eyes narrowed. Then, with a derisive shake of his head, he turned and strode out arm-in-arm with Peter Thomas.

David stood alone, staring up at the glowing red EXIT sign over the rear door when a hand touched his shoulder. He whirled round and met the concerned, pale-blue eyes of Margaret Armstrong.

"Are you all right?" she asked.

"Yeah, sure, great." He made no attempt to clear the huskiness in his voice.

"David, I am sorry for what just happened here. If I had known how heavily Lt. Dockerty was going to pounce on you, I never would have allowed the whole thing to happen. He said he wanted to check the spontaneous reactions of several people. You were just one of them. All of a sudden, you erupted, and there wasn't even a chance for me to . . . " She gave up trying to explain. "Look, David," she went on finally, "I like you very much. Have done since the day you got here. Just give me the benefit of a hearing. After what's just happened to you, I know that won't be easy, but please try. I want to help."

David looked at her, then bit back his anger and nodded.

"How about an hour or so at Popeye's?" Her smile was warm and sincere.

"Popeye's it is," David said, picking up his jacket. Together, the new allies left the hospital.

Popeye's, a local landmark, had seen nearly thirty years of doctors and nurses bringing their problems and their lives to its tables. Outside the tavern, an animated neon sign, the pride and joy of the management, depicted characters from the comic strip chasing Wimpy and his armload of hamburgers across the building. As they entered, David caught sight of four of the nurses who had been at the inquiry. Neither Dotty Dalrymple nor Christine was among them.

"I haven't been here for years," Dr. Armstrong said after they had settled at a rear table. "My husband and I courted in some of these booths. Nothing has really changed, except for that garish sign outside."

David glanced down at her hands folded across the wooden table. She wore no wedding ring. "Is your husband still alive?" he asked.

"Arne? No, he died eight, no, nine years ago."

"Oh, yes, of course." David paused. "His death was a great loss." Arne Armstrong had been a world famous neurophysiologist and a possible Nobel laureate had he lived long enough to complete his work. "I'm sorry."

"Don't be silly . . . " Dr. Armstrong said, stopping in midsentence as a shapely blonde in a black mini-skirt and skin-tight red sweater arrived to take their order. "I'll have a beer, draught not bottled. And my date here?" She smiled over at David.

"Coke," he said. "Extra large, lots of ice."

The waitress left and Armstrong looked at David. "Not even with all that's happened to you tonight?"

She knew. Of course she knew. Everyone did. But she wasn't testing him. There was, David realised, admiration in her voice.

"It's been nearly eight years since I touched a drop of alcohol. Or a pill," he added. "It's going to take a hell of a lot more than Dockerty could ever dish out to get me back there. Even though I'm sure my teeth will finally disintegrate from all the cola I drink." His voice drifted away. Thoughts of John Dockerty staring expressionlessly through him were followed by images of other confrontations he had endured over the years since Ginny and Becky were killed.

As if reading his thoughts, Armstrong said, "David, you know that I'm aware of much that has happened to you in the past." He nodded. "Well, Lieutenant Dockerty has made it his business to find out as well. I'm not sure how he learned so much so quickly – he's just very good at his job, I suppose. And you know what a giant glasshouse a hospital is. Everybody's life is everybody else's business and what people can't gossip about for sure, they'll usually fill in with their imagination."

David gave a rueful laugh. "I've been the centre of hospital rumour before," he said. "I know exactly what you mean. This time, though, it's not just harmless gossip. They're talking about murder . . . But I would never – "

"Of course not," she said. "I know you wouldn't. As I said before, I think Lt. Dockerty is very thorough and very good at his job. I'm sure that will work in your favour. He doesn't seem the type who would stop until his case was airtight."

Their drinks arrived, and David welcomed the break in conversation. "Maybe I should voluntarily take myself off the staff until this whole thing blows over," he said at last.

Armstrong slammed her glass on the table splashing some of its contents and startling the couple in the next booth. "Dammit, young man," she said. "Never in all my days have I run into anyone who was more his own worst enemy than you are. Based on what I heard tonight, and what I believe to be true, our Lieutenant friend had better come up with a great deal more in the way of incriminating evidence before I'll allow anyone, including you, to move for your suspension. And if you don't think I have that kind of power around here, then just watch."

David's smile came more easily than it had all evening. "Thank you," he said. "Thank you very much."

"Well, now." She glanced at her watch. "This old bird has a full day at the office tomorrow, so I suggest we call it quits for the night. We'll talk again. Meanwhile, you've got to make yourself relax. Be patient. People like Lt. Dockerty, and also your friend Wallace Huttner won't be told much about anything. They have to find it out for themselves." She smoothed a five dollar bill on the table, and without waiting for change, walked with him to her car.

As she got in and rolled down the window, David said, "I've repeated myself so many times, I feel like a broken record, but . . . thank you. I guess there simply aren't any better words. Thank you."

"Just take care of yourself, David," she said, "and get through this in good shape. That will be all the thanks I need."

He watched until her car had disappeared around the corner, then walked numbly to the adjacent lot where his was parked. The car, a yellow Saab he had owned for less than a year, rested on its rims. All four tyres had been viciously slashed. Across the driver's side, in crudely sprayed red paint was the word MURDERER.

"A big glasshouse," David muttered as he stared at the sabotaged car. "You said it, lady. A big, fucking, animal of a glasshouse."

13

Barbara Littlejohn was an attractive woman in her late forties, tall, tanned, and nearly as thin as in the days when she'd worked her way through nursing school as a fashion model.

As she caught the taxi from the TWA terminal to the Copley Plaza, and then dashed through the cold Boston drizzle, she wondered how she could once have thought New England weather whimsical and charming.

"I'm with the Donald Knight Clinton Foundation," she said slightly breathlessly to the leering desk clerk. "We have a Board of Directors meeting here."

"Oh, yes, ma'am. Room 133. Across the lobby to the elevators, one floor up." He looked her up and down appraisingly, but she turned on her heel and strode towards the lift aware that she was late.

It was Monday, not yet twenty-four hours after the inquiry at Boston Doctors Hospital. Sixteen women had hastily rearranged their schedules and travelled to the Copley meeting from all parts of the country — New York, Philadelphia, San Francisco, Miami. They came because Peggy Donner had sent for them, and because of their commitment as Regional Directors of The Sisterhood of Life.

Co-ordinating Director of The Sisterhood of Life, Barbara Littlejohn was also administrator of the Donald Knight Clinton Foundation, the visible arm of the movement, and as such was in charge of the voluntary contributions of some half a million dollars made each year by Sisterhood nurses. She knew, as did all the others, that her lofty position in the California medical world was due in part to her involvement with the Sisterhood, and that although these titles were hers, the influence and much of the power still rested with Peggy Donner. Peggy Donner had spawned the Sisterhood in Boston and it had spread rapidly to hospitals throughout the country. Functioning through the

Clinton Foundation, the movement published a monthly newsletter updating the progress of Sisterhood projects and outlining available upper echelon nursing positions for which members would receive special consideration.

This emergency meeting convened at short notice was unprecedented. Of those who would be present, only Barbara knew its purpose in detail. She looked fleetingly at her watch as the lift doors opened, and hurried into room 133. It was a plush room with forest-green crushed velvet wall-covering, lithographs of the Punchestown Races of 1862 on the walls and a large oval mahogany conference table in the centre, around which now sat her Sisterhood colleagues. They looked up as she entered.

"I'm sorry I'm late. My flight from L.A. was delayed." Her apology was directed at Peggy Donner, who sat at the head of the table. Peggy nodded curtly and Barbara took the chair at the other end of the table between Susan Berger from the Hospital Consortium of San Francisco and June Ullrich, administrator for the largest pharmaceutical company in the country. Having concluded the general Foundation business, the women were having a short coffee break. As she poured herself a cup of rich dark coffee, Barbara asked Susan Berger what had been discussed in the half hour she had missed. Day care centres for children of working nurses, modern equipment for underfinanced hospitals, scholarships for advanced degrees in nursing, and continuing efforts to upgrade the function and image of hospital nurses had been some of the topics, explained Susan.

"Also, there's a letter from Karen who used to be on the board but who's now in Paris. Here, have a look." She opened a folder and pulled out a letter. "She's located five Sisterhood members who have moved to Europe. She says they're close to organising a screening committee, but they can't agree whether the European branch should be named in English, French, Dutch or German."

"Perhaps we should find out what Sisterhood of Life is in Esperanto," joked Barbara, and the women next to Susan laughed. They were the Boston contingent – Ruth Serafini, Dean of the White Memorial Hospital Nursing School, Sara Duhey, a striking, young black nurse, and Dotty Dalrymple.

"What beautiful flowers," Barbara continued, motioning to

the vase of dahlias at the end of the table, from which Peggy was lifting a pure, regal white bloom. The others agreed. Only one person in the room would see the flowers not simply as a beautiful arrangement, but as something else — a warning. The Garden would be watching and listening; the offspring appraising the parent.

Still holding the flower, Peggy Donner got to her feet.

"If we could resume now, Sisters." She paused, looking slowly from woman to woman around the table and waiting for silence. "I have something very important to discuss with you all. It has been nearly forty years, *forty years,* since four other nurses and I formed the secret society which was to grow into our Sisterhood." Her voice had a hypnotic quality to it. "Recently, one of those four nurses, Charlotte Thomas, died at Boston Doctors Hospital. She was so vital, so very special. She remained active in our movement for only a decade or so, but during that time, she was responsible, as much as anyone, for our remarkable growth.

"She had a terminal illness, and expressed both to me and to her physician her desperate desire for the freedom of death. As too often happens, however, her physician turned a deaf ear and was using the most aggressive methods to prolong her hopeless agony.

"Several days ago, I called an exceptional young nurse in our Sisterhood, Christine Beall, and asked her to evaluate Charlotte for presentation to our Regional Screening Committee. For many reasons, personal and professional, it was impossible for me to do so myself. The committee approved and recommended intravenous morphine. Through a series of unforeseeable and unfortunate circumstances, an unusually thorough autopsy was performed and a critically high blood morphine level was found."

The nurses sat in stunned silence as Peggy outlined the investigation that followed, and John Dockerty's session in the West Wing conference room. She paced as she talked, absently using the flower as a prop. Her tone was even and calm, and only when she came to discuss David Shelton did emotion appear in her voice. She described his background in great detail, stressing the difficulties he had encountered through his use of alcohol and drugs. "A disturbed young man," she said categorically. "One who would be doing the medical profession a great service by leaving it."

Peggy's pacing became more rapid as she searched for words. "My sisters," she said gravely, "it has been over twenty years since our system of Regional Screening Committees was established. Over those years, more than thirty-five hundred cases have been handled without the slightest hint of our — or anyone's — involvement. Unfortunately, it has now happened. Although Lt. Dockerty suspects Shelton is guilty of Charlotte's death, he is not convinced. Since he had learned of the special relationship which existed between Christine Beall and Charlotte, he had turned his attention to her. He has even mentioned the possibility of requesting her to submit to a polygraph test. I will not allow that to happen!"

For the first time, several at the table exchanged concerned glances. None had ever seen Peggy so close to losing control. The atmosphere in the room became increasingly uncomfortable.

She continued. "We are a Sisterhood. Our bond is as sacred and immutable as if it were blood. When one of us suffers, we must all share her pain. When one of us is threatened with exposure, as Christine is now, we must all fly to her aid. I, and each of you, should expect as much from your sisters. We must protect her!" The woman's voice had risen to a strangled, desperate stridency. For a time, there was silence, save for pulses of leaden rain clattering across the window behind her. Around the room, uneasiness gave way to strain and, for some, an icy foreboding. Petals dropped from the flower, mangled in Peggy's hands.

"I want that man found guilty." Peggy's words, barely audible, were spoken through clenched teeth.

The women gaped at her in disbelief. Dotty Dalrymple buried her face in her hands.

"What do you mean?" Susan Berger was the first to react. There was incredulity and anger in her voice.

Peggy glared at her. "Susan, I want the pressure off Christine Beall. There is no telling what might happen to her, or to our Sisterhood if the police try to break her down. I've worked too hard to allow anything like that to happen. Our work is too important. I want the Board's approval to take whatever steps are necessary to protect Christine and our interests. With a little ingenuity, I'm sure we can convince the police of Dr. Shelton's guilt. Considering his background, the most that would happen to him is a few months in some hospital and a year or two away from medicine. That seems a small price to pay for – "

"Peggy, I can't go along with this," Ruth Serafini spoke up. "I don't care what Shelton has done. Something like this works against the dignity of a man's life, against everything we stand for." Her assertion brought mutters of agreement and support from several others. She glanced around the table. Of the fifteen women, seven would support Peggy no matter what she asked of them. The others? A vote would be very close.

"Why don't we just let things be and see what happens," she continued. "If necessary, we can supply Christine Beall with money, lawyers, anything she needs. At this point it's not even a certainty that – "

"No!" The word was like a slap. "Don't you understand? One piece at a time, no matter how hard she resists, Christine will tell them about us. Can't you see the distortions that would appear in the press? It would ruin us. It would be the end of The Sisterhood. I will never allow that to happen!" and with this, Peggy turned to the window. Her shoulders heaved with each rapid breath. For a time, the only sounds were her breathing and the eerie music of the autumn storm. Yet, when she turned back, she was calm and smiling. Her voice was soft. "My sisters, a year ago I presented a plan by which I felt we could at last inform the public of our existence, and of the holy task we have undertaken. With several thousand taped case reports from the finest, most respected nurses in the world, I felt we could mount a campaign for acceptance so intense that those opposed to our beliefs would have no choice but to acquiesce. It would have been the culmination of a life's work, for me and all of you. I submitted my belief to a vote, but was defeated. I accepted the wishes of the Sisterhood then, but I promise you now that if we do not act tonight to protect this woman I shall move ahead with that plan rather than risk a debasing, distorted, sensationalist disclosure by the police and the press. I will release the tapes. I have them – all of them – and *I will do it.*"

Peggy turned to Barbara Littlejohn. "Barbara, I would like a vote giving me authority to do whatever is necessary to insure the guilt of Dr. David Shelton, and to protect the interests of Christine Beall and The Sisterhood of Life."

Barbara knew that further argument was fruitless. All the

women knew that the reports represented their bond, their conscious and total commitment, from which there was no turning back. With a shrug, Barbara called the question. To her left, Sara Duhey slowly lifted her hand. Barbara's eyes called on each one, and like a ripple, their hands came up. The vote of support was unanimous.

Breaking the silence that followed, Dotty Dalrymple cleared her throat and spoke for the first time. "Peggy, as you well know, Christine Beall is a nurse on my service. I have come to know her fairly well, although I have not yet chosen to tell her of my commitment to The Sisterhood. She is, as you have described, a remarkable nurse, devoted to the ideals we all share. Can we be certain she'll let this man answer for what she has done, regardless of our decision here tonight?"

The question had been on everyone's mind.

"That, Dorothy, must be our responsibility — yours and mine. When the time is right, you must go to her. Explain the situation as only you can. I know that you will make her understand. You may have to share your secret with her, but I think she has earned that confidence. If necessary, the rest of us here will share our secret with her as well. Is that acceptable to you?"

Dalrymple smiled. "I've known you far too long and too well to ask if I have a choice. I'll talk to her."

Peggy nodded and returned the smile.

Dorothy Dalrymple did indeed know Peggy well. From the beginning, Dotty had followed her rise, had even been party to her decision to enter medical school at a time when it was difficult enough for a woman, let alone a nurse, to do so. She had followed Peg's astounding success in the field of cardiology, to her marriage to one of the most famous scientists and human rights advocates in the world. She had watched her assume the leadership of the medical staff of one of the largest hospitals in the country. She knew from experience that Margaret Donner Armstrong could accomplish anything. The sentence they had voted for David Shelton was as good as carried out.

With a few parting words from Barbara Littlejohn, the meeting was dismissed. As she said her goodbyes, Dotty paused by the lavish bouquet, bending to inhale its strong perfume and briefly touch a feathery petal. Then, with a final glance at Peggy, she left.

The room emptied quickly. Soon, only two remained – Peggy Donner, gazing serenely out of the window, and Sara Duhey, who paused outside the doorway, then returned. Turning towards her with a warm smile, Peggy said, "Sara, how nice of you to stay. We so seldom get a chance to talk." Sara had been a personal recruit of hers. "I see a troubled look in those beautiful eyes of yours, Sara. Are you concerned about what happened here tonight?"

"A little. But that's not what I stayed to talk to you about. Something else has happened which bothers me. Terrifies me might be a better way to put it."

"Oh?"

"Peggy, a few days ago Johnny Chapman died at your hospital of a massive allergic reaction – probably to one of the drugs used, they're saying. Have you heard of him and the work he's done?" Margaret Armstrong nodded. "Well, I've known Johnny for years. Served on so many committees with him I've lost count."

"And?"

"Well, I've talked to a few people about his death – you know, people from my community. At least one of them felt quite certain there was nothing accidental about it. You can probably guess that as a black rights campaigner Johnny's been a thorn in the side of a lot of important people over the years."

"My dear. Every time an important or influential person dies, someone has a theory about why it couldn't have been a natural or accidental occurrence. Invariably, their theories prove to be unfounded."

"I understand," Sara said, "and I hope what you say is true in this case. We'll never know for certain, because Johnny's church forbids autopsies. His wife told me that. She had it written in big red letters on the front of his chart, along with a list of the things he was allergic to."

Dr. Armstrong shifted uncomfortably. "And exactly what is it that you're driving at?"

"Peggy, the person I mentioned told me that he had heard ahead of time that Johnny Chapman would not leave Doctors Hospital alive. He didn't. Then, two days after Johnny suddenly goes into anaphylaxis and dies, Senator Cormier has a fatal cardiac arrest on the operating table. The papers said it was a heart attack, but they also said that because the attack was instantly fatal, there was no definite cardiac damage found at his autopsy."

"Sara, I still don't see what – "

"Peggy, you do. I can see it in your eyes. Two of the cases I have handled through The Sisterhood involved intravenous ouabain. Both of them looked like heart attacks. The drug is impossible to detect. What if someone in The Sisterhood has gone off the deep end? What if she is using our methods to carry out some sort of vendetta? What if – "

"Whoa! Slow down, young lady. Just slow down. I understand how you must feel losing a friend and ally like John Chapman, but that is no reason to allow your imagination to override your common sense. These are your sisters you're talking about. Women you've known for years."

"Many of them, yes. That's true," Sara said. "But there are new recruits, a number at your hospital, whom I've never met. All I am afraid of is that one of them has begun using our methods on people who – "

"*You* may not know them all," Dr. Armstrong cut in, "but I do. They are superb nurses and completely honourable people. Every one of them. I think that unless you have some concrete proof, I would suggest – no, I would insist that you keep these notions to yourself. We have much more pressing concerns, you and I, starting with the man who is posing a threat to our entire movement." She sensed the impact of her outburst and softened. "Sara. I'm sorry for snapping. Look, after this Shelton business is cleared up, we can discuss your concerns in more detail. All right?"

Sara Duhey studied the older woman, then nodded. "All right."

"Thank you," Dr. Armstrong whispered.

The two women left room 133 together. Outside, the storm had intensified, and wind gusted with a fury that shook buildings.

14

"A crack that had the habit of looking like a rabbit . . . " David repeated the words over and over as he studied the series of thin lines that made crazy-paving of his living room ceiling.

" . . . had the *funny* habit of looking like a rabbit." Where had he read that? What were the exact words? No matter, he decided. None of the cracks looked anything like a rabbit really. Besides, the caretaker had promised they would be plastered over, so it was a fruitless exercise, anyhow.

He rolled to one side, tucked an arm under his head and stared out of the window. The outlines of buildings across the alley undulated through a cold, driving rain.

It had been nearly two days since the nightmarish session with Dockerty. The morning after the inquiry, David had tried to conduct his affairs at the hospital as usual. It was like working in an ice box. No virus could have spread through the wards faster than news of the tacit indictment brought against him. Most of the nurses and medical staff took special pains to avoid him. Some whispered as he walked past and one nurse actually pointed. Those few who spoke to him picked their words with the deliberateness of soldiers traversing a mine field.

By early afternoon, he could take no more. Aldous Butterworth and Edwina Burroughs were the only two patients he had in the hospital. Butterworth was essentially Dr. Armstrong's problem again. The circulation in his operated leg was better than in his other one. Edwina Burroughs was anxious to go home, and probably as ready for discharge now as she would be in the morning. David wrote a note in Butterworth's chart instructing Dr. Armstrong to arrange for his sutures to be removed in three days, then he made out a list of directions for Edwina Burroughs and sent her home.

He was walking, head down, towards the main exit when he collided with Dotty Dalrymple. They exchanged apologies, then

130

Dalrymple said, "Heading to the office?"

David fought the impulse to brush aside her courtesy with a dismissive reply. "No," he said. "I've cancelled the rest of the day. Actually, I'm going home."

He was surprised at the interest and concern in her eyes. Although the two of them were acquainted, they had never talked at length.

"Dr. Shelton, I want you to know how distressed I am about last night." She was, David realised, the first person all day who had openly said anything to him about the session.

"Me, too," he muttered.

"We haven't had the chance to get to know one another very well, but I've heard a great deal about your work from my nurses – all of it highly complimentary." David's face tightened in a half-smile. "My praise plus a dime gets you a phone call. That's what you are thinking, isn't it?" she said. David's smile became more open and relaxed. Dalrymple rested a fleshy arm against the wall. "Well, I'm afraid I don't have much in the way of cheery news for you, but I can tell you that Lt. Dockerty was in to see me this morning. Your name came up only briefly and, for what it's worth, I think he is not at all convinced of your guilt despite the circus last night."

"From the reaction around the wards this morning, Sister Dalrymple, I'd say that if that's the case, he's in a tiny minority. All of a sudden, I feel I have about as much control over what happens to me as a laboratory mouse. At the moment, Lt. Dockerty is very low on my list of favourite people."

"I guess if I were in your position, I'd probably be feeling the same." Dalrymple said. She paused as if searching for words to prolong their conversation. Finally, she shrugged, nodded a "good day," and headed off.

She was several steps down the hall when David started after her. "Sister Dalrymple, please," he called out. "If you can spare another minute, there is something you might be able to help with." The Nursing Director slowed, then came about like a schooner, smiling expectantly. "You had Charlotte Thomas's chart last evening," David said. "If it would be possible, I'd like to borrow it for a day. I have no idea what to look for, but maybe there's something in there that will give me a clue."

Dalrymple's expression darkened. "I'm sorry, Dr. Shelton,"

131

she said. "The chart I had last night was only a copy. The Lieutenant has the original." She hesitated. "Now, I don't even have the copy." David looked at her quizzically. He felt uneasy with the way she was weighing each word. "I . . . ah . . . gave it away, Doctor . . . this morning . . . Wallace Huttner, and the woman's husband . . . and a lawyer. They came to me with a court order for my copy of the chart. Apparently it was the only one the Lieutenant would allow to be made."

David's hands went cold. A damp chill spread from them throughout his body. He had little doubt as to what they were trying to pin on him. There was only one explanation. He carried a million dollars in liability. Peter Thomas wanted to be prepared to move as soon as any action was taken against him. David shuddered. On top of everything else, Thomas was going to sue him for malpractice. And his own Chief of Surgery was helping him to do it.

Dalrymple reached out to touch his shoulder and then seemed to change her mind. "I'm sorry, Doctor," she said coolly. "I wish I could help you, but I can't."

David tightened his lips. "Thanks," he mumbled, then hurried towards the exit.

By the time he arrived home, he was beset with a feeling of total frustration. He paced the apartment several times. Then, overwhelmed by his impotence, he threw himself across his bed and grabbed the telephone. He would call Dr. Armstrong, or Dockerty, or even Peter Thomas. Anyone, as long as it felt as though he was doing something. Indecision kept him from dialling. His address book lay on the bedside table. He opened it and flipped through the pages, hoping half-heartedly that someone's name would leap out at him. Anyone who might help.

Most of the pages were blank.

His brothers were listed — one in California, and one in Chicago. But even if they were next door, he wouldn't have called them. After the accident, the alcohol, the pills and finally the hospital, they had quietly separated him from their lives. Christmas cards and a call every six months or so were all that remained.

A few associates from his days at White Memorial were listed. From time to time over the past eight years some of them even invited him to parties. He was fun to be around . . . as long as he

132

was fun to be around. The more he had chanced talking about the course his life had taken, the fewer the invitations had become. There would be no real help from any of them.

The shroud of isolation grew heavier. There was no one. No one except Lauren, and she was five hundred miles away, probably having lunch with some congressman and . . . Wait! There *was* somebody. There was Rosetti. Of course. For ten years, whenever he was down or needed advice, there had always been Joey Rosetti. Joey, and Terry, too. Over the months with Lauren he hadn't seen them very much, but Joey was the kind of friend to whom that really didn't matter.

Excited, David looked up the number of Joey's Northside Tavern. Even if Rosetti didn't have any advice – which was doubtful since he had advice for everything – he would have encouragement, probably even a new story or two. Just the prospect of talking to him was cheering.

A curt, gravelly voice at the Northside Tavern informed David that Mr. Rosetti was not available. David's spirits immediately plummeted.

"This is Dr. Shelton. Dr. David Shelton." David emphasised the title in the manner he reserved only for making dinner and hotel reservations, or for working his way past the switchboard operator at an unfamiliar hospital. "I'm a close friend of Mr. Rosetti's. Could you tell me when he'll be back, or where I can reach him?"

The voice called someone without bothering to cover the mouthpiece. "Hey, some doctor's on the phone. Says he's a friend of Mr. Rosetti's. Can I tell him where he's gone?"

In a few moments it spoke to David. "Ah, sir, Mr. Rosetti and his wife've gone to their house on the North Shore. They'll be back late tonight."

David heard the voice ask, "Any message?", but he was already hanging up. In less than a minute, the silence and inaction were intolerable. David switched on the radio and tried to force himself to sleep.

When David awoke still dressed at five thirty the next morning, the radio batteries were dead and he felt as uneasy as the night before. Had he been dreaming about the accident again?

133

He couldn't remember.

He amused himself for nearly an hour by counting the seconds between a flash of lightning in the alley and the subsequent clap of thunder. Three calculations in a row agreed exactly – the electrical discharge was a mile and a half away. Measured against the disappointments of the past two days, his mathematical triumph was like winning an olympic medal. Fifteen minutes reading a mindless paperback. Two with the weights. Another few with the book. They were, he realised, the random, anxious movements of someone with no place to go. The same sort of restlessness that had characterised his first few weeks of hospitalisation in the Briggs Institute.

He stared at the phone and considered trying Lauren again. He had tried earlier in the day – her home number and even the hotels in Washington where she usually stayed. She'll be here soon, he told himself. If not today then tomorrow. Their only contact after she left had been a brief conversation just before the hideous session with Dockerty in the West Wing. Lauren had called to explain that she would be on the move, covering reaction to the death of Senator Cormier. In fact, she confessed, her main reason for calling (other than "just to say hi,") was to see if David could talk to people at his hospital, and get some inside information on the sudden tragedy. At the time, he'd felt certain he could learn something. Of course, there had been no way of knowing that within a few hours he would become a pariah at Boston Doctors.

David went to the kitchen for some water, then to the bathroom for some more.

She'd said she'd be in Springfield today covering the funeral. Possibly for a day or two after that. Perhaps she would call and they could meet in Springfield. Maybe they could even drive to New York or . . . or maybe up to Montreal.

Random movements, random thoughts.

He re-opened the mystery novel, read for a time, then discovered that the last ten pages of the tattered paperback were missing. He barely reacted, just shrugged, and shuffled off to take a shower, his second of the day. As he turned on the water, the telephone rang.

David skidded into the hallway and raced to the bedroom. "Hey, where have you been?" he panted into the receiver. "I've

134

been worried. I didn't even know for sure what city you were in.''

"David, it's Dr. Armstrong. Are you all right?''

"Huh?'' . . . oh, damn. "I'm sorry, Dr. Armstrong. No, I'm fine. I was expecting a call from Lauren . . . uh . . . my girlfriend . . . ''

"David. Take a minute and relax. Do you want me to call back?''

"No, no, I'm fine. Really.'' He stretched the phone cord to reach his chest of drawers and pulled on a pair of scrub trousers. Then he sighed and sank to the bed. "Actually, I'm not fine. I've been sitting around here all day. Half the time I wait, and the other half I try to figure out what I'm waiting for.''

"But you haven't . . . ?'' She let the question drift.

"No, not even close,'' he said forcing a laugh. "Not a pill or a drop of anything. I told you the other night that nothing was going to get me back there.'' Actually, the urge had been there several times – fleeting, but unmistakable. It never lasted long enough to pose a major threat, but after so many years, any sense of it at all was frightening.

"Good. I'm glad to hear it,'' Armstrong said. "I'm truly sorry to have taken so long to get back to you.''

"I understand.'' He cut in, hoping to spare her any uncomfortable explanations of the turmoil he knew was surrounding him – and her – at the hospital. "Any news?''

"Not really. Our friend the Lieutenant has been on and off since Sunday. He checks in with me or Ed Lipton to let us know he's around, but that's about it.''

"Well, I bumped into Sister Dalrymple yesterday and asked for her copy of Charlotte Thomas's chart. I thought perhaps I could get some brainstorm from studying it.''

"And did she give it to you?'' David missed the chord of heightened interest in her voice.

"No. I think she would have, but she didn't have it any more.'' Briefly, he reviewed the conversation with Dotty Dalrymple.

"So,'' she said after a moment's pause, "the buzzards circle.''

David smiled ruefully at the image. "Circle and wait,'' he said. "I feel so damn helpless. I want to do something to show them all I'm alive and fighting, but I can't even find a stick to wave.''

135

"I understand," she said. "If I were you, I would just sit tight and see what develops."

"You're probably right, Dr. Armstrong, but unfortunately, passivity has never been one of my strong suits. If I don't do something to sort this whole mess out, who will?"

"I will, David."

"What?"

"I told you the other night I would do what I could."

"I remember."

"Well, I have a friend in personnel who's checking the hospital computer for any former mental patients or drug problems or prison records. That sort of thing."

David became excited. "That's a great idea. How about past employment at Charlotte Thomas's nursing agency?"

"We could try that."

"And graduates of her nursing school. And . . . and activists supporting patients' rights, living wills, things like that. And . . ."

"Whoa! Slow down, David. First things first. You just stay where I can get in touch with you, and fight that self-destruct impulse of yours. I'll do the rest, don't worry. Are you coming back to work?"

"Tomorrow. I thought I'd try tomorrow. Anything would be better than sitting around like this waiting for the bell to toll. Thanks to you, it'll be much easier to concentrate on my job knowing at least that something's being done."

"Something's being done," Armstrong echoed.

Margaret Armstrong set the receiver down and glanced through her partially open office door at the patients in her waiting room - half a dozen complex problems which she would, almost certainly, unravel and deal with. Even after so many years, her own capabilities awed her.

"Mama, please. Tell me what I can do to help?"

She understood now. She had the knowledge and the power and she understood. But how could she have been expected to know then what was right? She was still a girl, barely fifteen years old.

"Kill me, Peggy. For God's sake, kill me."

136

"Mama, please. You don't know what you're saying. Let me get you something for the pain. When you feel better, you'll stop saying such things. I know you will."

"No, Peggy. It doesn't help. Nothing has helped the pain for days. Only you can help me. You must help me."

"Mama, I'm frightened. I can't think straight. I'm so frightened. I . . . I hate this place."

"The pillow, Peg. Just set it over my face and lean on it as hard as you can. It won't take long."

"Mama, please. I can't do that. There must be another way. Something. Please help me to understand. Help me to know what to do . . ."

Margaret Armstrong's receptionist buzzed several times on the intercom, then crossed to the office door and knocked. "Dr. Armstrong?"

The door swung open, and the receptionist knew immediately that she should have been more patient. It was just one of those times when the cardiac chief was totally lost in thought. One of those times when she sat fingering a small strip of linen, staring across the room. They came infrequently and never lasted long.

The receptionist eased the door closed and returned to her desk. Minutes later, her intercom buzzed.

The talk with Margaret Armstrong and their plan of action, however ragtag, injected a note of optimism into David's day. Some Bach organ music and twenty minutes of hard, almost vicious weight-lifting nurtured the mood. He was showered, dressed, and stretched out thumbing through a journal when a key clicked in the front door. He charged down the hall and was almost to the door when Lauren entered. She was carrying her raincoat and a floppy hat, but otherwise looked as if she had just come in from a garden party. Her light blue dress clung to her body, more out of will, it seemed, than design. A thin, gold necklace glowed on the autumn brown of her chest.

In those first few moments, standing there, looking at her, nothing else mattered. Then as he focused on her face, she looked away. Suddenly, David felt frightened even to touch her. "Welcome home," he said uncertainly, reaching a tentative hand towards her. She took it and moved to him, but there was no warmth in her embrace. Her coolness, and the scent of her

137

perfume – the same fragrance she had worn the morning she left – filled him with a sense of emptiness and apprehension. "I had no idea when you'd be coming back," he said, hoping that something in her response would dispel the feeling.

"I told you when I called the other day that I'd be tied up with the Cormier story," she said, settling into an easy chair in the living room. "What a shitty thing to happen," she went on. "Of all the people I ever interviewed in Washington, Dick Cormier was the only one I really trusted. Everyone did. His funeral was very moving. The President spoke, and the Chief Justice, and . . ."

David could no longer stand the tension inside him and in her nervous chatter. "Lauren," he said, "there's more, isn't there? I mean it's not just the Senator. Something else is eating at you. Please talk to me." Another man, he thought suddenly. She's met another man. Lauren stared out the window, biting at her lower lip. For a moment David thought she was about to cry, but when she finally spoke, her voice held far more irritation than sadness.

"David," she said, "a policeman was waiting for me when I arrived home. I spent more than two hours at the police station answering questions from Lt. Dockerty – some of them very personal – about you, and about us."

"Did Dockerty tell you what it was all about?" he asked.

Lauren shook her head. "Only briefly. He was nice enough at first, but his questions got more and more pointed – more and more offensive. Finally, I just stalked out and told him I wouldn't talk to him again without a lawyer. He made it sound like you were really sick and I was protecting you in some way. David, I can't have – "

"Damn that man!" David shouted. "When this is all over, he's going to answer for this shit. I've had about all I can take." His fists were white and tight against his thighs. "Lauren, this is a nightmare. The man's on some kind of vendetta. Ever since he came on the scene, he's gone after me like he had blinders on. I didn't do anything. He's taken a pile of circumstantial horseshit, and he's been trying to mould it into some kind of case against me." His control was disappearing. He sensed it, but was unable to back off. One after another his words tumbled out, each louder and higher pitched than the last. "I could handle the crap

138

he's been laying down at the hospital. That I could handle. But hauling you in . . . The bastard's gone too far." He was pacing now, thumping his fist against his side.

"David, please!" Lauren screamed. "You're acting crazy. Please get hold of yourself. It frightens me to see you like this."

He stopped in his tracks and forced his hands open. A deep breath, then he said, "I'm sorry, babe. I am. First I'm a jester, now I'm a madman." He managed a thin smile, and sank numbly onto the couch. "Lauren, could you hold me for a minute?" he asked, reaching his hands to her.

Lauren's lips tightened. She looked at the floor and shook her head. "David, we've got to talk."

"So, talk." He folded his hands in his lap.

"My wire service has people all over, David. Including the police department here. Business like this – being questioned at the police station and all . . . My boss is very straight and very conservative. If he gets wind of this – "

"Jesus Christ!" David exploded. "You make it sound as if I'm doing all this to give you a black eye. Can't you understand that I haven't done anything? My God, here I am being harassed up and down by some monomaniac, in danger of losing my career – or worse – and my girlfriend is worried about being embarrassed in front of her bureau chief. This is insane. Absolutely insane!"

"David," Lauren's voice was low and measured with anger. "I've told you over and over again how much I dislike the label 'girlfriend'. Now please calm down, and try to understand my position in this thing, too."

Speechless, David could only look at her, and shake his head. Lauren straightened her dress, sat rigidly upright, and met his incredulity with defiance. "I know you'll be pleased to hear," she said, "that of all the things you have to worry about, having to endure the Art Society dinner dance on Thursday will not be one of them. After the Lieutenant brought me home, Elliot May called and asked if I was planning on going. I knew how little you were looking forward to the affair, so I took the opportunity of relieving you of the burden." The wildness in David's eyes was frightening. She forced her lips into a proud pout and turned towards the window.

He rose and took a step towards her. In that frozen, terrifying moment, Lauren was sure he was going to strike her.

Suddenly, the buzzer from the downstairs foyer sounded. David whirled and half stalked, half stumbled to the intercom in the hall.

"Yes?" he shouted.

"It's Lt. Dockerty, Dr. Shelton." The policeman's voice crackled from four floors below. "May I come up, please?"

"Do I have any choice?" David said as he pressed the door release.

For the next half minute, the only sound David was aware of was his own breathing – bitter, frantic gulps, gradually slowing down as he fought for composure. He had been expecting a visit from Dockerty for the past two days. Typical of the man to pick a time like this to show up. He heard the clank as the gears of the rickety lift engaged. Standing by the door, he shook his head disdainfully at the groan from the straining cables. The antiquated box took more than a minute to make the four floor trip. A second clank, and the rattle of the automatic inside gate signalled its arrival. David stepped from his apartment just as Dockerty pushed open the heavy outside door of the lift. He was accompanied by a tall, uniformed officer.

"Dr. Shelton, this is Officer Kolb," Dockerty said. "May we come in, please?" It was an order. David thought for a moment about Lauren, then shrugged and led them into the living room.

"Miss Nichols." Dockerty nodded, but made no move to introduce Kolb to her.

Lauren stood and picked up her raincoat. "If you'll excuse me," she said formally, "I was just leaving."

She had taken one step towards the door when Dockerty said, "I think perhaps you had better stay, Miss Nichols." Lauren's eyes narrowed. She stiffened, then strode back to her chair.

Inside David, confusion and panic began to mount.

Dockerty stared at the floor for a few silent seconds, then reached into his coat pocket and produced a manilla-covered pad. The forms inside it were green. "Dr. Shelton," he said, handing the pad to David, "do you recognise these?"

David flipped through the sheets, then stammered, "Yes, they're my C222 order forms. But I don't see what . . . "

"For ordering narcotics?" Dockerty asked.

"Yes, but . . . "

140

"They're reprinted with your name, aren't they?"

"Yes, they are! Look, I've had enough of this sort of treatment. Say what you came to say, or leave!"

David's words were full of anger. Inside his gut, inside his chest, huge knots formed and began to tighten.

"Dr. Shelton, I sent notice to all the pharmacies in the city, asking for the names of everyone who purchased injectable morphine in the last month." He produced a single green form from his breast pocket. "This form C222 was used to purchase three twenty millilitre vials of morphine sulphate from the Quigg Pharmacy in West Roxbury. It's dated October 2nd, the day Charlotte Thomas was murdered. It's your form, Dr. Shelton. There's your signature at the bottom."

David snatched the form away. "That's not my signature," he said automatically. He stared at the writing, then closed his eyes. For years he had been kidded – had himself made jokes – about the scrawl that was his signature. "An unscrupulous chimp could prescribe for my patients," he had once quipped. The signature on the C222 would have passed his desk without a second notice.

"Perhaps," Dockerty responded tonelessly. "But I suspect that it is. You see, Doctor, there's more. The warrant I obtained to search your office allowed me to remove not only your forms, but this." He reached in his pocket again, and produced a small, gold-framed photo. "Mr. Quigg at the pharmacy has positively identified you from this photo as the one who purchased the morphine from him."

David stared down at the picture. It was one he had never been able to put away. The whole family — David, Ginny and three-year-old Becky — posing by the swan boats in Boston's Public Garden. It had been taken only two months before the accident.

For a time, Dockerty said nothing. Finally he shook his head. "David Shelton, I am placing you under arrest for the murder of Charlotte Thomas."

The words fell on David like hammers. An uncomfortable, high pitched buzzing began to fill his head. He tried to shake the sound loose as the tall policeman read him his rights from a frayed, cardboard card. The man's words seemed jumbled and slurred. David watched, a detached observer, as uniformed arms reached out and handcuffed his wrists behind him.

David was disoriented, frightened almost beyond functioning. He tried to pull away. Without a flicker of expression, the patrolman tightened his grip.

Bewildered and mortified, Lauren backed away as David, needing support to stand, was led out the door.

Dockerty moved to follow, then turned to her. "He's going to need a lawyer, Miss Nichols," he said grimly. "If I were you, I'd make sure it was a damn good one." With a nod, he headed down the corridor.

The wind had died down, but a cold, heavy rain was still falling. Dockerty threw a windbreaker around David's shoulders and zipped it up the front. Even so, by the time they propelled him the short distance to the squad car, he was soaked to the skin. In bizarre, disconnected scenes, David watched the events of his own arrest. The eerie blue light, a strobe atop the squad car . . . tiny, perfect diamond shapes in the metal screen . . . pedestrians bundled against the downpour, motionless through the screen and the front windshield. David saw them all as if frozen on camera. A grotesque slide show.

The station house . . . the lights . . . the uniforms. Then, it was the voices. "Empty your pockets . . . " ". . . son, can you hear me? Son? . . . " " . . . here's his wallet. Get the shit you need from his licence . . . " "Give me your right hand, thumb first . . . " "Over here, stand over here . . . " " . . . the other hand now . . . " "Look, fella, it's just a number. Let it hang there . . . " "Face straight ahead . . . now turn . . . no, this way, this way . . . " "Three's empty. Put him in there . . . "

Next it was the noises. Scraping of metal on metal . . . a loud clang – the lift? – no, not here. Can't be the lift . . . music . . . from where? . . . where is the music coming from? . . . More voices . . . " . . . here, boss, over here . . . " " . . . a light, I need another light. My fucking cigarette's soggy . . . " "When the fuck's dinner? Don't we even get fed here? . . . "

Finally, the wide, blurry bands . . . up and down in front of him. Gradually, the blurs narrowed and darkened . . . Bars! They were bars!

Again, the buzzing crescendo. Images of other bars, other

screens exploded through his mind.

"No! Please, God, no!" he screamed. He whirled and dropped to his knees by the toilet, retching uncontrollably into water already murky with disinfectant.

Barely aware of the bile stinging his nose and throat, David crawled across the stone floor and pulled himself onto a metal-framed cot. He descended into a cold, unnatural sleep long before his sobs had faded.

15

"Time to move out, son. There's some Listerine in this cup. Splash some cold water on your face and swish this stuff around in your mouth for a minute. It'll help you wake up."

David worked his eyes open a crack. His first sight of the morning was the same as his last the night before. Bars. This time, they were the narrow blue and white bars of the sweat-stained pillow beneath his face.

The officer was a red-faced man of fifty or so, with a belly that hung several inches over his belt. He leaned against the door-frame of the cell and watched patiently while David pulled himself up and wiped grimy sleep from his eyes. "Are you able to talk, son?" he asked.

David nodded, squinted at the man, then took the mouth-wash. The officer seemed in no great hurry, so David took a minute to stretch the ache from the muscles in his neck and back, trying at the same time to take stock of himself. For the moment, at least, the terror and confusion of the past night were gone. In their place was a strange but quite comfortable feeling of well-being. Knees locked, he bent forward and put the tips of all ten fingers on the floor. Peaceful, he thought. This shithole, all the madness, and here I am feeling peaceful. It was the same detached sense of peace a drowning man feels the moment before death, after the struggle is over.

The sergeant's ruddy cheeks puffed out in a grin. "Glad to see you're feelin' better," he said. "The night boys were worried. Said you weren't even able to hold a dime, much less make the phone call they tried to give you." When David didn't answer, he added, "You are feelin' better, aren't you?"

"Oh, yeah, I'm okay, thanks," David said distantly, still testing his body and his emotions for pain. "Wh . . . where am I, anyway?"

"District One," the man answered. He looked at David with

renewed concern. "You're in the jail at District One in Boston. Do you understand that?" David nodded. "We have to go now. You've got to go to court. The judge and the people at the court will help you. Don't you worry."

David watched with bemused interest as the policeman clicked a handcuff on his right wrist and led him out of the cell. He smiled politely at the black, silver-haired prisoner who was snapped into the other cuff. Calmly, with vacant eyes, he tried to focus on the manacled hands – black and white – and followed them into the back seat of a squad car.

"Name's Lyons," the black man said as the car pulled away. "Reggie Lyons." His wise face was etched with the lines of hard living and marked with the old furrows of an enemy's steel.

"David. I'm David," he answered.

"You ain't never been this route before, David, have you?" Lyons asked. David shrugged, looked out the window, and shook his head. "Well, you is in for *a* treat. The tank at Suffolk is the worst, man, I mean the pits." David stared at the motor-cycle cruising next to them and nodded. "Hey, you all right? Well it don't matter much one way or tuther. Crazy's prob'ly better. You just stick close to ol' Reggie. He'll take care of you."

The tank was, in fact, a cage. The holding room for prisoners awaiting court appearances. Twenty men, all "presumed innocent" were packed inside – rapists, drunks, vagrants, murderers, flashers. Around the outside, half a dozen lawyers were vying to be heard over one another and over the din inside. "Perkins, which one of you is Perkins? . . . " "Frankly, Arnold, I don't give a flying fuck if the kid is guilty or innocent. He either cops the first charge and saves us a trial or he ends up going down for both and spending three-to-five in Walpole . . . " "Look, kid, I know what you've seen on Perry Mason, but that just ain't the way it works. Today we don't talk guilty or not guilty. Today we talk money. If you have some or can get some, we bail you out. Otherwise, you wait for your trial in Charles Street. Nobody cares about your story today. This is just for bail. Understand? Just for bail . . . "

David wedged himself in one corner of the tank, and stared through the chain link at a high window that was opaque with grime. Bit by bit, reality – and terror – was returning. He thought about the hospital. The operation rooms would already be on their second cases of the day.

"Hey, David, you got a lawyer?" Reggie Lyons stood next to him, leaning against the cage. As he spoke, a wrinkled cigarette jumped up and down at the corner of his mouth.

"Er, no Reggie, I haven't," David said absently. "At least not that I know of." An uncomfortable pressure grew beneath his breast bone. He tried to remember when he had last eaten. When he had last run by the river. He looked about the cage, reality returning to him and with it an abysmal despair.

"Shelton? David Shelton. Which one of you is Shelton?" The bailiff was a dumpy man in his late fifties. There was an air about him – a look in his eyes – that suggested his favourite pastime out of court might be pulling the wings off insects.

Reggie Lyons leaned over and whispered, "David, don't you be scared now. Jus' go in there an' think about the beach or your favourite broad or somethin'. All the uniforms an' robes is jus' dress-up. A game they play to impress one another an' scare the shit out of us."

David turned and looked at Reggie's aged but timeless face. "Thanks," he said hoarsely. "Thanks a lot."

The man stared at him curiously, then took one of David's hands in both of his. His palms were tough and callous-roughened. "Good luck, man," he whispered. "Don't give in to 'em."

The paunchy bailiff snapped handcuffs on David as he stepped out of the tank. Moments later, he was seated in the prisoners' dock. The three-foot high, four-foot square pen was a wooden island, separating him from the rest of the courtroom. Told to stand, he braced his legs against a low panel as new words, new voices and scenes penetrated his nightmare.

The clerk who read the charges was a spinsterish woman who looked as if she had been born into the ornate old courtroom.

"As to complaint number 31947, your complainant, John Dockerty, respectfully represents that in the City of Boston in the County of Suffolk in behalf of said Commonwealth, David Edward Shelton of Boston in the County of Suffolk on the second day of October, in violation of the General Laws, chapter two six five, section one, did wrongfully murder one Charlotte Winthrop Thomas with intent to murder her by injecting into

146

her body a quantity of morphine sulphate. The court has entered a plea for the defendant of not guilty.''

David leaned more heavily against the panel as the district attorney, a slick young man with two rings on each hand, briefly outlined the case against him. Disconnected words and phrases were all that registered. " . . . premeditated . . . unconscionable misuse of his skill and knowledge . . . clandestine injection . . . positively identified as . . . murder, as heinous as any committed in passion . . . ''

"Dr. Shelton, do you understand the charges that have been brought against you?'' the judge said mechanically. David nodded. "Speak up, please. Do you understand the charges?''

"Yes,'' David managed.

"And do you have a lawyer?''

For several seconds there was total silence in the room. Then a voice called out from the last row of seats. "Yes, yes, he does, your Honour.'' A thin man, dressed in a three-piece pinstripe suit rose and walked briskly down the aisle towards the judge.

"You're representing this man, Mr. Glass?''

"Yes, your Honour.''

"Let the record show the defendant is represented by Mr. Benjamin Glass.''

David's eyes narrowed as he studied the man who had come forward to champion him. They alighted on the thinning, black hair, strands combed carefully across the top, a scuffed brown leather briefcase, a broad, intricately carved gold wedding band.

Glass walked to him and smiled encouragement. "You okay?'' he asked softly. David managed a nod. "You're white as a sheet. Do you need to see a doctor or anything?'' This time a shake. The lawyer's face was dark, nearly olive coloured, youthful, yet assured. Dark circles accentuated the intensity in his eyes. "Sorry I'm late. Lauren didn't get through to me until this morning. Let me get you out of here, then we'll talk.''

Ben Glass approached the judge. "Your Honour, I would like to move for bail and petition for a probable cause hearing.'' He looked slight to David, almost frail. But his stance, the tilt of his head exuded confidence.

This was Glass's world, David realised, his operating room. "Thank you, Lauren,'' he whispered. For the first time a flicker of hope broke through his nightmare.

"On what grounds?" the judge said.

"Your Honour, Dr. Shelton is a respected surgeon with no criminal record, and no recent history that would suggest the need for psychiatric observation and evaluation."

"Very well. Fifty thousand dollars cash."

"Your Honour," Glass said with just the right incredulity, "This man may be an M.D., but I assure you, he is no millionaire. Please save us a trip this afternoon for review by a supreme court justice. Make it a hundred thousand, but let me pay a bondsman."

The judge tapped his fingertips together for a few minutes, then said, "All right, Mr. Glass. One hundred thousand dollars bail it is."

"Thank you, your Honour."

Ben took David by the arm and, with the bailiff close behind, led him from the courtroom. "You're almost home, David," he said. "My friend the bondsman will want ten thousand dollars. Have you got it?"

"I . . . don't think so," David said.

"Family? Can you get it from your parents or someone?"

"My parents are dead. I . . . I have two brothers and . . . ah . . . oh, an aunt who might help. What if I can't come up with the money?"

"Believe me, you don't want that to happen. The place you stayed last night is a palace compared to Charles Street where they'll send you now. Tell you what. Maury Kaufman, the bondsman has gotten so fat off my clients that he owes me. He'll agree to cuff this one for a day rather than risk losing my trade. Today is Wednesday. I'll get you until Friday morning to come up with the cash. Okay?"

"Okay," David said as the bailiff removed his handcuffs and motioned him back into the tank. "And Mr. Glass, thank you."

"David, I hope this doesn't shake your confidence too much, but while you were taking Godliness 101 in medical school, I was one of those hippie weirdo flower children getting pushed around at anti-war demonstrations. It's Ben. You can only call me Mr. Glass if it makes it easier for you to come to grips with the fee you're going to have to pay me." He turned and headed down the hall as the bailiff clanged the tank door shut.

"Hey, David, is that Glass dude your lawyer?" A toothpick

148

had replaced the cigarette in the corner of Reggie Lyon's mouth.

"He seems to think so," David said, feeling his heart lifting slightly.

"Well, then, I guess I can stop gettin' all worked up 'n' worried about you. He don't look like much, but I seen him prancin' around in court a few times. The dude's a tiger. I mean he is *the* man."

"Thanks for telling me, Reggie." David actually grinned. "You've really been great to me. Say, what are you here for anyway?"

Lyons smiled and winked. "Jus' bein', pal," he said. "I is here jus' for bein'."

The sign over the bar said "Paddy O'Brien's Delicatessen: Home of the world's best chopped liver, and the most famous Irish Jew since Mayor Briscoe."

"I've never even heard of this place." David smiled as he slid onto the wooden bench across from Ben. Shamrocks and Stars of David were everywhere. On the wall over their booth, the photograph of a ragamuffin group of Irish revolutionaries hung side-by-side with one of a spit-and-polish Israeli tank unit.

"Are you Jewish?" Ben asked.

"No."

"Are you Irish?"

"No."

"I rest my case. It's no wonder you've never found your way here. Sooner or later, though, most people do. And here you are."

"Thanks to you."

"It's just my job," Ben responded matter-of-factly. "If my appendix bursts someday, then it may be thanks to *you* that I get back here to enjoy the chopped liver . . . That's the way it all works, right?"

"Right," David said. He knew that the easy talk they'd shared since leaving the courtroom had been as carefully orchestrated by Ben as his choice of this gritty, vibrant restaurant. He also knew they were wise choices. Slowly he was relaxing. Slowly he sensed the resurgence of hope.

Ben ordered a "sampler of delights" that could easily have fed ten. They ate in silence for a while, then he said, "It's probably unfair to have waited until after you've eaten to discuss my fee, but it is how the wee ones at home get fed. It's ten thousand dollars, David."

David started momentarily, then shrugged it off and took a sip of water. "In for $10 grand, in for $20 grand . . . " he joked with bravado, then added flatly, "I don't have it."

"I'm a bit more lenient in my payment schedule than Maury-the-Bondsman," Ben said, "but I do expect to get paid."

David's lips tightened. "I guess that after being accused of murder and spending the night in a cell, there's really not much place for false pride. I expect I could borrow the money if I can just sit on my vanity long enough to ask. My brothers would probably be willing to help. And I have this friend who owns the Northside Tavern – "

"Joey Rosetti?"

"You know Joey?"

"Not well, but enough to know that he's a good kind of friend to have. Somehow Rosetti's always been able to straddle the fence between the North End boys and the establishment without falling off on either side. If he's your friend, I say give him a call."

"If I need to, I will."

"Well, like I said, I expect to get paid." David nodded. "We're in business, then," Ben said reaching over to shake his hand. "Now I can tell you what you get for your money – and what you have to do to keep me. You get everything I can give you, David. Time, friends, influence, sweat – whatever you need. In exchange, I want only one thing from you – beside the fee, that is." He paused for emphasis. "Honesty. I mean total, no-crap, no-bullshit honesty. There are no second chances. If I catch you in even a tiny fib, you find yourself another lawyer. There are enough unpleasant surprises in this job as it is, without constantly worrying whether I'm going to get one from my client."

"We're still in business," David said.

"Fine. Why don't you start by giving me some background on yourself. Assume I don't know anything."

At that moment, a sprightly little man with freckles and greying red hair bounced over and leaned on the table. He wore a grease-stained apron with a large, green Star-of-David on the front. His high pitched brogue made every word a song. "Benjy, me boy. Openin' the annex to your office again, I see."

"Hi, Paddy. It's been a while." Ben shook his hand. "Place looks good. Listen, this is my friend, David, He's a surgeon, so you'd best keep this rowdy lot quiet while we're working, or I'll have him graft your precious parts to your dart board."

Paddy O'Brien laughed and patted David on the shoulder. "Go ahead, if it'll make 'm work any better. Benjy here's the best there is at lawyerin' *and* at bummin' the check, so watch out. You boys go on about your business. I'll have two pints sent over – courtesy of the house."

"Make that one, Paddy," Ben said. His eyes met David's for an instant. "For me."

"One pint, and one Coke comin' up," the little man said without batting an eye.

"So, assume you don't know anything, huh?" David was smiling.

"I was late this morning because I was talking to John Dockerty," Ben explained. "I didn't stay long enough to learn too much, but I will tell you he hasn't put this thing in the drawer. Please, play it my way and just assume I know nothing, okay?"

"Okay," David shrugged. "How far back?"

"It's your story," Ben said.

"My story . . . " For a moment, David's voice drifted away as events, people flashed through his thoughts. "Began innocently enough, I guess." He shrugged. "Two older brothers. Decent, loving parents. White picket fence. The works. When I was about fourteen, the whole thing unravelled. Mother got cancer. It was in her brain before anyone even knew she had it. Even so, she lived for eight pitiful months. My dad owned a small store. Appliances. He ended up selling it so he could nurse mother — in between her hospitalisations, that is. A few weeks before she died, *he* had a coronary. Dead before he hit the floor, they told me.

"I'm still not sure why, but from that time on all I wanted to be was a doctor. A surgeon. Even back then."

It had been years since David had sat and gone through the whole thing. He felt surprised at how easily the words came. "Is this the kind of stuff you want to know?'' he asked. Ben nodded.

"My aunt and uncle took care of me until college, then I was essentially on my own. I was never any great genius, but I knew what I wanted and I clawed and scraped to get it. Scholarships and jobs all the way through medical school. I'd find what I thought was my limit, then I'd push myself past it. By the middle of my internship, it was starting to get to me. I was sort of a wunderkind in the hospital, but outside I was coming unglued. Too many cigarettes, sleepless nights, relentless depressions. I fought the problem the only way I knew how. I pushed myself even harder at work. Looking back, I feel sure that if it weren't for a stop sign some kids had stolen, I would have gone off the deep end."

Ben started at the strange association, then he smiled. "A woman?"

David nodded. "Ginny. Her car and mine smacked into each other at an intersection. The sign her way was missing. The irony of it all is still really painful. I met her through a car accident, then . . . " For the first time, words became difficult.

Ben raised a hand. "David, if this is too hard for you right now, we can do it another time. Sooner or later, though, there are things I have to know."

David toyed with his glass, then said, "Nope, I'm okay. Just stop me if it gets too maudlin – or too boring." Ben grinned and waved him on. "We got married six months later. She was an interior decorator. A rare and gentle person. My whole life changed, just by having her there. Over the next four years, there was magic in everything I did. The head of the surgical department at White Memorial asked me to stay on an extra year as Chief Resident. That job is about the only way a surgeon can get a staff appointment at WMH. So, it was all there. For a little while at least.

"We had a little girl, Becky. I finished the residency and started in practice. Then, there was the accident. I was driving. I . . . well, let's skip the details. Becky and Ginny were dead. Just like that. I had scrapes and cuts, but really nothing. Except that in my own way, I died too. I never really got back to work. I went from being a social drinker, a teetotaller almost, to being a drunkard and it was one long bender. Thank God I had enough

152

sense to stay away from the operating room.

"I tried seeing minor cases at the office, though. That's when I started on the pills. My version of changing seats on the *Titanic.* Ups to get started, downs to sleep. You know the story. At first my associates were tolerant. Helpful, even. One at a time, though, I managed to work over their faith brutally enough to drive them away. It went on like that for almost a year. In the end, I was removed from the staff. I didn't even know it had happened because I was lost in another bender."

"It's a bitch of a cycle to break out of," Ben said.

"Alone it is. That's for sure. Well, one morning I woke up in a cage. My last friend couldn't stand it any more. Actually, it was a hospital he brought me to. Briggs Institute?" Ben nodded that he knew the place. "It turned out to be a great place for me, but those first few weeks were hell. No handle on the door. Bars on the windows. The whole scene . . . Are you still awake?"

Ben managed a short laugh. "I got snatches of your story from Lauren and Dockerty," he said shaking his head, "but not like this. Getting locked up last night must have revived unpleasant memories . . ."

"It did." David shuddered, but gulped down half a glass of water to slake the dusty dryness in his throat, and forced himself to continue. "Let's see . . . There's not much left to tell. Several months at the institute and I was ready to go back to medicine. But not to surgery. I spent almost three years as a G.P. in one of the inner city clinics, then went back and repeated the last two years of my surgical residency. I made the staff at Boston Doctors nearly two years ago. It hasn't been easy, but things have been picking up. At least until a week ago."

"David, this is much more than I ever hoped you would be able to tell me at this point," Ben said. "I'm grateful to you for doing it. Makes my job much easier."

David looked at him quizzically. "I'm curious," he said. "Why is it you haven't asked me whether I killed her?"

Ben grinned and set his chin in his hands. "I don't need to, my friend. You've already told me. A dozen different times in a dozen different ways. You've hauled yourself too far for me not to move hell and earth to get that court to admit your innocence."

"Thank you." David whispered the words. He paused.

"Ben, when you talked to Lauren, what did she say? You see, we had a fight and . . . "

"David, I don't want to get in the middle of anything like this, but I do have something to say. I've known Lauren Nichols for years. She's a bright, incredibly beautiful woman who, by choice or circumstances, has not had to face too much adversity in her life. She . . . ah . . . she asked me to give you this." He pulled out a pink envelope – Lauren's stationery – and handed it to David.

David looked at the envelope for a long moment. "No prizes for guessing what it says, I'm sure." His voice was flat as he folded the envelope and stuffed it in his pocket.

"I'm sorry," Ben said softly. "Are you all right to go home? I mean if you need a place to stay for the night . . . "

"No, thanks, Ben. I'll be okay. Really,"

"I'll call you tomorrow," Ben said.

"Tomorrow," David echoed.

The steely afternoon sky was threatening, but the steady rain of the past several days had let up. The walk from Paddy O'Brien's to his apartment was about two miles, and with nothing to hurry home for, David took it at a leisurely pace, stopping once to wander through the old cemetery where Paul Revere was buried. He reasoned that the graveyard would be an appropriate place to read Lauren's letter.

He needn't, he decided afterwards, have bothered. The note was what he expected: — one-third thank-you-for-everything, and two-thirds just-doesn't-seem-like-things-will-work-out-for-us. "I guess she took me for better or for better," David said as he tore the note into tiny pieces and ceremoniously tossed the pink petals over an ancient grave. He was surprised at how little hurt he felt. Perhaps it was because the loss of the relationship was just another brick in the wall that seemed to be closing him off from life. Then, as he trudged towards Boston Common, he began to realise that he had rarely been totally at ease with Lauren. It was largely his fault for trying to force her into the spaces Ginny had filled in his life. Even before it had started, he had doomed the relationship with his hopes.

The advance unit of the rush hour had begun filling the

walkways of the Common. Haggard businessmen, giggling groups of secretaries and stylish career women were all crossing the grassy park on the way home. David was lost in thought.

By the time he reached Commonwealth Avenue, a light, misty rain had started falling again. He squinted upwards and picked up his pace. Half a block ahead, a thin elderly gentleman stood up from the bench where he had been reading the early evening edition of the Boston *Globe*. He tested the rain with an outstretched palm, then folded his paper under his arm and headed home. On page three of that paper was a two column spread on David and his arrest.

16

"Chrissy, check the bathroom out. Does it look okay?" Lisa called out as she pulled on a skirt and zipped it up the side.

"Lisa, the bathroom looks fine. I told you, don't worry about the place. I've got an hour before she's due. That's plenty of time to clean up." Christine dropped a record into its jacket and replaced it on the shelf, taking a moment to straighten the row of albums. She had felt increasingly jittery and apprehensive since Dotty Dalrymple's late afternoon call, and now wished her roommates would head off for the evening so she could have some time to herself before the woman arrived.

The Nursing Director had given no hint as to why she wanted to stop by, but it was hard for Christine to believe the visit related to anything other than the death of Charlotte Thomas. She had given some thought to calling the Regional Screening Committee for advice on how to handle the situation but decided it was foolish when she wasn't at all certain of what, exactly, the situation was.

Lisa popped into the living room, naked from the waist up. "Carole, bra or no bra for this guy?"

"He's a *blind* date, Lisa," Carole shouted from her room. "Just don't let him touch you and he'll never be able to tell whether you have one on or not."

"What do you think, Chrissy? Bra or no bra?"

Christine appraised her for a moment. "It's been a dull season," she said. "I think you should go for it." Her voice held far less cheer than she intended.

Lisa shrugged and slipped on a blouse. "You seem tense as a drum. Anything you want to talk about?"

"Believe me," Christine said, "if I had something to talk about, I would. I've never had Sister Dalrymple visit me like this, that's all. She could want to promote me, she could want to fire me. I just have no idea. Listen, you guys, have fun. I hope he's

156

nice. And thanks for helping me tidy up the place."

"Ooh, wait a minute!" Lisa snapped her fingers and dashed to her room, talking as she ran. "These came earlier this afternoon. I guess while you were out." She returned with a vase of flowers. "I think they'll be the perfect touch over here by the window . . . no, on the table . . . no, I think perhaps over the . . ."

"Lisa, those are lovely. Who sent them?"

"The mantel. Yes. They're perfect for the mantel."

"Lisa, *who?*"

"Oh, they're from Arnold. Arnold Ringer, the office heart throb. The fool believes these are a short cut to my body. And you know what?"

"He's right!" The two of them said the words in unison, then laughed.

Christine was straightening the kitchen when the doorbell rang. Moments later, Carole and Lisa called their good-byes, and she was alone.

Her solitude lasted a sigh and one pace to the living room and back. With a purely perfunctory knock, Ida Fine slipped in the back door. Folded under her arm was a copy of the evening *Globe*. She started talking before Christine could explain that her visit was ill-timed.

"So, where are my other two? Gone for the evening? So, why not you?" Ida seldom asked a question without answering it herself or at least following it with another, often unrelated, query.

"They've got dates, Ida," Christine said, hoping that the flatness in her voice would get the message across without being offensive.

"And you, the prettiest of the three, have none? You're sick, is that it? You're not feeling well. I have some soup upstairs. I know you nurses are too sophisticated to believe in such things, but . . ."

"No, Ida, I'm fine." There was no stopping the woman short of a frontal assault. "I'm just busy tonight. My nursing supervisor is coming over soon, so I've got to get ready. Maybe tomorrow, or even later tonight we can talk, okay?"

Ida slapped the newspaper on the table. "I'll bet it's about that doctor who murdered the woman at your hospital," she

157

said. "A doctor, yet. My mother always wanted me to marry a doctor, but no, I had to be pig-headed and marry my husband, God-rest-his-soul . . . "

Christine's eyes widened and fixed on Ida, who just kept talking. " . . . not that Harry was a bad man, mind you. He was a very good man. But sometimes – "

"Ida, what are you talking about?"

"The murder. David somebody. Must be Jewish. No, he can't be Jewish. A Jewish boy murdering a patient? I can't – "

"Ida, please!" Christine's shout produced instant silence. "What on earth are you talking about?"

"It's right here. In the *Globe.* I thought you knew. Here, keep the paper. Just leave me the T.V. section. I forgot to get a T.V. guide while I was at the market."

She talked on, but Christine no longer heard her. The newspaper rustled in her hands even after she had folded back the page. "Surgeon Charged with Mercy Killing; Released on Bail."

Colour flushed in her cheeks, then drained away. "Oh, my God," she said softly as she read the account of David's arrest and arraignment. "Oh, my God . . . "

Ida's verbal onslaught continued for another minute, then slowed and finally stopped. Christine read the article one word at a time, unaware that her landlady's gaze was now riveted on her.

Ida brought a chair from the kitchen table, and Christine sank down numbly as she read the last few lines.

Reliable Globe sources report that Shelton filled prescriptions for large quantities of morphine on the day of Mrs. Thomas's death. Attorney Glass declined to comment on the evidence, but reasserted his confidence in the innocence of his client. 'When all the facts are in,' he said, 'I am sure the truth will be learned and my client will be vindicated.' Dr. Shelton has been released on $100,000 bail. No date for trial has been set.

158

Ida rushed to the sink, wet a washcloth and rubbed the cold compress over Christine's forehead. For almost a minute, Christine made no move to stop her. Finally, she nodded and gently pushed Ida's hand away.

"I guess you hadn't heard?" Ida said. "You know this David?" Miraculously, she stopped at two questions.

"Yes. I . . . know him," Christine said. David Shelton had been in and out of her thoughts since the day they'd first met on Four South. Nothing persistent or overwhelming – or even well defined – but he was there. Dockerty's inquiry had given her reason to talk about him with other nurses without seeming too obvious or interested.

Ida Fine rubbed her hands together anxiously. "Chrissy, your face is the colour of my Swedish ivy. You want me to help you to bed, or . . . or call a doctor?"

Christine shook her head. "Ida, I'm all right. Really. But I have got to be alone for a while. Please?"

"Okay, I'm going. I'm going," Ida said. The pout invaded her voice more by reflex than by intention. "If you need me, I'm right upstairs. Also food, if you need food . . . keep the paper . . . " She was still talking as she backed out the door.

Christine read the article a second time, then wrote Ben Glass's name and law firm in her address book. Why had David purchased so much morphine? And on the day Charlotte died. A coincidence? Perhaps, but certainly not an easy one to accept. Maybe the hospital rumours were true this time. Maybe he does use drugs. Or deal them. Possibly both. But what little she knew of him would not permit her to believe that was true.

She pressed her fingers against her temples as a dull, pulsing ache began accompanying each heartbeat. It really made no difference, she realised, why David had purchased morphine. She knew what she had done with the vials left for her by The Sisterhood, and there was simply no way she could allow him to suffer for that. It had seemed so right, she thought. Damn it, it *was* right. Charlotte wanted it. The Committee approved. She hadn't acted alone. She closed her eyes tightly against the pulses, which had become hammers. Every tiny movement of her head made the pounding worse.

"Lie down," she told herself. "Find some aspirin, some Valium, something, and lie down." She blinked at the kitchen light, which suddenly seemed painfully bright, then pulled herself to her feet. At that instant, the doorbell rang.

She moved awkwardly to the stove. Tea, must make her some tea, she thought. The bell sounded again, more insistently.

With a groan, Christine turned and raced through the hallway to the front door.

Dotty Dalrymple, wearing a purple overcoat, looked more imposing than usual. She smiled warmly from beneath a broad-brimmed, purple rainhat, and stepped inside. "This is wet," she said, holding her black umbrella like a baton. "Is there somewhere I can leave it?" She seemed totally at ease.

The pounding in Christine's head began to recede as she set the umbrella by the door and hung up the tent-sized coat. "Tea," she said, forgetting to invite the woman in. "Would you like some tea?"

"Tea would be fine, Christine." Dalrymple's smile broadened as she motioned at the hallway. "In the living room?"

Christine calmed down a bit more. "Oh, I'm sorry, Sister Dalrymple," she said. "I didn't mean to be so impolite. Come in. I . . . I'm sorry for the mess the place is in but . . . "

"Nonsense." The Director cut her off. "It's a lovely apartment. Please, Christine, relax. I promise not to bite you." She surveyed the living room briefly, selected an armless, uphol-stered chair opposite the couch, and settled herself down. "You mentioned tea?"

"Oh, yes, there's water on the stove. Let me heat it up."

"Lemon if you have it," Dalrymple called out. "Otherwise plain."

"It'll only be a minute," Christine said, bustling about the kitchen. She bit into a biscuit from the only box she could find. "Damn," she hissed, spitting the stale cookie into the trash.

In the few minutes it took to arrange two cups of tea and some lemon slices on a tray, Christine singed her forearm and put a thin cut in the corner of one thumb. Two steps inside the living room she froze, barely preventing the cups from toppling over. Dotty Dalrymple had a copy of the evening *Globe* unfolded on her lap.

"I assume from your reaction that you have read this evening's paper," Dalrymple said.

Christine closed her eyes and inhaled sharply. If her nursing

160

director had made the connection between her and Charlotte, something was very wrong. Now, she wished she had called the Sisterhood Screening Committee for advice. "I . . . my landlady showed it to me a little while ago," she stammered. "It's awful."

"Do you know Dr. Shelton well?" Dalrymple asked, motioning her to the couch.

"No, not really. We've barely even talked. I . . . I just met him for the first time last week." Too many words, she thought. What could she want?

"Do you know his background?"

His background? The question caught Christine off guard. Why would Dalrymple ask about that? Does she suspect? Was she trying to cover for her somehow? Christine decided to continue the verbal joust until the woman's purpose was clearer. "His background? Well, not much really. No more than some hospital rumours."

"The man is a known drug addict and probably an alcoholic," Dalrymple cut in bluntly. "Did you know that?" Christine was too shaken by the Nursing Director's statement to answer. After a moment, the woman continued. "Several years ago he was removed from the staff at White Memorial. His appointment to the staff of our hospital was made over the loud protests of many of the other physicians. David Shelton is not a credit to his profession."

David's face formed in Christine's thoughts – gentle and intense, with kind, honest eyes. Dalrymple's words did not fit that picture. "I . . . I don't know what to say."

Dalrymple leaned forward in her chair and stared at her intently. "Obviously I am here sharing these facts with you for a reason." Her voice held a strange, mystical quality. "Christine, we are sisters, you and I. Sisters." Christine gasped. "I wanted so much to tell you that afternoon on Four South, but our rules forbid it. I have been part of The Sisterhood of Life since my earliest days in nursing. In fact, I represent the Northeast on our Board of Directors."

"I never would have thought . . . what I mean is I never suspected . . . ."

Dalrymple laughed. "There are several thousand of us, Christine. All over the country. The very best nursing has to

161

offer. Joined by ideals and our pledge to forward the cause of human dignity.''

"Then you know about Charlotte?"

"Yes, my dear, I know. All the directors know, the New England Screening Committee knows, and of course, Peggy knows. I am here representing all of them. I am here to help.''

"Help me?"

"Yes."

Christine shook her head. "Who's going to help Dr. Shelton?" she asked sullenly.

"My dear, you don't seem to have understood what I said." Dalrymple leaned forward for emphasis. "The man is a — "

Christine cut her off with a raised hand and a finger to her lips. She stared towards the side of the house. Dalrymple looked at her quizzically, then followed the line of her sight to the spot.

"I heard something," Christine whispered. "Out there, by the window.''

Dalrymple cocked her head to one side and listened. "Nothing," she said softly.

Christine wasn't convinced. She tiptoed to the side of the window and peered out at the night. The driveway and as much of the street as she could see were quiet. She stood there, pressed against the wall for several minutes. Still nothing. Finally, with a shrug, she pulled the blinds and returned to the couch. "There was a noise out there," she said. "A thud.''

"Probably a cat," Dalrymple said.

"Probably." Her voice was doubtful. Dalrymple sipped her tea patiently, waiting for Christine's concentration to return enough to continue their discussion.

"I'm . . . I'm sorry," Christine said at last.

Dalrymple smiled. "I understand what you're going through, dear," she said. "We all do, even though a situation such as yours has never arisen before, and probably never will again. Ours is not an easy task. Everywhere along the way there are choices to make, and few if any of them are painless." There was an edge in her voice that Christine found unsettling.

"Just what are you suggesting I do?" she asked.

"Why nothing, dear," Dalrymple said. "Nothing at all.''

Christine stared at her with disbelief. "Miss Dalrymple, I can't let that man suffer for something I've done. I could never

162

live with myself."

Dalrymple looked back impassively and shook her head. "I'm afraid, Christine, that many more would suffer if you made any attempt to clear him."

Foreboding tightened in Christine's gut. "Wh . . . what do you mean?"

"Peg – the woman you spoke to – is Peggy Donner. Almost forty years ago, she founded The Sisterhood of Life. She has dedicated her entire life to its growth."

"And?"

"Christine, she will not allow you, or any other Sister, to be hurt for doing what is right. She fears that your exposure will, sooner or later, lead to the exposure of the entire movement."

"But that's not true!" Christine cried. "I would never disclose anything about . . . "

"Please. What matters is not what you think would happen, but what Peggy thinks would happen. You see, before she would risk having the public learn of us through a sordid police investigation and sensationalist press, she will move to inform them herself." Dalrymple's expression was grave. "She has our tapes, Christine. All of them. If you go to the police, she has promised the Board of Directors that she will make them public in her own fashion. For several years now, she has wanted to do so anyway. Only pressure from the rest of us has kept her in check. We did not feel it was time."

The throbbing in Christine's head began anew. "This . . . this can't be happening," she murmured. "It just can't be."

"But it is, Christine. And the careers of all those in The Sisterhood hang by the thread that you control. I'm not at all happy with the situation, despite my personal dislike for degenerate physicians such as Dr. Shelton. However, you must believe me as one who has known Peggy for many years. She will do it."

Christine could only shake her head.

"We would like you to take a vacation from the hospital," Dalrymple continued softly. "I'll have no trouble granting you a leave for say, three or four weeks. When you return, a shift supervisor's slot will be waiting for you. Perhaps Greece? The islands are beautiful this time of year. A month in the sun for you and the whole matter will have blown over."

"I . . . I don't think I could do that."

"For all our sakes, Christine, you must. Please believe me, Peggy's threat is not an idle one. With our numbers, and the positive image she would project, she feels certain that The Sisterhood can now withstand exposure. If you go to the authorities, nothing and nobody will be able to stop her. She may even be right, but I for one do not wish to risk my career and life on that chance."

"There would be chaos," Christine said.

Dalrymple nodded.

"I need some time. Some time to think."

"The sooner you take your trip, the better," Dalrymple said. "I promise that getting away from all this will make the whole process much easier on you." She stood up, took an envelope from her purse and handed it to Christine. "This should help you do what you must. Please call me if I can be of any further help. It is a difficult situation, Christine, having to hurt one to avoid hurting many. But the choice is clear."

Christine followed her to the hallway, and stood numbly to one side as she put on her coat. "Your sisters," Dalrymple said, "all of us, are grateful for what you are doing." She reached out and squeezed Christine's hand then turned and let herself out.

The blue sedan, parked in an islet of darkness between two street lights, was virtually invisible. Slouched behind the wheel, Leonard Vincent kept his attention fixed on the house as he struggled to catch his breath. The close call beneath the window and his dash to the car had left him winded and, despite the chill night air, soaked with sweat. On his lap, his right hand moved in continuous circles, working the blade of a knife over a whetstone with the loving strokes of a concert violinist. The blade was eight inches long, tapered and slightly curved at the tip. The handle of carved bone was nearly lost in his thick fist. It was Leonard Vincent's pride – the perfect instrument for close work.

The front door opened. Vincent sniggered at the sight of the huge woman manoeuvring herself down the concrete front steps. As she crossed the street to her car, he amused himself by planning the description he would use in his report. "At precisely five thirty, a blimp floated into the house." Vincent's sallow face bunched in a mirthless grin. "She rolled out of the

164

house and bounced down the stairs to her car. At precisely six fifteen she started getting behind the wheel. At six thirty she made it!''

Distracted by his own wit, Vincent was slow to react when the woman made a sudden U-turn and came towards him. An instant before her headlights flashed by, he dived across the front seat, striking his forehead on the passenger door handle. He cursed the handle, then the door, and then the fat bitch who had made him hit it. But mostly, he cursed himself for taking a job without knowing exactly who was hiring him or even what he was expected to do.

It had started with a call from a bartender friend. ''Leonard,'' he had said, ''I think I may have something for you. There's this broad in here askin' me if I know of anyone who's interested in makin' some big bucks. She says that whoever it is will have to be able to keep his mouth shut and do what he's told. I tried to find out some details, but she just gives me this fucking look, shoves a fifty across the counter, and says that there'll be more if I can get her someone who asks less questions than I do. You interested? I'll tell you Leonard, the broad's weird, but I think she's on the level. Also, she's got great tits.''

Right away, Vincent hadn't liked her or the set-up. The name she had given him, Hyacinth, was a phony, he was sure of that. But no matter. Except for setting up the job, all she would do is deliver the money.

So he had ended up with twenty-five hundred bucks up front, a phone number, and a name – Dahlia. Another phony.

Vincent rubbed the lump that was rising over his left eye. ''Face it, Leonard,'' he told himself, ''You've really hit bottom this time, no matter how good the fucking money is.''

He watched the house until he was reasonably sure Christine Beall was not coming out, then he shoved the knife into a hand-tooled leather case and drove around the corner to a phone booth. A woman answered on the second ring.

''Yes?''

''This is Leonard.'' His voice was a toneless rasp.

''Yes?''

''You wanted a report on everyone who talks to this Christine.''

''And?''

"Well, a big fat woman just left. She got here about forty-five minutes ago."

"Mr. Vincent, your instructions were to call as soon as she met someone, not to wait until they had left."

"Hey, you don't sound like Dahlia. Is this Dahlia?"

"Mr. Vincent, please. When Hyacinth paid you, she told you to call this number and report. Now, you will either do exactly as instructed, or I promise you trouble. Big trouble. Is that clear?"

The threat was effective. Leonard Vincent feared nothing that he could see, but an icy, disembodied voice was something else. He cursed himself again for taking the job. "Yeah, it's clear," he said.

"All right. How long did you watch the house after the woman left?"

"Ten, fifteen minutes. I don't know exactly. Long enough, though. She's staying put."

"Very well. Return to your post, please."

"What about sleep?"

"You are being paid, and paid well, to watch that woman and report on her movements, Mr. Vincent. Now return to your post. And remember, we wish to know the minute she talks to anyone, *not* after they have already left. Call this number at two o'clock, and we shall discuss your sleep then. Oh, and one last thing. We've done some checking around. We know your tendency to hurt people, sometimes without provocation. No-one, I repeat, no-one is to be touched without our say-so. Is that clear?"

Vincent shrugged. "Like you said, it's your money." He hung up the phone, stared at it for a moment, then spat on the receiver. A reflex check of the coin return, and he drove back to watch the house.

The only lights in the apartment shone through the blinds of the living room window. Every few minutes, Christine's silhouette appeared, then vanished. Leonard Vincent picked up his whetstone, and began clucking a one note melody as he withdrew another knife from the glove compartment.

Christine had been unable to sit still since Dotty Dalrymple's departure. She paced from room to room tapping the unopened

166

envelope against her palm. Suddenly, she looked down, as if noticing it for the first time. Then she tore it open.

Inside were five neatly banded packets of hundred dollar bills – ten in each.

"The choice is clear," she said out loud, testing her nursing director's words. Again the image of David's face formed in her mind. She stared at the packets, then threw them on her bureau.

"The choice *is* clear," she whispered.

17

On Thursday, the ninth of October, as on the previous three days, Boston forecasters predicted an end to the persistent low pressure system and the rain. For the fourth day straight, they were wrong.

In Huddleston, New Hampshire, ninety minutes north of the city, a one-hundred-and-fifty-year-old covered bridge washed away before Crystal Brook – little more than a trickle in August.

Accidents on frenetic Route 128, never a rarity, more than tripled.

On David Shelton, however, as on most in the area, the effects of the unrelenting downpour were even more insidious. It was more than a mile from his apartment to the financial district, and the law offices of Wellman, MacConnell, Enright and Glass. Irritable, and frustrated by inactivity, he chose to defy the storm and walk to his appointment with Ben. Within a block, he was soaked. "Oh, what the hell," he pronounced testily, trudging on head down into the wind, "wet is wet."

The suite of offices occupied most of the twenty-third floor of a mirror-glass building whose name and address were both One Bay State Square. "No wonder he charges $10,000," muttered David as he approached the reception area. Three women were directing people with practised calm in a space nearly as big as David's whole office.

He looked and felt like a drowned rat. For a moment, he thought of asking the severe receptionist for some towels and a change of clothes, but nothing in her expression encouraged that kind of frivolity. "Mr. Glass," he said meekly. "I have an appointment with Mr. Glass." The woman, barely masking her disdain, motioned him to a bank of leather easy chairs.

Whatever the goals of the interior decorators, David decided, making clients who looked like drowned rats feel less conspicuous was not one of them. The gold carpeting was thick, the oils on the walls originals, and a jungle of bamboo palms and huge ferns sprouted from shiny, gold-rimmed pots.

Ben popped around a corner, smiled at David then extended both hands. "Either you walked over, or this is autumn's answer to the Blizzard of '78," he said.

"Both." He took the lawyer's hands in his and squeezed them tightly. Ben was like a thin break in the clouds, an island in the madness and confusion.

"Had lunch yet?" he asked as they walked to his office.

"Yesterday. But please, nothing for me. You go ahead if you want."

"Meatloaf à la Amy?" He produced a brown bag from his desk. "There's plenty here. You sure?"

David shook his head. "No thanks. Really." He looked around the room. Ben's cluttered office was in sharp contrast to the rest of the austere suite. Books and journals were everywhere, many of them open or marked with folded sheets of legal paper. The walls were cluttered with framed photographs and pen and ink drawings. "Your partners let you get away with all this earthiness?" he asked, gesturing at the disarray.

"They think I'm camp." Ben grinned. "One of my partners once called my office 'funky'. A thousand a month just for this room, and he calls it funky!" He took a bite of sandwich, then spoke around chews. "Even soaked, you look better than yesterday. Are you holding up all right?"

David shrugged. "I got suspended from the staff at the hospital," he said flatly.

"What?"

"Suspended. I had a visit this morning from Dr. Armstrong – she's the Chief of Staff, and the only one at that place who really seems to give a shit about what happens to me. Anyhow, she called and asked to stop by. I knew what she had to say, and suggested she tell me over the phone, but she insisted on doing it in person. That's the kind of woman she is."

"So?"

"So, last night the executive committee voted, over her objection, to ask me to voluntarily suspend my staff and O.R. duties until this whole business is cleared up."

Ben shook his head. "Not ones to waste any time, this executive committee of yours!"

"According to Dr. Armstrong, Wallace Huttner, the Chief of Surgery, led the push. He's also helping the murdered woman's husband put together a malpractice case against me. If I'm found guilty, they want to be ready to move right in and sue. Dr. Armstrong said they made my suspension voluntary as a favour to me – to keep me having an enforced suspension on my record. I think they did it because it's less paper work for them."

"Shit," Ben muttered.

"It's probably just as well. Even before I was arrested, the place froze the minute I set foot in the door. It's all crazy. I . . . I don't know what the hell to do. I'd fight back if I had even a faint idea of who or what I was fighting, but . . . "

"Hey, easy," Ben urged. "The fight's just starting. For now, I'll throw the punches, but you'll get your chance. This afternoon, we share ideas about who and why. Tomorrow, we'll start planning what to do. Somewhere out there is an answer. Just be patient, and don't do anything rash or crazy. We'll find it."

David nodded and managed a tense smile. "Hey, I almost forgot this." He pulled a soggy envelope from his trouser pocket. "Good thing pencil doesn't run," he said, passing it over. "Dr. Armstrong didn't want me to get into any more trouble at the hospital, so in exchange for my promise to stay put, she did some checking for me. There are four names on the sheet inside. She got them from the hospital personnel computer. Two orderlies with prison records, a nurse with a drug use history, and another nurse who is pressuring the hospital to post a Patients' Bill of Rights. I don't know any of them. It's not much, but Dr. Armstrong said she would get the names to Lt. Dockerty."

Ben cut him off. "She already has, David."

"What?"

"The Lieutenant called a short time ago. I talked to him for half an hour. He wants you – and Dr. Armstrong – to quit playing Holmes and Watson and let him do the work."

"Let him do the work?" David's voice was incredulous. "Ben, the man has spent almost a week tarring and feathering me. He's the other side. He's the one we should be fighting."

Ben shook his head. "No, pal, he's not," he said firmly. "He's a damn good cop. I've known him for as long as I've been in practice. Whether you believe it or not, he doesn't want to see you fall."

"Then why the fuck did he arrest me?"

"Had to." Ben shrugged. "Pressure from all sides and a ton of circumstantial evidence. Motive, opportunity, weapon – you know all that."

David clenched his fists. "I also know that I didn't kill that woman," he said.

"Well, John Dockerty's not one hundred per cent convinced you did either. Otherwise, he wouldn't be trying to work on Marcus Quigg, the pharmacist who – "

"Dockerty told me who he is," David broke in. "But Ben, I never met the man. Why would he want to do this to me?"

"One of the big three," Ben said. "Vengeance, fear, money."

David shook his head. "Ben, until Dockerty said his name, I'm sure I never heard it before. Marcus Quigg isn't exactly John Jones you know. If I treated a Quigg, I'd remember . . . No, vengeance doesn't make any sense at all."

"Unless it was a sister or daughter," Ben said. "Different name."

"I guess." David slapped the desk in exasperation. "But there are just too many unpredictable events to believe anyone could have planned to frame me. Far too many."

"David, right now it can't do anything but harm to try and over-think this thing. There simply isn't enough information . . . yet." Ben paused, twisting his wedding ring as he searched for words. "David," he said finally, "I wasn't going to bring this up today, but maybe it's best that I do. I told you yesterday that I wanted complete honesty from you, yes?" David nodded. "You didn't mention to me that you were once accused of deliberately over-medicating a cancer patient of yours. Is that true?"

David stiffened, and his eyes widened in disbelief. "Ben, I . . . this is crazy," he stammered. "That was at least nine years ago. I was completely exonerated. I . . . how do you know about it?"

"Lt. Dockerty knows. I don't know who, but someone tipped him off."

"The nurse, it must have been that goddamn nurse. How in the hell? . . . "

"What happened?"

"It was nothing. Really. I ordered pain killers for a dying old lady – every four hours as needed. And believe me, she had plenty of pain. Well, I found that this one nurse was too damn lazy to check on whether she needed it. So I changed the order to every two hours, lowered the dose, and took out the 'as needed' part so the woman had to receive it. The next day the nurse reported me. There was an inquiry, and I think *she* ended up getting censured.''

''Well, now it seems she's getting even,'' Ben said. ''Listen, David, you must tell me everything. No matter how insignificant it might seem to you. Everything. This nurse coming forward after nine years may be yet another coincidence. There *was* the article in last night's paper. But if someone put her up to it, we've got even more problems than we realised. And maybe, just maybe, you have the answer inside you without even knowing it.''

''Maybe . . . '' David's voice drifted off. For a few seconds, he squinted and scratched his ear.

''What? What is it? Do you remember something?''

David shook his head. ''I could swear something popped in and out of my mind. Something someone said about Charlotte Thomas. I . . . '' He shrugged. ''Whatever it was – if it *was* anything – is gone.''

''Well, go home and take it easy, pal. We'll meet again tomorrow. Same time?''

''Same time,'' David said weakly.

''Say, listen, if you're free tomorrow night, why don't you plan on coming here at four. We can talk, then you can come home and have dinner with us. You can meet Amy and the kids and get a good meal in the bargain. She'd love to get to know you. Would even if I hadn't told her you were paying for little Barry's orthodontia.''

''Sounds fine,'' David said with little enthusiasm.

''Do you good,'' Ben added. ''Besides, Amy has this sister . . . '' He smiled, then suddenly the two of them were laughing. David couldn't remember the last time he had laughed.

''You're losing it, Shelton,'' David said as he paced through the apartment. ''You're losing it and you know it.'' The two hours following his departure from Ben's office had seemed like ten.

172

Outside, the steady rain continued, punctuated now and then by the muted tympani of distant thunder. It was becoming harder and harder to sit still; more and more difficult to concentrate – to focus in on anything. Call someone, he thought. Call someone or else ignore the rain and go for a run. But stop pacing. He picked up his running shoes and stepped to the window. Sheets of rain blurred the sombre afternoon sky. Then, as if in warning, a lightning flash coloured the room an eerie blue-white. Seconds later, a soft rumble crescendoed, reverberating through the apartment. He threw the shoes in his closet.

This is how it felt before, he remembered. After the accident. This is how it all started. The frustration. The growing restlessness.

Is there anything in the medicine chest? Didn't Lauren always keep something there for her headaches? Just in case the pacing won't stop. In case the loneliness gets too bad. In case sleep doesn't come. In case the night won't end.

He paced from one end of the hall to the other, then back. Each time he paused by the bathroom door. Just in case . . .

All at once he was there – reaching for the mirrored door of the medicine chest. Reaching, he suddenly realised, towards himself. He froze as his outstretched hand touched its reflection. His eyes, glazed with fear and solitude, locked on themselves and held. A minute passed. Then another. Gradually, the trembling in his lips began to subside. His breathing slowed and deepened. "Take hold of yourself," he said softly, gazing into his own eyes. "Over the last eight years you've found yourself again. They've been eight hard years. Open that door, touch one fucking pill, and you'll lose it all. You'll have nothing. You'll *be* nothing."

His hand dropped away from the mirror. Resolve tightened across his face, then pulled at the corners of his mouth until he was smiling. He nodded at himself – once, then again. He saw the strength, the determination grow in his eyes.

"I don't need them," he said quietly, as he turned from the mirror and walked to the living room. "No, I don't need them," he repeated more loudly as he stretched out on the sofa. "No, sirree . . . "

Twenty minutes later, when the phone rang, he was still on the sofa. He skimmed over the last few lines of the Frost poem he was reading, then rolled over and picked up the receiver.

"David, I was afraid you hadn't got home yet." It was Ben.

"Oh, no, I'm here," David said. He smiled, then added, "I'm very much here."

"Well, enjoy your free time while you have it," Ben said excitedly, "because I think within a day or two you'll be back to work."

David's spirits instantly soared. "Ben, what's happened? Talk slowly so it registers."

"I've just had a call, David, from a nurse at your hospital. She said that she can positively clear you of the murder of Charlotte Thomas. I'm meeting her at a coffee shop in a couple of hours. I think she's for real, pal, and if I'm right, the nightmare's over."

"Thank God," David said, half to the phone, and half to himself. "Ben, can I come? Shouldn't I be there?"

"Until I know what this woman has to say, I don't want you involved. Tell you what. Expect me at your place at nine – no, make that nine-thirty tonight. I'll fill you in then. With luck, our dinner tomorrow night will turn out to be a celebration."

"That would be wonderful," David said wistfully. "Tell me, who's the nurse?"

"Oh, she said she'd met you. Her name's Beall. Christine Beall."

At the mention of her name, David's spirits soared again. "Ben, I've just realised, that's what I was trying to think of in your office. Remember? When something popped in and out of my head?"

"I remember."

"Well it was something *she* said. Christine Beall. Right after I shot my mouth off to Charlotte's husband. She whispered to me that she was proud of the way I stood up to Huttner, and . . . and then she said, 'Don't worry. Things have a way of working out.' Then all of a sudden she was gone. Ben do you think . . . ?"

"Listen, pal, do us both a favour if you can. Try not to get too worked up. A few hours, then we'll know. Okay?"

"Okay," David said. "But I will anyway, you know."

"Yeah, I know," Ben said. "Nine-thirty."

"Right." David checked his watch. "Will you at least synchronise with me so I don't go nuts waiting for you?''

Ben laughed. "Five to five, pal. I make it five to five."

"Four fifty-five, it is," David sang. He set down the receiver.

His elation was brief. Over the past few days, conscious thoughts of Christine had been submerged in the nightmare. At that moment, David realised they had never been far from the surface.

"It wasn't you, was it?" he said softly. "You know who did it, but it couldn't have been you."

His concern for Christine faded quickly as the impact of Ben's call began to sink in. He clenched his fists, and grinned, then whooped loudly. He rushed to his record recollection, and seconds later he was bouncing through the living room, throwing jabs and uppercuts at the air. The music from *Rocky* filled the apartment.

Fanfare still in his ears, he walked down the hall and into the bathroom. He stood before the medicine cabinet and looked at himself. "You made it, buddy," he said to his reflection. "Stronger than ever, now. I'm proud of you. Really."

Out of curiosity, not need, he reached up and pulled open the cabinet door.

The shelves were empty.

A shower and long overdue letters to his brothers killed an hour and a half. Feasting on spaghetti with Ragu sauce did in another thirty minutes. The seven o'clock news made it two hours until Ben was due.

David paced impatiently for a while, then pulled his chess set from the closet along with his copy of *Chess Openings Made Simple*. Within a short time, he gave up. Thoughts of Christine made it impossible to concentrate. Somehow, in the short time they had talked, in their brief contacts, she had touched him deeply. There was a disarming, innocent intensity about her – an energy he had seldom seen survive the years in medical or nursing school. Then too, there were her eyes – wide and warm, smiling one moment, flashing with anger the next. He found himself hoping, even praying with renewed intensity that she had no direct involvement in the death of Charlotte Thomas. By nine o'clock, he had convinced himself that there was no way she

175

could have, and returned to the chessboard.

By nine-fifteen he was pacing again. Once he heard the lift gears engage and raced out into the hall. Then he remembered that he would have to buzz Ben through the downstairs foyer door. Still he waited out there just in case. The lift stopped one floor below.

At precisely nine-thirty, the downstairs buzzer sounded. David leaped to the intercom.

"Yes?"

"David, it's me." The excitement in Ben's voice was apparent despite the barely functional intercom. "The woman is for real. Sad, but very much for real. It's over, pal, it's over."

The word "sad" stood out from all the others. "Come on up," David said as he pressed the door release. His voice held surprisingly little enthusiasm.

Thirty seconds later the lift clattered into use. Shit, David thought, it *was* her. He stood in the open doorway and listened to the groaning cables. Turning his nightmare over to Christine Beall was not the way he had wanted it to end, no matter what her actions had put him through. He was half-way to the lift when the car light appeared in the diamond-shaped window of the outside door. A second later, the car crunched to a halt. The automatic inside gate rattled open.

David stopped several feet away and waited for Ben. Five seconds passed. Then another five. He took a tentative step forward. The door remained closed. Finally, he peered through the grimy window. Ben stood to one side, leaning calmly against the wall.

"Hey, what's going on?" David asked, swinging open the heavy door. The lawyer's eyes stared at him – moist and vacant. His face was bone white. Suddenly the corners of his mouth crinkled upward in a half smile.

"Ben, not funny," David said. "Now cut the crap and come on out of there. I wanna hear."

Ben's lips parted as he took a single step forward. Crimson gushed from his mouth and down his chin. David caught him half way to the floor. The back of Ben's tan raincoat was an expanding circle of blood. Protruding from the centre was the carved, white handle of a knife.

Sticky, warm life poured over David's hands and clothes as he dragged his friend from the elevator.

"Help!" he screamed. "Someone, please help me!"

He pulled the knife free and threw it on the carpet, then rolled Ben's body face up. The lawyer's dark eyes stared unblinkingly at the ceiling. David checked for a carotid pulse, but knew that the blood, now oozing from one corner of Ben's mouth, was the sign of a fatal wound to the heart or a main artery.

"Please help." David's plea was a whimper. Please . . . "

The stairway door at the far end of the hall burst open. Leonard Vincent stood there, his massive frame darkened by the light behind him. Almost casually, he reached to his waistband and withdrew a revolver. The ugly silhouette of a silencer protruded from one end.

"It's your turn, Dr. Shelton," Vincent rasped, certain he was facing the man Dahlia had described. He had followed Christine Beall to a coffee shop, and recognised the criminal lawyer whom she was meeting. Dahlia's response to his call was immediate: Glass first, then Shelton and later the girl. Now, thanks to the lawyer, he could handle the first two almost at once. Light from an overhead bulb caught the huge man's face. He was smiling. His smile broadened as he slowly raised the silenced revolver.

David stumbled backward and tried to straighten up, but his hand, covered with blood, slid off the wall and he spun to the carpet. Inches away was the knife. He grabbed it by the tip and hurled it at the advancing figure. It fell two yards short, but as Vincent was picking it up and wiping the blade on his trousers, David scrambled to his feet and made a mad dash to the living room, slamming the door behind him.

David looked wildly about, his heart racing. The fire escape! Opening the window, he looked down at his stockinged feet. For a moment he thought of his running shoes in the closet. No chance, he decided. With a groan of resignation, he jumped out onto the metal landing. There was a crash from inside the apartment, as the front door burst open. An instant later, David was racing down four flights to the alley below.

The night was tar black and cold. The metal steps, slippery in the driving downpour, hurt his feet, but the discomfort barely registered. Just beyond the third floor, his heel caught the edge of a step and shot out from under him. He fell hard, tumbling down half a flight. He gasped with pain as several inches of skin ripped from his right forearm. Above him, there was a loud clank as Leonard Vincent stepped onto the fourth floor landing, and David heard a muffled shot ring out. At that moment he had the absurd notion that he should have opened the window to the fire escape then hidden in the closet.

"I'll bet it would've worked," he thought, as he scrambled, panting, towards the second floor landing. He slipped again, electricity shooting up his spine as he slid the final few stairs. Through the metal slats overhead, he saw the man, a faint dark shadow moving against the night sky.

On his hands and knees, David struggled to release the ladder from the second floor landing to the alley. Through his soaked shirt, needles of rain stung his back. The metal slats dug into his knees. The ladder release would not budge.

With a glance above him, David grabbed the side of the landing and rolled off. He hung there for a moment, trying to judge the distance to the pavement, then dropped. He felt and heard the crunch in his left ankle as he hit. The leg gave way instantly. He screamed, then bit down on the edge of a finger so hard that he drew blood.

Lying on the wet pavement, he heard the clanging footsteps and grunting breaths of the man overhead. The killer was nearing the second landing.

David stumbled to one foot, then hesitated. If the ankle were sprained, there would be discomfort, but he could move. If it was broken, he was about to die. Teeth clenched, he set his foot down. Pain seared through the ankle, but it held – once, then again and again. Suddenly he was running.

At the end of the alley, he looked back. The man had lowered the ladder and was stepping off the bottom rung.

Clarendon Street was nearly deserted. David paused uncertainly, then decided to try for the heavy traffic of Boylston Street. At that instant, he saw a figure half a block from him, walking in the opposite direction towards the river. Instinctively, he ran that way. His gait was awkward. Every other stride was agony. Still, he closed on the figure.

"Help," he called out. "Please help." His cry was instantly lost in the night storm. "Please help me."

He was ten feet away when the figure lurched around to face

178

him. It was an old man – toothless, unshaven, and drunk. Water dripped from the brim of his tattered hat. David started to speak, but could only shake his head. Gasping, he supported himself against a parked car. Without sound or warning, the rear window of the car shattered. David spun around. Through the gloom and the rain, he saw his pursuer's shadow, down on one knee in position to fire once more. He was running when flame spit from the silencer. Running when the bullet meant for him slammed into the old man, propelling him to the pavement.

He pushed himself forward, through the pain and the downpour. Pushed himself harder than ever in his life. His heels slammed down on small stones, sending dagger thrusts up each leg. Still, he ran: across Marlborough Street, across Beacon Street and on towards the river. It was his route, his run – the path he had jogged so many sunlit, promising mornings. Now, he was running for his life. Behind him, the huge killer gained ground with every stride.

Traffic on Storrow Drive was light. David splashed across without slowing down – onto the stone foot bridge and over the reflecting basin. Ahead of him, the lights of Cambridge shimmered through the rain, and danced on the pitch black Charles.

He risked a glance over his shoulder. The man, delayed by several cars on Storrow Drive, had lost some ground, but not enough. David knew the chase was almost over. With fear his only driving force and flailing strides, he was near collapse. He scanned the deserted esplanade for somewhere to hide. The killer was too close. His only hope was the river. Stones along the bank tore away what was left of his socks as he scrambled over them and plunged into the frigid, oily water.

The needle-sharp cold hit him like a wall, and David's whole body screamed in agony. Behind him, Leonard Vincent crossed the footbridge and neared the bank. As deeply as he could manage, David sucked in air and dropped below the surface. He was twenty feet from shore, pushing himself along the muddy bottom. His clothes became leaden, at first helping him stay down, then threatening to hold him there. He broke once for air. Then again. Still he drove himself. The water stung his eyes and made it impossible to see. Its taste, acrid and repugnant, filled his nose and mouth.

All at once his head struck something solid. Dazed and near

blind, he explored the obstacle with his hands. It was a dock – a floating wooden "T," laid on the river to tether some of the dozens of small sailboats that spent the warm months darting over reflections of the city.

For a minute, two, all was silent, save for the drumming of the rain on the dock and on the river. David crouched by the dock in four feet of water, rubbing the silt in his eyes. His feet and legs were numb. Then he heard footsteps – careful, measured thumps. The killer was on the dock! David pressed the side of his face against the coarse slimy wood. The footsteps grew louder, closer. He slid his hand under the dock. Did it break water? Was there room enough to breathe? If he ducked under he might be trapped without air. If he didn't . . .

He inhaled, slowly, deeply, realising this breath might be his last. Eyes closed tightly, he pulled himself beneath the dock. His head immediately hit wood. Terror shot through him. He was trapped, his lungs near empty. Pawing desperately overhead, his hands struck the side of a beam. An undersupport! He pushed to one side, and instantly his face popped free of the water. There were four inches of air. Relief shot through him, then vanished. The footsteps were directly over his face. Through the narrow slits between timbers he could have touched the bottom of the man's shoes, now inches from his eyes. The pacing stopped. David bent his neck back as far as he could and pressed his forehead against the bottom of the dock. Through pursed lips, he sucked in air slowly, soundlessly.

Above his face, the shoes scraped, first one way and then another, as Vincent scanned the river. Then, with agonising slowness, the man headed towards the other arm of the "T".

In the icy water, David began to shake. He clenched down with all his strength to keep from chattering and wedged himself more tightly between the river bottom and the dock. All feeling from his neck down was gone. The footsteps receded further and further, then disappeared. The closed space began to exert its own ghastly terror. Is he just sitting up there, David wondered? Sitting and waiting? *How much longer can I stay here like this?*

He counted. To one hundred, then back to zero. He sang songs to himself in his head – silly little songs from his childhood. Gradually, inexorably, he lost control over the soft staccato of his teeth. Still he did not move. " . . . this old man he played two, he played knick knack on my shoe . . . " " . . . I knew a man with seven wives and seven cats and seven lives . . . " " . . . Red Sox, White Sox, Yankees, Dodgers, Phillies, Pirates . . ."

The chill penetrated to the core. He could no longer stop shaking. How long had it been? His legs seemed paralysed. " . . . Red Rover, Red Rover, come over, come over . . . " " . . . I'll bet you can't catch me, betcha can't betcha can't . . . "

"I'll bet . . . I'll bet . . . I'll bet I'm going to die."

18

Joey Rosetti closed his eyes and breathed in the fragrance of Terry's excitement. That scent, her taste, the way her dark nipples grew firm beneath his hand – even after twelve years, the sensations were as fresh and arousing as they were warm and comfortable.

He rubbed his cheeks against the silky skin between her thighs, then drew his tongue upward between her moist folds.

"It's good, Joey. So good," Terry moaned, drawing his face more tightly against her. She smiled down at him and dug her fingers through the jet-black waves of his hair.

Shuddering, she brought his mouth up to hers. Her heels slid around his body as the hunger in their kiss grew. He entered her with slow, deepening thrusts.

"Joey, I love you," Terry whispered. "I love you so much."

She sucked on his tongue and caressed the fold between his buttocks. The heavy muscles tensed as her fingers worked deeper.

Joey's thrusts grew quicker, more forceful. It would be soon, they knew, for both of them.

Suddenly, the telephone on the bedside table began ringing. "No," Terry groaned. "Let it ring." But already, she felt a let-up in Joey's intensity. "Let it ring," she begged again. Six times, seven – the intrusive jangling was not going to stop. The pressure inside her lessened. An eighth ring, then a ninth.

"Damn," Joey hissed, popping free of her as he rolled over. "This better not be a fucking wrong number." He mumbled a greeting, listened for half a minute, then said a single word, "Where?" A moment later he kicked the covers off and scrambled out of bed.

"Terry, it's the doc," he said. "Doc Shelton. He's hurt and he needs help." He flicked on the bedside light and raced to the closet.

"I'm coming with you," Terry demanded, pulling herself upright.

"No, honey. Please." He held up a hand. "He sounded crazed. I could barely understand him. But he did say there was trouble. I don't want you there. Call the tavern. See if Rudy Fisher's still working. If he is, tell him to get his ass over to the esplanade by the Charles River. The Hatch Shell. I'll meet him there."

"Joey, can't you call someone else? You know how I feel about that m — "

"Look, I don't have time to debate. Rudy's been with me longer than y . . . for a long time. If there's trouble, I want him around."

Twelve years had taught Terry the uselessness of arguing with her husband over such matters. Still, his insistence on Rudy Fisher, a giant who doted on violence, frightened her. "Joey, please," she urged. "Just be careful. No rough stuff. Please promise me. If he's hurt, then just get him to a hospital and come home."

"Baby, the man saved my life," he said, pulling on a pair of pants. "Whatever he needs from me he gets."

"But you promised . . . "

"Listen," Joey snapped, "I'll be careful. Don't worry." He forced a more relaxed tone. "I'm a businessman now, you know that. If he's hurt, I'll get him to the hospital. Don't worry. Just do what I asked you." He grabbed a shirt from the closet.

Terry sat on the edge of the bed admiring him as he dressed. At forty-two, he still had the cleanly chiselled features and sinewy body of a matinée idol. There was a calm, unflappable air about him that gave no hint of the deadly situations he had survived in his life. Reminders were there though, in the burgundy scars that crisscrossed his abdomen. One, an eighteen inch crescent around his left flank, was a memento from his days as a youth gang leader in Boston's North End. Intersecting it just above his navel was another scar – ten years old – the result of a gunshot wound sustained while thwarting a hold-up at the Northside.

Rosetti had been one of David's first private patients at White Memorial. It had been a twelve hour operation that some of the O.R. staff still spoke of reverently. During Joey's convalescence, a lasting friendship had developed between the two men.

"Terry, will you stop gawking and make that call," Joey said tersely as he stepped into a pair of black loafers. He waited until her back was turned, then snatched his revolver and shoulder holster from beneath the sweaters on his closet shelf.

He was walking to the door when Terry said, "Joey, don't use it, please."

Rosetti turned back and kissed her gently. "I won't, honey. Unless I absolutely have to, I won't. Promise."

Terry Rosetti waited until the door slammed shut, then sighed and picked up the phone.

David sat on the ground of the esplanade, hanging over the dangling payphone receiver to keep from falling over. He shook uncontrollably, drifting in and out of consciousness as the driving rain splattered him with mud. Squinting through the downpour, he could see the Hatch Shell Amphitheatre. The mountainous half-dome, looming several hundred yards away, was the only landmark he'd been able to think of to give Joey.

Slowly, painfully, he released the phone, rolled over in the muddy puddle, and began crawling towards a night light at one side of the dome. For ten minutes, fifteen minutes, he clawed his way over the sodden ground. The tiny bulb, at first a beacon, soon became his entire world. It seemed farther away with each agonising inch. Again and again he tried to stand, only to crumple beneath the pain in his ankle and the paralysing chill throughout his body. Each time, he got to his hands and knees and pushed on. Twice he doubled over as spasms knotted his gut, forcing fetid river water and bile out of his nose and mouth. The taunting light grew dimmer, more distant.

"It can't end like this." David said the words over and over, using them as a rhythm to force one hand, then one knee in front of the other. "It can't end like this . . . "

Suddenly, the grass turned to concrete, then to smooth slick marble. He was on the stairs at the base of the Shell. His shivering gave way to paroxysmal spasms in his hands, shoulders, and neck – the harbingers of a full blown seizure. Blood dribbled from the corner of his mouth as his teeth, chattering like jackhammers, minced the edges of his tongue. Overhead, the nightlight flickered for a moment, then went black. David felt the incongruous peace of death seeping through

184

him in advancing waves. He fought the sensation with what little strength and concentration he had left. Christine knows, he thought. She knows why Ben is dead and now she'll die, too. Must hang on. Hang on and help her. It can't end like this . . . It can't.

The emptiness had set in only minutes after Christine declined Ben's offer of a ride and started home. It was as if a tap had opened, draining from her every drop of emotion and feeling. She had abandoned her attempt to shelter beneath the overhangs of buildings and wandered along the centre of the sidewalk, oblivious to the downpour.

The session with Ben had been easy – at least easier than she had anticipated. In his comfortable, unjudging manner, he had assured her again and again that her decision to confess was the right thing, the *only* thing to do. He had accepted the explanation she chose to give; that she, acting alone, had honoured the wishes of a close, special friend who was dying painfully. The most difficult moment came when he brought up the forged C222 order form.

"The what?" Christine said, stalling for a little time.

"The form. The one Quigg, the pharmacist, claimed Dr. Shelton filled at his store."

Christine's mind raced. Clearly, Sister Dalrymple or one of the others had used the form to protect her. Unaware of what had transpired, she had no ready response. "I . . . I used it and . . . and then I bribed the pharmacist."

"How did you come by it in the first place?" Ben asked. There was no trace of disbelief in his face.

"I'd rather not say just yet." Christine held her breath, hoping the lawyer would push no further. Given a few days, she could think of something. If Sister Dalrymple still wished to protect The Sisterhood, she would have to do whatever she could to ensure that the pharmacist did not contradict her. She would also have to convince Peggy that Christine was determined to keep the movement out of her confession.

Ben studied her for a moment, then nodded. "Very well, then," he said. "Let's talk about how I believe you should handle things. That is, if you want my advice."

185

"I'd like more than that, Mr. Gl . . . I mean, Ben. If it's possible, I would like you to represent me."

"I'll have to think it over, Christine. Just to be sure there wouldn't be any conflict of interest involved." He smiled. "There shouldn't be. But anyway meet me Monday morning at my office. Nine o'clock. I'll see to it that Lt. Dockerty is there. Don't worry, I'll tell you ahead of time exactly what to say to him. Monday okay?"

Christine nodded.

Monday. Christine repeated the word over and over again as she scuffed through the rain. Three days before her life would, to all intents, come to an end. A bus careered past, spraying her boots and trench coat with muddy water. She did not even break stride. In a flood of images, she pictured what was to follow for her: the arrest . . . the judge . . . Sister Dalrymple . . . her brothers and sisters . . . the newspapers . . . her father, already confined to a nursing home . . . the nicknames – Death Angel, Mercy Murderer . . . her roommates and their families . . . But most punishing of all, perhaps, were the images of David and the hatred she knew he would feel for her.

She walked past the turn-off for her street. Little by little, the great emptiness within her grew. The relief and the peace she had felt while talking with Ben were gone. Drops of rain supplanted the tears she could not cry.

With unseeing eyes, she gazed at the windows of shops and stores as she passed. All at once, she realised she was standing in front of a pharmacy – her pharmacy. The elderly pharmacist knew her, knew and liked all three roommates, in fact. Dreamlike, she entered, exchanged a few pleasantries, then asked the man for a new supply of the Darvon she occasionally took for cramps. Her last prescription, filled six months ago, was at home in her bureau, the bottle still nearly full. After briefly checking her file, the man handed her a new bottle.

On the walk home, Christine began to compose the note she would write.

"Rudy, he's up here!" Joey cried out. "Mother of God, what a mess! I think he's dead."

David's motionless form lay face down in a puddle to one side

186

of the amphitheatre steps. He had crawled up the stairs and wedged himself behind a marble slab, hidden from the sidewalk below. Gently, Joey rolled his friend over to his back. The driving rain splattered filth and blood from David's face. At that instant, he moaned, a soft whine, nearly lost in the night wind.

"Jesus, go get a blanket!" Joey screamed. "He's alive!" He cradled David's head in one hand and began patting his cheek, then hitting it faster and faster. "Doc, it's Joey. Can you hear me? You're gonna be all right. Doc . . . ?"

"Christine . . ." David's first word was an almost indistinct gurgle. "Christine . . . must find Christine." His eyes fluttered open for a moment, strained to focus on Joey's face, then closed. Rosetti set a hand on David's chest. He nodded excitedly at the shallow but rhythmic rise and fall.

"Hang on," he said. "We'll get you to the hospital. You're gonna be all right, Doc. Just hang on." He looked up and muttered a curse at the downpour. In moments, the wind died off. The heavy rain gave way to a light, misty spray. Joey stared overhead in amazement, then nodded his approval.

"First thing in the morning You get a raise in pay," he grinned.

David heard Rosetti's voice, but understood only the word "hospital". No, he thought. Not the hospital. He struggled to hang onto the thought, to put it into words, but consciousness drifted away from him and he slid into darkness.

Five minutes later, he was bundled in a blanket, propped against Joey on the back seat of Rudy Fisher's Chrysler. His uncontrollable shaking continued but, moment by moment, he was regaining consciousness. Joey ordered Fisher to the Doctors Hospital emergency ward. Like echoes down a long tunnel, David heard his own fragmented words. "Ben is dead . . . Christine is dead . . . No hospital, please . . . Must find Christine . . . I'm cold . . . so cold . . . Please help me get warm . . ."

Several ambulances were lined up in front of the emergency entrance, their lights flashing in hypnotic counterpoint. Joey jumped out and returned moments later with a wheelchair.

"Place is a fucking zoo," he said as they eased David out of the car. "Must be the rain. Looks like a scene from some war movie. Rudy, wait for me in that space over there. You all right, Doc?"

David tried to nod but the lights and the signs and the faces spun into a nauseating blur. He was retching as Joey pushed him through the automatic doors into the artificial brilliance of the reception area. The atmosphere and action were reminiscent of a battleground infirmary. A constant stream of patients, some bleeding, some doubled over in pain, flowed in through several doors. Stretchers lay everywhere. Joey took in the scene, then pushed his way through the crowd surrounding the nurse on reception.

The woman, a trim brunette in only her second month of screening duty, listened to him incredulously and then rushed over to David. He was moaning softly, his head rolling from side to side as he struggled to steady it. "My God, he's cold as ice," she said, holding a hand beneath his chin. "Keep his head still while I get an orderly. What happened to him?" She rushed away before Joey could answer. A matronly intake clerk, clipboard in hand, arrived seconds later and began firing questions at him.

"Name?"

"Joseph Rosetti."

She looked at David. "That's not Joseph Rosetti, that's Dr. Shelton."

"Oh, I thought you meant my name. If you already knew his, why did you ask?"

The clerk flashed him an ugly look and tore off the top sheet of her clipboard. "Name?" she said in the identical voice as before.

Joey fished out David's soggy wallet and found some of the information the woman requested. He came near to losing control several times, but held his temper for fear that she would rip off another sheet and start over again. In answer to "Name and address of next of kin," he was about to say he had no idea, but thought about the chaos his answer might cause and gave his own.

"Religion of preference?" The woman asked blandly.

Joey looked down at David whose skin now had a pea-green cast. "Look," he snapped, "this man is seriously hurt. Can't the questions wait until the doctor sees him?"

"I'm sorry, sir," she bristled, "I don't make hospital regulations, I only carry them out. Religion of preference?"

Joey fought the impulse to grab the woman by the throat. The

188

dark haired nurse returned at that moment with an orderly. "I've emptied out Trauma Twelve," she said briskly. "Take Dr. Shelton there. Sir, if you'll finish signing him in, you can wait in one of those seats. I'll let you know as soon as someone has examined him." She looked at Joey's face and realised for the first time how very handsome he was. Her smile broadened. "Any questions?"

"No," Joey said. "But could you tell this – ah – nice lady here that I do *not* possess the knowledge of Dr. Shelton's religion of preference?" He winked at the young nurse, whose cheeks reddened instantly, then took the intake clerk by the arm and led her back to the reception desk.

In the feverish emergency ward, only one pair of eyes followed attentively as the orderly wheeled David away. They belonged to Janet Poulos. Only her ears heard and understood the single word he moaned: "Christine."

With multiple accidents and two gunshot wounds tying up regular staff, she had agreed to work overtime until the crush of patients diminished. Now, she realised, that decision might pay off in unexpected ways. Her mind raced as she tried to sort out the significance of what she had just seen and heard.

Leonard Vincent had been hired by The Garden to watch Christine Beall and to intervene only if it looked to Dahlia as if the woman had decided to confess and expose The Sisterhood. That much Janet knew. Dahlia had made the decision to protect The Garden at all costs; every flower was also a member of The Sisterhood, whether they were active in that movement or not.

Beall and Shelton must have talked, Janet reasoned. She must have gone to him. Must have told him about The Sisterhood. Why else would he be here in this condition calling out her name? Dahlia had turned Leonard Vincent loose, but Shelton had somehow escaped. It was the only explanation that made any sense. If it were true, then it was Hyacinth's good fortune to be in just the right place at the right time. Janet began to tremble with excited anticipation. The opportunity had been laid in her lap. If she handled things well, made the proper decisions, Dahlia might see fit to involve her in the innermost workings of The Garden. The rewards would be enormous.

Janet glanced about. The police, always present in the emergency ward, were occupied with the gunshot and accident victims. She sensed she could move through the chaos unnoticed, but she had to act quickly. Was there time to call Dahlia? She checked the hallway to Trauma Room 12. The area outside the room was deserted. There might not be another chance.

Adrenalin. Potassium. Insulin. Digitalis. Pancuronium. Janet ticked off the possibilities as she hurried to the nurses' station. She wondered about Christine Beall. Had Vincent already accounted for her? No matter, she decided. The only problem she could do anything about at the moment was waiting in Trauma 12.

"Dr. Shelton, my name is Clifford. Can you lift up your bum so I can pull these trousers off you?" The pudgy orderly was past thirty, but looked like he had yet to shave for the first time.

David grunted his reply but, with consummate effort, was actually able to do what the man requested. Gradually, ripples of warmth washed over the deep chill inside him. As feeling returned, so did the throbbing pain in his ankle and arm, and the raw aching above his right ear and on the soles of his feet.

"You look like you've had quite a time of it," Clifford said cheerfully, spreading David's sodden trousers over the back of a chair.

"The river . . . I . . . was in the river." David's voice was distant and flat. "Ben is dead . . . "

"Can you hold this under your tongue?" the orderly asked, shoving a thermometer into David's mouth. "Ben?" David mumbled and struggled to reach the thermometer. "No, no, don't touch that," Clifford scolded. "Doctor will be in shortly to check you over. You just keep that under your tongue until I get back."

Never take an oral temp on someone who's freezing to death, idiot! The unspoken disapproval flashed through David's mind as the corpulent orderly left the room. Then his lips tightened in a half smile. He was coming round. Bit by bit his random thoughts were connecting. Suddenly, Ben's face appeared in his mind, blood pouring from his mouth. Renewed terror took hold. Desperately, he pulled himself up, first on to one elbow, then on to his outstretched hand. "Christine," he gasped, spitting the thermometer out. "I've got to get to her." As he lifted his head, the walls began to swirl in front of his eyes.

He fought the spinning and the nausea, and forced himself to a sitting position. Sweat poured from his forehead and dripped down his sides. The floor blurred beneath him. As he leaned forward, the room began to dim, and he knew that he was falling. For an incredible moment, he was weightless, floating in a sea of brilliant light. Then there was nothing.

Janet Poulos caught David by the shoulders as he toppled forward, and eased him back onto the stretcher bed. His breathing was rapid and shallow, the pulse at his wrist faint. Briefly, she thought about sitting him up again. The precipitious blood pressure drop from such a manoeuvre might well remove the need for the syringe full of adrenalin in her pocket. Too chancy, she decided, pulling his feet up on the stretcher bed. She checked the corridor again. There was a crisis of some sort several rooms away and the emergency trolley was being rushed in. Perfect, she thought, stepping back into the room and closing the door behind her. Everyone just stay where you are for a little while.

"Dr. Shelton, can you hear me?" she asked. "I'm going to put a tourniquet on your arm to draw some blood. It will only take a minute."

David moaned and pulled his arm away as she looped the rubber tubing around it. "Now, now, David," she said sweetly. "Just hold still. This isn't going to hurt a bit." She slapped the skin over the crook of his elbow and looked for a vein. The area was blanched and cold, every skin vessel constricted to the maximum. Janet groaned and slapped more frantically, cursing herself for forgetting about the body's response to hypothermia and shock.

David's head lolled back and forth as his consciousness began to return. Panicking, Janet jammed the needle into his arm, hoping for a chance to hit a vein. At that instant Clifford burst into the room. The syringe popped free and slipped from Janet's hand as she whirled round. A drop of blood appeared at the puncture site.

"Well, doctor, I'm back. Sorry to have . . . " Clifford stopped short, aghast at Janet's withering glare.

"Damn you," she hissed, ripping off the tourniquet and quickly retrieving the syringe. Shielding Clifford from view, she

191

squirted the adrenalin beneath the stretcher bed, then turned back to him. "Haven't you learned to knock when doors are closed? I was in the middle of drawing blood from this man and you just screwed it up."

"I . . . I'm sorry." The orderly shifted nervously from one foot to the other and stared at the floor.

"You'll be hearing from me about this," she spat. Her mind was swirling with thoughts of what to do next. Then she froze. Harry Weiss, the surgical resident was standing in the doorway.

"Is everything all right?" he asked calmly.

Janet nodded. "I . . . I didn't know when someone was going to get in to see Dr. Shelton, here, so I thought I'd draw some blood just to get things started."

"Thank you. That was good thinking." Weiss smiled. "If you haven't taken any yet, why don't we wait until I've finished having a look at him."

"Very well, Doctor." Janet shot another icy glare at Clifford, then walked from the room before racing to the telephone.

"Dr. Shelton, it's me, Harry Weiss." The hawk-nosed resident David had guided through the difficult hand case looked at him anxiously. David's eyes were open, but he was having difficulty focusing. Weiss leaned closer. "Can you see me all right?"

David squinted, then nodded. Moments later he was struggling to sit up. "Christine. Let me call Christine," he heard himself say. The dizziness began anew, but he battled against it, flailing with both hands.

Harry Weiss grabbed his wrists and pushed him back. "Please, Dr. Shelton, I don't want to have to tie you down," he begged. He looked about for Clifford as David's thrashing increased, but the man had left. "Nurse," he called out, "would someone please get an orderly and a set of four point restraints in here on the double."

In less than a minute, David was lashed to the stretcher by leather arm and ankle cuffs. His efforts weakened, giving way to sobs. "Please . . . just let me find her . . . just let me call." His words were unintelligible.

Weiss looked down at him and shook his head sadly. "I think

we're all right now," he said to the small group who had rushed in to help. "Leave us alone so I can examine him. Call the lab and tell them I want a complete screen and CBC. Have them do a scan for drugs of abuse as well. When I'm finished, start an I.V. — normal saline at 300 cc an hour, at least until we know what's going on. One of you find out who's on for psych tonight and let me know. If he's any good we might call him down. If he's one of those turkeys who's sicker than the patients, we probably won't." The group smiled at his remark, but only the orderly laughed out loud. Harry Weiss glared at him, picked up a piece of the shattered thermometer, then said, "And Clifford, when are you going to learn that we never take oral temperatures on someone with hypothermia. It's too inaccurate. Rectal temps only. I don't want to hear of you doing that again." He nodded that his orders were complete and the room quickly emptied.

"Atta boy, Harry." David wanted to say, but he was unable to get words out. The terror, shock, and hypothermia were taking their toll. Even if the orderly had used a rectal thermometer, David's temperature would not have registered. Still, his eyes were open. He watched as the tall resident began examining him. Tell the man, David thought. Sit up and tell him that you don't need a fucking shrink. Tell him that Ben is dead. Tell him that you must find Christine. That she might already be dead. Tell him you're not crazy. Or are you? Maybe this is how it is. How it feels. There he is poking and grabbing you all over, and you can't even talk to him. Maybe this is what crazy is . . . Where the hell is Joey? Joey was here a while ago. Where the hell is he now?

Pain shot up his leg from where Weiss was examining his ankle. David groaned and fought to sit up. The leather restraints held fast. "Sorry," Weiss said gently. "I didn't mean to hurt you. Dr. Shelton, can you understand me? Can you tell me what happened?"

Yes, yes, David thought. I can tell you. Just give me a minute. Don't rush me. I can tell you everything.

Harry Weiss saw him nod and waited for more of a response. Finally he said, "Well, you're beginning to feel warmer. I've ordered some tests. We're going to get X-rays of your ankle, your arm and, just in case, a set of skull films. I think everything's okay, but I can't say for sure about your ankle. Understand?"

"Joey," David mumbled. "Where is my friend Joey?" For a moment he was unsure of whether he had actually said the words or only thought that he had said them.

The resident's face brightened. "Joey? Is he the guy who brought you here?" David nodded. "Great, well, it sounds like you may be coming around. I'll go and talk to your friend. Then I'll send him in to stay with you until X-ray is ready. We're very busy tonight, so there'll probably be a bit of a wait. I'm going to turn off the overhead light. Try to get some rest and don't shake this blanket off."

"Thank you," David whispered. "Thank you." Weiss looked down at him briefly, shook his head, and left the room, flipping the light off on his way.

David tested the restraints one at a time. No chance. He took a deep breath, exhaled slowly, then settled back. The shaking had stopped and the deep chill had disappeared. There was something soothing about the dim quiet of the room and the familiar clamour from outside. "Time to rest," he told himself. "Rest and get your strength back. When Joey gets here we'll go after Christine. When Joey gets here . . . " Slowly, his eyes closed. His breathing became more shallow and regular.

Through a peaceful, twilight sleep, David heard his friend enter the room. Don't wake me up, Joey, David thought. Give me another minute or two, then we'll get going. But, Christine, we must get to her. His eyes blinked open an instant before Leonard Vincent's massive hand clamped down over his mouth, pinning him roughly against the litter.

Dressed in the orderly's whites Hyacinth had provided, Vincent had encountered no problem making his way from a rear entrance to Trauma 12. He grudgingly acknowledged Dahlia's wisdom in ordering him to wait by a phone near Doctors Hospital. "A hunch," she had called it. He had baulked at the prospect of strolling into the emergency ward, but assurances that the emergency ward police were all occupied, and the promise of a bonus had convinced him to try. Now, he silently applauded himself for the decision.

"You've been a great pain in the ass, Dr. Shelton," he growled. "I have half a mind to make this hurt more than it should. But because at least you tried, I'm gonna make it quick and easy."

David watched helplessly, his eyes circles of terror as Vincent raised a knife over his face, giving him a clear view of the ugly, tapered blade.

With his hand still pressed over David's mouth, the killer hooked two thick fingers beneath his chin and pulled it up. "One slice, just like a surgeon," he whispered, drawing the dull side of the blade slowly across David's exposed neck.

"For God's sake, wait! I didn't do anything," was all David could think of in that final moment. Eyes closed, he listened for his own death scream. Instead, he heard a loud thud, and the clatter of Vincent's knife on the floor. His eyes opened in time to see the killer's body lurch sideways, then crumple over. Behind him, Joey Rosetti lifted the heavy revolver he had used as a club ready, if necessary, to deliver another blow.

"Nice place you run here, Doc," Joey said, quickly undoing the restraints. "If I ever need another operation, remind me to go back to White Memorial."

"He's the man," David blurted. "The man who killed Ben. He . . . he was going to . . . "

"I know exactly what he was going to do," Joey said. "Leonard an' me have met before. He does it for a living. The shit. If he's after you, my friend, then you are into some serious business."

David sat up. This time, the dizziness was bearable. Instinctively, he rubbed his hand over his throat. The rush of terror had done more to bring him around than anything else. "Joey, get me out of here," he begged. "Shoot that animal then get me out of here. We've got to find Christine."

Joey glanced at Vincent, who was lying on one side, face contorted, on the tiled floor. "We'll let the cops take care of Leonard," he said. "I promised Terry I wouldn't use my gun – at least the other end of it – unless I had to. Someone will find him here. Can you walk. Where the hell are your trousers."

"There, over there on the chair. I . . . I think I can walk with a little help." David slipped off the table and steadied himself against Joey's arm. His ankle throbbed, but held weight as he wriggled into his damp, muddy jeans. "Joey, there's this woman, Christine Beall. She's the only one who can straighten out the mess I'm in. We've got to find her." He sighed relief at the realisation that, at last, his words were coming out intelligibly.

"Okay," Joey said, "but first we've got to drift out of this place with as little commotion as possible. I saw this gorilla here dressed up like a doctor or something heading for your room. Nobody else even looked twice at him. I figured he wasn't going in to give you a check-up. Now listen, my manager's parked by the front door. Let me get a wheelchair. We'll go as far as we can with that, then run like hell. It's a red car, an Olds or Chrysler or some ox like that. Do you remember it?"

David shook his head. "I'll find it, Joey, don't worry. Let's just get the hell out of here."

The electronic front doors slid open. A woman's voice behind them called out, "Hey, you two, where are you going?"

David scrambled out of the chair and hung onto Joey's arm as they raced the last few yards to the Chrysler. "Let's go," Joey panted as they dived into the back seat. "But no need to burn rubber."

Janet Poulos stood helplessly to one side of the reception area and watched them go. She had told Dahlia nothing of her abortive attempt to handle matters. Now, she must decide whether or not to see if Leonard Vincent was alive and needed help. Since she was the only person the man could identify if he were arrested, the decision was not difficult.

She stopped at the emergency trolley, took several ampoules of pancuronium, then dropped them into her pocket. The respiratory paralysis caused by the drug helped maintain respirator patients. Well, now it would help her, too, provided she had the chance to use it. If not, she would have to find a way to help the man escape. Perhaps she could still salvage some heightened prestige in Dahlia's eyes.

Janet cursed her rotten luck, and David Shelton for causing her so much difficulty. Then she stalked down the hall to Trauma 12 hoping she would find Leonard Vincent dead.

196

"Ouch! What is that stuff?" David winced as Terry Rosetti scrubbed at the dirt embedded in the deep gouge along his arm.

"Just something I use to clean the windows," she said. "Now sit still and let me finish."

The Rosettis' North End apartment was old, but spacious and newly renovated. Terry had decorated the place with grace, making full use of a collection of family furniture that would have been welcome in any of the smart antique shops on Newbury Street.

David lay stretched out on the large oak guest bed, savouring the smell and texture of fresh linen and wondering if he would ever feel warm again. He was weak, lightheaded, and aching in a half dozen different places. Still, he could sense his concentration improving as the mental fog brought on by hypothermia began to lift. He silently thanked Joey for reasoning him out of an immediate search for Christine in favour of a hot shower.

Terry Rosetti, a full-breasted, vibrant beauty, expertly wrapped his arm in gauze. "Fetuccini and first aid," David said. "You are truly the complete woman."

Terry's smile lit up the room. "Tell that to your friend out there. I think he's starting to take me for granted. Do you know he was actually able to stop in the middle of making love to me to answer the phone when you called?"

"No wonder it seemed to be ringing forever," he said. "I almost hung up."

"It's a lucky thing you didn't," Terry said, then frowned. "David, Joey didn't *kill* that man, did he?"

The fear in her eyes left no doubt of the importance his answer held for her. "I wanted him to pull the trigger back there, Terry. I really did. That animal killed my friend. But Joey said he'd promised you and backed off."

Terry Rosetti swallowed the lump in her throat.

At that moment, Joey marched into the room, carrying a pile of clothes, a pair of crutches, and the Boston phone directory. "I think this must be the woman," he said. "C. Beall; 391 Belknap, Brookline. I checked the other books and this is the only name that fits. By the way, the clothes and shit are courtesy of the North End Businessman's Association."

"What's that?" asked David.

"Oh, just some simple business types like me who like to help poor, unfortunate folks that get chased into the river by gorillas.'' Joey smiled conspiratorily at Terry and winked. ''You feel up to travelling, Doc?'' he asked.

''Yeah, sure. What time is it anyway?''

''Twelve-thirty. It's a new day.''

''Three hours.'' David shook his head in amazement. ''It's only been three hours . . . ''

''What?''

''Nothing, hand me the phone, please. I only hope she's all right.''

Joey squinted down at him. ''You *positive* you're all right?'' he asked.

''Sure, why?''

''Well, you're the one with the education an' the degrees an' shit. All I got goin' for me is my street smarts. Just the same, I can think of at least six or seven good reasons why we would want to tell this C. Beall what we have to tell her face to face, not over the phone. Remember, you've already been arrested for murder. Right now, that woman's your only hope of gettin' off.''

David understood instantly. If Christine had nothing to do with Ben's death, the news could panic her into a hasty, possibly fatal move. If she was somehow involved, or knew who might have hired Leonard Vincent . . . He wouldn't allow himself to complete the thought. ''When this is all over,'' he said, ''I'm going to write to my medical school and tell them to bring you in as a guest lecturer. You could teach medical students about making it in the real world. Let's go find her.''

Ten minutes later, they were back in Rudy Fisher's car headed towards Brookline. ''Don't push it too hard, Rudy,'' Rosetti ordered. ''We don't want to get stopped. If Vincent's already got to the woman, all the fancy driving in the world isn't gonna help.'' David grimaced and looked out the window.

After a mile of silence, Joey said, ''Doc, there's somethin' I want to tell you. Call it a lesson if you want, since you're gonna make me a teacher.'' David turned towards his friend, expecting to see the wry glint which usually accompanied one of his stories. Joey's eyes were narrowed, dark, and deadly serious. ''Go on,'' David said.

''Leonard Vincent may not be the slickest operator in the

198

world, but he is a pro. And as long as he or someone like him's in the picture, you're gonna be playing by his rules. Understand?'' David nodded. ''Well, we don't have much time, so I'm gonna make the lesson simple for you. There's only one rule you gotta know. One main rule for survival in Vincent's game. I didn't follow it back there in the hospital because Terry made me promise not to. But you got no Terry, so you pay attention and do what I say. If you think someone's gonna do it to you, you damn well better do it to him first. Understand?'' He slipped his gun into David's pocket. ''Here. Whatever happens, I got a feelin' you're gonna need this more than me. Terry'll cook you something real special when she hears you got it away from me.''

John Dockerty knelt by the door to David's apartment and watched as the medical examiner's team finished working around Ben's body and wheeled it into the lift. He looked up at the patrolman who had been making inquiries in the other apartments on the floor. The man shrugged and shook his head. ''Nothing,'' he mouthed.

The news came as no surprise to Dockerty. Survival in the city meant hearing, seeing, and reporting as little as possible. He picked at the bullet holes in the doorjamb, then retraced the steps it seemed the action had taken. There was blood smeared on the hallway floor and wall of David's apartment, and along the bottom of the open bedroom window. He made a note to check David's military and health records for mention of his blood type.

A fatal knife wound, bullet holes, blood all over, an old drunk shot to death two blocks away, and not one witness. Dockerty rubbed the fatigue stinging his eyes, and tried to recreate the scenario. There were several possibilities, none of which looked good for Shelton. He had little doubt the man was dead.

At that moment, David's phone began ringing. Dockerty hesitated, then answered it.

''Hello?''

''Lt. Dockerty, please.''

''This is Dockerty.''

''Lieutenant, it's Sgt. McIlroy at the Fourth. We just got a call from one of our people at the Doctors Hospital. Apparently this David Shelton, you know, the one you busted for that mercy killing?''

"Yeah, I know, I know."

"Well, this Shelton showed up a little while ago on the emergency ward all smashed up. I called your precinct and they said you'd want to know about it right away."

"Tell your people to hold him at the hospital," Dockerty barked.

"Too late. He took off with some guy a few minutes after he arrived. No-one realised it until he'd split. Our men were off taking statements from two assholes who had a shoot-out at the High Five Bar."

"Who the hell was the other guy?" Dockerty's head began to throb.

"Don't know."

"Well, isn't it on Shelton's emergency sheet?"

"That's just it. There *is* no emergency sheet. The clerk swears she typed one out, but now no-one can find it."

"Jesus Christ. What in the hell is going on?"

"Don't know, sir."

"Well, tell the men at the hospital I'll be right over. They're not to let anyone who saw Shelton leave. No one. Got that?"

"Yes, sir."

"Jesus Christ." Dockerty dropped the receiver in place and swept some strands of hair off his eyes and back under his hat. It was going to be a long goddamn night.

Rudy Fisher cruised up and down Christine's street three times before Rosetti felt certain there were no "surprises". He directed the giant to wait half a block away, then he helped David up the concrete steps to the house. "Old Leonard's probably having a time of it right now," Joey laughed. "I can just imagine him trying to weasel his way out of that situation in the hospital with the only ten or twelve words that he knows."

David braced himself on his crutches and peered through the row of small panes next to the door. He moved gingerly, but even a slight turn or drop of his head brought a wave of dizziness and nausea. The prolonged hypothermia, he realised, had somehow impaired his balance, or perhaps his body's ability to make quick blood pressure adjustments.

The house was dark, save for a dim light coming from a room on the right — the living room, David guessed. He glanced at his watch. Nearly one a.m.

"I guess we ring the bell, huh?" David asked nervously.

"Well, Doc, given the options, I'd say that was your best bet. I'm glad you're not this tense in the operating room."

David gave a laugh, then pressed the bell. They waited, listening for a response. Nothing. David shivered and rang again. Ten seconds passed. Then twenty.

"Do we break in?" he asked.

"We may have to, but I'd suggest trying the back door first." Joey walked to the street and motioned to Rudy Fisher that they were going around to the back. David gave the button a final press, then fought an attack of queasiness and followed.

It was that third ring which woke Christine. She was stretched across her bed, careening through one grisly dream after another. On the floor, shards of torn note paper were strewn about two pill bottles. Both of them were full.

"Wait a minute, I'm coming," she called out. Could both her roommates have forgotten their keys? Knowing them, a likely possibility. She pushed herself off the bed, then stared at the floor. The shredded note, the bottles, the pills . . . how close she had come. She threw the pills into a drawer, then swept up the scraps with her hands and dropped them in the basket. By the end of the terrible, dark hour that had followed her return home, Christine had resolved that nothing would ever make her take her own life. Nothing, except perhaps a situation such as Charlotte Thomas's. She would face whatever she had to face.

Again, the doorbell sounded. This time, it was the buzzer from the back door. "I'm coming, I'm coming." She rushed through the kitchen and was half way down the short back staircase when she stopped dead. It was him, David, propped on crutches and peering through the window. She reached down and flipped on the outside light, then she gasped. His face was drawn and cadaverous, his eyes totally lost in wide, dark hollows. A second man, his back turned, was standing behind him. Christine's pulse quickened as first confusion, then mounting apprehension gripped her.

"Christine, it's me, David Shelton." His voice sounded weak and distant, through the windowpane.

"Yes . . . yes, I know. What do you want?" She felt frightened, unable to move.

"Please, Christine, I must talk to you. Something has happened. Something terrible . . . ."

Joey grabbed his arm. "Are you crazy?" he whispered, working his way in front of the window. "Miss Beall," he said calmly, "my name is Joseph Rosetti. I'm a close friend of the Doc's. He's been hurt." He paused, gauging Christine's expression to see if any further explanation was necessary before she let them in.

Christine hesitated, then descended the final two stairs and undid the double lock. "I . . . I'm sorry," she said as they entered the hallway. "You took me by surprise and . . . Please, come up to the living room. Can you make it all right? Are you badly hurt?"

For the next fifteen minutes, she did not say another word as the two men recounted the events of the night. With each detail, a new emotion flashed in her eyes. Surprise, astonishment, terror, pain, sorrow. David studied them as they appeared. He wondered if she were even capable of a successful lie. Whatever she might have done, he was now certain that in no way was she responsible for Ben's murder.

Still, she was somehow involved. That reality pulled David's attention from her face. "Christine, what did you tell Ben?" She seemed unable to speak. "Please, tell me what you said to him." There was a note of urgency and anger in his voice.

"I . . . I told him that it was me. That I was the one who . . . who gave the morphine to Charlotte."

David's heart pounded. His arrest, the filth and degradation of his night in jail, the loss of everything he had fought so hard for in his career, Ben Glass's death – *she was responsible.* "And the forged prescription?" There was bitterness in his words now. "Were you responsible for that, too?"

"No! . . . I mean, I don't know." The muscles in her face tensed. Her lips quivered. The only explanation she could think to give him was the truth, but what was the truth? The Sisterhood had sacrificed David to protect her, she felt certain of that.

202

But why Ben? It was hard enough to accept that they would choose to send an innocent man to prison, but murder? "Oh, my God," she stammered. "I'm so confused. I don't know what's happening. I don't understand."

"What?" David demanded. "What don't you understand?" His eyes flashed at her.

Christine began to cry. "I don't understand," she sobbed. "So much is happening and nothing makes sense. It's horrible. The pain I've caused you. And Ben . . . they've killed Ben. Why? Why? I . . . I need time. Time to sort this all out. It's crazy. Why would they do it?"

"Who're *they*?" David asked. Christine didn't answer. "Dammit," he screamed, "what are you talking about? Who're they?"

"Now just hold it a minute." Joey put up a hand to each of them. "You're both gonna have to calm down, or we could all find ourselves in trouble. Leonard Vincent's probably out of the picture, but there's no guarantee he was working alone. The longer you two spend goin' at one another like this, the more chance there is that some goon's gonna crash in here and do it good to all three of us." He paused, allowing the thought to sink in, and waited until he sensed the tension easing. "Okay. Now, Miss Beall, I don't know you, but I do know the Doc here, and I know the shit he's been through. The way I see it, you're both in hot water until this whole business is straightened out. I can see that the news we've brought has shaken you, but this man here deserves an explanation."

"I . . . I don't know what to say." She spoke the words softly as much as to herself as to them.

Joey could see that she was coming apart. He glanced at David, whose expression suggested that he sensed the same thing. "Look," Joey said finally, "maybe what we should do is just call the cops and – "

"No!" Christine blurted. "Please no. Not yet. There's so much I don't understand. A lot of innocent people could be hurt if I do the wrong thing." She stopped and breathed deeply. When she continued, there was a new calm in her voice. "Please, you must believe me. I had nothing to do with Ben's death. I liked him very much. He was going to help me."

David leaned forward and buried his face in his hands.

"Okay." He looked up slowly. "No police . . . yet. What do you want?"

"Some time," she said. "Just a little time to work this whole thing through. I'll tell you everything I know. I promise."

David sensed himself soften before the sadness in her eyes and turned away.

"Look, Doc," Rosetti said impatiently, "I meant what I said before. We're just not smart stayin' here any longer than we have to. If it's no police, then it's no police. If it's some time to talk, then it's some time to talk. Only not here."

David heard the urgency in Rosetti's voice, and saw, for the first time, a flash of fear in his eyes. "Okay, we'll get out," he said. "But where can we go? Certainly not to my apartment. How about the tavern . . . or your place? Do you think Terry would be upset if we went there?"

"I have a better idea. Terry and me have this little hideaway up on the North Shore. I think if you two can keep from rippin' each other apart without me for a referee it would be a perfect place. Doc, you can't see yourself, but let me tell you, you look about ready for an embalmer. Why don't you go on up there tonight and get some sleep. Tomorrow you can take all the time you need to talk things through." David started to protest, but Rosetti stopped him. "This ain't the time for arguin' pal. You're my friend. Terry's friend too. So I know you'll understand that I don't want her mixed up in anything this messy. It's the North Shore or you're both on your own. Now what do you say?"

David looked over at Christine. She was slumped in her chair, staring at the floor. There was an innocence about her – a defencelessness that was difficult to reconcile with his anger, and the hell she had caused him. Who are you, he wondered. Exactly what have you done? And why?

"I . . . I guess if it's okay with Christine, it's okay with me," he said finally.

Christine tightened her lips and nodded.

"It's decided, then," Joey announced. "There's food in the house. This time of year, there's not too many folks on Rocky Point, so you shouldn't be bothered. I'll draw you a map. Take Christine's car. We'll follow you to the highway just in case. It's nice up there. Especially if the rain is through for good.

204

There's an old jalopy jeep in the garage. The keys are in the tool box by the back wall. Use it if you want. Okay?''

"Give me a minute to pack a couple of things," Christine said. "And to leave a note for my roommates that I won't be home tonight."

"Okay, but be quick about it," Joey replied. "And Christine? Tell your friends to keep the door locked – just in case."

"Mr. Vincent, you have bungled things badly. Possibly beyond repair. Hyacinth took a great risk helping you escape that mess in the hospital, but never again. This time I want results. The girl first, then Dr. Shelton. Understand?''

"Yeah, yeah, I understand." Leonard Vincent slammed the receiver down then rubbed the thin mat of dried blood that covered the stitches in his head. Hyacinth wasn't his type but for being cool in a crunch he had to hand it to her. After regaining consciousness, he had been unable to keep to his feet. He remembered her helping him to a stretcher. Seconds later, a doctor arrived. It was then that the woman really put on her show, explaining how this poor orderly had slipped and smacked his head on the floor, and how she would take care of all the paper work if the guy would just throw some stitches into the gash.

Yes sir, Vincent thought, he certainly did have to hand it to ol' Hyacinth. Then he remembered the way she had looked at him just before she sent him out of the hospital – the hatred in her eyes. "You asshole," she had said. "You absolute asshole."

The memory triggered a flush of nausea and another fit of dry heaves – his third since leaving the hospital. Vincent held onto a tree until the retching subsided. "People are gonna die," he spat, fighting the frustration and the pain with the only weapon he knew. "People are gonna fuckin' die."

Carefully, he eased himself behind the wheel of his car and drove to Brookline. He turned onto Belknap Street just as another car, heading away from him, neared the corner at the far end. Vincent tensed as he peered through the darkness, trying to focus on the car before it disappeared around the corner. It was red – bright red. The killer relaxed and settled back into the seat.

He stopped across from Christine's house and scanned the drive-way. The blue Mustang was gone.

Muttering an obscenity, he reached inside the glove compart-ment and pulled out the envelope Hyacinth had given him. "Well, Dahlia, whoever the fuck you are," he said, "I guess you get the doctor first whether you want it that way or not. If I can find him . . ."

He tore open the envelope and spread David's emergency ward sheet on the passenger seat. Across the space marked "Physician's Report" the words, "ELOPED WITHOUT TREATMENT" were printed in red. The information boxes at the top were all neatly typed in. With an unsteady hand, Vincent drew a circle around the line of type identifying next of kin.

19

The wharf was dark, quiet, and even more eerie than usual. John Dockerty backed inside a doorway and listened until the echo of his footsteps had been absorbed by the heavy night. It took several minutes to sort out the random sounds that surrounded him. Clinking mooring chains. Gulls caterwauling over a midnight feast. The lap of harbour swells against thick pilings. The reassuring drone of a foghorn.

Through the silver-black mist he scanned the row of warehouses, ghostly sentinels guarding the inner harbour. Then he crossed the narrow strip of road and ducked into a small alley. At the far end, a slit of dim light glowed from beneath an unmarked warehouse door. Dockerty knocked softly and waited.

"Come in, Dock, it's open." Ted Ulansky's voice boomed in the silence.

Dockerty slipped inside closing the heavy metal door quickly behind him. "Christ, Ted," he said. "I spend twenty fucking minutes sneaking around to be sure I'm not followed, and you bellow at me louder than the foghorn out there."

"Just goes to show what confidence I have in you, Dock. Come on over and park your duff." Ulansky pumped Dockerty's hand, then motioned him to a high-backed oak chair beside his desk. He was an expansive man, with a physique that bore only a faint resemblance to the All-American linebacker he had been at Boston College two and a half decades before.

"Nice place," Dockerty said sarcastically, looking around the large, poorly lit office. "Is this it?"

"This is it," answered Ulansky with mock pride. "The legendary Massachusetts Drug Investigation Force Headquarters. Want a tour?"

"No thanks, I think I can manage to take it all in from here."

In fact, the MDIF, while not publicised, had gained an almost fabled reputation for quiet efficiency and airtight arrests.

Ulansky, as head of the unit, was gradually acquiring a super-human reputation of his own. The office, however, was hardly the stuff of which legends are made. It was stark and cold. Bare cement walls were lined with filing cabinets – more than two dozen of them – all olive green, standard government issue. Inside the metal drawers, Dockerty knew, was virtually every piece of information available on illegal drug traffic in the state.

In one corner of the room, partially covered by Ulansky's carelessly thrown jacket, was a computer terminal, connected through Washington to drug investigation and enforcement agencies throughout the country.

Ulansky lowered himself into his desk chair. "A drink? Some coffee?" Dockerty shook his head. "Must be serious business for you to come out here in this rat's ass weather then refuse a drink."

"I guess," Dockerty said distractedly, battling with some obstinate strands of hair. "I appreciate your coming out speci-ally."

Ulansky buried a shot glass of Old Grand Dad in a single gulp. "Believe me, with the Czernewicz fight on live from the coast tonight, you're about the only one of the precinct boys who could have gotten me out of the house. Jackie Czernewicz, the Pummelling Pole. You follow the fights?"

Dockerty shook his head again. "Too much like a day at the office for me."

Ulansky smiled. "Tell me then," he said, "what prompts a visit from you to this Hyatt Regency of law enforcement?"

"I'm involved in a really weird case, Ted." Dockerty scratched the tip of his nose. "An old lady got murdered while she was a patient at Boston Doctors Hospital. Morphine. So far, I've narrowed the field of suspects down to about three dozen. Even made one arrest."

"Yeah, I read about that," Ulansky said. "A doctor, right?"

"Right. A ton of circumstantial stuff against him, but way too neat if you know what I mean. The captain, that pillar of justice, got pressure from some fat cat at the hospital and insisted that I bust the doctor. I did it, but I've never been convinced. Now the guy's lawyer has been murdered. Ben Glass. You know him?" Ulansky grimaced and nodded. "Well, he was knifed. Outside the doc's apartment door no less. There are bullet holes all over, and the apartment door's smashed in. There's blood in the hallway and even on the wall.

"A little while ago the doctor gets brought to the emergency ward at the hospital soaked and freezing and half crazy. Then, before he can get any treatment, he splits with another guy. By the time I hear about it and get to the hospital, there's no record he was ever there. For all I know he may be dead by now. I've got the usual lines out for him, but I'm at a brick wall with the rest of the case. I feel like the whole fucked-up mess is partly my fault for letting the captain talk me into arresting him."

"How can we help?"

"My only hope of breaking something open is a pharmacist named Quigg. Marcus Quigg. Owns a little drug store in West Roxbury. He swears that this Dr. Shelton collected a big prescription for morphine the day this woman was O.D.'ed."

Ulansky's moon face crinkled as he worked the name through the memory. "We've got something on the man some place," he said. "I'm almost sure of it. What about a C222?"

"Quigg's got one. The doctor claims it was stolen from his office, that he never ordered any morphine."

"Signature?"

"Only a maybe from the guys at ident. They tell me Shelton's signature is a scrawl. Easy to duplicate."

"So, maybe it *is* his," Ulansky said.

"Maybe," Dockerty shrugged. "My hunches have been wrong before."

"Sure, about as often as a solar eclipse."

Dockerty accepted the compliment with a tired grin. "I need a handle on that pharmacist, Ted," he said. "The man bends, but he won't break. I figure if he'd take a pay-off to do something like this, he must have dirtied his hands on something else at one time or another."

"Well," Ulansky offered, "we can go through the files and check the computer for you. I have a feeling something's down on paper about him." He paused, then continued in a softer voice. "Dock, you know that if we can't find anything on him, we can easily set something up that will work just as well. Maybe better. You want that?"

Dockerty tensed, then rose and walked slowly to the far side of the room. Ulansky was about to add something, then sat back and let the silence continue. Dockerty rested one arm on a filing cabinet. For more than a minute he studied the blank wall. "You know, Ted," he said finally, "In all these years on the force I've never once purposely set anyone up. If I did it this time, I know it would be to make up for mistakes I've already made." He shook his head and turned back to Ulansky. "I don't want to do it, Ted. No matter what my cock-ups may have put that doctor through, I don't want to do it." Ulansky nodded his understanding. "Look," Dockerty added, "check everything you can to dig something up on Quigg. Call me first thing tomorrow. If I've got nothing and you've got nothing, we'll talk again."

"Don't worry, Dock," Ulansky said stonily. "If Marcus Quigg has so much as pissed on a public toilet seat, I'll find out. Don't worry your ass about that at all."

"We just passed it. That was the exit. I told you one twenty seven, and you just breezed right past it." David, bundled in an army blanket, sat wedged against the passenger door. He glared at Christine, but turned away before she noticed.

"Sorry," she said flatly. "My mind was on other things." She took the next turn-off and doubled back. Traffic was light, but her difficulty concentrating was such that she kept their speed below fifty. For a time, they drove in silence; the tension between them was building.

Finally Christine could stand no more. She pulled into the dirt parking lot of a boarded-up diner and swung around to face him. "Look, maybe this wasn't a good idea, maybe we should go back."

David stared out the window, struggling to comprehend the existence and the incredible scope of The Sisterhood of Life. Christine had given him only the roughest sketch of the movement, along with the promise of more details in the morning. Still, what she had told him already was awesome. Several thousand nurses! Dorothy Dalrymple one of them! He had listened, his eyes shut, his head close to exploding, as her factual, curiously dispassionate voice divulged secrets that could easily annihilate the hospital system to which he had dedicated so much of his life.

210

Now, he felt sick. Tired and angry and sick.

Christine sensed his mood, but could not contain her own growing frustration. "Dammit, David," she said, "I've been trying to explain to you as best as possible what has happened. I didn't expect a reward, but I didn't expect the silent treatment either."

"And just what did you expect?" Irritation sparked in his voice.

"Understanding?" she said softly.

"My God. She kills one of my patients, gets me thrown into jail for it, my friend is murdered practically in my arms, and she wants me to understand. And . . . and that Sisterhood of yours. Of all the presumptious, insane . . . "

"David, I told you about The Sisterhood of Life because I thought you deserved to know. Back there at my house you seemed willing to listen and at least try to understand. Instead, all you've done is pull into a shell and come out every few miles to snap at me. I'll tell you one last time. I had nothing to do with your arrest. I didn't even know it had happened until I read it in the papers. I imagine The Sisterhood is responsible, and that sickens me. I joined the movement because of its dedication to mercy. Now I discover it's involved in despicable crimes – against you, against Ben, and God knows who else. If I had known beforehand, I would never have allowed any of this to happen. Why else do you think I went to Ben to confess?"

She paused for a response, but David was staring out the window. "I thought you might be able to help me work things out," she continued, "but that was foolish of me. You have every right to be angry. Every right to hate me. I'm going home."

She started the engine. David reached across and turned it off. "Wait, please. I . . . I'm sorry." His speech was halting and thick. "I've been listening to my own bitterness and anger, and trying to understand where they're coming from. I thought it was my pain talking, or frustration, or even fear, but I'm starting to know better. I liked you – maybe more than I would allow myself to accept. That's what's doing it. I didn't want to believe you were any part of this. Now you tell me that you *were* part of it, but you ask me to believe you didn't know what your Sisterhood was capable of doing. Well, I want to believe that. I do. It's just that . . . " He gave up fumbling for words. How

211

much of what she had told him had actually sunk in? "Look," he said finally, "I'm absolutely exhausted. I can't seem to hold onto anything. Please, let's call a truce for the night and just get up to Rosetti's place. We'll see what things are like tomorrow, Okay?"

Christine sighed, then nodded. "Okay, truce." Hesitantly, she extended her hand towards him. He clasped it, first in one, then in both of his. The warmth in her touch only added to his confusion. Why did it have to be her? Why? The question floated through his thoughts like a mantra, over and over again, easing his eyes closed and blanketing the turmoil within him. He heard the engine engage and felt the Mustang swing onto the roadway in the instant before he surrendered to exhaustion.

"David? . . . I'm sorry, but you have to wake up." Christine pulled the blanket away from his face and waited as he pawed his eyes open. "Are you feeling better?"

"Only if there are degrees of deceased," he mumbled. He pushed the blanket to his lap and peered through the windscreen. They were parked on the shoulder of a narrow, pitch black road. "Where are we?"

"We're in lost," she said matter-of-factly.

Her humour, unexpected, nearly eluded him. He glared at her for a moment, then stammered. "But . . . but we weren't going there. I think we should take the next right, or at least the next left."

"At least . . . " They both laughed.

"What time is it?"

"Two. A little after. We were right where the map said we were supposed to be, then all of a sudden, about fifteen or twenty minutes ago, the landmarks disappeared." She handed him Joey's drawing.

David opened his window and breathed deeply. The air, scrubbed by four days of rain, was cool and sweet with the scents of autumn. An almost invisible mist hung low over the roadway. Within a few breaths, he could taste the salt captured in its droplets. Then he heard the sea, like the thrum of an endless train, up through the woods to their right. "Have we passed Gloucester?" he asked.

"Yes, just before I got lost."

He smiled. "You did fine, Christine. The ocean's over there through the trees. It sounds as if we're pretty high above it. I'll bet a Devil Hot-dog we're near this place Joey marked as 'cliffs'."

"Bet a what?"

"A Devil Hot-dog. You see I . . . never mind. I'll explain tomorrow. Assuming I'm not too foggy to figure out what this map says, and if there are no other roads between us and the ocean, we should be close to the turn-off for Rocky Point. I vote straight ahead."

She eased the Mustang back onto the road and into the darkness.

After a quarter of a mile, the pavement rose sharply to the right. Moments later, they broke free of the woods. The sight below was breathtaking. The steep slope, dotted with trees and boulders, dropped several hundred feet before reaching the jet black Atlantic. Overhead, a large gap appeared between the clouds, revealing several stars and the perfect white scimitar of a waxing moon. Christine pulled to the side and cut the engine. Her hands were shaking.

"Even if we had no idea where we were, we wouldn't be lost," David said gently. "See that dark mass on the other side of the cove? I think that's Rocky Point."

Christine did not respond. She stepped from the car and walked to the edge of the drop. For several minutes she stood there, an ebony statue against the blue-black of the sky. When she returned, tears glistened in her eyes. The rest of their drive was made in silence.

The little hideaway, as Joey had called it, was splendid — a hexagonal glass and redwood lodge suspended over the very tip of the point.

"David, it's just beautiful," she said.

"You go ahead and open the place up," David said, "I'll be along."

"Do you need help?"

David shook his head, then realised he was not at all sure he could make it on his own. He pushed himself out of the car and onto the crutches. Immediately, dizziness and nausea rushed back. He struggled to the bottom of the short flight of steps leading to the front door. For hours, tension and nervous energy had helped him overcome the pain and the after-effects of hypothermia. Now, it seemed, he had no strength left. He grabbed the railing, but spun off it and fell heavily. In seconds, Christine was beside him, supporting him, guiding him inside.

The huge picture windows and high beamed ceilings were little more than hazy, whirling shapes as she helped him past a large fieldstone fireplace to the bedroom. As she lowered him onto the bed, the telephone in the living room began ringing.

"Go on and answer it, I'll be all right," he said, eyes closed. "It's probably Joey."

He heard her leave, and for several minutes, he fought encroaching darkness and waited. By the time she returned, he was losing to oncoming sleep.

"David are you awake?" A single nod. "You were right, that was Joey. He wanted to make sure we got here in one piece. Please nod if you understand what I'm saying, okay? Good. He called some friends of his on the police force. David, no one knows anything about Leonard Vincent being picked up tonight. Everyone in Boston is looking for you, but Vincent must have escaped the hospital before he was noticed. Joey said he would keep checking around and call us later today or else Saturday morning. We're okay as long as we're up here, but he said to be careful if we drive back to the city. David?"

This time, he did not nod.

Hours later, David's eyes blinked open in twilight wakefulness.

He was undressed and under the covers, his torn, swollen ankle was propped up on pillows. Nestled beside it was a plastic bag of water, the remains of an improvised ice pack.

He lifted himself to one elbow and looked out through the ceiling-to-floor windows. An endless field of stars now glittered across the clearing night sky.

A cry came from outside the room. David grabbed his crutches and limped towards the sound. Christine was asleep on the living room couch. She cried out again, more softly this time. David went to rouse her. Then he stopped. He could wake her for a minute or ten or even an hour, but it would make no difference. He knew the resilience of nightmares.

20

The sizzle and aroma of frying bacon lured David from a dreamless sleep, and kept his first thoughts of the morning away from the horror of the past night.

Sunlight, streaming through the huge windows, bathed him in an almost uncomfortable warmth. Sun! David opened his eyes and squinted into the glare. For nearly a week, the world had been a damp, monotonous grey. Now, he could almost taste the blue-white sky.

His forearm was throbbing beneath Terry's bulky dressing, but not unbearably so. He dangled his legs over the edge of the bed and flexed his ankle. A numb ache, also tolerable. In fact, he realised, there was a strange, reassuring comfort about the pain – perhaps because feeling this pain was itself testimony that he was still alive. The notion brought with it a fleeting smile. How many times had he encountered patients who seemed to be actually enjoying their pain? Next time, he would be more understanding.

He heard Christine moving about the kitchen, then suddenly there was music from a radio. Classical music! Telemann? Absolutely, he decided. A jumbo pizza and six mindless hours of uninterrupted T.V. said it was Telemann. For a time he listened, thinking about Christine and the fantastic story she had told him. Last night he had been furious. As angry and frustrated as he could ever remember. But now, in the sunlight and the music, he realised she was in many ways as innocent – caught in the same nightmare – as he was. True, she had given the morphine to Charlotte Thomas, but in no way could she have anticipated the events to follow. He had to believe that. For his own sanity, he *had* to believe that.

He closed his eyes, savouring the promise of a new day. Then he picked up one crutch and hobbled out of the bedroom.

The kitchen, separated from the living/dining area by a

butcher-block counter, was on the west side of the hexagon. Christine stood by the sink, whisking a wire beater through a bowl of pancake mix. The sight of her triggered a warm rush through David's body. No morning sun could have brightened the room as she did that moment. Her hair, in a loose, sandy braid, dangled half way down her back. A light blue man's shirt, knotted at the bottom, accentuated the curve of her breasts and exposed a band of honeyed skin at her waist. Below that, faded jeans clung to her hips and buttocks.

As he watched, David sensed the pounding in his chest, and willed it to stop. "Mornin'," he said casually, wondering if he looked more at ease than he felt.

She turned. "I couldn't decide whether to wake you or to wait and risk ruining breakfast, so I took the coward's way out and turned on the radio. Did you get enough sleep?"

David searched her expression. Was she asking for their truce to continue, to be allowed to bring things up in her own time and her own way? "I slept fine," he said. "Thanks for putting me to bed."

"I was afraid you might be upset about my doing that." Christine set the beater down.

"Only that I wasn't conscious when you did," he said. Her laugh gave him his cue. He would keep things light until she was ready to talk. "Listen, can I help in there? I'm a wonderful cook . . . for any type of meal whose main ingredient is water."

"I think things are under control. You could light a fire. It's a little chilly on this side of the house. There's wood already laid in the fireplace. This afternoon, if you want, you can be in charge of lunch."

"Fair enough." He headed for the hearth.

As Christine returned to the sink she heard him mumble, "Maybe some Cup-O-Soup and instant mashed potatoes . . . or perhaps beef jerky in white wine sauce . . . " Silently, she thanked him. A rueful smile crossed her face as she remembered Dotty Dalrymple's assessment. "A degenerate," she'd called him. And just what are *we*? Christine wondered. We who have taken it on ourselves to weigh the value of a human life. We who can believe so mightily in our commitment to end it whenever we think appropriate. What are we?

She glanced into the living room. David was sitting by a low

216

fire, his swollen ankle propped on a hassock. "Show me how to make it through, David," she whispered. "Show me how you survived the hell you went through. I know it's a lot to ask, but please, please try."

Joey Rosetti's jeep was old in body and spirit if not in years. From the passenger seat, David watched with admiration as Christine manoeuvred the snorting beast around rocks and muddy puddles on the steep grade to the ocean.

Conversation during the morning had been light, with only oblique references to the horrors that had brought them together. When Christine suggested a picnic by the water, David started to object — to insist that they confront the issues facing them. Quickly, though, he realised that he, too, wanted the respite to continue. There would be time enough to talk after lunch.

The stony dirt track they had chosen wound through a tangled fairy-tale forest of beach plum, wild rose, and scrub pine. After several hundred yards, it deteriorated into a series of partly overgrown, hairpin turns.

"Maybe we should back up and try to find another road," David said.

"Maybe . . . " She bounced round a vicious loop that he had felt certain would be impassable. "But I'll bet you a . . . a fruit pie we make it on this one."

Moments later, the thick brush fell away to either side. A final hairpin and the road spilled on to a sandy oval, scarcely thirty yards long, a perfect white-gold medallion resting on the breast of the Atlantic. Christine skidded to a dusty stop. The engine noise faded. They sat soaking in the silence and the colours.

"A penny . . . ?" David asked finally.

"For my thoughts?"

"Uh huh."

"You'll want change."

"Try me."

"Well, I was just deciding which spot would be best to spread the blanket and set our lunch."

"That's it?"

"That's it." She took the bag of food and the blanket, then kicked off her shoes and hopped onto the sand. "After we eat,

217

we can talk, okay?'' He nodded. ''Well, are you coming?''

''In a minute. You go ahead.''

Concern darkened her face then vanished. With a delighted whoop, she raced across the beach.

David sank back in his seat, aware of a heavy, husky tightness in his upper chest. In the minutes that followed, the feeling intensified. He struggled to pin it down – to label it. Gradually, he understood. He was caring more for her, his affection growing by the minute. Caring for the woman whose actions, whose hubris, had triggered his nightmare and had somehow led to the death of his friend. Caring for a woman who had confessed to murder, for a woman whose situation was . . . hopeless.

This is crazy, he thought. Absolutely insane. Falling in love with a woman with no future beyond the turmoil of an arrest and trial, and possibly jail. So different from Lauren. How could he be falling for her?

''David?'' Christine's voice startled him, and for a moment he couldn't locate her. Then, through the window, he saw her, elbows resting on the hood of the jeep studying him. ''Are you all right?''

''Huh? Oh, sure, I'm fine.''

''Good. I couldn't tell if you were in a trance or just in a huff because I forgot to let you put lunch together. It's ready whenever you are.''

David smiled thinly, lowered himself from the jeep, and limped across the sand to the partly shaded niche where she had spread their blanket.

They were silent as they tucked into the amalgam of foods Christine had found – sardines, marinated artichoke hearts, Wheat Thins, boiled eggs, black olives, string cheese, and Portuguese sweet bread.

''That was delicious,'' David said finally. ''Want to flip for that last artichoke?''

''No, thanks, I'm full. You go ahead.'' She paused, then continued with almost no change in her tone. ''Charlotte wasn't dying of cancer, was she?'' It was a statement more than a question.

So much for Camelot, David thought. With a deliberateness that he hoped would help him form a response, he set his fork in an empty jar, then swung around to face her.

"You mean the autopsy findings?" he said. She swallowed hard and nodded. "Well, then, the simple answer to your question is probably not. On autopsy there was no obvious cancer. For sure it could have popped up again in six months or a year, or even two. But for now, no is your answer."

Christine started to reply, then bit her lips and turned away. Without the slightest warning, David snapped, "Damn it, Christine, don't do this to yourself. If you're going to work this whole business out, then you must do it objectively, and not stop to blame yourself at every turn. Either we take a hard look at it from every angle, or we might as well go back to small talk. Okay?"

Christine nodded. Her eyes were glazed and vacant. "I . . . I just feel so damn lost," she said hoarsely. "So frightened, so . . . so hopeless."

That word again. This time it was David who looked away. He could not contradict her. What *did* she have to look forward to? Then he thought of Lauren. For better or for better. That was how he had described her commitment to him. Now it was his turn to decide.

But, he thought angrily again, hadn't Christine made her own decisions – decisions which had caused people to get hurt, to get killed? Surely, feeling hopeless was no more than she deserved?

No more than she deserved. David shook his head. How many of his colleagues thought that his getting arrested, then suspended from the Doctors Hospital staff was no more than *he* deserved? Did he have any more right to pass judgment than they did?

He reached out and took Christine's hand. Her fingers tightened about his. He could feel her despair.

All at once, he crossed his arms in a rigid, professorial pose. "And just what makes you think you have the right to make that diagnosis?" he asked haughtily.

"What diagnosis?"

"Hopelessness. Here you are in the presence of perhaps the world's greatest expert on the subject, and you have the temerity to diagnose yourself without asking for a consultation? That is unacceptable. I am taking over this case." The emptiness in her eyes began to lift. "We must take an inventory," he said. "First the basics. I see ten fingers, ten toes, and two of all the parts

219

there are supposed to be two of. Are they all in working order, miss?'' She suppressed a giggle and nodded. ''So far, this sounds very hopeful. Are you perchance aware of the classic Zurich study on the subject? They measured hopelessness on a scale of zero to ten in over a thousand subjects, half of them living and half dead. A hopelessness index of ten was considered absolute. Can you guess the outcome of that research?'' She was laughing now. ''Can't guess? Well, I'll tell you. A marked statistically significant difference was found between the groups. In fact, those in the deceased group invariably rated ten, the rest, invariably zero.'' He rubbed his chin and eyed her up and down. ''I'm sorry, miss. I really am, but I'm afraid that no matter how much you want to be, you are simply not hopeless. Thank you very much for coming. My bill's in the mail. Next?''

She threw her arms around his neck. ''Thank you.'' Her lips brushed his ears as she spoke. ''Thank you for the consultation.'' She drew her head back to look at him. Their kiss simply happened – a gentle, comfortable touching that neither of them wanted to end. A minute passed, and then another. Finally, she drew away.

''It all went wrong,'' she said softly. ''It seemed so right, and it all went . . . crazy. Why, David? Tell me. How the hell can I ever trust my feelings again when something I believed in so very much turned out so sour?'' She sank down to the sand and stared out at the Atlantic.

''You want to know why?'' he said dropping next to her. ''Because you're not perfect, that's why. Because nobody's perfect. Because every equation involving human beings is unsolvable, or at least never solvable the same way twice. I believe in euthanasia just as much as you do. I always have. The concept is absolutely right to my mind. But I have come to understand that while it is absolutely right in theory, in practice there is simply no way to do it right. Sooner or later, the human element, the unpredictable, uncontrollable 'X-factor' rears its ugly head, and wham, things come apart.''

''And innocent people die,'' she said.

''Chris, as far as I'm concerned, when it comes to dying, we're all innocent. That's the problem. Someone in your Sisterhood, possibly this Peggy woman, has snatched up the good, honest beliefs of some wonderful, idealistic nurses and has run away with them. Again, the human element. Money, greed, lust, fanatacism. Who knows what will pluck that special string hidden within someone and set him off? You were about to expose The Sisterhood, or at least that's what somebody thought. That string gets plucked and crazy, insane decisions get made.

"There's this riddle I once heard," he continued. "It asks a person what he would do if he was presented with a healthy newborn infant and promised that by slaying that infant he could instantly cure the ills of all mankind. Someone in your Sisterhood has answered that riddle for herself. Ben, you, me — none of us is as important to that person as her ideals. The individual, sacrificed for the greater good. It happens all the time."

"That's horrible," she said.

"Maybe. But more important, it's human. You can shoulder the burden of responsibilities for my suffering, or even Ben's death if you want to, but that's being awfully tough on yourself for just doing what you believed in, and for trusting that other human beings were just as constant, just as pure in their belief as you were.

"You have decisions to make, Chris. Huge, crunching, God-awful decisions. If you want, I'll help. But don't expect me to stand by holding the matches while you pour petrol over yourself. I . . . I care too much."

Slowly, she turned to him. Her eyes held his as they had during their first meeting. Her hands caressed the sides of his face. Their kiss, this time warm and deep and sweet, carried them to the sand. Moment by moment, as they undressed each other, the world beyond their beach drifted away. David kissed her eyes, then buried his lips in the soft hollow of her neck. Her hands flowed over his body, feeling him, exciting him, exciting her.

With every kiss, every touch, the loneliness and fear inside them lessened. With each new discovery, the sense of hopelessness faded.

Christine's face glowed golden in the late afternoon sun as she lifted herself on top of him. He stroked her firm breasts, first with his hands, then with his tongue. She was smiling as she reached down and guided him inside her.

"Barbara, just stop fretting and give me the names. I'll take care of it."

"But . . . "

"The names please." Margaret Armstrong snapped the words, then balled the small piece of fabric in her fist and forced herself to relax.

Barbara Littlejohn hesitated. Finally, she opened a manilla folder and passed one letter at a time across the cardiologist's desk. "Ruth Serafini," she said. "Resigned from both the board of directors and the movement. Says that she understands you are doing what you think is right, but that she cannot, in all good conscience, go along with it."

"Not even a copy to me," Peggy muttered, scanning the letter then tossing it aside.

"Susan Berger," Barbara continued. "Says essentially the same thing as Ruth, but goes on to state that until matters are resolved, she intends to curtail all Sisterhood operations in Northern California. No approval for new cases, and also her recommendation that all contributions to the Clinton Foundation be held up."

Peggy set the letter on top of the other without reading it. "Susan will listen to reason," she said evenly, weighing the possibility of doctoring the half dozen tapes of Susan's which were locked in her basement vault. Without any reference to The Sisterhood of Life, the tapes would contribute a chilling confession. "She's far too ambitious a woman not to listen to reason." Peggy unravelled the square of linen, and absently rubbed it between her fingertips.

Barbara Littlejohn, appearing grey and drawn despite her carefully applied make-up, passed the third letter. "This is the one that upset me the most," she said. "It's from Sara."

"Damn!" the expletive was thought more than spoken.

"She says that she will reconsider her resignation if we conduct a careful investigation into involvement of The Sisterhood or its members in the deaths of John Chapman and Senator Cormier – both at this hospital. Peggy, we didn't have anything to do with – "

"Of course not," Peggy said. "John Chapman was a friend of Sara's. She's just upset. Senator Cormier was autopsied, and has already been thoroughly discussed at a death conference. I made it a point to attend. He had extensive coronary artery disease, and simply had a fatal heart attack during surgery. That's all there is to that."

"I'm glad." There was genuine relief in Barbara's face and voice. "Peggy, I don't know what I would have done if you hadn't been available to discuss this. Everything seemed to be coming apart."

"Nonsense. You're doing a wonderful job. Our Sisterhood has not only survived for forty years, it has grown. A situation like this Shelton business may dent our solidarity, but it won't break it. Just leave those letters with me. By day's end I'll have the whole matter under control."

"Thank you," Barbara said, taking Peggy's hand. "Thank you." She let herself out.

Margaret Armstrong's eyes were closed even before the outside door of her office clicked shut behind Barbara. Suddenly the sense of that evening so many years ago – the hospital room, the pain on her mother's face, was real once again.

"The pillow, baby. Just set it over my face and lean on it as hard as you can. It won't take long."

"Mama, I . . . " Please Mama. Please don't make me do it.

"Peggy, I love you. If you love me too, you won't let me hurt so anymore. They all say it's hopeless . . . Don't let it hurt so anymore."

"I love you, Mama. I love you." Peggy Donner whispered the words over and over again in Margaret Armstrong's mind.

"I love you, Mama . . . " she said as she placed the pillow over the narrow face and leaned on it with all the strength she could manage . . .

Margaret Armstrong was shaking. She looked at the square of fabric as if discovering it for the first time, and pressed it to her lips.

John Dockerty paced from one side of the cluttered back room of Marcus Quigg's pharmacy to the other. Slouching against a wall, Ted Ulansky watched, his broad face an expressionless mask. They had been grilling Quigg for nearly two hours after finding enough improprieties in his records at least to have his licence suspended. Dockerty's hunch had been right. There was no need to manufacture evidence against the squirrel-like pharmacist. In just a few hours, checking his prescriptions and calling a few doctors, they had gained the kind of clout that should have brought Quigg to his knees begging for some kind of a deal. However, the little man had proved surprisingly resistant – or frightened.

"Mr. Quigg," Dockerty said irritably, "let's start all over again." The detective smacked a small stack of Quigg's bogus prescriptions against the palm of his hand. He and Ulansky had agreed beforehand that Dockerty would assume the role of tough, threatening bully during the interrogation and Ulansky would wait until he felt the time was right, then ride to Quigg's defence like a knight errant.

"Whatever you say," Quigg mumbled. He was maintaining what composure he had left by chain smoking and avoiding any eye contact. However, from his vantage point, Ted Ulansky noticed that, for the first time, Quigg's hand was shaking. It would not be long.

"I've laid it all out for you," Dockerty spat. "These prescriptions tell me that you are, at best, a crook. At worst, you're a fucking dope pusher who is putting bread on his table by dealing pills to kids. Now either you tell us what we want to know – who paid you to finger David Shelton – or I'll see to it that your pharmacy licence is chopped up and stuffed down your throat as your first prison meal. Got that?" Quigg bit at his lower lip. The shaking increased.

From the corner of his eye, Dockerty saw Ulansky nod. Time for the finale. He tightened his jaw and spoke through clenched teeth. "I want a name, Quigg, and I want it now. Otherwise, there's a cell waiting for you at Walpole. And believe me, a cute little fellow like you is dog meat to those guys. After a week, your asshole is going to be so wide from getting screwed that you'll shit your pants every time you take a step." His voice was booming now. "The name, Quigg, I want the name."

"Enough!" Ulansky cracked the word like a whip. Quigg's ashen face spun towards him. The narcotics investigator inserted himself between the two men like the referee in a prize fight. He put a calming hand on Dockerty's chest, only to have it slapped aside. For an instant he wasn't certain the Irishman was acting. "John, calm down. Just calm down. That temper of yours has gotten you in enough hot water with internal affairs as it is, so just

224

get a hold of yourself." He turned benevolently to Quigg, noting with satisfaction that a trace of colour had returned to the man's cheeks.

"Marcus, I want to help you out, I really do," he said, reassurance flowing from every word. "But you've got to realise what you're up against. You're sitting here balancing your career, your freedom and your health against a name. Just a name. That's all the lieutenant is asking for. I know you're frightened about what will happen if you give it to us, but just think about what will happen to you if you don't. At least the detective here can offer you some hope. Can the name we want offer you that?"

Ulansky scrutinised the man's face. He saw fear and uncertainty, but not defeat – not the capitulation he had expected by now. He looked at Dockerty and shook his head.

"I . . . I want to speak to my lawyer," Quigg said.

Dockerty shot across the room, grabbed the man by his lapels and pulled him to his feet. "You get nothing until I get some answers." Reluctantly, he released his grip. "We're taking you with us, Quigg," he said. "I want you to see first hand what jail is all about. We still have business, you and me. Come on, you creep, let's go."

Marcus Quigg felt the knife-like pain beneath his breast bone, and thought for a moment that it was all going to end right there. The wafer-thin aneurysm that had replaced much of the muscle of his heart was stretching. He had wanted to tell them at the outset that he was no crook. He wanted to tell them now that the illegal prescriptions were strictly nickel-and-dime stuff — bandaids to try to hold together his failing business and his failing health and his wife, terrified of being left alone with four children. He wanted to tell them, but he couldn't.

What difference did it make, anyway? He asked himself the question over and over as Dockerty snapped handcuffs on him and led him from the store. So this Shelton was in trouble because of what he was doing. Well *he* was in trouble, too. Big trouble. The goddamn balloon in his chest was stretching, and his doctor had said it could be a year or a month . . . or an hour. She had said there was nothing that could be done for him. Would Dockerty understand? Would he understand that after a whole life of trying to do what was right, all he had to show for

225

it was a frightened wife, four kids who needed to eat, and a ball of blood in his chest that could explode any time?

Quigg felt the knot in his gut, and tasted acid rising up in his throat. He wanted to tell them, and just go home to his own bed. But he knew what would happen. He knew the money would stop. He knew the additional thousands of dollars he had been promised when the whole mess was over would never come.

As he was shoved into the back seat of the detective's car, Marcus Quigg silently cursed Dr. Margaret Armstrong, and the misery she had brought him.

A pot of coffee, a shower together, and suddenly the evening had passed into crystal night. A birch log fire bathed Joey's living room in a crackling, flickering glow. Stretched on the couch, David and Christine alternated brief conversations with prolonged gazes at the velvet sky.

"Red silk," David said, fingering the robe he had borrowed from Rosetti's closet. "I never thought of myself as the silk dressing gown type, but it sure does feel fine."

Christine sat up, then pulled the edge of her robe across her lap. "David, I want you to know how much this day has meant to me." His eyes narrowed. "You know I didn't plan it this way, don't you?" He nodded. She saw the tightness in his face and the moist film over his eyes. "All of a sudden I feel . . . sort of selfish, even cruel."

"That's nonsense."

"No, it's not. I've allowed this to happen, knowing every minute it was going to end."

"I had some part in it too," he said huskily.

"Yes, I guess you're right . . . " Her voice trailed away. "David," she said at last, "I'm going back in the morning."

"Just one more day." His response was so quick that they both knew the thought had already been in his mind.

Christine shook her head. "I don't think that would be fair - to either of us. I know what you're feeling. I've been feeling i' too. All day. My mind keeps flip-flopping from fantasies of wha I want to happen to the reality of what I know is going t happen. Staying here - even another day - will only make it hur

226

more when I go. I've caused you enough pain already."

"I don't want you to leave." He knew what she had said was true, yet he was unable to stem the torrent of words. "It . . . it just isn't safe. Joey told you that last night. Vincent is loose somewhere in Boston. He's looking for me, and as likely as not, for you, too. If we go back, we'd have to go straight to Dockerty. And what would we tell him? We can't go back yet. Hell, Christ, we don't have to go back ever. We could take off. Right now. Tonight. We could go to Canada or . . . or to Mexico. I speak some Spanish. Maybe we could open a little clinic somewhere. Practise together. What good would it possibly do to go back now?"

She kissed him lightly. "It wouldn't work, David. You know that as well as I do. My Sisterhood has done some terrible things. I couldn't live with myself if I didn't try to stop them. I only hope I can find a way to do it without hurting all those nurses like me who believed – "

"Dammit, there must be another way!" David muttered angrily, but then sighed and sank back against the cushion. She was right. The rational, logical part of him understood that. If their circumstances were reversed, he knew he would be saying the same things. But at that moment, the rational, logical part of him was not controlling his words.

"Look," he said, "maybe there *is* another way. Maybe we could go off somewhere safe and you could send what information you have to Dockerty or . . . or to Dr. Armstrong. Of course, that's it – Dr. Armstrong." In spite of himself, the idea actually began to take hold. "She'd be perfect. You heard it yourself, Chris. Armstrong's absolutely set against euthanasia. She said it that night on Four South. And she's got clout. We could write her and she could – "

"David, please. Don't do this."

"No, wait, hear me out. Just let me finish. Charlotte Thomas wanted to die. As far as we can tell she was going to die no matter what. Oh, maybe another day of misery, or a few agonising weeks, but she was going to die." He shut his mind to the thoughtlessness of what he was saying, to the pressure he was putting on her. "From what you know of the woman, do you think she would want you, want us, to have our chance together snuffed out because you helped her accomplish what she simply

227

didn't have the strength to do herself? Just another day or two to think things over. That's all I'm asking. We'll find another way, or we'll go back and face things together. At least let's wait until we hear from Joey. Maybe we'll find out Vincent's in jail somewhere after all.''

She closed her eyes and held him with all her strength. In the silence that followed, the scene David had started to paint took form in her thoughts. It was a dusty village, nestled in a horseshoe of craggy mountains. She even saw their clinic, a white-clay building at the end of a sunbaked dirt street. She could feel the warmth and serenity of their life. She sensed the peace that would come from devoting herself to such a place and such a man.

Christine pressed her lips together and nodded. ''Okay. Another day. But no promises.''

''No promises.''

They made love in soft, unhurried harmony. For nearly an hour their eyes and mouths and fingertips explored one another. At last, when it felt as if neither of them could tolerate another touch without exploding, he entered her.

Marion Anderson Cooper was tough. Not only a tough cop, although he was that too, but in ways that only boys growing up with a girlish name on the streets of Roxbury could be tough. His toughness had been forged by rat bites as he lay on the shabby mattress he shared with his two brothers, and tempered by two years amid the mud and death of Vietnam. It was tested again and again by situations encountered as one of the first black sergeants assigned to the Little Italy section of Boston – the North End.

In the early morning hours of October 11th, Cooper was making his second round through the largely deserted streets of his patrol. From time to time, he stopped the cruiser to shine his light in the window of a store or restaurant where he sensed something out of the ordinary. Each time, he identified the source of his uneasiness – a new product display or repositioned table – and moved on.

The purple Fiat, parked inconspicuously by a rubbish skip in one of the back alleys had not been there on his earlier swing through the area. Cooper blocked the alley with the patrol car, flashed his spot on the licence plate and radioed the dispatcher.

"This is Alpha Nine-Twenty one," he said, "requesting stolen check and listing on a purple Fiat, Massachusetts licence number three-five-three, Mike, Whiskey, Quebec. Any back-up units available?"

"Negative, Alpha Nine-Twenty one. Repeat licence, please."

Cooper repeated the number and waited. The car was hot, he felt certain of that. In fact, he was surprised there hadn't been other redistributed vehicles on the first night of decent weather in over a week. If it were stolen, it was kids, not the pros. Had it been the pros, the little Fiat would have already been painted, supplied with new numbers and on its way to fill an order in Springfield or Fall River or someplace.

The delay seemed longer than usual. Cooper drummed impatiently on the wheel. He flipped on his walkie-talkie and was stepping out of the car when the radio crackled to life.

"Alpha Nine-Twenty one, I have information on 1979 Fiat sedan, Massachusetts licence three-five-three, Mike, Whiskey, Quebec." The woman's voice, sensuous and tantalising, was one Cooper recognised as belonging to a fat, mustachioed mother of five.

"This is Alpha Nine, Gladys," he said. "What have you got?"

"So far the car is clean as your whistle, Alpha nine, no wants, no warrants. Registered to Joseph Rosetti, twenty-one Damon Street, Apartment C."

"Alpha Nine out," Cooper said. As he entered the alley, he instinctively unsnapped the flap of his service revolver.

The driver's side door of the Fiat was open. Cooper shined his flashlight on the seats, then the floor. Nothing. Suddenly, he tensed. The thick, nauseating stench of blood – the perfume of death – filled his nostrils. Wedged behind the seats, covered by a scruffy tan blanket was a body. He took a quick breath and pulled the blanket aside. At that moment, all the toughness, all the gruesome battles in the rice paddies, the jungles and the city streets did not help.

Marion Anderson Cooper spun away from the car and puked on the pavement.

Joey's hands and feet were bound. He had been stabbed dozens of times before he died. Arranged neatly on his chest were one of his ears and parts of three fingers. The morning papers would dismiss his grisly death as "A probable gangland slaying".

Twenty miles north of the city, the real reason, a crudely sketched blood-smeared map, extracted after an hour of torture, rested on the passenger seat of Leonard Vincent's sedan.

21

Moving soundlessly, Christine set her suitcase by the front door and returned to the bedroom. Through eyes reddened by nearly an hour of crying, she peered across the pale early morning light at David. He was sleeping peacefully, his bushy hair partly buried in the pillow clutched to his face. With a painful glance at the letter wedged alongside the dresser mirror, she tiptoed out of the house.

The morning was chilly and still. Her breath, faintly visible, hung in the air. Far below, a thick mantle of silver covered the ocean as far as she could see. With movements as dreamlike as the world about her, she took the key from the jeep, dropped it in an envelope and walked slowly to her own car. Any moment, she expected to hear his voice calling to her from the balcony. The sight of him now, she knew, would snap her resolve like a dry twig.

Without a backward look, she slid onto the driver's seat of the Mustang and rolled it down the drive before starting the engine. At the end of the turn-off to Rocky Point, a quarter of a mile from the house, she stopped and placed the envelope with the key in a small pile of rocks. A final check to be certain David would have no trouble spotting it, then she turned left onto the winding ocean road, heading south to Boston.

The thoughts and feelings whirling inside her made it impossible to concentrate. She took no notice of the dark sedan that cruised past her in the other direction, nor of the huge, nondescript man behind the wheel. No notice, that is, until the car suddenly appeared in her rear-view mirror only a few yards behind and closing.

Leonard Vincent manoeuvred his car close to the smaller Mustang. Christine's momentary anger at being tailgated changed to terror as their bumpers made contact. At first, it was just a scrape, then a crunch. Suddenly, Vincent sped inside her on the right and began forcing her off the road. Christine's knuckles whitened on the wheel as she strained to keep from spinning out of control. She searched to her left for an escape route and instantly broke out into a terrified, icy sweat.

Not ten feet away was the edge of the drop — the high slope of rocks and trees where thirty-six hours ago she had stood and gazed for the first time at Rocky Point. The cliff plunged several hundred feet before reaching the Atlantic.

Suddenly there was another crunch, louder than before. Christine's head spun to the right to see the front of Vincent's car even with her passenger door. Beyond him, a shallow gully, then a sheer wall of sandstone. The Mustang vibrated mercilessly as its tyres bounced sideways. Christine slammed on the brake. The acrid smell of burning rubber filled the car.

Leonard Vincent's expression was bland, dispassionate as he forced her closer and closer to the drop. Less than five feet remained between the Mustang and the edge of the road when Christine released the brake and floored the accelerator. Her car shot forward. Out of the corner of her eye, she saw the sedan slip away. Then, the bumpers of the two cars locked.

In an instant, they were both out of control, spinning in a wild death dance across the road. Christine fought the wheel with all her strength, but it ripped from her hands. Her right arm slammed down against the gear shift and shattered just above the wrist. At the moment the white-hot pain registered, Christine's car hit the sandstone wall. Her head shot forward, smashing into the windshield. The glass exploded and instantly her world went black.

She did not hear the screech of tearing metal as the two cars separated. She did not see the wide-eyed terror in Leonard Vincent's face as his car snapped free of hers like a whip then catapulted towards the ocean, hitting the steep slope nose-down, and bouncing off trees and boulders, somersaulting until it disappeared in the thick fog. She did not feel her own car ricochet off the rock face, spin full circle, then roll towards the drop.

She lay unconscious on the seat when the rear wheels of the Mustang dropped over the embankment. The car stopped, its chassis teetering on the soft dirt. Then, it slid slowly over the edge.

David felt the emptiness even before he was fully awake. He opened his eyes a slit, then closed them tightly, trying to will what he knew was true not to be so. She's in the living room, sitting quietly, looking out at the ocean. A dollar says she's in the living room. He held his breath. The silence in the house was more than the simple absence of sound. It was a void, a nothingness. There was no movement of air, no sense of energy, no life.

She's gone for a walk, he reasoned desperately. He rolled towards the window, blinking at the sunless glare. The sky was a thin sheet of pearl – the sort of overcast that would miraculously disappear by mid-morning, opening like a curtain on the extravaganza of a new day. A morning walk, that's all.

He pushed himself to one elbow and scanned the room. The realisation that her clothes were gone sank in only moments before he saw the envelope wedged along side the mirror. It was the scene from countless grade B movies, only this time it was real. Sadness as flat as the morning sky swept through him.

"Shit," was his first word of the day. Then his second and third. He pulled himself out of bed and walked purposefully past the dresser into the bathroom. He peed, then washed, then shaved. He limped to the kitchen and put on water for coffee. The ankle was stiff and slow, but almost free of pain. His nurse had done her job well.

He tidied the living room and waited for the water to boil. In one final surge of hope, he checked the driveway. The Mustang was gone. Christine was gone. Mexico and any chance for a new life together were gone.

Numbly, he shuffled back to the bedroom.

His name was printed in the centre of the plain, white envelope. He watched his hands tear it open. Another note. The second one in less than a week. This time, though, he felt the anguish in every word.

Dear David,
    I couldn't chance waiting for you to wake up and talk me out of doing this. I tried all night to make myself believe there was another way. God, how I tried. In the end, though, all I could think of was how much pain and sadness I've caused you.
It's all so very crazy. Something that seemed so good, so right. And now . . . I am going to see Lt. Dockerty to make a full confession about Charlotte. Before I do, I am going to meet

Dr. Armstrong. What you said last night made so much sense. I know she can help me. Despite what has happened, I know in my heart that most of us are only following principles we believe in. With luck, Dr. Armstrong can help put matters to rest with as little public disclosure as possible. I have three names to give her for starters, plus some phone numbers and a few Clinton Foundation newsletters. That's not much, but it's a start.

Maybe, we can find a way of getting inside the secrecy.

Then there is the matter of who is responsible for hiring Ben's killer. I'll do what I can to find out before involving the police.

Finally, there is you – a special, magic man. In so short a time, you have reached places inside me that I'm not sure I even knew existed. For that, and much more, I owe you. I owe you a life free from running, from constantly looking over my shoulder. I owe you a chance to fulfil the dreams you've worked so hard for.

If the circumstances were any different, sweet, gentle David, I would have risked it. Gone wherever we decided. But circumstances are not different . . . Don't worry about me. I'll go straight to Dockerty after I see Dr. Armstrong. Just be careful yourself.

Please understand, be strong, and most of all, forgive me for causing you so much hurt.

Love,
Christine

P.S. The key to the jeep will be at the end of the turn-off for Rocky Point. It's in an envelope like this one.

The jeep. David laughed in spite of himself. From an even start it was doubtful the jeep could stay with Christine's Mustang for more than a few yards. She was certainly determined not to be dissuaded. Well, he would not be dissuaded either. He could not change the situation, so he would simply change his expectations. Whatever she had to face, he would face with her as long as she wanted him there.

David dressed, playing through in his mind the situations the two of them might encounter in the days and weeks ahead. He noticed the bulky sweater he had worn on the ride to Rocky Point. Christine had placed it neatly folded on a chair by the bureau. David grinned. Perhaps he could return it to Joey as a contribution towards the wardrobe of the next man chased into the Charles River. As he picked it up, Rosetti's heavy revolver fell out. David had completely forgotten about it.

He weighed the revolver in one hand, and felt the queasy tension he had come to expect when handling guns of any kind. When was Joey to call again. Last night? This morning? A moment of reflection, and he went to the phone. Rosetti's Boston number was printed on a small card taped to the receiver.

The woman's voice that answered his call was older than Terry's.

"Hello, is that the Rosetti's residence?" he asked.

"Yes. Can I help you?"

"Well, could I speak with Mr. or Mrs. Rosetti, please?" For a time there was silence on the other end.

"Who is that, please?" the woman asked finally. Her voice was cold and flat.

David began to shift nervously from one foot to the other. "My name is David Shelton. I'm a friend of Joey and Terry's, and I'm stay – "

"I know who you are, Dr. Shelton," the woman said dully. Again there was silence. David felt an awful sinking in his gut. "This is Mrs. D'Ambrosio, Terry's mother. Terry can't come to the phone. The doctor's given her some medicine and . . ." Suddenly, the woman began to cry. "Joey's dead . . . murdered," she sobbed. David dropped to the couch and stared unseeing across the room. "Terry hasn't been able to talk to the police, but she's talked to me, and she said it's because Joey helped you that's he dead." She broke down completely, any pretext of anger at him lost in her grief.

"But that's . . . impossible," he mumbled, his mind whirling. It was Leonard Vincent. It had to be. He pressed his eyes shut, trying to stop the spinning. First Ben, now Joey . . . and Christine out there somewhere. "When did this happen?" The words came out woodenly.

"Early this morning. They found him in his car, stabbed and cut and . . . Dr. Shelton, I just don't want to talk to you any more. Joey's funeral is Tuesday, you can speak with my daughter after that."

"But wait . . . " The woman hung up.

For several minutes, David sat motionless, oblivious to the bleating of the receiver in his lap. Then he grabbed the sweater and the revolver, along with his crutches, and raced from the house. Hoping against hope, he checked the jeep. There was no key. He threw the gun on the seat and pushed himself down the road in long, swinging arcs. By the time he returned, nearly half an hour had passed. He was soaked with perspiration, gasping for air. His ribs, battered by the unpadded arm supports, screamed as he pulled himself up behind the wheel.

"Calm down," he panted to himself. "She's fine. She's all right." He started the motor. She was probably in Dr. Armstrong's office right now, or even with Dockerty. All he had to do was cool down and get to Boston in one piece.

He glanced over at the revolver and thought about Rosetti's advice. How had he put it? Do it unto others if you even think they're gonna do it unto you? Something like that. David shuddered, then cradled the gun in his hands. Had Joey died because he didn't have the revolver when he needed it? The possibility drained what little spirit David had left. All that remained was anger. Anger, and a consuming hatred. He would find Vincent, or whoever had murdered Joey. He would find them and kill them or die trying. He pummelled his clenched fist into the palm of his other hand until both began to hurt. Finally, he put the jeep in gear and started down the driveway.

Concern for Christine diluted his anger with a sense of urgency. He glanced at his watch. It was after nine. He tried accelerating, but the carburettor, choked on dust and sand, flooded. Above, the frail overcast was showing the first signs of surrender to the autumn sun. He forced himself to loosen up, and restarted the engine. By the time he reached the ocean road, he had mastered a rhythm of shifting and acceleration that was acceptable to the old jalopy. His thoughts returned to Christine. Perhaps he should have called the police. If she didn't have too great a start, at least they could detain her long enough for him to catch up. But who? The State Police? Would she be upset if he involved them before she was ready. He turned the notion over in his mind. He had decided to stop at the first phone booth when he saw the flashing lights and barriers of a roadblock ahead.

A battered maroon pick-up truck in front of him was struggling to do a U-turn, its grizzled driver mouthing obscenities. David leaned out of the jeep and called to him.

"Hey, what's going on up there?"

"Eh?" The man stopped the truck mid-manoeuvre, blocking the road.

236

"Up ahead, what's happened?" David tried again, this time shouting.

"Accident. Bad one too, damn it." The old man's tone left no doubt that he was taking the inconvenience personally. "Two cars over the side. One they just hauled up. One's comin' from way at the bottom. Fifteen, twenty minutes more, they said. Probably be an hour the way Mac Perkins works that old tow rig of his."

Uneasily, David strained to see past the truck. "Did you see either of the cars involved?" he called.

"Eh?"

David groaned. "The cars," he yelled, "did you see either . . . ? Oh, never mind. Could I get by please?"

"Sure, but you ain't goin' nowhere. An' there's no need for you to go snappin' about it neither." All at once, David's questions registered. "The cars, you say? Did I see the cars?" Totally exasperated, David nodded. "Only the little blue one," the man called out. "Smashed to smithereens it is, too."

David's hands clenched the wheel, and terror knotted his stomach. He closed his eyes as the old man worked his pick-up out of the way. In that instant, the photo-like image of another accident appeared in his mind. The rain, the lights, Becky's and Ginny's faces, even their screams. Now, Christine . . . He had no doubt that the blue car the old man had seen was hers.

"Mister, road's closed. I'm afraid you'll have to turn around."

David whirled towards the voice. It was a State Trooper, tall and thin, with a schoolboy face that made him look slightly ridiculous in his authoritative blue and grey uniform. Before David could respond, his gaze swung past the spot where the truck had been to the cluster of police cars, trucks and ambulances ahead. In the midst of them, resting on flattened tyres, was the shattered, twisted wreck of Christine's Mustang.

"Mister . . . ?" The young trooper's voice held some concern.

David's face was ashen. "I . . . I know the woman who was driving that car," he said in a remote, hollow voice. "She was a . . . friend."

"Mister, are you all right?" When David did not answer the trooper called down the road, "Gus, send one of the paramedics over here. I think this guy's gonna pass out or something." He opened the door of the jeep. As he did, David pushed past him and began a hobbling run towards the car, oblivious to the jagged salvos of pain from his ankle. He stumbled the last five yards, falling heavily against the door. Gasping, he stretched his arm across the roof and held on. The car was empty. The windshield was blown out, and the engine had been smashed backwards into the body of the car. An ugly brown bloodstain stood out against the soft blue seat cover.

"God damn it," he cried softly. "God damn it . . . God damn it!" He was screaming.

Several men rushed towards him just as the trooper took his arm.

"Mister, please calm down," he said in more of a plea than an order. He led David to the side of the road and propped him against the trunk of a half-dead birch.

After a minute, David managed to speak. "Wh . . . where is she ?" he stammered.

"What?"

"Her body, damn it," he screamed. "What have they done with it?"

The young man grinned suddenly with relief. "Mister, there isn't any body. Not from this car anyway."

David sank to one knee and stared up at him.

"Passerby found the lady wanderin' down the road," the trooper explained. "Pretty battered up, with a nasty cut or two, and probably a broken arm, but nowhere near dead. Now, can you calm down enough to tell me who you are?"

Kensington Community Hospital, a twenty minute drive according to the trooper, took thirty-five in the jeep. David had stayed at the accident scene for a short while, learning what he could. Christine's survival was miraculous. A couple had come upon her, bloodied and incoherent, wandering along the road. Later, the rescue team found her Mustang wedged upside down against a tree fifty feet down the rocky slope and nearly half a mile from where she was picked up.

David remained long enough to watch with total dispassion as Leonard Vincent's mangled corpse was prised from his car and transferred to an ambulance. He left during the commotion that followed the discovery in the wreckage of a silenced revolver and a variety of knives. As he drove to the hospital, he felt renewed hatred not for Leonard Vincent, but for those who had hired him.

The hospital was fairly new and very small – fifty beds or less, David guessed. He paused for a moment inside the front door trying to get the feel of the place. The lobby was deserted save for the salmon-coated volunteer behind the desk, rearranging the contents of her handbag. To her right, an impressive brass board listed the two dozen or so physicians on the hospital staff. Beside each name was a small amber bulb which the physician could switch on when he was "in the house." Only one had a glowing amber light. No one could accuse Kensington Community Hospital of being overstaffed, he thought sardonically.

The emergency wing was labelled with black, paste-on letters above a set of automatic doors. As they slid shut behind him, David heard the volunteer say, "Can I help you, sir?" He shook his head without bothering to look back.

The physician on duty, an Indian woman with dark, tired eyes met him half way down the corridor. She wore a light orange sari beneath her clinic coat, and had a White Memorial Hospital name tag that identified her as Dr. T. Ranganathan.

"Excuse me," David said anxiously, "my name is Dr. David Shelton. I'm a surgeon at Boston Doctors. A friend of mine, Christine Beall, was brought in here a short time ago."

"Ah, yes, the automobile accident," she said in precise English. "I saw her only briefly before Dr. St. Onge arrived and . . . ah . . . took over the case. She has a fractured wrist and possibly some fractured ribs on the left side. Also two scalp lacerations. However, at the time Dr. St. Onge dismissed me, she seemed in no immediate danger. You will find her in there." She pointed at one of the rooms.

In addition to St. Onge, three others were in the room with Christine – an orderly, the lab technician, and a second nurse. David ignored them all and rushed to the examining table. "Dr. St. Onge, I'm Dr. David Shelton," he said looking only at Christine. She was lying on her side, sterile drapes over her head. A large patch of hair had been shaved away from above her left ear. The drapes surrounded an ugly, three-inch gash which was nearly sutured shut.

"David?" Christine's voice was the empty whimper of a lost child.

He knelt by the table a safe distance from the sterile field. "Yes, hon, it's me." The reassurance in his voice belied the anger and sadness inside him. "You're doin' fine. A few dents, but you're doin' just fine."

"We're a pair, aren't we," she said weakly. The few words were all she could manage.

"And who the hell are you?" St. Onge was obviously not satisfied with David's introduction. He was a heavy man, barrel-chested with thick hands. His tan was still mid-summer dark and his clothes custom-made. David guessed him to be about fifty.

"Oh, I'm sorry," he said, backing off a step. "My name is Shelton, David Shelton. I'm on the surgical staff at Boston Doctors. Christine is a . . . close friend."

"Well, right now she's my patient," St. Onge growled. "I'm sure you wouldn't take too kindly to someone barging in on your work. Even if he was a fellow surgeon."

David swallowed his instinctive reply, and mumbled, "I'm sorry. Could you tell me how she is?"

St. Onge rummaged through his set of instruments, found a needle holder, and returned to the cut.

"She has another gash I've already closed above this one. She's got a busted arm that Stan Keyes will probably have to reduce in the operating room. That is providing he doesn't capsize and drown in that stupid regatta he's racing in today."

David stiffened. "Is he the only orthopaedist available?"

"Yup. But don't worry. Fortunately, he's a damn sight better orthopaedic surgeon than he is a sailor." St. Onge chuckled. "The arm will keep until he gets back."

David grit his teeth, and turned his attention to the bank of four X-ray view boxes on the wall across from the bed litter and studied the views taken of Christine's chest, abdomen, ribs, forearm and skull. The forearm fracture was a bad one, with multiple fragments, but fortunately did not involve the joint space. The function of her hand would probably be unimpaired. He thought about the superb orthopaedic staff at Boston Doctors, and began wondering if a transfer there would be possible.

St. Onge finished suturing the laceration as David was

snapping the four films of Christine's skull into place. The man whipped off his gloves with a flourish, letting them fall to the floor. "Use one of my standard head injury order sheets, Tammy," he said, "Keyes will probably want to transfer her to his service anyway when he does the wrist. Any questions, Dr. . . . "

"Shelton," David said icily, brushing past him and kneeling by Christine. The sterile drape had been discarded and David could appreciate for the first time the extent of the battering she had absorbed. Despite some attempt to clean her up, patches of dried, cracking blood still covered her face and neck. Almost the entire left side of her scalp had been shaved, exposing the two angry gashes. Tiny diamonds of glass sparkled in the rest of her hair. Her upper lip was the size and colour of a small plum.

"Christine," he said softly. "How're you holding up?"

"Oh David . . . " Her words were agonised, tearless sobs. David's fists tightened against his thighs.

"Dr. St. Onge, has a radiologist gone over her films?" He rose with deliberate slowness and turned towards the man.

"Why, no. The radiologist has left for the day. On call if necessary, but I didn't see any reason to call him in for findings as obvious as . . . "

"Excuse me, Miss," David cut in. "Could I have an otoscope please. And while you're at it an ophthalmoscope." The woman had a bemused expression on her face as she handed the instruments over. St. Onge was speechless.

David slipped the otoscope tip in Christine's left ear. At that moment St. Onge found his tongue. "Now you just wait one goddamn minute," he said. "That woman is still my patient, and if you . . . "

"No!" David snarled the word. "*You* wait one goddamn minute. This woman is being transferred to Boston."

"Why you have a fucking nerve!" St. Onge was crimson. "I'll have you up before the medical board for this, big city credentials and all."

"Please do," David bellowed sarcastically. The marginal control he had maintained disappeared completely. "And while we're there, we'll ask why you were too arrogant to call in a radiologist to look at these films. We'll ask why you missed the basilar skull fracture in two of the views. We'll also ask how you overlooked the blood behind her left ear drum caused by that fracture. Okay?" The silence in the room was painful. He lowered his voice and turned to the nurses. "Could one of you call an ambulance for us, please?"

The nurse hesitated, then with an unmistakable glint in her eye said, "Yes, Doctor," and rushed out. St. Onge looked apoplectic.

David turned to the remaining nurse. "I'm going to need some meds and equipment for the trip. I'll send the stuff back with the ambulance. Meanwhile, could you hang a Ringer's lactate I.V., please. Fifty cc's per hour."

"I'll have your ass for this, Shelton." St. Onge hissed each word then stalked away.

David used the phone at the nurses' station to call Dr. Armstrong. As he was dialling, he heard giggles and a muted cheer from the staff in Christine's room.

"David, I've been worried sick about you," Dr. Armstrong said. "What's going on? Are you all right?"

"I'm fine, Dr. Armstrong. Really," he said. "But Christine Beall isn't. Do you remember her? The nurse on Four South?"

"I think . . . yes, of course I do. A lovely girl. What's wrong?"

"She's had an accident. Automobile. We're at Kensington Community Hospital now, but I'm on my way with her to the Doctors Hospital E.R. Could you meet us there and take over? She's got a fractured arm, a basilar skull fracture, and some chest trauma, so you'll probably end up being traffic cop for a three ring circus of consultants. Will you do it?"

"Of course I'll do it," Dr. Armstrong said. "Are you sure she can handle the trip?"

"Sure enough to try. Any risk is worth taking to get her out of here. Especially with you there waiting for her. I have a lot to talk to you about, but all of it can wait until you get Christine taken care of. We'll be there within an hour."

"That will be fine," Dr. Armstrong said softly. "I'll be waiting."

22

At David's instructions, the ambulance ride was made at a steady fifty. No lights, no sirens. The fifty-five minute drive seemed interminable, but what little time they might save by a dramatic dash to the city was hardly worth the risk of an accident.

During the trip Christine slipped in and out of consciousness. David, seated at her right hand, systematically checked her pulse, respiration, blood pressure, and pupil size, looking for changes that might indicate a sudden rise in the pressure against her brain. Any significant increase, either from bleeding or swelling, and he would have only minutes to reverse the process before permanent damage began.

The tension was suffocating. He had acted decisively in dealing with St. Onge, but had he been too hasty? The thought ate away at him. Any crisis in the moving ambulance would be immeasurably more difficult to handle than in the hospital. It was the sort of decision he had spent years in training to deal with, the sort of decision he had unflinchingly made many times over the years. But this was different.

"Christine?" He squeezed her hand. There was no response. "Let's go over the equipment again," he said to the paramedic riding alongside him. Out of David's field of vision, the man shook his head in exasperation. Granted it was the first time he had ever carried instruments for drilling cranial burr holes, but this was the third check David had asked him to make.

On the off-chance Christine could hear, David turned his back to her and whispered the list of instruments and medications. The paramedic held each one up, or signalled that he knew exactly where it was. Scalpels, drill bits, anaesthetic, laryngoscope, tubes, breathing bag, adrenalin, cortisone, suction catheters, intracardiac needle: they were prepared for the worst.

"Pulse: one ten and firm; respiration: twenty; B.P.: One sixty over sixty; pupils four millimetres, equal and reactive." The words became a litany, every two minutes. Dutifully, the paramedic repeated then charted them. There was no banter between the two men. No communication at all, in fact, other than the numbers, every two minutes. Pulse . . . respiration . . . B.P. . . . pupils.

As they entered the outskirts of Boston, the tension mounted. David, constantly moving, checking, re-checking, rousing Christine. The paramedic, nervous in spite of himself, fingering the instruments of crisis. The driver, a burly young man with thick brown curls, growled a few words into the two-way radio and toyed with the control switches for the lights and siren. They were close enough now. Any sign of trouble in the back and he would make a run for it, doctor's orders or not.

Suddenly, the trip was over. The ambulance swung a sharp U-turn and backed up to the raised receiving platform. The doors flew open. A nurse burst into the ambulance and, with a glance at Christine, went straight for the intravenous bag. Right behind her, an orderly grabbed one side of the collapsible stretcher. A quick nod from the paramedic and they were gone, the nurse, running to keep up, holding the I.V. bag aloft.

David was about to follow when he caught a brief glimpse of Margaret Armstrong. She met the team half-way across the cement platform and began her examination even before they reached the entrance. Her white clinic coat, unbuttoned, swung behind her like a queen's cape. Her every movement, every expression exuded control and competence. David sank back onto the seat. They had made it. They were home. The decision to move, however hasty, had held up. As relief swept through him, David began to shake.

He wove his way across the busy reception area and headed straight to the trauma wing. Was he imagining it, or was everyone – staff and patients – staring at him? Phoenix, rising from the ashes; Lazarus from the dead.

Pausing outside Trauma Room 12 he glanced inside. The room was empty. He shuddered at the memory of Leonard Vincent's knife gliding across his throat. Then he thought about Rosetti. As soon as Christine was out of immediate danger and he had finished speaking with Dr. Armstrong, he would go and see Terry.

As David approached Trauma 1, Dr. Armstrong emerged and

beckoned him inside. Christine was awake. Through a sea of white coats – residents, technicians and nurses – her eyes, sunken shadows, met his. For a moment, all he saw was pain. Then, as he drew closer, he saw the sparkle – the flicker of strength. Her swollen, discoloured lips pulled tightly as she tried to smile.

"We made it," she whispered. David nodded. "I . . . I'm glad we're here."

Her eyes closed. A reed-thin surgical resident moved in, swabbed russet antiseptic over her right upper chest and prepared to insert a sub-clavian intravenous line. As the man slipped the needle beneath Christine's collarbone, David grimaced and turned away. He came face to face with Margaret Armstrong, who was standing several feet behind him watching quietly.

"David, I'm so relieved to see that you're all right," she said. "The stories that followed your brief visit here the other night were quite frightening."

"There's trouble in this hospital – in a lot of hospitals, in fact. I have a great deal to talk to you about, Dr. Armstrong," David said. He glanced over his shoulder at the resident, who was calmly suturing the plastic intravenous catheter in place with a stitch through the skin of Christine's chest. "What about Christine?"

"Well," said Dr. Armstrong, leading him out of the room, "I'll examine her more carefully as soon as the crowd in there has finished. My initial impressions add little to yours. She has a definite skull fracture, and some blood behind that drum, but so far she seems neurologically stable. I have both a neurosurgeon and an orthopaedic man waiting in the house, but I think we'll hold off on the wrist until we've had a chance to watch her. Ivan Rudnick is the neurosurgeon. Do you know him?" David nodded. Rudnick was the best on the staff, if not in the city. "Well, Ivan will see her and do a CAT scan as soon as possible. If there's no evidence of active bleeding, we'll wait and hope."

"What about her chest trauma?" David asked.

"No problem as far as I can see. ECG shows no cardiac injury pattern. My more extensive exam should help confirm it."

"Dr. Armstrong, I'm really grateful to you for handling this."

"Nonsense," she said. "I can't tell you how flattered – and pleased – I am that you would ask me. By the way," she added, "there is one small problem."

"Oh?" David's eyes narrowed.

"Nothing critical, David, but there are no ICU beds. We're checking on one post-op patient now, but he's been very unstable and I doubt we'll be able to move him. I've decided we'll be all right putting Christine in a private room. There's one available on Four South. I know the girls up there will give her closer attention than she could ever get anywhere else, including the ICU. She'll be moved up there as soon as possible."

"That sounds fine," David said. "If the nurses don't mind, I'll hang around and do what I can to help monitor her. That is, after you and I have had our discussion."

"Yes," said Dr. Armstrong distantly.

"Well, you go ahead and finish. I'll wait in the doctors' lounge until you're free to talk. By the way, which room will she be going to?"

"Pardon?"

"The room," David said. "What room is she going to?"

"Oh, ah, I have it right here. It's four-twelve. Four South room four-twelve." The cardiologist smiled then disappeared into Trauma 1.

412! David swallowed hard. Charlotte Thomas's room! Step one on the road that had led through one land of madness after another. He fought his sense of superstition and pondered instead on the irony. Room 412 would serve as the first command post in their battle to bring The Sisterhood of Life to an end. He wandered across the reception area to the doctors' lounge and stretched out with a copy of the monthly periodical, *Medical Economics.* The lead article was entitled "Ten Tax Shelters Even Your Accountant May Not Know". Before he had settled into shelter number one, David was asleep.

An hour later, the phone above his head jangled him free of a frightening series of dreams in which Christine died again and again in one grisly manner after another.

His clothes were uncomfortably damp and the sandpaper feeling in his mouth made it difficult to speak.

"On-call room. Shelton here," he said thickly.

"David? It's Margaret Armstrong. Did I wake you?"

"No, I mean, yes. I mean I wasn't exactly . . ."

"Well," she cut in, "our Christine is safely in her room.

246

Nothing new for me to add to what we already know. I think she'll be all right."

"Wonderful."

"Yes . . . it is." Armstrong paused. "You said you wanted to talk with me?"

"Oh yes, I certainly do. That is if you . . . "

"This would be an excellent time," she interrupted again. "I'm in my office – not the one in the office tower, the one on North Two."

"I know where it is," said David, at last fully awake. "I can be there in five minutes."

The cardiac exercise laboratory doubled as Margaret Armstrong's "in house" office.

David knocked once on the door marked "Stress and Exercise Testing", then walked in. The small, comfortable waiting room was empty. He hesitated then called, "Dr. Armstrong? It's me, David."

"David, come in." Armstrong appeared at the door. "I was just making some coffee."

As he passed where she had been standing, David breathed in the distinctive smell of liquor.

Instinctively, he checked his watch. It was not yet noon. He ran through a number of explanations as to why the Chief of Cardiology might be drinking under such circumstances, especially at such an hour. None really fitted. Still, the woman seemed quite in control. For the moment, at least, he forced the concern to the back of his mind.

The lab was spacious and well equipped. Several treadmills and exercise bicycles each with a set of monitoring instruments were lined up across the room. The required emergency equipment and defibrillator unit were placed discreetly to one side – an effort, David knew, to avoid alarming patients already nervous about their cardiac testing.

One end of the suite had been set aside as a conference area, with a maple love seat and several hard-backed chairs encircling a low, round coffee table. Armstrong motioned David to the love seat, then brought a percolator and two cups. She seemed more subdued than David could ever remember.

"You seem tired," he said. "If it would be better for us to talk later, I could . . ."

"No, no. This is fine," she said sharply. "Hospital politics, you know. But for a change, I get to sit back and listen. Let me pour us some coffee, then you can fill me in on what has been going on."

She pushed a carton of cream towards him, but he shook his head. "Where to start," he said, using a few sips to sort out his words.

"The beginning?" She encouraged him with a comfortable smile.

"The beginning. Yes. Well, I guess the beginning is that I didn't give the morphine to Charlotte Thomas. Christine did." He sipped some tea. "Dr. Armstrong, what I've got to tell you is incredible, potentially explosive stuff. Christine and I have decided to share it with you because . . . well, because we hoped you might use your position and influence to help us."

"David, you know that I'll put myself and whatever influence I have at your disposal." She leaned forward to give him a closer view of the reassurance in her eyes.

In minutes, he was totally immersed in relating the story of Charlotte Thomas and the Sisterhood of Life.

Initially Armstrong encouraged him with a series of nods, gestures and smiles, interrupting occasionally to clarify a point. Soon, though, her posture grew more rigid, her gaze more impassive. Gradually, subtly, the warm blue invitation in her eyes turned cold. Still, David talked on, relieved at unburdening himself of the awesome secrets that, until now, he was the only outsider to know. Nearly half an hour passed before he first sensed the change in her.

"Is . . . is something the matter?" he asked.

Without responding, Armstrong rose and walked unsteadily to a telephone resting on a small desk at the opposite end of the lab. After a brief, hushed conversation, she worked her way back and settled heavily into a chair across the table from him. All at once, she seemed frail, and very much older.

"David," she said gravely, "have you discussed all this with anyone else?"

"Why no. I told you that earlier. We were hoping you could help us, without involving - "

"I'd like you to start over again. There are some points you must clarify for me."

"Chris, are you awake? Can you hear me?"

The voice seemed to be echoing from a great distance. Christine opened her eyes, then blinked several times, straining to focus. She recognised the woman as a nurse though her features remained blurred. She tried to turn to the side. Waves of nausea and an excruciating pressure in her head made it impossible. The room was dark, but even the light from the hallway was unbearable. "I'm awake," she said. "The light hurts my eyes." Slowly, she closed them.

"Chris, Dr. Armstrong ordered your pupils to be checked every hour. I'll do it as quickly as I can."

Christine felt the nurse's fingers on her right eye, then a searing pain as the beam from the penlight hit her pupil. A brief respite, then a second stab on the left. She tried to lift her hands, but they would not move. Was she restrained? Her right arm, especially, felt heavy and numb. For a moment, she worried that it was gone. Then she remembered being told by Dr. Armstrong that it was broken. She settled back on the pillow and tried to relax.

"Listen, I'm going to let you sleep for a while," the nurse said. "You're due for a new I.V. in about twenty minutes. I'm going to wake you up then and we'll try to get some more of this glass out of your hair. Okay?" Christine nodded as best she could. "Hey, I almost forgot. Only a few hours in the hospital, and already you're getting flowers. These were delivered a couple of minutes ago. They're beautiful. I'm going to put them on the table here. I know you can't see them, but maybe by tonight you'll be able to. There's a card. Do you want me to read it?"

"Yes, please," Christine said weakly.

"It says best wishes for a speedy recovery, Dahlia."

Dahlia? The pain and the swelling in her brain made it difficult to concentrate. "But . . . I . . . don't . . . know . . . any . . . Dahlia," she said.

The woman had already left.

"David, this killer, this . . . this Vincent, you must tell me again how you think he found you on the emergency ward, and then was able to locate your friend."

David toyed with the cover of a magazine, then dropped it on the coffee table and rubbed his eyes. What had started as a comfortable, long-awaited unburdening had mutated into a tense interrogation as Dr. Armstrong probed for every possible detail. He felt off-balance, bewildered and threatened by the persistence of her questions, and the strain in her voice.

"Look," he said, no longer trying to conceal his mounting apprehension. "I've told you everything I know. Twice. My theories about how Vincent found Ben and me, and then Joey, are just that – theories. Dr. Armstrong, I know something is going on here. Something that I've said has upset you. I'm not going to tell you any more until you level with me. Now please, what is the matter?"

The look in her eyes was glacial. "Young man, much of what you have told me is impossible. Preposterous. A series of sick, misguided conclusions that can only cause pain and suffering to many good, innocent people." David stared at her in disbelief. "You are stirring flames of a fire whose scope you do not understand. This so-called killer you have described, it is impossible that he is connected in any way with The Sisterhood of Life."

"But . . ."

"Impossible, I say!" She screamed the words.

"Just what is impossible?" Their heads spun in unison towards the door. Dotty Dalrymple stood calmly watching, her hands buried in the pockets of her uniform. David's skin began to crawl at the sight of her.

"Oh, Dorothy, I'm glad you could make it down this quickly." Armstrong's voice was tense, but composed. "I phoned you because Dr. Shelton here has been telling me an astounding tale about an organisation called The Sisterhood of Life."

"Oh?" Dalrymple said.

"Yes. He maintains that both you and Christine Beall belong to the group, along with Janet Poulos and other nurses at this hospital. But most disturbing is that he believes The Sisterhood of Life is responsible for hiring the man who killed his lawyer and one of his friends.''

''And?''

''And I told him that simply couldn't be so. I suggested that he confront you with his preposterous theories, so that together you might go to Christine and explain to her the impossibility of any organisation to which you might belong being involved in hiring murderers.''

''I'm afraid I can't do that,'' Dalrymple said, still resting some of her weight against the door frame. She smiled at the two of them and shrugged. ''I would be lying.'' The nursing director lifted her right hand free. Nearly lost in the fleshy ball of her fist was a snub-nosed revolver.

''The light . . . please turn it off.'' Christine felt the glare even through tightly closed eyes.

Two women – a nurse and an aide – were picking fragments of glass from her hair with tweezers. ''All right, Chris,'' one of them said. ''I guess we've put you through enough for now. I have to rouse you in forty minutes. We can do a little more then. Okay?'' She shut off the overhead light. ''Wait a minute. I'm sorry, but I have to turn it back on. Just a few seconds to adjust the flow of your new I.V.

''Prime rib of beef and pheasant were on your little menu sheet, but since you didn't circle anything, we decided to serve you the speciality of the house: dextrose and water.''

A ten second blaze of light and, again, the room dimmed. Christine tried to ignore the throbbing in her skull.

''By the way,'' the nurse said. ''Ol' Tweedledum was on the floor a few minutes ago. She herded all of us into the conference room just to make it clear that heads would roll if you didn't get first class service from everyone. As if we would give you anything else. Well . . . see you later.''

Christine heard the woman leave. ''Tweedledum.'' For a time, she wrestled with the name. Then she remembered. Dalrymple! Suddenly bits and pieces of information were swirling about in her head. Dalrymple condemning David. Dalrymple offering a bribe. Her mind, working sluggishly through bruised, swollen tissues struggled to slot them together. Apprehension began to rise in her, and fuelled the already

251

unbearable pounding in her head. Dalrymple! Could she have been responsible? Nothing made sense. Nothing, except that she had to find David. Had to talk to him. She tried to move, to reach the bedside phone. Her free hand touched it, then knocked it clattering to the floor.

She searched for the call button. They had pinned it somewhere. Where? Where did they say it was?

From the darkness over the bed, the intravenous fluid flowed inexorably from the plastic bag, through the tubing, and into her chest.

Christine was fumbling through the bedclothes for the call button when her pain began to abate. An uncomfortable warmth took hold and spread deep within her. David . . . call David. Christine battled to maintain her resolve. Her eyelids closed, then refused to open again. So much to do, she thought. David . . . Sisterhood . . . so much to do.

Thirty seconds alone at the nurses' station were all Dotty Dalrymple had needed to empty the vial into Christine's new I.V. fluid.

Christine's head sank back on the pillow. Her hand relaxed and fell to her side. Suddenly nothing seemed to matter. Nothing at all. She listened for a time to the strange hum that filled the room. Then, with an inaudible sigh, she surrendered to the darkness.

Dalrymple motioned Armstrong to the chair next to David. Her brown eyes flashed hatred at both of them. Her fat, dimpled finger moved nervously against the trigger.

"Dorothy, please," Armstrong begged. "We've come so far. Shared so much. You're just overtired. Perhaps . . . ''

"Oh, Peggy, just sit back and shut up," she snapped.

David looked at Armstrong. "Peggy? You? But you're a . . . ''

"Doctor?" Armstrong filled in the word. "A few more years of studying, that's the only difference for me between being a nurse and a doctor." She turned back to Dalrymple. "Dorothy, you know I'm on your side."

"Are you? Are you really on anyone's side but your own? Even now you've been trying to dodge admitting to Dr. Shelton here exactly who you are. You never did go to see Christine Beall. It's not your name she associates with The Sisterhood. It's not you whose life would have gone down the drain if that lawyer Beall spoke to had gone to the police. Believe me, Peggy, I have far too much going for me to sit back and let that happen.''

"But you . . . you hired a killer?" Dalrymple nodded. "Dorothy, how could you do a thing like that?"

"Now don't start getting high and mighty with me. Killing's our game, isn't it? You taught it to me. You draw your line one place, and I draw mine another. No real difference. You were perfectly willing to forge prescriptions and sacrifice Shelton here to save your precious Sisterhood. I'll bet if *you* had gone to see Beall – if it had been *your* neck on the block – you would have done the same things to protect yourself as I did."

"Perhaps," Armstrong said somewhat nervously. "Yes, yes, perhaps I would."

"Really?" Dalrymple sneered. "And just what did you plan to do with Shelton here while I was off pulling the noose tighter around my neck with Beall? Would you have what it takes to use this gun? To pull the trigger?" Armstrong's response was too slow. "You're weak, Peggy," Dalrymple spat. "Selfish and weak. All you've thought about for years is the glory you would reap from having The Sisterhood become public knowledge. I would never have allowed that to happen, Peggy. Never!"

Armstrong raised her hands in protest, but Dalrymple silenced her with a flick of the gun. "I'm afraid you have both become unacceptable liabilities," she said. She reached into her pocket and, smiling, withdrew a large syringe filled to capacity. Then she checked her watch. "One o'clock. If my nurses are as efficient at their jobs as I have trained them to be, the I.V. ordered on young Miss Beall should be up and running."

Christine's death sentence! David stared at Dalrymple with sudden panic. "What did you give her?" He shifted his feet for better leverage and began searching for an opening, however slight.

Dalrymple sensed his thoughts and levelled the revolver at his face. "It would be useless to try anything." She glanced again at her watch. "Besides, it's too late." She set the syringe on

253

the table in front of him. "The two of you will be a murder/suicide," she said calmly. "I really don't care which is which, as long as the police are satisfied there are no loose ends. Doctor, I give you the choice. The needle or a bullet. Astute clinician that you are, I'm sure you can deduce that one will be considerably more painful than the other."

"Dotty, please, you don't know what you're doing," Armstrong begged, moving off her chair to grab Dalrymple's free hand. Before David could react, the Nursing Director pulled her arm free and swung a full backhand arc, catching the woman flush on the side of the face. With a loud snap, Armstrong's left cheekbone shattered. Her slender body shot across the room and slammed against the wall fifteen feet away.

Her revolver still levelled at a spot between David's eyes, Dalrymple glanced over her shoulder at Armstrong's crumpled form. "I've wanted to do that for so long." She smiled. "Now, Doctor, you have a choice to make." She moved around the table, pushing it back with a trunk-like leg to allow herself room. The muzzle of the revolver was only a foot from David's forehead as she offered him the syringe. "Please decide," she urged softly.

David was staring at her face when, out of the corner of his eye, he saw Margaret Armstrong moving. On hands and knees, she was inching across the floor. Desperately, David forced his eyes to maintain contact with Dalrymple's.

"Well?" said Dalrymple. "My patience is running out."

David took the syringe and studied it. "I . . . I don't think I can get this in without a tourniquet," he stammered. In the moment Dalrymple looked down, he was able to catch another glimpse of Armstrong. The cardiologist was drawing closer. Then he noticed her hands. Each one held a small metal shield. The defibrillator! Armstrong had activated the machine. The paddles, connected to the unit by coiled wires carried 400 joules.

David rolled up his sleeve and pumped his fist several times. The wires were almost out straight and Armstrong was still ten feet away. Dalrymple's hand tightened on the revolver.

"Now," she demanded.

"Dotty!" Armstrong yelled.

Dalrymple spun to the sound at the instant David made his

lunge. He threw his shoulder full against her vast chest. The woman stumbled backwards, catching the low coffee table just behind her knees. She fell like a giant redwood, shattering the table. As her bulk touched the floor, Armstrong was upon her, jamming one paddle on either side of her face, and, in the same motion, depressing the discharge button.

The muffled pop and spark from the paddles were followed instantly by a puff of smoke. Dalrymple's arms flew upwards as her huge body convulsed several inches off the floor. A smell of searing flesh filled the air, and vomit splashed from her mouth as her head snapped back. At the moment of her death, the sphincters of her bladder and bowel released.

For several seconds, David stood motionless, staring at the two women on the floor. Then, with resurgent panic, he broke from the room in an awkward painful dash towards Four South.

Margaret Armstrong, rubber-legged, leaned against the sink, patting cold water on her face. She felt drugged, unable to sharpen the focus of her mind. Behind her lay the monstrous corpse of Dorothy Dalrymple.

With great difficulty, she forced herself to concentrate. If Christine were dead, she realised, David Shelton was all that stood in the way of the continuation of her Sisterhood. Could he be eliminated? Should he be? Margaret Armstrong knew she would gladly confess to murder – sacrifice herself – to save the movement. But was she capable of killing as Dorothy had killed?

She walked unsteadily towards the door, then turned and looked back in disgust at Dalrymple. If a woman she thought she knew so well, trusted so implicitly, could have tried to buy her own security at such a price, how could she be sure that in a time of crisis there wouldn't be others? Would the ideals of The Sisterhood be debased for individual self-preservation at every turn? Trembling, more from her thoughts than her injury, Armstrong supported herself against a wall. Was it over? After so many years, so many dreams, was it all over?

She slipped out of the office and locked the door. The janitor would not be in until sometime the following morning. Less than twenty-four hours. If she wished to salvage The Sisterhood, she had only that long to plan, to prepare, to act. Questions, one after another, raced through her mind. Was it worth the price of another life? Could she do it? Was there an explanation that would hold up? At the moment, the answers were not at all apparent.

23

Using the banister for leverage, David vaulted down the stairs from North Two to North One. Pulses of adrenalin muffled the jagged pain from his ankle. He crashed through the doorway to the central corridor, scattering a trio of horrified nuns.

The main lobby was in its usual midday chaos. David weaved and bumped his way across it like a halfback in open field, leaving two men sprawled and cursing in his wake.

"Hang on, baby, please hang on," he gasped, scrambling up the stairs in the South Wing. Even two at a time they seemed endless, doubling back on themselves between each landing. "Fight the bitch. Fight her fucking poison. Please . . . "

His feet grew leaden. His legs gave way between the third and fourth floors, then again as he stumbled on to Four South.

The corridor was empty except for one aide struggling to tie an old man safely to his wheelchair. In the seconds she spent staring at the figure limping towards her, the patient, a stroke victim, squirmed free and fell heavily to the floor. Seeing David's distraught expression, the aide, sensing the emergency, waved him past. "Go on," she urged. "Don't worry, Clarence does this all the time."

David raced to the nurses' station. "Code Ninety-nine room four-twelve," he panted. "Call it and get me some help. Code Ninety-nine room four-twelve."

The astonished ward secretary froze for a moment, then grabbed the phone.

For David, the scene in room 412 was the return of a horrible dream. The dim light, the bubbling oxygen, the intravenous set-up, the motionless body. He flicked on the lights and raced to the bed. Christine, lying serenely on her back, was the dusky colour of death. Through the hallway speaker, the page operator began calling with uncharacteristic urgency, "Code Ninety-nine, Four South . . . Code Ninety-nine, Four South . . ."

For a desperate second, David's fingers probed Christine's neck for a carotid artery pulse. There it was! The faint, rhythmic tap of life against the pad of his first and second fingers. But, was it his own pulse or hers? At that moment, as if in answer to his uncertainty, Christine took a breath – a single, shallow, wonderful whisper of a breath. Frantically, David went into action. He clamped the intravenous tubing shut, then bent over and gave two deep mouth-to-mouth breaths.

Before he had finished, a nurse burst into the room, pulling the emergency trolley behind her. Over the minutes that followed, the two of them, surgeon and nurse, worked as one. The young woman was a marvel – a controlled whirlwind, providing a needed drug or instrument almost before the words were out of his mouth.

Battling an unknown poison, David's approach was shotgun: a fresh intravenous solution at full speed to dilute the toxin and support Christine's blood pressure; an oral airway and several breaths from an Ambu bag to maintain ventilation; bicarbonate to counteract lactic acid build-up.

Christine's colour darkened even more. He risked a few seconds away from the breathing bag and lifted her eyelids. Her pupils were tiny black dots, nearly lost in the brown rings that constricted them. They were the pin-point pupils of a narcotic overdose. God, let it be morphine, David prayed. Let it be something reversible like morphine. He ordered naloxone, the highly effective antidote for all narcotic drugs. Within seconds, the nurse had injected it.

A few more breaths, and David stopped again. This time to recheck Christine's carotid pulse. With a deep, sinking sensation, he realised there was none.

"Slip a board under her, please," he said, lifting Christine's shoulders free from the bed. "Forget about the meds and just do closed chest compression until we get some more help. Christ, where is everyone?" His speech was rushed and anxious.

"One nurse went home sick." The woman said the words in rhythm to the downward thrusts of her hands against Christine's breastbone. "Two more are at lunch. They'll be here."

David continued the artificial breathing. "We need someone on the trolley," he muttered. "We need someone on the goddamn trolley." With the nurse unable to stop her cardiac massage, the trays of critical medications might as well have been on the moon.

An orderly wandered in. David snapped at him to take a blood pressure. The man tried twice. "Nothing," he said.

"Can you do CPR?" David asked, hoping he might free the nurse to return to the emergency trolley. The man shook his head. "Shit!" David hissed.

He looked down at Christine. There was no more spontaneous respirations, no signs of life. Her body was covered with deep blue mottling. Unless he could get help very soon – one more pair of skilled hands – Christine would slip beyond resuscitation. For five seconds, ten seconds, he stood motionless. The young nurse watched him, her eyes narrowed in mounting concern.

Suddenly, a woman's voice called out, "Whatever you need, Doctor, just order it."

Margaret Armstrong stood poised by the emergency trolley. Her left eye was nearly swollen shut by a huge bruise covering the side of her face. Blood trickled from one nostril. Still she held herself regally, indifferent to the stares from around the room.

David's decisiveness, already dulled by Christine's lack of response, became further blunted by fear and uncertainty. "You . . . you can take over the cardiac massage," he said, wishing she were not standing so close to the medication trolley. There were any number of drugs there that could be fatal.

Armstrong shook her head. "No, no. You're both stronger than I am. Besides I'm a nurse, and a good one. I'll handle meds. Now dammit, let's get on with it!"

David hesitated another moment, then shifted into high gear, calling out for antidotes to the substances Dalrymple would have been most likely to use. The crunching blow Armstrong had been dealt had no apparent effect on her reaction or efficiency. She was, as she had claimed, an incredibly good nurse. Adrenalin, concentrated glucose, more nalaxone, calcium, more bicarbonate – she drew them up and administered them with speed and total economy of movement.

More help arrived. Another nurse offered to relieve Armstrong, but was directed to the blood pressure cuff.

"She's still not breathing on her own," David said. "I think we should intubate."

Armstrong reached up and pressed her fingers against Christine's groin, searching for a femoral artery pulse. She looked at David grimly and shook her head. "Nothing."

"All right. Give me a laryngoscope and seven-point-five tube."

"Hold it!" Armstrong's eyes lit up. "Wait . . . wait . . . It's here, Doctor," she said. "It's here."

Seconds later, the nurse operating the blood pressure cuff sang out, "I've got one! I hear a pressure! Faint at sixty. No, wait, eighty. Getting louder! Getting louder!"

David rechecked Christine's pupils. They were definitely wider. Fifteen seconds later she began to breathe. The young nurse who had helped from the beginning gave David a thumbs-up sign and pumped her fists exultantly in the air. Colour slowly returned to Christine's cheeks. She moaned softly, rolled her head from side to side, then fluttered her eyes open. They fixed immediately on David.

"Hi," she whispered.

"Hi, yourself," he answered.

Around the room, people congratulated one another.

"I . . . I feel much better. My headache's almost gone." Her expression clouded. "David, Miss Dalrymple. I think she might be the one who . . . "

He silenced her with a finger against her lips. "I know, hon," he said with soft reassurance. "I know everything."

She looked puzzled for a moment, then relaxed. "I do feel better. Much better, David. Dr. Armstrong is a miracle worker."

David glanced over at Armstrong. "Yeah," he said stonily, "a miracle worker."

Margaret Armstrong met his gaze, and for a few moments, held it. Then, one at a time, she whispered a thank-you to those in the room and motioned each to leave.

The young nurse was the last to go. Armstrong walked her into the hall, then said, "You did wonderful work in there. I'm very proud of you."

The nurse flushed. "You . . . you've been hurt. Can I get you anything?"

"I'll be fine," Armstrong said. "You go on along and get back to your patients." Then she turned and re-entered room 412. She knew that at the moment she had stepped to the emer-

260

gency trolley and had drawn up the correct medication, she had sealed the fate of The Sisterhood.

Christine was asleep. Across the room, David had opened the curtains half-way and was looking out at the hazy afternoon. His hands hung heavily by his sides, his slumped shoulders reflecting none of the victory he had just won. Armstrong walked quietly to his side. He would not look at her. For a time, the only sounds in the room were the gurgle of oxygen through the safety bottle, and the steady sighs of Christine's breathing.

"That's a hell of a bruise you've got," David said, his gaze still fixed on the city below. "I think you should have someone look at it."

"I will," she said. "Later."

"That woman, that . . . that beast lying in your office, was your creation, you know."

"Perhaps. I suppose that in some ways she was. Does it make any difference to know that I still truly believe in the good of what The Sisterhood of Life has been doing? That the struggle for dignity in human death is just?"

"Sure." David snorted the word. "It makes a difference. Like it makes a difference to the fracture in Christine's skull. To the crap she faces when – *if* – she recovers. To the fucking judge and the prosecutor and the newspapers who are going to try her for murdering Charlotte Thomas. To my friends who are dead just because . . . " His frustration and fury choked off the words.

A silent minute passed before Armstrong said, "David, I know how you are feeling. I really do. I know my help with Christine and what I did to Dorothy can't take away the pain you both have suffered. But I also know something else. Something that will do much to soothe your wounds." She hesitated. "I know that Christine will never have to stand trial for murder."

David whirled round and stared at her. "What did you say?"

"Christine did not murder Charlotte Thomas." Her eyes levelled with his, her gaze and expression deadly serious.

"How . . . how can you say that?"

"She didn't," Armstrong said flatly, "because I did. And I can prove it."

261

24

Armstrong closed the door to room 412 as David first checked Christine's blood pressure then slowly raised the head of her bed. He had listened to the woman's story for only a minute or two before realising the importance of letting Christine hear it for herself.

Sitting on the edge of the bed, he slipped a hand beneath her head. The room was dark, save for a splash of pale sunlight through the partially closed curtains. David shook with excitement as he reached up and stroked her bruised, swollen face. "Chris, honey, wake up," he said. "Wake up."

Armstrong pulled a chair to the head of the bed.

Christine opened her eyes, smiled at David then closed them again. "I'm awake," she said weakly. "It just hurts less with my eyes shut. I'll be okay, though. A few days and I'll be okay."

"You bet you will," he said. "Chris, Dr. Armstrong is here. She has something to tell you. I . . . I thought you would want to hear."

"Christine? Can you hear me? It's Margaret Armstrong."

Christine turned towards the voice and again opened her eyes.

For several seconds, the women looked at one another. Then Armstrong said softly, "Christine, I am Peggy. Peggy Donner."

Christine gasped, then reached out and clutched her hand. "The Sisterhood . . . is it over?"

"Not yet, dear. But . . . but soon."

David searched Christine's face for anger, or even surprise, but neither was there. A bond was forming between the two women — a connection that was beyond his understanding. He watched in silent fascination, transfixed by the scene.

"Christine," Armstrong said, forcing each word, "after I leave here, I am going to begin the dissolution of The Sisterhood. It will be done in such a way that none of the members will be hurt. That is, provided you and David can live with the secrets we share. Do you understand?"

Christine managed a nod. "I understand. But the reports — the tapes . . . ?"

"They will all be destroyed. All, that is, except one. That one I shall send to you. It was made by me after I injected Charlotte with a fatal dose of potassium. Christine, the morphine you gave her was not enough. She was stronger, far stronger, than anyone suspected. Charlotte was my friend. She was . . . she was our sister. I had promised her a peaceful death. After you left her room, I went in to say good-bye. One last good-bye. She was breathing easily. I waited, but she only seemed to get stronger. Once she actually opened her eyes. I had promised her. I loved her as . . . I loved her as I did my mother. I . . . " Armstrong could go no further. For the first time in almost fifty years, she wept.

Christine loosened her fingers and brushed them across the older woman's tears. "I love you, Peggy," she said haltingly. "I love you for what you tried to do for Charlotte."

A minute passed before Armstrong continued. "After I've done what is necessary for our Sisterhood, I'll go to see Lt. Dockerty and take full responsibility for Charlotte's death. Believe me, Christine, I *was* the one who did it." She turned to David. "I shall also take responsibility for Dorothy and for the deaths of your friends. I think there would be fewer questions if there is no suggestion of more than one person involved in all this."

David saw the concern in Christine's face at the word "friends". "I'll explain later, Chris," he said. "Dr. Armstrong, I do appreciate what you did during the resuscitation. For that, I promise that as long as you do what you've said, there will be no interference from me."

"Thank you." Armstrong studied the coldness in his eyes, then bent down and kissed Christine on the forehead. Moments later she was gone.

David knelt by the bed. The scant light in the room glinted off the tears in Christine's eyes. "When you get out of here," he said, "we're going to take a trip to that dusty little village in Mexico."

"But we get to come back?" There was both joy and sadness in her smile.

"We get to come back."

She closed her eyes. For a moment, it seemed she had fallen back to sleep, but as he moved away she grasped his hand. "David, could you tell me one more thing now?" she asked.

"What's that?"

"Do you have vanity plates on your car?"

John Dockerty gulped at what remained of the cold coffee in his mug and sank back in his chair. It had taken the entire night, and most of the morning, but at last Marcus Quigg had broken and had given him the name. The triumph – if that is what it was – felt hollow. Images of the frightened, sick little man would haunt him, possibly forever.

That it was Margaret Armstrong who was responsible for the murders, the mistakes, and the pathetic pharmacist only made things worse. She was someone he respected, and even more depressing, someone he had trusted.

"John Dockerty, master sleuth," he said scornfully. "Danced around the barn by a lady who turns out to be another goddamn Ma Barker." Well, at least he had had the pleasure of telling the Captain – though not in so many words – what an ass the man had been to order the hasty arrest of David Shelton.

Dockerty checked his watch. It had been nearly an hour since the Captain had promised to get a magistrate's warrant for Armstrong's arrest. He rubbed the stubble on his face, and was deciding whether to shave or not when the phone rang.

"Investigations, Dockerty," he said. " . . . Yes, Captain . . . that's fine, sir . . . I'll be down to get it right away . . . Yes, sir, I know he looked guilty as sin. If I were in your position, I would have done the same . . . Thank you, I'll be down in five minutes . . . Turkey." Dockerty delivered the last word to the dial tone. He combed his hair with his fingers, and pushed himself out of his chair. At that moment, with a soft knock, Margaret Armstrong stepped into his office.

"Lt. Dockerty, I have some things to talk to you about," she said.

"Yes," he replied, settling back on the edge of his desk, "you certainly do."

Within thirty minutes, Dockerty had heard enough of Armstrong's confession to call in a stenographer. With a certain relish, he rang the Captain and asked him to witness the proceedings. The man, a suave half-politician, half-policeman with jet-black hair listened in dumbfounded silence as Armstrong calmly admitted responsibility for the murders of Charlotte Thomas and Dotty Dalrymple, as well as for hiring the killer of Ben Glass and Joseph Rosetti. It was a story she had rehearsed carefully before driving to Station 1; an explanation she hoped would leave Dockerty satisfied that she had acted totally on her own. It disgusted her to have to paint Dalrymple as a heroine who had died because she had stumbled onto the truth, but any hint of conspiracy would have risked exposure of the movement. She knew what policemen like Dockerty could do. Besides, Margaret was sure that up until the end, Dotty had been just as dedicated to The Sisterhood as she was. The woman was frightened of losing her position and her influence, that's all.

Armstrong's confession held together well enough, but there was a vagueness about the details that made Dockerty uncomfortable. He attempted to pin her down, but was silenced by the Captain who found his tongue in time to say, "Now, Lieutenant, I'm sure the doctor will fill in some of these details in good time. As you can see, she's had a rather rough go of it."

Armstrong thanked him, giving him a look that clearly made Dockerty an outsider in the exchange between two people of stature.

Dockerty decided to push his luck. "Just one thing," he ventured. "Exactly how did you go about hiring a killer like Leonard Vincent?"

"I shall cover that in a moment," she said, giving him her most withering, authoritative stare. "But first, if you would direct me to your ladies' room."

"If you'll wait," Dockerty said, "I'll get a matron to go . . ."

"Nonsense," the Captain cut in. "Dr. Armstrong has been officially charged with nothing as yet. The . . . ah . . . ladies' room is just down the corridor to the right. You can't miss it."

Armstrong again acknowledged the Captain's understanding, and carefully adjusted her skirt before striding from the room.

The ladies' room was a sty. The institutional tiled floor was stained and cracked. Paper towels overflowed from the metal wastebasket to one side of the sink. The air reeked of urine and disinfectant.

Margaret Donner Armstrong did not notice the filth. She scanned the room then went directly to the toilet stall, hooked the plywood door shut, and sat down.

She felt pleased at the way she had manipulated Dockerty and the Captain. If David and Christine were true to their word, The Sisterhood of Life would die with dignity. The irony in that realisation brought her some solace.

After leaving the hospital, Armstrong had gone home and honoured her promise. The tapes - all but one - had been incinerated. Now and again she had stopped to listen to a particular report, or to reflect on her friendship with a particular woman. Her dream - her ultimate dream - had nearly come true. If only Dorothy hadn't cracked.

Barbara Littlejohn had agreed that it was no longer possible for the movement to continue. At times during their telephone conversation, the woman had actually sounded relieved. Armstrong wondered if Barbara would have reacted the same way as Dalrymple had her own reputation and career been at stake. The painful fact was that she simply did not know for certain - about Barbara or any of them.

So it had been decided. Barbara would make the calls and write the letters, then do what she could to continue the Clinton Foundation projects. And, as the receiver dropped to its cradle, Armstrong knew that after forty years it was over.

Now, she sat looking at the sordid messages and crude drawings on the door in front of her, remembering back fifty years to the last time she had been in such a place. She had felt frightened then. Frightened and dirty. She had feared the detectives, and the way they stared at her breasts. She had taken her mind to special, hidden places to keep from telling them what they wanted her to say. Hour after hour she had resisted their control, at one point choosing to wet herself rather than ask to leave the room. And in the end, she had won. And with her victory had come the chance to strike out on a holy mission - a journey she had come close, oh, so close, to completing.

Now, it was time to embark on another.

Armstrong reached inside her blouse to the waistband of her skirt, and withdrew the syringe Dotty Dalrymple had almost forced David to use. For a few moments, she fingered the deadly tube. Then, she rolled up one sleeve and skilfully slipped the needle into a vein. She rested her head against the wall and closed her eyes. With a fine, slim finger, she depressed the plunger.

"It's all right, Mama . . . I'm here, Mama," she said.

EPILOGUE

The breeze, which had been little more than a zephyr all day, picked up suddenly, sending noisy flocks of dry leaves swirling about the grey stones.

Dora Dalrymple paused on the narrow path to pull her great-coat tightly about her. She was, in face, size, manner and dress, a virtual mirror of her late twin. Her incongruously tiny feet handled the steep downgrade with a sureness born of having taken the same walk each evening for three weeks.

The grave, still a fresh mound of dirt, was encompassed by a ring of pines. In the same grove, a small uncarved block of marble marked the plot where some day she herself would be buried. Ritually, she picked up the metal folding chair she had left there the first day, and positioned it next to the dark soil. Then she placed a single flower over the spot where she knew her sister's heart to be.

"It's a 'mum, Dotty," she said, 'sort of rust coloured. I know 'mums aren't one of your favourites, but this one's so pretty and so like autumn. You're not upset by my choice today, are you? It just caught my eye, and I felt sure you'd under-stand.

"People at the hospital are being very nice to me now. I think they've even stopped calling me Tweedledee behind my back . . . yes, I know. Well, it's out of respect for you that they don't, I think. Dotty, you got a call today from Violet in Detroit. I told her you were out for the afternoon and to call back later. I . . . I don't know if I can continue The Garden without you. I mean, I helped and all, but you were the one who started it and kept it growing . . . But The Sisterhood is finished. All of the nurses, including our flowers have been notified. None of the flowers wants the Garden to die, but to survive, we must grow. How will I find new nurses to join us . . . 'Tall oaks from little acorns' . . . I know you used to joke. You always understood human nature better than I did . . . So, I cook better than you, what does that prove? It's apples and oranges as far as I'm concerned . . .

"I checked today with Mr. Stevens. Your stone is almost ready. It's beautiful. You'll love it, I know you will . . . Okay, okay, so I'm changing the subject. I'm frightened of making a wrong decision, that's all. I'll do my best. You were always so confident, so decisive . . . You must promise to keep giving me strength – I can feel it, you know – but you must help me.

"I think I'll follow your suggestion and ask that lovely Janet to move in with me. Is that a good idea? I'll call Hyacinth today, then. But remember, we'll both be counting on you every step of the way."

The conversation over, Dora placed the chair to one side of the grove and returned to her car, oblivious to the light rain that had begun to fall.

Inside the Tudor mansion she and Dotty had purchased shortly after the inception of The Garden, she brewed a pot of tea and settled into an oversized easy chair, one of a pair they had designed themselves. Fifteen minutes later, the telephone rang.

"I'm calling Dahlia," the young woman's voice said.

"I'm sorry, but Dahlia is not readily available," Dora said, assuming the whispered tone she had heard Dotty use on so many occasions. "However, this is her sister . . . Chrysanthemum. You may, if you wish, confide in me just as you did in Dahlia."

"Well . . . all right, I guess," the woman said uncertainly. "This is Violet calling again from Detroit. Saint Bart's Hospital. A situation has come up here that I think could use some further research."

"Go on," Dora said reassuringly.

"It's a woman named Agnes Morgan. Her husband is Carter Morgan, one of the executive directors at Ford. She's only forty-two, but is drying out in our hospital for the third time this year. Rumour has it that her husband's been trying to get a divorce for several years so he could marry his secretary. Apparently, Mrs. Morgan won't let him have one without bleeding him dry and doing what she can to ruin his career."

"Sounds very promising," Dora said, doodling the picture of a car on a yellow legal pad, and overlaying it with an ornately

269

inscribed dollar sign. "I'll do some checking up on the situation and call you. Meanwhile, dig up as much information as you can on this Mr. Morgan and his wife. It sounds like the benefits in this case would be quite substantial, assuming the gentleman decides to do business with us."

"I think he just might," Violet said. "When can I expect to hear from you?"

"Within a day or so, I think," Dora answered. "As you know, Dahlia and I will take care of any business dealings. You'll have all the help you need."

She replaced the receiver and picked up a gold-framed photo of Dotty from the table. The likeness to herself was such that she might have been holding a looking glass.

"Well, love, we're still in business," she said, resting the picture on her massive lap. "I can't do it without your help, though, so you'd better not forget your promise. Anyhow, that's what sisters are for, aren't they?"

JOHN SAUL

SUFFER THE CHILDREN

One hundred years ago in Port Arbello a pretty little girl began to scream. And struggle. And die. No one heard. No one saw. Just one man whose guilty heart burst in pain as he dashed himself to death in the sea ...

Now something peculiar is happening in Port Arbello. The children are disappearing, one by one. An evil history is repeating itself. And one strange, terrified child has ended her silence with a scream that began a hundred years ago.

POST A LITTLE HAPPINESS

Post·A·Book

A Royal Mail service in association with the Book Marketing Council & The Booksellers Association.

Post-A-Book is a Post Office trademark.

MORE EXCITING FICTION FROM CORONET

JOHN SAUL

☐	22687 0	Suffer The Children	£1.50
☐	24262 0	Punish The Sinners	£1.50
☐	25548 X	Cry For The Strangers	£1.50
☐	26680 5	Comes The Blind Fury	£1.50
☐	28107 3	When The Wind Blows	£1.50

TERENCE STRONG

| ☐ | 27908 7 | Whisper Who Dares | £1.75 |
| ☐ | 32120 2 | The Fifth Hostage | £1.75 |

PETER TONKIN

| ☐ | 32045 1 | The Journal of Edwin Underhill | £1.60 |

GEORGE MacBETH

| ☐ | 32803 7 | A Kind Of Treason | £1.75 |

All these books are available at your local bookshop or newsagent, or can be ordered direct from the publisher. Just tick the titles you want and fill in the form below.

Prices and availability subject to change without notice.

CORONET BOOKS, P.O. Box 11, Falmouth, Cornwall.

Please send cheque or postal order, and allow the following for postage and packing:

U.K. – 45p for one book, plus 20p for the second book, and 14p for each additional book ordered up to a £1.63 maximum.

B.F.P.O. and EIRE – 45p for the first book, plus 20p for the second book, and 14p per copy for the next 7 books, 8p per book thereafter.

OTHER OVERSEAS CUSTOMERS – 75p for the first book, plus 21p per copy for each additional book.

Name ....

Address..

....